MW00627520

Amazing Adventures
Of

The Tramp Prince

'A Philosophic Fantasy'

*38 Anecdotal Odysseys Exploring
the Diversity of Human Absurdity*

By "Hobo" Jack Sophir

DEDICATION

This work is dedicated to my immediate family (what little is left of it), to my extended family of former classmates, friends and hobo pals (what little is left of them), and to my "Family of Man".

In addition, I want to dedicate this book to the memory of Antoine De Saint Exupery, whose 1943 children's book, *The Little Prince* served as an inspiration for, though in no sense as a *basis* for, the *Tramp Prince*.

And, I wish also, to dedicate this book to the memory of Judy Wasserman, who, in 1951, first introduced me to *The Little Prince*. Judy herself, was the most whimsical person I ever met. She lived and died in her own world of fantasy.

ACKNOWLEDGEMENTS

Special thanks to Charles Hershey for both the computer data entry for this book and for numerous valuable suggestions.

Cover Design, Re-formatting and Notes By:
Robert Whiteside
www.ArchivalProductions.com

PREFACE

Every Writer draws upon personal experience in order to create situations and characters for a work of fiction — and I am no different. I wish to state emphatically, however, that this work is *not* in any way autobiographical, except perhaps in some very marginal sense. But there are seventeen of the characters in this fantasy with real-life counterparts who served as a basis or model for the fictional personalities. Only one person, Albert Carter Savage is depicted somewhat biographically.

The seventeen real persons are as follows:

        Lawrence Altman
        Warren Barnett
        "Ramblin' Rose" Dahlin
        Larry "the barber" Feldmeyer
        Stanley "Pre-Pre" Gavander
        Annie Graham
        Ollie Hartzel
        Oliver Kassabaum
        Edward Lanwermeyer
        Dan Leavitt
        William Larkin McKibbin
        Brenda Pace
        Janet Regan Robertson
        Sheila Rosenthal (a.k.a. Tiffany)
        Albert Carter Savage
        Fred Summers
        Judy Wasserman

Since several of those on this list are now deceased, they will, unfortunately, never be able to read how they have been honored — or, as they might have thought, *dis*honored. The others, in the unlikely event that they will ever obtain a copy of this remarkable absurdity, may decide for themselves.

Print Version: ISBN 978-0-9625074-2-7

Digital Edition: ISBN 978-0-9625074-3-4
Available as a download from: www.hobojack.com
and major eBook retail websites.

CONTENTS

PROLOGUE "A Tepid Appraisal"

Ah, dear reader…if you have been, like me, a little, old hobo, tramp, bum or a beggar (and I have probably been them all), then you may understand the story better, than those who have not been.

I say that because the following story takes place in 1910-11, a time that was still rife with many little ragged vagabonds and transient workers. It was a time that was long before many parts of the world became filled with veritable giants of the human kind.

You see, there are many references to "smallness" in the first few paragraphs of my story; and I, myself, am a "little" person. All of my life, I have often felt like a midget living in a land of giants; so, when I write of smallness, it is with a consciousness of that feeling of inadequacy that the word may imply.

Yet, the good aspects of smallness — like being able to live on mere scraps of food or being able to sleep in the cramped back of an automobile — those aspects (familiar to any hobo) never escape my thoughts.

The reader who sees my following words, may think that I am a weaver of outrageous and fanciful tales. Perhaps I am. However that may be, I will let the reader view my random thoughts as they come spilling pell-mell out of my head — as they often do!

So, now that you have read through these paragraphs, I welcome you to the sometimes diminutive world of…the Tramp Prince.

AMAZING ADVENTURES OF THE TRAMP PRINCE

Chapter One: The Garden

Not terribly many years ago, in a rather remote, forested land that may have been far away (or may not have been), there lived a small family in a small house. The small house had a small garden and it was next to a small orchard.

The father of that small family was called, "King Of The Garden" and the mother was called, "Queen Of The Garden". Not surprisingly, their son and daughter were called respectively: "Prince Of The Garden" and "Princess Of The Garden".

The small family worked their small garden and small orchard diligently, and were able to raise most of the food they ate. When they had a surplus, they would sell it in the nearby village so that they could buy food that they did not grow, as well as the few manufactured items they could not make for themselves.

Since they had decided not to complicate their lives with farm animals, the four family members lived all alone in their remote garden surrounded by a dense forest.

I should say, though, that they were not entirely alone, for wild animals occasionally wandered into the area to try to avail themselves of ripening melons or corn or apples. Once a house cat suddenly appeared and took up residence in a shed. "It may as well stay," said the King Of The Garden, "and help keep down mice and voles." Later, an old dog with a lame leg limped in and everyone felt too sorry for the old fellow to drive him off. So, he also became a family member.

One fine autumn day, when the wind was spinning yellow leaves along the ground and the sky was bright with an incandescent aura of sunshine yellows and cloudless blue, there ambled up the path to the house, a rather portly figure of a little man dressed in a striped business suit and tie. He was mopping his brow with a handkerchief and panting heavily.

"Hello!" said the King Of The Garden.

"Good day," replied the Plump Little Man With The Bald Spot. "I am afraid I am not used to walking such great distances over such rough terrain."

"Ah well," said the King of the Garden, " I seldom walk that path myself, unless I push my high wheel cart to market in town. I'm sorry, but that is why I don't keep down the weeds. You look to be overheated. Would you like a cool glass of fresh apple cider from the spring house?"

"Oh, yes indeed!" exclaimed the Plump Little Man With The Bald Spot.

"Mother, please bring this man a glass of cider," said the King Of The Garden.

After the stranger had drunk the cider, the King Of The Garden invited him to sit on a bench in the shade of the porch.

"I am most grateful for that cool drink," said the Plump Little Man With The Bald Spot, "however, I must be brief and tell you why I have come here and then be on my way."

The King Of The Garden and his family stood in rapt attention as the Plump Little Man With The Bald Spot continued.

"You see," he began, " I am the administrator of my family's many properties, and I have come here to tell you that you people are occupying a part of a property to which my family has the deed. We have owned this property for many years, paying the property tax on it each year all that time, and it is my regrettable duty to inform you that you must vacate the premises in a reasonable amount of time. This is a beautiful spot and I would like to move in here myself."

The small family stood in silent amazement, until the almost deathly still was finally broken by the King Of The Garden.

"But when we came here twenty years ago, this place had been abandoned and been deteriorating for at least a couple of generations. This house was a shambles; the roof had caved in and many windows were broken out; the floor had huge holes in it and the porch had rotted away. There were oak and hickory trees growing up between the apple trees in the orchard and the apple trees themselves were covered in wild grape vines; the trees were thick with unpruned and dead branches. The few apples the trees produced were small and knotted and gnarled. The springhouse had collapsed into the spring and the lane up here from the road had narrowed into an overgrown rabbit trail. I thought that property abandoned that long belonged to anyone who claimed it and was willing to work on it. I guess like 'squatter's rights'."

"With *moveable* property," replied the Plump Little Man With The Bald Spot, "what you say is quite true. If someone leaves something by the roadside — or even in your care — then does not come back for it in a reasonable amount of time, it belongs to whoever finds it or possesses it. With even something quite valuable, like a bag of money the same is true if one has made considerable effort to locate the owner with no success. But with real estate properties, there is a deed to the land and as long as the deed holder pays the yearly property tax, the land still belongs to the deed holder. My family has owned and paid tax on this land for decades."

"My goodness!" exclaimed the King Of The Garden, "I am at complete loss as to what to say — or as to what to do!"

"Please understand," said the Plump Little Man With The Bald Spot, "that I'm not accusing you of having done something bad — immoral…but you were, unfortunately ignorant of the law and while ignorance of the law is not considered an excuse, most people don't understand it any better than you did and certainly don't understand the underlying implications. You see," he went on, "although I am not trained as an attorney, since I've been the administrator of my family's properties for several years, it has been necessary for me to study the statute books on numerous occasions. So I'm fairly well versed in the laws governing real estate."

"But it would seem to me," said the King Of The Garden, "That when a house has been abandoned, that it would make much more sense for someone who has a need for a place to live, to be allowed to live in it — rather than just let it continue to go to waste and rot and ruin."

The Plump Little Man With The Bald Spot frowned. "Actually, what is important is not what *you* think — or what anyone else thinks, for that matter. It is what the government *decrees*. It's the law of the land. Even if it makes no logical sense."

"One other thing," he continued, "that almost no one understands, is that even the deed holder of a piece of real estate does not in the final sense *own* that property."

"And how could that possibly be?" interrupted the King Of The Garden in further amazement.

The Plump Little Man With The Bald Spot went on: "The government records the deed to a property a purchaser of real estate has just bought. That way, no one else can claim that it's theirs. But then, if the deed holder does not or cannot, for any reason, pay the government's yearly property tax on that parcel, the government will eventually evict the "owner" and resell the property to someone else for back taxes. That means, in essence, that it is the *government* which, in reality, *owns* all real estate. And further, the 'right of eminent domain'— that is, the taking of property for projects of public good — retained by the government, is another reason why the government actually owns your land. The deed holder is merely a 'lessee' of the property and pays a yearly rental or tribute that the government calls the property tax. The truth of actual ownership is hidden from the deed holder by use of the term 'property tax' and the term 'property owner'."

"Ah," said the King Of The Garden, completely perplexed, "I simply do not know *what* to do now."

"My suggestion," said the Plump Little Man With The Bald Spot, "is that since you found this abandoned garden and house and have lived here for twenty years, you could look for and find another like it somewhere else and possibly live there another twenty years without being bothered. That would take you well into your old age. Since you have not paid any rent here for all the years you have lived here, but have done a great deal to improve the property, I will consider the improvement in lieu of a monetary rental fee.

"My chauffeur is waiting for me in my motor car down on the road and, if I stay any longer, he will be wondering why I have not returned. I shall come back here in about six months and expect to find the property vacated. Good day!"

With that the Plump Little Man With The Bald Spot ambled away down the path from the garden and was soon out of sight.

"Oh dear! Oh dear! Whatever shall we do?" asked the Queen Of The Garden, wringing her hands in intense exasperation.

The Prince Of The Garden spoke up: "I know what to do, Mother," he said. You and Father and Sister should stay here and continue your lives as usual and I'll go out in search of another abandoned garden. After all, I've lived for eighteen years and am fully grown and strong and I'm confident that I can take care of myself out in the world."

"My son," said the King Of The Garden, "you don't realize that you are still very young and untried in the ways of this world. But I have great faith in your resourcefulness — and I think that your plan is the only practical solution we have. It would take us years of saving every penny from the sale of crop surpluses to have enough to buy even a run down piece of land. And obviously we do not have that kind of time. So you may go with my blessing."

That very evening, the Queen Of The Garden began sewing a warm blanket roll together and a tough canvas sack in which to hold it, and the few other necessities for life on the road. The King Of The Garden searched for and found an old folding knife with many kinds of blades and implements. He handed it to the Prince Of The Garden saying: "This is the knife that was given to me by *my* father many years ago when I set out on my own search for a place in this world. I know that it will serve you just as well as it served me."

Then the Prince Of The Garden sorted through all of his clothes and picked out the strongest looking shirts and trousers and shoes, choosing two of each and two pairs of shoes. He found a small metal water bottle and placed it with the clothes.

In the morning, dressed in one of the sets of tough clothing, the Prince Of The Garden began packing all the rest of the items he would take with him into the canvas sack. The Queen Of The Garden had stitched some shoulder straps onto the sack and she added a few more stitches for safety.

With a small brown bag in her hand, the Princess Of The Garden lifted the lids of the family's jars of dried fruits, vegetables and nuts and placed a few of each into the sack until it was almost filled. She then tied the top and placed the bag into the Prince's large canvas sack.

"These will give you just a little bit to eat sometime when there's no other food," she said.

The Prince smiled and gave his little sister a hug. "That's a wonderful idea!" he told her.

When everything had been prepared for the Prince's departure, the little family gathered around him to bid him farewell and good luck.

After many hugs and tearful goodbyes, the Prince Of The Garden, with his backpack firmly mounted, strode briskly down the path toward the ancient stone gatepost. Like some silent sentry, the gatepost marked the edge of the garden. But its ornate iron gate lay rusted and half-cocked to one side with the bars almost forming a ladder.

The Princess Of The Garden ran alongside the Prince until they reached the gatepost. She quickly scrambled up the bars of the gate and stood atop the stone post.

"Now — you see, I'm even taller than you are!" laughed the Princess. I can hug you without you even having to bend over!" And she gave her brother another hug.

"Big brother..." began the Princess, "won't you be awfully lonely just by yourself? If I came along with you, I could keep you company." The little girl looked at her brother with a quizzical and pleading expression in her eyes. "I could help you gather firewood at night. I'd look through one part of a woods while you looked at another. And I could...I could..."

"Oh dear little Princess," said the Prince, "I would *love* to have your company on this journey, but you must know that you're entirely too young. How would you continue your schooling? And there may be times when I will not be able to have enough to eat; you're still growing. Surely you must realize that Father and Mother would never allow you to go."

The little child looked down with disappointment.

"Oh well," she said, "maybe you should take a dog — Limpy."

"That wouldn't be right," laughed the Prince. "Old Limpy is just barely able to get himself around the garden here. He would never be able to take the rigors of a very long road trip."

The Princess Of The Garden jumped down from the gatepost and almost landed on a large toad.

"Here," she cried, "here's a companion to take with you!" And she handed the wiggling toad to the Prince.

The Prince gave another loud laugh. "Oh yes," he said cynically, "I'm sure he would *want* to go with me."

"Well," said the toad, "it might not be a bad idea."

"What?!" exclaimed the Prince with unrestrained amazement. Did you hear what that toad said?"

The Princess frowned at her brother. "You're trying to play mean tricks on me. That's silly — you know that a toad can't talk!"

"Tell her that I'm not like other toads," said the toad. "She can't hear me because I'm speaking to you telepathically — and she's not tuned into my thoughts. I must have been a human in a past life and somehow mistakenly reincarnated into a toad's body. When I try to talk, all that comes out of me is little 'grump', 'grump' sounds. It's such a relief to be able to speak to someone telepathically. Actually, since I've been a toad, you're the only one I've encountered who can communicate with me."

The Prince Of The Garden simply stood there, not knowing quite what to say to his sister.

"I'm not trying to play a trick on you," the Prince offered. "Let's just say that I would have a *very* difficult time trying to explain all of this to you about that toad — but I will take the toad along as a companion, that is, if he really wants to go."

As a test, to see if he were truly communicating with the toad telepathically, the Prince then thought very hard, trying to transmit an idea to the toad: "If you want to go with me, I'll crouch down and hold open my jacket pocket and you jump into it. Alright?"

The toad immediately leaped off the ground into the Prince's pocket.

The Prince then arose and blew a kiss to his little sister as he began tramping on down to the main road. At the last tree in the orchard, he filled all his pockets with apples that had dropped on the ground.

"Watch it there!" said the toad. "You're not giving me any space to move around in here!"So the Prince took a large apple out of that pocket and began munching on it as he walked.

Chapter 2: The Farmer's Daughter

For several hours along the dusty road, the Prince Of The Garden walked briskly in the bright sun of that cool autumn morning, passing farms and forests, ponds and streams — but no abandoned gardens.

As he was passing one farmhouse, a pack of dogs ran out from it barking viciously. When he passed them, one of the dogs came up to him growling and snarling. The Prince then moved to the other side of the road, but the dog followed, getting closer and closer to the Prince's leg. Suddenly the dog attacked and the Prince quickly leaped the low fence of the field on the left of him. But the dogs teeth had nipped the Prince's leg and put a small rip in his pants.

"Wow!" thought the Prince, "That was close!"

"Did that dog hurt you?" the toad inquired.

"No, not really," the Prince said aloud. He reached down to feel the small tear in his pants leg as he continued walking in the field long past the farm where the dogs still stood barking.

"My pants leg has a slight rip from the dog's teeth, but other than that, I'll be alright. I know now why tramps are always pictured with walking sticks. It's not to help them walk — it's to fend off vicious farm dogs!"

The toad winked one of his bright little eyes. "Why don't you stop at the next grove of sassafras saplings and cut a stick for yourself? Then you'll be a true tramp and we'll have to call you the 'Tramp Prince'."

"Alright...but if I have a road name, then you need one too. How about 'Road Toad'?"

"Hmm. I don't know...well, why not? It's probably as good as any other."

At the next grove of sassafras, the Tramp Prince got out his knife and cut through a straight sapling, trimming off the top so that it was just about the same height as his own head.

"When this dries out and cures, it will be very light weight and strong," he said to Road Toad.

"Yes, indeed!" replied his amphibious friend.

So, on they traveled down the road, until the Tramp Prince decided to sit and rest by a bridge over a sparkling, clear stream. As he sat eating one of his apples, Road Toad jumped out of the jacket pocket.

"I'll be right back," said Road Toad. I'm just going to look for a few grubs and slugs to eat."

"Grubs and slugs?" said the Prince with a questioning hesitancy in his mental voice.

"Certainly!" Road Toad advised him. "They're really quite delicious! You should try them yourself sometime — if you haven't already."

"Ah...I don't think so!" said the Tramp Prince. "I would have to be *very* hungry, indeed!"

"Hmm...yum, yum!" Road Toad exclaimed as he gobbled down a couple of slugs that were chewing away on a little plant. "You don't know what you're missing!"

"And...I shall continue not to know," the Tramp Prince thought to himself.

"I heard that!" Road Toad told him. "You can't keep secrets from me!"

With that, Road Toad jumped back into the jacket pocket and they were soon, again on their way down the road.

As the afternoon progressed and became warmer, the Tramp Prince slowed his pace. He was not moving very rapidly when they came to another group of barking farm dogs.

The leader of the pack came out to challenge the Tramp Prince, snarling and snapping his teeth. When the dog lunged at him, the Tramp Prince swung his stick, catching the dog lightly under its jaw, and the animal went yipeing and yipping back toward the farmhouse from which it had come. The others of the pack followed in quick retreat.

"Ha! Served him right!" said Road Toad.

"Oh, now — that dog just thought he was defending his territory," the Tramp Prince replied. "I didn't like hitting him, but dog bites on the leg don't help you any to walk."

Several hours further on down the road, at the edge of a field where it met a wooded hillside, a cow stood with its head caught between the rails of a wooden fence. The animal bellowed as the Tramp Prince passed, as if to say: "Please help me!"

When he attempted to free the cow's head, the Tramp Prince found that the wooden rails had been securely nailed to each other and could not be lifted apart.

"Silly thing," said the Tramp Prince, "you must have thought the grass looked greener on the other side of the fence." The cow's head, being wedge shaped, had pushed through the narrow space between the rails, but would not pull back in the reverse direction.

"I need to try to find the farmer to let him know about this," said the Tramp Prince.

"Just another delay," telepathized Road Toad with a touch of sarcasm.

"I've got to do it," the Tramp Prince replied.

A quarter of a mile further along the road, in another small hollow, they came to a lane leading to a farmhouse. The Tramp Prince proceeded along the lane toward the house, where he met a rough-looking farmer carrying a double-bit axe. The farmer raised the axe menacingly.

"We don't feed tramps here!" the farmer shouted, even before the Tramp Prince was within speaking distance. When the two were a few feet apart, the farmer angrily shook his axe.

"See this?" he nearly shouted, with his brushy brown beard flapping like a flag in a breeze. "I cuts my *own* wood! Don't need no help around here, so skeedaddle back the way you come in!"

"I just came to tell you that one of your cows has its head caught between the rails of the fence down there at the far edge of your property. I couldn't free it because the rails were too tight."

"Well I'll be danged! I'll bet it's that same goldurned fool cow as did it a couple weeks ago."

The farmer laid his axe down at the wood pile and went to the barn for a hammer and a pry bar.

"I'll show you where the cow is caught," the Tramp Prince told the farmer when he returned. "You can't hear her bellowing up here, I guess because of the shape of the hill and all the trees."

As they walked back down the road to where the cow had become caught, the late afternoon breezes began whipping little swirls of brownish dust into miniature funnel clouds that died along the edge of the road. The cow still stood with its head locked between the fence rails and the Farmer With The Brushy Beard quickly took his pry bar to the rails, wedging them apart enough for the Tramp Prince to help the animal slip its head back through. Then, the Tramp Prince hammered back the nails that held the wooden fence rails together.

As the pair walked to the farm lane, the farmer thanked the Tramp Prince.

"Young feller, I hafta 'polergize. I thought you were just another one a' them no 'count tramps come in fer a handout, but I sure wuz wrong."

"That's okay," said the Tramp Prince. "I fully understand. I'm just glad that I was able to help you free your cow."

"So where'd yuh come from, anyhow?" the farmer queried.

Then, as briefly as he could condense the happenings of the day before, the Tramp Prince explained where he had been living and what had happened that set him on his journey.

"Well ain't that awful!" said the Farmer With The Brushy Beard. "Ef I had a larger house, I'd invite you folks to come stay here, 'till you kin find another home. But as you'll see, the house is mighty small; we don't even have one spare bed. Say, it's near supper time an' you've walked a good many miles, so why don't you join us fer a bit o' food. We ain't got nuthin' fancy — Jus' mainly cornbread 'n' beans t'night; yer welcome to some."

So the Tramp Prince accompanied the Farmer With The Brushy Beard to his house where he was introduced to the farmer's wife and daughter.

"This here young feller," explained the Farmer With The Brushy Beard, "found the ol' brown cow caught with her head 'tween the fence rails again — 'n' he helped me get her out, so I invited him fer supper. Momma, kin you rustle up enough grub fer him t' eat with us?"

The exquisitely plain-looking woman nodded her head, yes. "Ah think so, Pa." And she went swiftly into the kitchen.

"I'm goin' to the hen house to gather the eggs, Pa," the farmer's daughter told her father. "If this fella helps me, I can get through a lot quicker," she advised. "There's that other basket hangin' on a nail inside the shed."

"Well, go ahead," said the Farmer With The Brushy Beard. "An jus' see that collectin' eggs is *all* y' do."

"Oh, fer hevin's sake, Pa!" the girl responded.

The Tramp Prince accompanied the farmer's daughter to the hen house and on the way, briefly explained how he happened to be on the road.

The girl then said to him: "I've been through the woods and farms all around here and I don't know of any 'bandoned gardens or houses. I'm really sorry. But I do want to show you something very beautiful when we finish gathering eggs. Its just a short walk."

The youths quickly sorted through the various nests and odd ledges and crevices in the hen house. When they had both filled their baskets, the farmer's daughter placed the egg baskets on a table near the hen house and grabbed the Tramp Prince's hand, leading him down a path into the woods. The path meandered to a small spring creek, which they followed a short distance into a fern-covered glen. There, water fell into the creek from a six foot high waterfall.

"Isn't this just beautiful?" exclaimed the farmer's daughter. "I come here almost every day to enjoy it — but I can never share it with anyone."

"Oh, yes!" agreed the Tramp Prince. "This is truly a work of art by Mother Nature. I'm so glad you showed it to me. My family's garden is beautiful too…but in a different way. And, of course, my father and mother and sister all share it with me each day."

"Sharing is so important," said the farmer's daughter wistfully. "I wish I had someone to share my walks through the fields and woods. But I don't even have a brother or sister. And the other farms are so far from here…You know what they say: 'A joy shared is twice a joy.'"

"And," completed the Tramp Prince, "'A sorrow shared is half a sorrow.'"

"Come on," urged the farmer's daughter as she grabbed the Tramp Prince by the hand again and tugged him along. "Let's go down by the big pond and then we can go back that way to the house."

When they had retrieved the egg baskets and arrived back at the house, the food was already on the table.

"I showed him the waterfall and all the ferns," the farmer's daughter told the Farmer With The Brushy Beard.

"Humpf!" returned the farmer, raising his eyebrows, "What else?"

The daughter looked a bit abashed. "Why…then we walked down to the big pond."

"Um hum…," the Farmer With The Brushy Beard ended his comment munching a mouthful of food.

"Papa," the farmer's wife advised him, "you know I don't like for yuh t' eat 'til the blessing's been said! Dear Lord," she began, "bless us fer havin' this here food an' help that young man t' find what he's a' lookin' fer. Amen."

The farmer's wife smiled warmly at the Tramp Prince. Though her widely spaced features showed little sign of ageing, her face was pleasant rather than pretty. She wore her graying hair long, drawn up into a bun at the back of her head; her old fashioned granny bonnet that she had been wearing, now hung on a nail in the wall.

"We just got real simple food here tonight," she directed to the Tramp Prince. "Guess we're too poor t' have much of anything else most the time."

"I'm used to simple fare at home," said the Tramp Prince. "We try to live mostly on what we can raise in our garden and orchard. And we even dry a lot of fruits and vegetables for the winter."

"I know what we shoulda done!" announced the Farmer With The Brushy Beard. "We shoulda butchered that durn ol' brown cow an' had some steaks t'night!"

"Oh," the Tramp Prince responded politely, "what you've served suits me quite well."

"Tell old whisker-face that humans aren't carnivores," Road Toad whispered a thought to the Tramp Prince. "Tell him the dogs and cats and lions and tigers are supposed to eat flesh, but that humans are supposed to eat fruits and vegetables with some nuts and seeds."

"Who told you *that*?" the Tramp Prince questioned.

"Why, *you* did…I think," replied Road Toad. "I don't know…maybe I learned it in my past life and just forgot where I heard it. What difference does it make, anyway?"

The Farmer's Wife continued her efforts to be friendly: "When yer folks has t' move out of where yer livin'—that's gonna be jus' terrible, movin all the farm equipment an' then all yer animals. My Lord! I sure hope you folks kin find another place close by."

"You see," said the Tramp Prince, "it won't be quite so bad as you might think. We have no machinery other than a few hoes, rakes and shovels...and some pruning hooks and cutters. And we don't have *any* farm animals."

"What?! No animals at all? Not even any chickens?" asked the astonished Farmer With The Brushy Beard.

"No," replied the Tramp Prince. "My father decided long ago that animals were an unnecessary burden and cost far more than they were worth. And he didn't like the idea of putting them into a kind of slave relationship to benefit our human desires."

The Tramp Prince then explained in more detail, "We get by quite well on our garden produce and the orchard fruit — and we go out in to the woods in the fall to collect bushels of nuts from the walnuts, hickories, pecan trees and the hazelnut bushes. That may be a rather simple kind of life, but it leaves us a lot of time to enjoy the beauty of the forest and the lovely fluffy clouds and the spectacular colors of the sunsets."

"Wal — I sure can't understan' someone livin' without steaks 'n' eggs 'n' butter 'n' cheeze 'n' all!" the Farmer With The Brushy Beard commented, shaking his head in bewilderment.

"Seems like he's doin' alright on it," the farmer's wife chimed in. "Looks pretty big 'n' strong t' me."

"Wal..." drawled the Farmer With The Brushy Beard again, "I guess I ain't gonna change what I'm doin'. But it gives me sumpthin' t' thnk about — when I ain't got nuthin else t' think about."

"Which is most of the time!" laughed his wife.

When the meal was finished, the Farmer With The Brushy Beard said to the Tramp Prince: "Look here. It's already near dark. You can't walk no further. Like I told you, there ain't no extra bed here, but you kin sleep down in the barn ef you want ta."

After thanking the farmer, the Tramp Prince walked down to the barn. When he reached the open stable door, he took Road Toad from the jacket pocket.

"I'll leave you out here for tonight so that you can find something to eat," he told his small friend. You'll probably be better off under a log than in my pocket. I might crush you if I rolled over on that side."

"Yes, indeed," said Road Toad. "I would much prefer not being crushed."

The Tramp Prince then went into the barn and climbed up to the loft. He found a crevice between straw bales and pulled two bales overhead, forming an almost sound-proof, tiny, straw room. During the night, the cows mooed and the horses whinnied, but the Tramp Prince slept soundly through their nocturnal concert.

When he awoke in the morning, just after daybreak, the Tramp Prince found Road Toad waiting for him at the barn door.

"Hop aboard," the Prince announced, kneeling down so that Road Toad could leap up into his pocket.

"Sleep well?" asked Road Toad.

"Yes, very well, thank you!" the Tramp Prince replied. "How about you?"

"I'm afraid I can't say the same. There was a cricket under that log right near me and he kept me awake with his singing all night long."

"Sorry about that," said the Tramp Prince. "But it's better you were kept awake one night than to have been put to sleep permanently, don't you think?"

Road Toad said nothing.

Since the farmer and his wife and daughter were already hard at work doing their morning chores, the Tramp Prince thanked them for their hospitality, said goodbye and began walking down the lane toward the road. The farmer's daughter came running after him.

"Do you think you'll ever come back by this way again?" she asked.

"I...I'm not really sure," replied the Tramp Prince.

"I wish you would..." said the farmer's daughter.

"I know...it would be nice to see you again. But I have no way of knowing where my travels will take me — or how long it will take to find an abandoned garden. Right now, my first commitment is to my family's needs, so I simply cannot make any promises."

"We could go away together and share the experience...I'm sixteen; I'm old enough."

The Tramp Prince looked deeply into the scintillating blue of the eyes of the farmer's daughter. "You must know that I am *very* tempted to do that. You *are* a beautiful girl — and even more important than that — you have a beautiful mind. But my common sense tells me that the rigors and hardships of a life on the road are no way to begin a relationship. In fact, it could well prove to be disastrous for both of us!"

"I will promise you this, though," he told her as an afterthought," when my life is more settled, I *will* try to come back again. But you should not plan your life around my return — so much that is unknown and unknowable can happen to any of us."

The farmer's daughter gave the Tramp Prince a light kiss on his cheek, then turned and walked away, wiping tears from her eyes. Suddenly, she looked back and called out: "I won't forget you; you're important to me."

Later, the Tramp Prince sent a thought to Road Toad, "An idea just occurred to me. Perhaps I should be asking everyone I meet exactly what they think is *truly* important in life. What do you think of that, Road Toad?"

"I think you might get a bunch of weird answers — but, on the other hand, why not?"

After the Tramp Prince had walked several miles on down the road, exploring to no avail each weed-grown drive and lane, he received a telepathic thought from Road Toad: "I'm hungry again. Couldn't find very many bugs last night at that late hour."

"Alright. I'll put you down at the next patch of woods and take a rest, myself," the Tramp Prince advised him.

"I'm curious," said Road Toad, "why you didn't tell that pretty farmer's daughter about *me*. I don't like being ignored!"

"Ah well..." sighed the Tramp Prince. "Let's just say that you are *not* exactly *easy* to explain!"

"No, I'm not — that's true," said Road Toad, "but you, yourself, are not so easy to explain and you seem to do a pretty good job of it."

"Look," he told Road Toad, "One long explanation is enough for one day. Besides, you need a toad girlfriend. Right"

"Yeah, sure...right!" grumbled Road Toad.

Chapter 3: The Rich Man With The Top Hat

After resting a while, the Tramp Prince put Road Toad into his pocket again and began walking. Several more miles along the road, he came upon a motor car, broken down with a flat tire. The owner of the car was a large, well-dressed rich man, wearing a top hat and white gloves. He seemed exasperated as he stood in the back of his huge convertible Berline, directing instructions to the chauffeur who was attempting to change the tire.

"How could you *possibly* be so stupid as to forget to put the jack in the tool box?" the Rich Man With The Top Hat shouted to his chauffeur.

"I don't know, sir," responded the chauffeur. "I could have sworn I saw it in there yesterday. Maybe someone stole it when we were parked on the street in town last night."

"Yes, that's possible," said the Rich Man With The Top Hat. "But it will certainly not happen again — because, when we get back to town, the first thing I intend to do is to have a locksmith install a padlock on that running board tool box. That is, *if* we ever get back to town! Why don't you go up to that nearest farmhouse and see if they have a jack that you can borrow?"

"I have an idea!" said the Tramp Prince, who had been observing the situation from behind the car."Why don't we get a fence rail from that broken down fence over there; then we'll get some large flat rocks and place them near the back end of the car and use the fence rail as a lever?"

"Wonderful idea!" said the Rich Man With The Top Hat. "I shall get out of the car so that you'll not have to lift my own considerable weight as well."

The Tramp Prince and the chauffeur collected several large stones, placing them just behind the rear of the axel housing and chose a still sound fence rail to use as a lever.

When the Tramp Prince pushed down on the fence rail, the back of the car went up easily, allowing the chauffeur to quickly replace the rim and tire.

"What a brilliantly innovative young man you are!" the Rich Man With The Top Hat said to the Tramp Prince, as they watched the chauffeur tighten the wheel bolts. "Would you like a ride into town with us? You appear to be a tramp, and I'm curious to know why someone so young and with such an obviously bright mind would have chosen to follow the tramp life."

The Tramp Prince, being very tired by now, got into the back of the big convertible Berline as the chauffeur closed the top. He sat down next to the Rich Man With The Top Hat so as to be able to talk easily above the road noise.

During the twenty minute ride into the town where the Rich Man With The Top Hat lived, the Tramp Prince was able to explain what had happened to his family and why he was on the road.

Stroking his large handle bar moustache, as he mused the Tramp Prince's problem, the Rich Man With The Top Hat finally reflected: "Perhaps tomorrow, if you would like to, I could let you have the use of my motor car and have my chauffeur drive you around to all of the rural areas surrounding this town. That might save you a great deal of time in making your search."

"Oh, definitely," the Tramp Prince replied enthusiastically, "but are you really sure you can afford to allow me that luxury of your car and chauffeur?"

"Of course, my boy! Why you've done me a great favor and I shall be most happy to return one to you. I own a large shoe factory here in town and all that I need in the morning is to be driven to my office; then you may have use of the car and chauffeur the rest of the day."

"Thank you so very much!" responded the Tramp Prince.

"And another thing," continued the Rich Man With The Top Hat, "since you have no place to stay for the night, you might like to come home with me and sleep at my house. There are two empty bedrooms so it would be no imposition on me. And I think my family would enjoy meeting such an interesting young man as yourself. You can see my house from here." And he pointed out a large Victorian mansion just ahead, with an expanse of well kept lawn.

A large circular drive led to the canopied front entrance and the chauffeur drove around stopping the vehicle beneath the canopy.

"This is where I live," the Rich Man With Top Hat commented with a light, almost jocular, tone.

The Tramp Prince then accompanied the Rich Man With The Top Hat into his house, where introductions were made to the rest of the family.

"This young man has a very quick and inventive mind the Rich Man With The Top Hat told his wife and daughters.

After having explained the Tramp Prince's family's situation and how the young man had solved the dilemma of the lack of a jack, the Rich Man With The Top Hat said: "I haven't told him this yet, but I'm hoping he'll consider staying on to become an assistant to my chauffeur...so that he can earn money to help his family."

The Tramp Prince stood there in his rough outfit, a bit perplexed and feeling somewhat uneasy in the presence of the family with their splendid clothing and in their home's gleaming ornate interior.

During a few moments of awkward silence, the Tramp Prince looked around at the hallway's interior; the stairway with its delicate, intricate spindles — the polished mahogany banister-rail and the floor-to-ceiling oak paneling topped by a fringe of fancifully carved floral designs and gargoyle faces. With its stained-glass windows and ornate blue newel post lamp, the staircase paraded its still shining and pristine Victorian opulence.

Suddenly the youngest daughter went running up to her father. "Papa! Papa! I want you to hear the song I just learned on the piano!"

So, everyone followed her into the drawing room, where she performed a simplified version of "Heliotrope Bouquet". As she sat at the glossy grand piano, she looked almost like a little doll in a marionette display. Everyone applauded the child's delicate, but accurate, interpretation.

"I'm very impressed," the Tramp Prince told the family. "We don't have a piano at my home — and the only musical instrument I've ever learned to play is a small flute of my own design. I carved it from a branch of a wild cherry tree."

"Oh," said the young daughter, "I wish I could see it!"

"Well you can," the Tramp Prince replied, "It's in my sack; I carried it along because I thought there might be some leisure time to practice on it."

"Oh, please play us something!" the rich man's wife and daughters implored.

The Tramp Prince dug into his canvas bag and pulled out the flute. He then played a few brief favorites on it.

"Where did you find the pattern to use so that you could carve this flute?" one of the daughters asked.

"I didn't have a pattern. Since we have plenty of wood, I simply made a few of these, until I got the hole sizes and shapes so that they produced the sounds and notes I wanted."

"Amazing!" said the Rich Man With The Top Hat. You are *truly* an innovator!"

Just then, the family's kitchen maid announced that dinner was served and everyone filed into the dining hall where they sat down at the long, linen-covered table.

The Tramp Prince looked around in awe, observing the finely carved oak fringe at the top of the room's wood paneled walls and the elaborate scroll-sawed decorative grille work, which spanned the doorway entrance. On each side, below the grille, hung a curtain with hand-carved wooden beads that alternated with colored glass ones and draped nearly to the floor. Above the dining table, at each end, were two large brass chandeliers, each fitted with several electric light bulbs.

The Rich Man With The Top Hat watched the Tramp Prince as he looked around at the decorations in the room. He smiled with pride.

"It *is* a finely appointed house, is it not?"

"Yes," replied the Tramp Prince. "The little village near my family's house doesn't even have any electric power yet."

"Electricity will soon be sent to every nook and cranny — everywhere," said the Rich Man With The Top Hat. "And automobiles will be swarming over the roads by the millions."

"I hope not," returned his young guest. "The motor car is such a smelly, noisy contraption that it could destroy the peace and quiet of the countryside."

"Well, there are advantages and disadvantages to every invention," observed the Rich Man With The Top Hat. "My own car is a Lozier, the finest make one can buy, and it's not plagued with the many problems that are so common among the less expensive motor cars. Tomorrow, you'll see what I mean."

As the servants brought in the dinner, there were platters heaped with many kinds of vegetables and one huge platter with a great slab of steaming roast beef, dripping with the juice and melted fat.

"How much of this roast beef would you like?" the Rich Man With The Top Hat asked his guest. He began carving off thick slices.

"The vegetables will do very well for me, sir," replied the Tramp Prince. "That's the simple fare I'm used to having at home."

"My, my..." the Rich Man With The Top Hat said in astonishment. "Why, I could not live without my roast beef and steaks!"

The Tramp Prince remained silent, not wishing to incite a philosophic confrontation at his host's dinner table.

After the dinner was through, the eldest daughter came over to the Tramp Prince: "One of my boyfriends, Reggie, is coming over tonight to take me out dancing. Actually I can't *stand* Reggie, and I've been trying to get rid of him for weeks. Maybe if you were to come along with us, it might discourage him. I could say that you're my cousin from out of town."

"But I'm *not* your cousin," said the Tramp Prince with naïve honesty.

"Well," smiled the daughter, "if we went far enough back into history, we'd find that we're *all* related — distant cousins at some point. I just don't have to tell him *how* distant that is, do I?"

The Tramp Prince laughed.

"See, the only reason I even started dating Reggie is because he does have a nice, shiny, new red Stutz Bearcat speedster with a mother-in-law seat. But he'll know he can't get fresh with me with someone watching him from behind."

"I see," the Tramp Prince reflected.

"But that's not the only reason I want you to come along. I'm...just sort of embarrassed to have to be seen with Reggie. It's not that he's ugly — he just parts his hair in the middle and plasters it down. Y' know what I mean?" And she wrinkled her nose.

The Tramp Prince chuckled again.

"Besides," the daughter went on, "I kinda like you — you're cute!"

"But, what about my clothes?" the Tramp Prince pointed out with some chagrin.

"I'll see to it that we don't go to any place that's fancy," the daughter reassured him.

When her date arrived at the door, the butler ushered him into the parlor where introductions were made. The young man's facial expression was obviously one of displeasure when he learned that they would be accompanied by the Tramp Prince.

"Well, my father wants me to return early tonight, anyway," he told the daughter.

"What a relief!" she thought to herself.

The Tramp Prince excused himself for a few moments before following the pair to the car.

"Road Toad," said the Tramp Prince to his friend, "I'm going to put you down here in the front of the house so that you can find yourself something to eat. I'll pick you up again when we return."

"Humpf!" responded Road Toad with obvious irritation. "Another late meal for me! Why couldn't you have slipped me something at the dinner table? Didn't you get my thought I sent you?"

"Sorry, I must have been too absorbed in conversation. Anyway, what would I have given you? There weren't any bugs — that house doesn't even have a single roach on the floor!" the Tramp Prince's mental voice was apologetic. "Well — I'll see you later."

The Stutz with its three passengers roared off down the street and onto a country lane.

"Why don't you stop at that roadhouse up ahead?" suggested the rich man's daughter. "Then you won't have to bother lighting the head lamps."

As they slowed to a stop near the roadhouse's half open door, they could hear ragtime piano music drifting out into the early evening still. After seating themselves in the tavern, Reggie ordered three glasses of beer.

"Hope you two don't mind just ordinary beer," Reggie sighed with just a touch of sarcasm. "Anyway, we can start with that."

When the waiter had brought three glasses and a pitcher of beer, Reggie filled a glass for each of them.

"Here's to you!" he asserted loudly as he swallowed down a big gulp.

The Tramp Prince watched as the daughter began to drink hers. He sat staring at his own glass, and then lifted it to his mouth, smelling the contents before taking a sip. Although the odor seemed a little unpleasant, the Tramp Prince took a small taste into his mouth. With a grimace of displeasure, he attempted to swallow the amber liquid.

Reggie looked at the Tramp Prince and laughed loudly.

"What's the matter — never taste beer before?"

"Un, uh…no…and I don't know if I'll ever want to again."

With loud guffaws, Reggie almost fell out of his seat with laughter.

"I didn't like the taste myself, when I first tried it, but you sort of get used to it after a few times," interjected the daughter.

"I," said the Tramp Prince, "think I will prefer not to ever get used to it. Frankly, it tastes *awful!*"

"It's the effect it has on you — that's why you drink it," Reggie told the Tramp Prince. "Here, want a cigarette?" he asked as he slipped from his pocket a shiny cigarette case with his name engraved on it. He flipped the lid up and withdrew three of the small white cylinders, lighting one from a burning candle on the table.

"Go on — take one," he commanded the Tramp Prince. "Haven't you ever smoked a cigarette either?"

"No!" said the Tramp Prince with complete honesty.

"Well, you may as well try now!" the haughty young antagonist advised him.

With that, the Tramp Prince took one of the cigarettes and lit it, watching the smoke curl up toward the ceiling.

"Go on — take a drag!" Reggie sat across from the Tramp Prince with a wickedly gleeful smile on his face. "Just suck on it and take a deep drag into your lungs!"

And that was exactly what the Tramp Prince did. Instantly he began coughing violently until he became almost prostrated trying to get his breath and eliminate the smoke from his lungs.

"That *hurts!*" said the Tramp Prince between coughs.

Reggie again laughed so hard that he was barely able to avoid falling out of his chair.

"Well, you just have to get used to it, old boy!"

"But who," asked the Tramp Prince, "would ever want to get used to something that hurts so much?"

"A lot of people do," the daughter advised him.

The Tramp Prince shook his head in disgust and disbelief: "A lot of people must be doing a lot of things that make no sense!"

The rich man's daughter shrugged her shoulders. "Can't argue with that! Hey! Let's dance!"

The ragtime 'professor' had begun playing a lively new Joplin composition and the crowd moved onto the dance floor — Reggie and his date among them. After several minutes of intensive gyrations of arms and legs and hips, the couples retired to their seats.

"Great dance, huh?" was the daughter's enthusiastic comment.

Reggie said nothing, but poured himself another glass of beer.

"I need a shot of whiskey!" announced the young man with the plastered-down hair.

After having obtained the hard liquor, Reggie swallowed it in one gulp and immediately followed it with a couple more glasses of beer. He slowly slumped down in his seat into a drunken stupor.

"Come on...!" shouted the daughter to the Tramp Prince. "Let's dance! That jerk's dead to the world!"

The Tramp Prince protested, "But the only dancing I've ever done is to the waltz — that's all I know."

"Well, I'll teach you the new one they're all doing, the 'Paris Trolley-hop'. It's the *rage!*"

The rich man's daughter grabbed the Tramp Prince by the arm and yanked him out onto the dance floor as the 'professor' swung his way into another fast-paced tune.

"See, it's simple! Just follow my steps. First stamp your right foot and swing it back behind your left. Then hop twice on your left foot and swing your girl. You get the idea?"

The Tramp Prince tried to follow the steps of his partner, tripping over his own feet and missing the rhythm. For several minutes he gamely participated until the song ended.

"I'm sorry," he told the rich man's daughter. "I must have been born with two left feet."

The girl laughed. "Hey — you did okay. We're all like that the first time we try a dance that's so different from anything we know."

"You're very kind to say that, but I know better." Then looking over at her date, he added, "but what I *don't* know, however, is how we're going to get back to town."

"Yes," said the young woman. "Reggie's in no condition to drive his car and I don't know how to drive. Do you?"

"No," admitted the Tramp Prince, "but I'd rather *try* to do it than to see you have to walk the three or four miles back to town this late at night."

The rich man's daughter and the Tramp Prince, after failing to rouse the drunken young man with the plastered-down hair, finally succeeded in getting him to stand up far enough so that they could each get under an arm. Then they half-carried, half-dragged their driver to his car.

"Can you start this thing?" the Tramp Prince said to the inebriated owner.

"Shurt'nly!" was the response, as the young tippler stumbled to the front seat and reached over, turning the switch on the coil box. Then, stumbling to the front of the car, he grabbed the crank and gave it a mighty twist, which threw him off balance, spinning to the side where he landed on his seat in the gravel.

Miraculously, the car's engine had caught immediately and was racing away as the car's owner was loaded into the mother-in-law seat with his legs hanging out. The rich man's daughter turned on the Prestolite tank and lit the carbide head lamps.

When they were seated, the Tramp Prince asked the rich man's daughter, "How do you make this thing go?"

"I think you push in on the clutch pedal — that's the one on the left; pull the gear shift lever and let out on the clutch. But I don't know which position on the shifter is which."

The Tramp Prince pushed in the clutch, pulled the shifter lever toward himself and let out the clutch. The shrieking car lurched and began bucking forward like some angry bronco.

"Give 'er shome *gas*!" shouted the incapacitated inhabitant of the mother-in-law seat. The Tramp Prince quickly began pulling levers and pushing pedals until the car suddenly roared out on the road. The vehicle continued picking up speed.

"You must have put it in high gear!" shouted the rich man's daughter as they raced away at a high rate toward town. "Whee! You're a *scorcher*!"

"Yes, but it's certainly not intentional," the Tramp Prince shouted back.

He soon found, though, that by moving the gas lever on the steering sector, that he could reduce the speed of the car. But when they got close to town, the Tramp Prince was even more perplexed: "The problem now is: How do I *stop* this thing?"

The rich man's daughter thought for a moment. "I guess you push on the brake and push in the clutch; or maybe it's the other way around. I don't know…"

As they came within sight of the rich man's mansion, the Tramp Prince pushed in pedals and moved levers and turned switches until the car's engine finally stopped and the speedster slowly rolled up to the curb, not far from the house.

"Whew! What an experience!" the Tramp Prince exclaimed. His hands were shaking as though he were still holding onto the vibrating steering wheel.

"Oh, you did just *great*, honey!" said the rich man's daughter. And she planted a big wet kiss on his lips as they walked up to the house.

Upon reaching the door, the Tramp Prince lagged a few paces behind as the rich man's daughter entered the house. Reaching down, he scooped up Road Toad and deposited his diminutive friend again into the jacket pocket.

"Well," said Road Toad with some irritation, "it's about time!"

"I know — I know," the Tramp Prince returned apologetically. "But that turned into *quite* an experience."

On the way upstairs as the butler showed him to his room, the Tramp Prince explained to Road Toad in a thought message what had happened that evening.

"Wow!" Road Toad thought back. "When are you going out like that again?"

"Not for a while…" responded the Tramp Prince, sardonically. "Not for a *very* long while."

"Aw…" mused Road Toad. "I'd just *love* to go with you and watch all the excitement. What fun!"

"Harrumph!" was the Tramp Prince's reaction. "You should know that *excitement* is not necessarily a synonym for fun!"

Road Toad did not respond as the Tramp Prince hung his jacket on the back of a large chair with carved lion's heads on each arm.

Then he kicked off his shoes and laid down on the bed, where he sank into its fluffy feather quilt. Before turning off the light, he carefully viewed the opulence of the room's interior.

"I just wonder," he thought, "if I should really be staying in a house that's such a conspicuous display of grandiose wealth. I wonder if I even deserve to be here."

Road Toad pushed one eye up above the edge of the jacket pocket and looked around.

"Well, of course you deserve it. Just like I, a lowly toad, deserve to be sleeping in a nice warm jacket pocket in the room."

"It's just that there are so many people out there in the world who have to sleep on straw mattresses in ramshackle houses that are cold and drafty," remarked the Tramp Prince.

"Enjoy your brief exposure to wealth — it won't last long!" Road Toad advised him.

The Tramp Prince shut off the light and enjoyed a comfortable, though somewhat troubled sleep.

In the morning, the Tramp Prince accompanied the Rich Man With The Top Hat to the shoe factory in his great Lozier motor car. There was no longer any sign of the Stutz or its owner in front of the house.

"I guess that drunken young fool finally sobered up enough to drive his automobile away from here," observed the Rich Man With The Top Hat. "My daughter told me what happened last night. You know, she thinks very highly of you. You're not only quite inventive, but you're also a young man with a lot of grit."

"Thank you for the compliment," returned the Tramp Prince. "In a situation like last night, though, it's not something you think a lot about — you just get in there and do what has to be done. Probably anyone else would have done the same thing under those circumstances."

"You're too modest about yourself, my boy," suggested the Rich Man With The Top Hat.

"I guess I'd rather be modest and somewhat successful, than to be puffed up with pride, thinking I could tackle anything that came along and then overstep my abilities and fail at something."

"Good thought, young man."

Just then, they reached the shoe factory, and The Rich Man With The Top Hat, true to his word, turned over the Lozier and the chauffeur to the Tramp Prince.

"Since I know that you're short on money," said the Rich Man With The Top Hat, "I'll give you enough to fill the tank. Let's see…five cents times twenty gallons…" And he handed the Tramp Prince a few coins from his pocket. "There's a petrol dealer only a short distance from here. The chauffeur knows where to go. Good luck!"

At the petrol dealer's station, the large, square, red tank with its huge hard-rubber-tired iron wheels was rolled out to the curb and the car's tank filled.

"You'd better fill the emergency tank on the running board too," the chauffeur advised the attendant.

After paying, the Tramp Prince had one shiny coin left, which he dropped into his pocket.

All morning, the Tramp Prince had the chauffeur drive him around from one country road to another in a pattern roughly beginning to encircle the town. At each weed-grown lane, he would hike until the remains of a house was found or until the lane ended in a farmer's field.

After several more hours, the Tramp Prince came upon an abandoned farm house that appeared to be relatively intact. As he walked onto the porch floor, the boards creaked and cracked. When he opened the unlocked front door, barely stepping inside, the interior of the house suddenly made a rumbling, grumbling noise as large sections of the floor and inside walls went crashing into the cellar. The boy had stepped back just in time to avoid falling in with the rubble.

"Great heavens!" telepathized Road Toad. "What was *that?*"

"A termite infested death trap!" the Tramp Prince retorted. "The rumbling that you heard was the inside of the house falling into the basement. It couldn't take the extra pressure of my weight."

"Put me down!" said Road Toad. "I shall gobble up those little devils."

"Too late now," the Tramp Prince advised. "They've been gone probably for years. They're smart. The eat only enough of the wood so that it doesn't fall in from its own weight. Then they go someplace else."

The Tramp Prince walked back to the waiting motor car, his clothes now almost completely covered with burrs and stick-tights from the hours of hiking through weeds. He again sat down in the front of the car where he had been riding.

"I hope these burrs and stick-tights don't come off on the seats," he told the chauffeur.

"They won't stick to leather, I'm sure; I'm just glad you're not riding in the back in that plush mohair! I'd have to spend all day tomorrow cleaning those stickers off!" And the chauffeur chuckled.

Of the three more abandoned farmhouses that the Tramp Prince found that day, all were so badly rotted by the rain and torn by the wind, that they held no hope for rehabilitation.

The chauffeur looked at the big Elgin car clock on the dash and gave it a few winds.

"I'm sorry," he said, "but it's late enough now that we need to return to the shoe factory to pick up the boss."

That evening, the Tramp Prince related the events of the day to the Rich Man With The Top Hat.

"I'm very sorry to know that you had no success today," he sympathized. "Have you considered my offer to let you work as an assistant to my chauffeur? I can pay you a salary and if you save most of it, you could take that back to your family."

"Sir, I'm afraid that amount would not be sufficient for it to make any difference quickly enough. Besides — I know almost nothing about motor cars."

"But you could learn. You're a smart boy."

"If the truth be known," the Tramp Prince sighed looking out the window at the setting sun, "I would much prefer spending my life leaning about plants and flowers and trees and the animals that run free in the woods."

"Ah well..." replied the Rich Man With The Top Hat. "Say..." he mused, "I could pay you more if you were to work at my shoe factory. We'd have to start you off as an office boy or dockworker, but you're such a bright fellow, you'd probably be able to work up to becoming an assistant manager in just a few weeks. With that kind of salary, you'd surely be able to help your family.

The Tramp Prince's immediate reaction was neither positive, nor negative, but he said nothing.

"Come down to the factory with me tomorrow and look around. Ask questions. Then you can think about it and make an intelligent decision."

"Alright," said the Tramp Prince. "I'll do that."

The next day, after the Rich Man With The Top Hat had shown the Tramp Prince the various sections of his factory and how to operate the elevator, he said to the Tramp Prince: "I must go into the office now and take care of some large contracts, but you're welcome to go anywhere you wish here and ask the workers any kinds of questions you might have."

"Thank you," the Tramp Prince replied.

The first worker that the Tramp Prince encountered was a last designer.

"Hello..." said the Tramp Prince.

"Um hum," returned the last designer, pulling his glasses down after having examined some figures on a piece of paper.

"I was just wondering if you could give me a very brief idea of what you do. See, I'm considering the possibility of working here."

"Uh...well — I'll be happy to do that, but you'll have to come back in a while. I'm about to meet with some of the other workers for a few minutes to talk about getting a union in here...you know? So that we can have collective bargaining on problems — and have some representatives to fight for a fair wage."

After the man had walked away, the Tramp Prince listened for a few moments to the whirring of motors and the clacking of leather drive belts — and the periodic thump-thump of leather stamping machines. He began following the shoe last designer from some distance.

A group of workers had gathered in a dim corner of the factory's main building. The Tramp Prince, in order not to be seen by them, walked around and stood behind a nearby pile of large bales of leather so that he could hear their conversation.

"I say we oughtta form our *own* union an' go out on strike right now!" one angry man expressed. "Why wait for a national union to get around to coming in here?"

"Because, we'd have better bargaining power... with other factories possibly going out on a sympathy strike," said the shoe last designer.

"That doesn't put no food on my table now!" the first worker responded.

"No, it don't!" chorused several others.

"I'm just makin' a pittance here!" the first man insisted. "You know most of the rest of the workers here ain't doin' no better than I am!"

The meeting of the workers lasted only a few more minutes without coming to any decision. The Tramp Prince then took an elevator to an upper floor where shoe assemblers were stitching leather tops onto the soles. He looked down the long line of shoe stitching machines, most operated by young women. Two of the stitchers were girls not too much older than his own sister. The paleness of their faces was accentuated by the dim overhead lights and years of dirt on the windows. Dust had accumulated in thick layers on everything not moved daily.

"What do you think Road Toad?" The Tramp Prince sent out a mental inquiry to his still pocketed friend.

"What I think," Road Toad responded, " is that shoes would be better made by the local cobbler. He might *be* just as poor as these folks, but he wouldn't have to work in these awful conditions."

"Yes, my sentiments also," was the Tramp Prince's thought response.

He then returned to the office of the Rich Man With The Top Hat. As he entered the office, the Rich Man With The Top Hat motioned toward a chair next to his desk.

"Sit here, my boy. I hope you won't mind waiting a few minutes before we talk, but there are three or four checks that I need to sign and a contract that needs to be reread before I signature it. I should have done this yesterday afternoon, but there wasn't time. You know how business is…"

"Oh, I don't mind at all, sir; I'm enjoying looking at the beautiful carvings on your desk — and the decorations on the woodwork around the ceiling."

"Hmmm…yes — glad you like them," the Rich Man With The Top Hat mumbled back as he gave his attention to the papers he was perusing. After signing several of them, he turned his attention back to the Tramp Prince.

"Well, have you made a decision?" asked the factory owner.

An elderly man with a large push broom came in front of where the Tramp Prince was sitting by the desk of the Rich Man With The Top Hat. The broom held a pile of dust and papers in front of it and the elderly man pulled a dust pan and brush off his belt, scooped up the dust and litter and deposited it into a nearby wastebasket. As the man moved about, the Tramp Prince could observe that the old fellow had a badly crippled leg and arm. When the broom pusher was out of earshot, the Rich Man With The Top Hat remarked softly: "I only keep him on out of the goodness of my heart. You see, he was injured when a large bale of leather fell from a crane a few years ago. He's really not worth much of anything now, but I let him sweep the floors and pay him enough that he can buy food and shelter."

"That is generous of you, I suppose, but what about the other workers?" asked the Tramp Prince. "Some of them say they can't live on what they're making here!"

"My boy," said the Rich Man With The Top Hat, "I'm paying the same wage per hour as all the rest of the shoe factories! I can't pay more and still be competitive."

Road Toad whispered a telepathic message to the Tramp Prince, "Tell him that the workers should be the owners!"

"What?!" thought back the Tramp Prince, "Why, he'll kick me out of the office door if I say that!"

"Do it!!" returned Road Toad.

"Maybe..." said the Tramp Prince to the Rich Man With The Top Hat, "if all of the workers owned a portion of the factory, when there were good profits, they could share some of it and perhaps enjoy a little better quality of life."

"Oh, my boy, you simply don't understand how business works!" I am the owner of this factory because I have dedicated my life to it and risked my wealth and reputation — put them on the line to build this business for *years*! Why should I give it all away to the workers?"

"Not *all* of it," clarified the Tramp Prince, "just enough so that the workers would each own a small share — and the extra money that they would get and knowing that they owned a small part of the factory might act as an incentive for them to work harder, be more productive and more careful and make suggestions that would cut costs and increase profits for all."

The Rich Man With The Top Hat smiled: "That's an interesting, thought-provoking idea," he said, "but it *won't* work. The *reason* it won't work is because most workers don't have the *incentive* to be owners. If they did, they would go out and start their own shoe factories like I did."

The Tramp Prince's face took on a look of exasperation: "But the average worker may have family commitments that you didn't have; he may not have access to the necessary capital; he probably doesn't have the advantage of your educational background... lots of other things are probably not the same..."

"Sir," said the Tramp Prince calmly, "you must be getting enough wealth from this factory that you wouldn't be able to spend it all in two lifetimes. Couldn't you share just a little of that wealth with your workers? *They're* the ones making your wealth possible and you would still be getting far more than any of them as primary owner...for all your expertise and investment."

"Ah, you see, my boy, I still also have to provide for *my* daughters."

"And won't they become productive members of some work force somewhere themselves?"

The Rich Man With The Top Hat wrinkled his brow, "Probably they will... but one must be prepared for unforeseen future emergencies. Life is very unpredictable; one can never tell what disaster may befall any of us!"

"Yes sir, I would be among the very first to agree with you about that. But life should not be based on remote possibilities, but on the obvious *probabilities*," the Tramp Prince philosophized.

"There's another thing you haven't considered, son." The Rich Man With The Top Hat stroked his great handlebar moustache. "Once you start giving these workers something, they just continue to want more — and more — and more...until you have nothing left for yourself!"

"Well then, sir, I'm wondering what you think really matters in life..."

The Rich Man With The Top Hat first acquired a puzzled look, then his brow compressed in anger.

"I'm disappointed in you," he sputtered gruffly, "why the answer to that is absolutely self-evident! Everyone knows — or should well know — that, in this kind of a world, *money* is the only thing that really matters; actually, having *lots* of money…so that you can not only buy everything you need to have a comfortable life, but also be able to insulate and protect yourself from all the thieves and confidence men out there just waiting to try to steal all you own."

"But sir…isn't it also true that the less one owns, the less of a target one becomes for these thieves?"

"Yes, yes, that's true. So what do you want us to do — all live like Saint Francis of Assisi? Not even have enough money to feed the birds — let alone ourselves? *Money*! That's what makes the world go 'round. Yes, money…and *lots* of it!

"And it's not true what they say about money not necessarily being able to buy you happiness. Why, I'm the happiest fellow you'll meet! Ha, ha, ha, ha… I'm the jolliest fellow in this factory — and the wealthiest. I'm the jolliest fellow in the whole town!"

"Tell me," said the Tramp Prince gravely, "if you didn't have your health, what difference would your money make?"

"But I *do* have my health and my money helps me afford to *keep* my health. And even if I lost my health, my money would certainly make my misery a lot more bearable."

"I suppose," said the Tramp Prince, with obvious dismay, "that I shouldn't have expected you to say anything different."

"No…no, why should you have?"

The Tramp Prince could see that this conversation had reached an abrupt end.

"I'm sorry, sir, but I don't see how it would benefit me spiritually to begin working here. In addition, even at a manger's salary, it would take me far longer than six months to save enough money to buy a property for my family. And until I was able to save enough, they would have to come to this city and live in some tenement apartment. They would never be able to tolerate that kind of life, having enjoyed the freedom of simple rural living for so long. I do appreciate your interest in me and your concern, but I must leave now." And the Tramp Prince shook the hand of the Rich Man With The Top Hat and walked out of the door.

"Come back…" called out the Rich Man With The Top Hat. "In a few years you might even become part owner here! Why, after you've learned the business, I'll open a branch factory in another city and make you the manager. Then you can do whatever you want."

The Tramp Prince continued on, smiling sadly, he turned and waved farewell.

"Thank you again... but I don't think so." Then he went out of the shoe factory, leaving behind the clicking and clacking and thumping of machinery and the slapping of the huge drive belts.

The Tramp Prince walked the mile and a half back to the mansion, where he retrieved his backpack and began again on his way down the road.

"Well," he asked Road Toad, " do you think I did the right thing, or do you think I threw away an opportunity?"

Road Toad, who had listened attentively to the conversation at the factory quickly perked up. "That man may be very sincere right now while he's making you the offer, but so much can change over a period of time. You have no assurance of anything. I doubt that he would have put it in writing — made a contract. If one has a gut feeling about something not being right, it's best to follow that feeling. Anyway, all I can say is that I, personally, would not have liked it a bit being cooped up in that dirty, noisy factory for eight or ten hours every day...but then...what do I know — I'm just an ignorant toad. No one pays attention to toads!"

Chapter 4: The Elderly Tramp and The Dancing Girl

By the time the Tramp Prince had walked a few more miles on another road leading toward the largest city in the area, he began to encounter many other people traveling in the same direction. Some of these people were on horseback, some sat in crude carts pulled by donkeys — some drove motor cars or trucks and then there were even a few foot tramps like himself.

It was at an old roadhouse that sold petrol where the Tramp Prince saw an elderly tramp sitting on a rough-hewn log bench in front of one of the front windows. He sat down next to the elderly tramp.

"Hello!" the Tramp Prince said cheerily.

"Yes, and hello to you as well, me b'y."

The Elderly Tramp spoke in an Irish brogue with a soft, sad intonation to his voice. "T'would look t'me like yer jost shtartin' out on th' road," the Elderly Tramp observed.

"You're right," the Tramp Prince told him and then asked: "Which way are you headed?"

"Ah, young lad... A'm headed whichever way the wind blows me. A've been travelin' the roads since Ay was not much older than you are now. At me age, Ay don't much care where Ay go or what happens when Ay gets there! Yuh wish t' wa'k along wi' me fer a bit? Thir's no bummin' a meal here at this place!"

The two tramps began walking on the country road toward the large city, but the Tramp Prince soon noticed that his newly acquired friend moved with an impediment of age.

"Y'd prob'ly be better off t'be movin' alang wi' out th' loiks a' me holdin' y' back," the Elderly Tramp admitted.

After having explained his purpose for being on the road, the Tramp Prince added: "You can rest whenever I need to explore an unused country lane. And I still have some pieces of dried fruit left in the bag I brought from home. You're welcome to that if you're as hungry as you look."

"Oh, me b'y," the Elderly Tramp said sadly, "that is kind o' yer t' offer t' share what little food y' have...but Ay haven't enough a' me teeth left t' be able t' be chewin' somthin' th' loiks a' that!" And he gave the Tramp Prince a broad smile showing why he had made the comment.

"We should seek some dental help for you in the city," the Tramp Prince said with enthusiasm.

The Elderly Tramp merely smiled again. "You'll learn, lad, that there's no dental assistance fer tramps." And he gave a bitter laugh. "Ay get along well enough whin th' food's well cooked —whin Ay kin bum somthin' t' eat, that is."

The Tramp Prince now looked more carefully at his elderly companion's long gray beard and ragged clothes and thought to himself that people must be sympathetic to the plight of an elderly, homeless man like that.

"No, I don't think so," Road Toad quickly telepathized back. "It seems to me, from what I've observed, that most folks don't like tramps...of *any* age!"

"Ah well," thought the Tramp Prince to Road Toad, I'm beginning to think that the best we can do late in life is to try to roll with the blows, so to speak."

"Ha!" replied Road Toad, sardonically. "You mean roll over and play dead!"

"Now, now," the Tramp Prince returned. "No sarcasm today! After all, someone had to exhibit plenty of enthusiasm for the great cathedrals to ever get built; for all the factories and the inventions they manufacture; for all the great works of art; for..."

"Hum-de-dum!" interrupted Road Toad. "The human race might just be better off without a lot of the 'great this' and 'great that' stuff. Look at all the wars people fight over it; the greed and hatred it can cause."

"Yes," the Tramp Prince agreed, "and I'll bet they did the same things back in the stone age over beads and birch bark canoes!"

"I wouldn't know," Road Toad countered, "so how do *you* know? 'Vas *you* dere, Charlie?'"

"Road Toad," the Tramp Prince confided, "you know something... you're like a thorn in my side."

"Really?" laughed Road Toad, "I didn't know my feet were pushing that far through your coat pocket!"

The Elderly Tramp had been sitting down resting—perhaps dreaming the dreams that only an old tramp can dream...of faraway castles, beautiful princesses; puffy clouds and delicate sunshine flickering through a wooded glen — where he sits throwing tiny pebbles into a pool of clear spring water as he munches the last handout that he procured at some kind woman's kitchen door.

"Maybe we ought to stop at the next farmhouse and I'll offer to do some work in exchange for our food," the Tramp Prince suggested.

"Oh laddie...Ay kin work. Ay'm just a bit slow about it. Ay've been all over this world bummin' an' Ay do know what's usually the best way t' beg a meal."

At the next farmhouse they came to, the Tramp Prince and the Elderly Tramp went to the back door and knocked.

"Yez niver wants t' go t' th' front o' th' house, me lad; 'specially in the cities. There's often a kindly disposed cook who'll be more agreeable than the lady of the house."

The Tramp Prince rapped on the back door.

"Yes, what is it that you want?" said a thin, grim-looking woman as she opened the door.

"Kind lady," the Elderly Tramp started out, "yer see, me n' me son here have fallen on some hard times. Our house was washed away in a great storm an' me wife wuz drowned in the flood, an..."

"An' don't you be tryin' t' soften me up with yer fanciful sob stories. There's a large pile of wood in the yard that needs cuttin' an' splittin'. When you've stacked enough of it up on the porch here, I might be able t' find somethin' for you to eat. And y' see this wood that's still up here? Well, the rest of it needs to be split up just like it — real fine! I'm a very delicate woman an' I can't carry large pieces," she squeaked, "Here's the axe an' the hatchet an' the saw." And the grim-faced woman pointed to the tools at the other end of the porch.

For the better part of an hour, the pair of tramps worked away, the Tramp Prince doing the more difficult sawing and the Elderly Tramp splitting and stacking the wood on the porch.

The Tramp Prince looked over at the stack: "I don't think you're splitting it up as fine as she wanted it; she said she couldn't carry much."

"Ah, lad, that takes too much time! The real reason she wants it split so small is 'cause this wood is still a bit green. It's easier to get uncured wood to burn when it's split thinner — you know that!"

The Tramp Prince shrugged: "But maybe she really does have a difficult time handling larger pieces."

"Ah, pish tosh! Ay'll bet she c'n handle a big heavy rollin' pin well enough if she wuz t' git mad at yuh n' come after yuh with it!"

The Elderly Tramp then split a few more of the logs into finer pieces and stacked them in front of the coarser splits, hiding the ends of the main stack.

"What she needs t' do, me b'y, is t' have a bunch of us tramps cut up an' split th' whole pile just normal like, then cover it so it can dry out."

"She's too cheap for that!" Road Toad telepathized to the Tramp Prince.

"Now how can you possibly say that?" the Tramp Prince responded aloud with cynicism.

"How can Ay possibly say *what*?" questioned the Elderly Tramp.

"I'm sorry. I wasn't talking to you," the Tramp Prince advised him. "I was talking to my friend, Road Toad, here and forgot — spoke out loud."

"What air ye tryin' t' say, lad — air y' daft?"

"Not yet!" laughed the Tramp Prince as he lifted the toad out of his pocket and tried to explain their telepathic form of communication.

"Sure an' I don't undershtan' what it is yer tryin' t' say t' me," the Elderly Tramp admitted.

"Maybe," said the Tramp Prince, "if you concentrate *very* hard on this little friend of mine, you'll start to pick up some of his messages."

The Elderly Tramp sat down on the splitting block and looked at the toad, frowning in a great effort of concentration.

"Ay don't hear nuthin' but the birds an' th' wind!" exclaimed the Elderly Tramp.

The grim-faced woman suddenly poked her head out the door.

"Get back to work on that wood pile or you get nothing to eat, you lazy bum! You hear *this*, don't you?"

The two tramps worked again for a few minutes until the stack of firewood on the back porch looked as though it might fall over if they added more to it. They knocked on the door until the grim-faced woman came out and looked approvingly at the stack. She went back into the kitchen and returned shortly with a plate containing a sandwich cut in half and two small gnarled carrots from the backyard vegetable garden. The woman abruptly set the plate on the porch floor and re-entered the house.

"Why that stingy old harpie!" said the Elderly Tramp, expressing his anger. "All that work fer half a sandwich! Sure an' I'll leave the proper mark on *her* gate so no other tramp will make the same mistake we did!"

"You take both halves of the sandwich," the Tramp Prince offered. "I'll take the carrots since you won't be able to chew them."

"But what else are you goin' t' eat, lad; you need more than that!"

The Tramp Prince reflected for a moment: "I think I saw a couple of large walnut trees at the edge of the field when we came up here. Maybe there'll still be some walnuts on the ground under them."

When the pair reached the walnut trees, the Tramp Prince kicked aside piles of fallen leaves and found numerous nuts that the squirrels had missed. He filled his pockets with the cured nuts. A little further along the road, they came to an outcropping of rock where the nuts could be cracked. Finding a rock to use as a hammer and a large flat stone for an anvil, the Tramp Prince broke open enough nuts to allow him to eat his fill.

On down the road toward the big city, the Tramp Prince and the Elderly Tramp continued. As they walked along the roadside, avoiding many roaring motor cars and an occasional truck loaded with produce or farm animals, the Elderly Tramp began to limp again.

"You need another rest," said the Tramp Prince.

"Ay — 'tis just a momentary lapse," returned the Elderly Tramp. "Ay'll be over it in a bit."

Foot-weary and dust covered, the two tramps watched as a large farm truck heavily loaded with pigs for the stockyard in the city, moved slowly up grade toward the pair. The truck's progress was only a modicum more rapid than the hikers' pace, and its odor preceded it. The driver stopped his vehicle at the top of the grade and waited for the two tramps to reach his truck.

"Say there!" the truck driver said to the Tramp Prince. "Looks like your friend could use a little lift, ridin' in the truck cab here. I seen him limpin' back there as I past yuhs."

"That, me friend," said the Elderly Tramp, "would be most welcome. Ay thank y' fer stoppin'."

"Well," the driver told him, "you probably won't get where you're goin' much faster, considerin' the weight of my load, but at least you won't have to walk."

The Tramp Prince stowed his canvas sack on the floor of the cab and the Elderly Tramp slid onto the seat, placing his feet on the sack. The Tramp Prince then tried to fit himself in next to his friend, but the truck cab was too narrow for all three men to sit comfortably.

"I'll just stand on the running board and hold onto that handle below the wind screen," he told the driver. And off they chugged toward town.

The late afternoon air was warmly perfumed with a fall fragrance — a pleasant relief from the overpowering pig stench, as a brisk breeze flooded the C-cab's open sides.

"This," said the Elderly Tramp, "is the kind o' day, makes me life worth livin'!" He smiled broadly and wrinkled his brow as the stiff breeze caught his long unkempt gray hair, flailing it in front of his face.

"And a good drink of cold ale is what makes *my* life worth livin'!" interjected the driver. "Hey — I'm in need of somethin' to drink!"

When they had traveled only a couple of miles, the driver pointed out another roadhouse ahead.

"I'm stoppin' up there; they got real good ale," he told his two passengers. The driver was a pleasant looking young man whose ample girth showed that he made a habit of availing himself of refreshments whenever the opportunity afforded itself.

When the truck reached the tavern, the driver stopped at the very edge of the parking area so that the wind would keep the pig-stench away from the building.

"Listen, I'll buy each of you guys a glass of the brew if you want," he offered.

"Ah, that's mighty generous o' y', me boy," responded the Elderly Tramp. "It's *just* what Ay been needin'."

After the trio had seated themselves at a table and placed an order, the Tramp Prince requesting cider, the attractive young waitress brought the drinks, smiling warmly at all. "If you boys stay a little longer, the band starts at six and I'll be doing some dances every couple of numbers."

"Yeah — sure, why not?" the truck driver agreed, jovially. "That ol' stock yard's open late, anyway. The farmer I'm deliverin' them pigs for is payin' me by the load, not the hour."

The young truck driver smiled and patted his rather vast abdominal dimension. "Anything *this* big needs more than just one drink!"

"The same again?" asked the Dancing Girl.

"Yep!"

"Okay — be right back, guy."

Nudging the Tramp Prince, the Elderly Tramp got up from his seat and said softly, "Let's go outside fer a while, lad." Then he assured the truck driver: "We'll be back in a bit."

When the pair got to the tavern's entrance, the Elderly Tramp began looking around at the ground.

"Ay wanted t' come out here t' see if thir might be any cigarette butts Ay'd be able t' pick up t' smoke in me pipe. Ay breaks 'em up an' uses 'em fer pipe t'backy. Ever smoke a pipe, lad?"

"No," replied the Tramp Prince. "Once I tried a cigarette, but that was a disaster."

The Elderly Tramp pulled out his pipe and crumbled the contents of several cigarette butts into it. "Ay made this one out o' a corn cob. The stem was from one o' those tiny bamboo canes they gives th' kiddies at carnivals. Ay just whittled down everything t' fit together." And he proudly displayed his craftsmanship. "Can't afford t' be buyin' smokes. This way Ay gets around payin' anythin'!"

The Tramp Prince nodded approvingly at the craftsmanship of the pipe.

"Maybe you could whittle out something else that you might be able to sell."

"Weel...A've thought about it before, lad — but kiddies toys is about all Ay ever tried, an no one wants t' pay much fer somethin' the likes o' that."

"Y' see," he continued, "Ay has me buttons an' shoelaces t' offer folks on th' street in th' cities." And he slipped out a few packs to show to the Tramp Prince.

"Th' idea is that y' offer a pack o' buttons er needles — er samethin' to a lady for a few cents — not much more thin y' pays fer 'em an' usually th' lady already has plenty at home, but she feels sorry fer y', so she gives y' th' price o' th' packet an tells y' t' keep it. That way y' kin 'sell' it many times again!"

The Tramp Prince laughed. "Why, you old rouge!"

"Oh, me b'y," the Elderly Tramp intoned with great pretended seriousness, "that's what most o' us tramps *do* fer a livin'!"

By then, the two tramps had walked close to the stock truck in which they had ridden. Pigs were squealing as they battered against each other in the fetid confines of the truck's double-layered bed.

"Agh!" the Tramp Prince exploded. "Look at how those poor things are cramped into the bed of the truck! They're slipping around on their own excrement!"

"Ah, me b'y," replied the Elderly Tramp, "the pigs is just t' be sent t' market. No one cares about *how* they get there."

"But they *should* care!" said the Tramp Prince. "And the people who eat them should care enough about themselves to not want to dine on the rotting carcasses of these animals."

"Oh...that's just the way the world is; see, lad, its not you or me as is goin' t' change it."

The Tramp Prince looked at the pin that held the back gate of the truck bed.

"It would be so easy for me to slip that pin out of the socket and open the gate! Let those animals have their rightful freedom."

"Ay know, lad, simple it would be...but then, even if y' was t' let th' load loose, people would just go roundin' 'em up an' put 'em back in the truck again. Either that, or if some *did* manage t' escape, dogs or coyotes would eventually kill 'em off anyway. An', th' truth of it is, a lot of 'em would probably be too injured from fallin' out o' the height o' that truck's bed, that they'd niver get away anyhow. So its not a good place t' shtart on what y' perceive as a problem. An' th' only way y' could make an issue about it would be t' make lots o' people aware o' *why* th' pigs was out — otherwise everyone'd think th' pin jist came loose somehow. Y'd have t' tell 'em that y' *let* 'em loose an' *why*. An' then, most likely, they'd put y' in jail fer weeks — maybe months, an' from what y've been telling me y' can't afford that."

"No, you're right. I couldn't." The Tramp Prince shook his head, his eyes closed in bitter agreement. "Another thing that stops me is all the trouble it would make for the poor truck driver. He's too nice a guy to do that to."

"Listen, lad, this 'ere world is not always such a pleasant place. Lots o' times in yer life yer gayin t' see things ye wish that thir was somethin' ye could do t' change. Thir's some things y' c'n change — an' some things y' can't. Th' things y' can't change —least not right then — y' put in th' back o' yer mind so y' can try t' do somethin' later."

"I won't put *this* in the back of my mind; its going right up in the very *front*. I don't know...maybe there's already some organization working to get legislation passed to protect animals. Anyway, I won't forget about it."

"Well, laddie, Ay wish Ay could help y' — but y' know that where Ay'm from in Ireland, pigs has been part o' th' landscape probably since people first settled thire. So Ay'm used t' seein' 'em everywhire. An' if Ay was t' pull that pin n' let 'em out, we'd still have t' tell 'em that we done it. Thin we'd *both* be in jail fer quite a spell. An' at me advanced age, Ay wouldn't like it — not a bit. Ay haven't got that much time left that Ay want t' waste iny b'hind bars! That's why Ay just tries t' slip by as best Ay can —an' shtay out th' way o' th' trouble makers."

The Tramp Prince grimaced and shook his head negatively again.

When the two tramps reentered the roadhouse, music was already being performed by a small band. The Dancing Girl pirouetted around on the dance floor to the delight of all the customers seated at the tables. At the end of the number, she walked over to the table occupied by the two tramps and the truck driver.

"Mind if I sit in the other chair?" she asked.

"Oh, no — not at all, me dear. Yer presence is most welcome!" replied the Elderly Tramp.

The four sat in animated conversation as the truck driver related a number of humorous snippets from his work experiences. When the Tramp Prince told about some of his own recent travels, the dancing girl sat in rapt attention.

"Wow — sort of like the adventures of Don Quixote and Marco Polo mixed up together!" the Dancing Girl suggested in an uneducated wonder.

"Hardly that!" Laughed the Tramp Prince. "But I do have to admit that I just don't ever seem to know what's going to be around the next curve in the road."

As the evening passed, the Dancing Girl kept returning to the table to talk to the Tramp Prince and his friends.

"You're really quite an excellent dancer," the Tramp Prince complimented her.

"Oh, why, thank you!" she replied, and then commenced to tell how she had learned her skill and something of her background.

By now, the Elderly tramp had begun dozing and the truck driver was mingling with other drivers at the bar. The Dancing Girl grabbed the Tramp Princes hand under the table.

"You know, I *really* like you," she said. "Where are you going to sleep tonight?"

The Tramp Prince explained that he and the Elderly Tramp did not have enough money for a room at the inn, so they would just have to try to slip into a barn with a hayloft or find an empty shed somewhere.

"You could sleep in my room," was the Dancing Girl's offer. "They pay me a little for waiting on tables and for dancing and give me a tiny room on the second floor. It's not much larger than a closet — just enough room for a bed and dresser and some space to stand in between them. You'd have to sleep in the bed with me," she giggled.

"But we hardly know each other." The Tramp Prince hesitated.

"Well, we know that you're a boy...and I'm a girl! What more do we need to know?" And she laughed.

"Besides, where would my friend sleep? I don't think they'd let him stay down here."

"No," admitted the Dancing Girl. "They won't let anyone stay in here after we close. But he's a grown man — he can take care of himself."

"He's an *old* man with a lame leg and I feel like I should see to it that he's not just turned out late at night with no one to assist him in trying to find some kind of place to sleep. I didn't have to encourage him to keep staying here. I can't just abandon him —that wouldn't be right!"

"Oh, you're a fool!" said the Dancing Girl with petulance. "Any other young man would be happy to have a girl like me offer to bring him into her bed! Aren't I attractive?" she asked, pushing out her ample bosom.

"Yes, you are a very attractive girl — but that's not the point," responded the Tramp Prince. "I've explained to you what the situation is. Don't you think I owe my elderly friend some responsibility in seeing that he stays safe late like this in the dark? He doesn't seem to see well at night."

"Stupid fool!" exploded the Dancing Girl. Why any other guy would give his right arm to go to bed with me! And she stamped off in a huff.

The Tramp Prince awakened the Elderly Tramp. "This place will be closing soon and we still need to find somewhere to sleep."

The two tramps then went over to the truck driver, explaining that they would have a better chance of finding a place to sleep in the country than by riding on with him to the city. They thanked him and left the tavern.

Moonlight shimmered brightly in the October night, the chill air penetrating each nostril like a jab of the wind in a storm.

As they walked back along the field that adjoined the roadhouse, the Elderly Tramp stopped at the edge of a small woodlot.

"Let me show yuh somethin' young lad, somethin' y' might not know... Y' see, since it's clear t'night, we c'n sleep out under the stars."

The old fellow then found a large forked stick which he used as a rake to gather up a huge pile of dry leaves.

"Here, now, lad — take this stick an' do th' same wheriver yer be findin' a lot more leaves; thin just bury yersilf in th' pile. Y'll stay plenty warm and it'll be soft as a fither bed."

The Tramp Prince gathered a pile of leaves onto a flat area and before sliding into it, removed Road Toad from his pocket.

"Oops...almost forgot about you; you were so quiet." He conveyed the thought to Road Toad. "You should be able to find some insects under all these leaves around here."

"Ha!" responded Road Toad with obvious irritation. "A late meal *again*! And having to search for it in the moonlight!"

"Well," said the Tramp Prince, "you were so quiet I completely forgot about you. When I get involved with a lot going on around me, I forget that I have a toad in my pocket."

"Next time, I won't let myself doze off and I'll give you a swift kick in the ribs!" Road Toad scooted off, trying to snag one of the unwary night bugs.

That autumn moon seemed to smile upon the silent, sleeping tramps and was still visible when the blue-black night began to melt into the light of dawn.

The Tramp Prince, the Elderly Tramp and Road Toad all slept soundly until the sun was beginning to peek above the tops of some of the foggy, distant, eastern hills.

"Time to get up!" announced the Tramp Prince with a voice as sparkling as the morning sun.

The Elderly Tramp and Road Toad crawled slowly out from under the leaves.

"Sure it's tame t' go faind a clear spot bay th' field an' make a fire, me b'y. While yer doin thet, Ay'll take me pot an' tray t' find some water an' we can brew a bit o' tea."

When the Elderly Tramp returned with water from a creek, the fire was already blazing between two large stones, which the Tramp Prince had placed on opposite sides of the flaming twigs. The Elderly Tramp then cut three green willow sticks and tied the tops together with strips of the willow bark, forming a tripod, which he placed over the fire. After hanging his cooking pot from the tripod by a hook on its handle, he smiled at the Tramp Prince:

"Ye see, lad, yer stones is a good idea, but its too easy fer th' pot t' slide off an' spill — that's why a tramp uses a tripod."

"Hmmm..." reflected the Tramp Prince, "Never thought about that."

"Ah," the Elderly Tramp laughed. "Ye'll learn! Least it won't hafta be th' hard way."

The two tramps got out their knives and went over to a small thicket of sassafras saplings where they proceeded to dig out a few roots. Then, taking the roots to the creek, they washed off the dirt and went back to the fire where the water was now nearly boiling. The Elderly Tramp removed the pot from the tripod and shaved sassafras root bark into the hot water. As the brew cooled, it became a beautifully fragrant red tea.

"'Twould be better with somethin' t' sweeten it," said the old Irishman with his brogue intentionally thickening. "But sure, now, tea *without* is better than no tea a'tall; right lad?"

The Tramp Prince nodded in agreement.

As the pair of tramps plodded along the road that morning, the unseasonable temperature soon began to rise and made walking in the sun's heat more than uncomfortable. Dust rose with each of their footsteps.

"Ah lad, Ay need t' take a bit o' a break — an' look, this clear stream comin' under the road... look off over there — it's comin' from a mill pond. And the old mill's still next to it — under all those nice cool trees. What say we stop fer a bit?"

An old, unused wagon trail led to the decaying mill, and though it was hardly ever traversed, the dryness of the season had powdered the dirt surface, so that as the two tramps walked it, minute wisps of dust fluffed up as they proceeded.

When they had reached the edge of the mill pond next to the mill, the Tramp Prince removed his back pack and placed it on the ground in the shade. Then he sat down on it, enjoying the cooler temperature.

"Ay'm goin' up t' the mill stream an' wash up a bit," the Irishman said as he continued along the pond.

"Yes… well, I'll join you in just a minute, but for now, I simply want to sit here and contemplate… and enjoy the beauty of this place."

After a few minutes, the Tramp Prince got up and removed his jacket, laying it across the bindle pack, still on the ground. Then he walked back toward the mill, curious to get a closer look at the slowly moving, slightly creaking water wheel. Crickets and a multitude of other insects abounded by the splashing water from the ancient wheel and the Tramp Prince immediately thought about Road Toad.

"Road Toad… you should see this!" the Tramp Prince telepathized to his small friend. But he got no answer. Suddenly, the boy realized that he no longer had his jacket on; he immediately went back to where he had left it. Then he reached inside his right side pocket, but the amphibian was not in it. Frightened, he began calling out telepathically: "Road Toad —Road Toad, where are you? Have you gone off some place? Come back. Come here!"

After standing by the bindle sack for a few moments, the Tramp Prince began quietly walking along the edge of the mill pond, calling out mentally: "Come here! Come here!"

Slowly, he began to notice many small green frogs swimming toward him to the pond's bank. He stopped, then took a few steps up, away from the pond, but more toward the mill. Again, he telepathized the message: "Come here, come here!"

Now, he began to notice that there were perhaps dozens of toads hopping toward him from all directions. Soon the ground was literally covered with hopping toads and frogs and the Tramp Prince had to step carefully to avoid crushing them.

"Road Toad — which one *are* you? Come over here to me! Oh, my God… this is insane! You all look alike!"

The Elderly Irish Tramp returned, directly into the swarming horde of amphibians, nearly falling over in his attempt to avoid squashing any of the jumping mass of toads and frogs.

"Fer hivens sake! What in earth? In all me borned days, Ay niver seen the likes uv it! Thir mus' be hundreds uv 'em! What's goin' on here?"

"I don't know," said the Tramp Prince. "I couldn't find Road Toad and I called to him telepathically to come to me — and then the next thing I know...*this*! The only thing I can think of is that I must be able to telepathically communicate with *all* toads and frogs — not just Road Toad! I must be sending out an unvocalized thought as well as the vocalized one, since they can't respond in a vocalized way like Road Toad does."

The Tramp Prince got down on his hands and knees and looked at one of the toads sitting in front of him.

"If you're Road Toad, blink twice, quickly."

The small brown creature continued staring, not even blinking once.

"This is horrible!" exclaimed the boy. "Road Toad is lost and I'll never be able to figure out which one he is out of all the dozens of toads here!"

"Ah well," the old Irishman reassured him philosophically, "Just pick out a healthy-lookin' specimin an' stick him in yer pocket. One uv 'em looks t' be about the same as the others t' me."

"You don't understand," the Tramp Prince told the Elderly Tramp in frustration, "Road Toad is my *friend*. I can't just leave him here!"

"Well, it's not like he won't be able t' make a good livin' around here. This place is full o' bugs."

"I *know* that — I just can't abandon my friend. He's not an ordinary toad."

"Ah well... maybe you could train one of these other toads if you spent some time at it." The old Irishman laughed at his own raw humor.

"That's a *very* unkind thing to say, and you know it!" exploded the Tramp Prince in final exasperation.

Y'll hafta pardon me laughin'," the old fellow replied, "this is about the silliest thing I ever did see. A Pied Piper of frogs 'n' toads."

"You may think its funny, but, to me, it's *tragic*!"

At that point, the Tramp Prince looked over at his bindle sack and saw a toad pushing its head up from behind the canvas.

"Is that you, Road Toad?" the Tramp Prince shot out a thought message.

"Yes, of course.   Why, who else would I be?" asked the amphibian.

"Oh… well, you just might have been any one of these hundreds of toads out here in the woods, that's all."

Road Toad looked around at all the disappearing multitude of toads and frogs.

"Huh?! What *is* this? I fall asleep for a few minutes under your bindle sack and suddenly the whole world turns upside down!"

"Yes," said the Tramp Prince, "it's as hard to explain as it is to understand. Anyway, I'm just thankful you're safe and not lost."

Road Toad attempted to grimace without success. "I'm no more lost than you are…and we'll probably both stay safe…if you can avoid falling into the mill pond!"

After having walked again alongside the road for another hour, avoiding the stream of motor trucks and wagons headed to market, the Tramp Prince and the Elderly Tramp slowed their pace to watch a sputting, coughing motor wagon moving leisurely in the opposite direction.

"Well now — Hi! … It's Blimey th' Limey!" the Elderly Tramp shouted.

As the Irishman crossed the road, the driver of the motor wagon waved a greeting and stopped his vehicle.

"Come over here, me b'y. Ay want y' t' meet an old friend!" The Elderly Tramp pointed to the driver, who tipped his ragged hat. "This is me old pal, 'Blimey th' Limey'. We once shared a room together in London!"

"Ha!" laughed the other. "Tell 'im the truth. It was the closed-in end under a loadin' dock where we stoied a few weeks… till the bobbies found us sleepin' ther and choised us off."

"Ah, we found a lot o' scrap metal layin' aroun' that ol' warehouse till they chased us out. Right, Blimey?"

"Righteo, mate!" exclaimed the Cockney. "Blimey! Oil bet we'd a' moid a bloody fortune sellin' scrap if they 'adn't found us."

"Well now, tell me this, Blimey," asked the Elderly Tramp. "Whatever in th' world would th' likes o' you be doin' drivin' down th' road in a motor wagon of all things?"

"Blimey! It was just a chance 'appenin', it was. Yer see, Oi was workin' for a farmer a couple weeks bringin' in 'ay. An' when the job was through, 'e says t' me, 'Look, mate, Oi'm 'appy with the way yer done yer work an' since Oi 'as a new motor truck, Oi only keeps me team fer 'mergencies, an' Oi sure don't need three 'orses fer a team. One's too old any 'ow an' if yer wants 'er yer can tike 'er along. That way yer kin ride where yer goin'.'"

The Tramp Prince and the Elderly Tramp stood in attentive anticipation of the rest of the story, as Blimey's pudgy, whisker-stubbled face took on a look of self-satisfied achievement; he raised an eyebrow and smiled on the left side of his mouth.

"As Oi was ridin' down the road, Oi comes upon a boy standin' there cursin' an' swearin' at this 'ere motor wagon. Then 'e 'it's the side of the bed wit' a 'ammer, crackin' a board in a fit erv anger. When 'e spots me 'orse 'e says, 'Oil trade yuh this 'ere motor wagon fer yer 'orse. Oi kin see that at least yer 'orse will move. So Oi looks over the engine a bit an' can see there's nothing much wrong with it, an' Oi goes ahead an troides 'im. Oi could see that the sparkin' plug wire wuz badly frayed an' after Oi toiped it up a bit, the engine cranked right up — an' so, 'ere Oi am!"

"So where is it y' be headin?" asked the Elderly Tramp.

"To the petrol seller in the next town 'fore she runs out of gas," responded Blimey. There's room enough fer the two a'yers, if yer wants ter ride along."

The Elderly Tramp looked at the Tramp Prince. "Well, me b'y," he said rather sadly. "Ay've enjoyed travelin' wi' y', but this is a chance t' ride again, an' — as Ay once told y', Ay goes whire the wind blows me. Ay know thirs no pint in yer goin' back th' same way y' jist came from, so goodbay an' good luck."

The Tramp Prince grasped the old Irishman's hand warmly.

"Good luck to you, too!" he said, with much emotion. "I've learned a lot from you. But before we part, please tell me what you think really matters in life."

"So what d' Ay think really matters? Well... it's simple, lad... jest havin' a warm dry place t lie down an' relax at the end o' a road-weary day. That's what really matters t' me. Oh... an Ay guess havin' enough t' fill me belly before Ay goes t' sleep. That too..."

The Elderly Tramp brushed away a tear forming at the corner of his eye.

"Laddie, y' know Ay've been bummin' all over this world an' Ay seldom have met someone Ay really lakes. But Ay do care about y' an' Ay want to' leave y' with jus' this one thought: Believe only half o' what people tell y' — then t' be on th' safe side, cut that half in half an' y' might come out at somewhere close t' th' truth!"

The Tramp Prince smiled at his friend and gave a slight chuckle, not knowing quite how the comment was meant or to whom he should apply it.

Blimey cranked the wagon's engine and the two reunited cronies chugged on down the road, leaving the Tramp Prince waving after them.

"What a couple of characters," observed Road Toad, who had been listening and watching all that took place.

"Yes," agreed the Tramp Prince, "they're almost as bad as the two of us!"

"Oh, no," responded Road Toad, "not like me, at least. I'm unique in all the world!"

The Tramp Prince laughed: "You're unique alright — you're a *card*."

"Yes...," agreed Road Toad, "I'm a card not to be dealt lightly with!"

"Oh... well, I guess we're all unique in our own ways," observed the Tramp Prince.

Road Toad quickly shot a thought back, "But how many *toads* in this world do you know of that are anything like me?"

"Hmm..." thought the Tramp Prince, "No others... fortunately."

As the Tramp Prince continued along the road, a young man on a motorcycle came roaring past with the machine's throttle wide open. Suddenly, a brisk gust of wind lifted the rider's cap off of his head and carried it spinning, far out into the brush. The cycle rider slowed his engine and after looking back and seeing no cap in the road, cracked the throttle wide open again.

"Boy! He sure was in a hurry!" the Tramp Prince relayed to Road Toad.

"Yeah... and he's probably some rich kid with a whole closet full of caps at home," observed Road Toad.

"And maybe a whole garage full of abused motorcycles at home — after he wrecks that one — the way he's driving it!" the Tramp Prince returned.

The Tramp Prince then began searching through the brush at the side of the road to see if he could find where the cap had landed.

"I see something that might be a cap, hanging on a branch over your head," said Road Toad, who had been looking up because it was easier for him than looking down.

"Yes!" the Tramp Prince exclaimed. "That's it! But it's hanging right over this huge patch of sticker bushes and brambles. There's no way I can get past the thorns on this bunch of wild rose in front of me."

"See if you can snag it with your walking stick," suggested Road Toad.

The Tramp Prince very carefully caught the tip of his walking stick under the bill of the cap and slowly lifted the cap off of the branch. Then he maneuvered the cap with delicate precision over the patch of wild rose and blackberry until he could lower it into his hand.

"Well done," said Road Toad, "See if it fits."

Placing the cap on his head and giving it a slight adjustment, the Tramp Prince observed: "Well what do you know — it's perfect! Just what I've been needing on these chilly days. And what an inexpensive way to get a cap!"

"Yes, the price was right! Now all you need is to find a motorcycle and some goggles that the wind blew away," Road Toad joked with a hardy laugh to his thought.

"What — a motorcycle that got blown away... how? In a tornado?" giggled the Tramp Prince. "You'd have to ride that one to the junk yard. And you certainly wouldn't need goggles!"

Chapter 5: The Girl with Long, Curly, Brown Hair

Early the next morning, the Tramp Prince reached the outskirts of the city. The streets were still almost empty as he began walking along them — not really certain of which direction he was heading

— or which way he *should* go. Slowly, he overtook a pretty young woman who was dragging behind her a piece of heavy string attached to nothing.

"Hello," said the Tramp Prince, tipping his cap politely as he came alongside the rather dainty girl. "It looks as though your dog must have gotten off his leash some distance back, because I didn't notice him anywhere as I came up the street."

"Oh no, he's still attached," said the Girl With Long, Curly, Brown Hair, giggling. "Don't you see him there? Look *very* closely."

The Tramp Prince slowed his pace and bent over to peer at the end of the string — not knowing what to expect.

"No...no, I really don't see anything at the end of the string..." And he smiled warmly with a somewhat perplexed expression on his face.

The Girl With Long, Curly, Brown Hair stopped and reached over.

"Oh look, the dear has fallen asleep again — that quickly." And she patted the air. "I'm going to release him and he'll just go home to where we live in Pfantassiland."

"Pfantassiland...?" mused the Tramp Prince. "I don't think I've ever heard of a place like that. Where is it?"

"Oh...it's...it's really somewhat difficult to try to explain; for a lot of people it's difficult to get to. It's kind of everywhere —and yet at the same time — nowhere. Do you know what I mean?" She giggled almost instinctively.

Thinking that the girl was playing a clever bit of trickery on him, the Tramp Prince decided to go along with the game.

"Well," he said thoughtfully, "I've probably been close to having been there at some point in my life!"

"I'm sure you have," responded the Girl With Long, Curly, Brown Hair, giving the Tramp Prince a wide, lovely smile.

Looking again at the little Girl With Long, Curly, Brown Hair, the Tramp Prince found himself smiling and chuckling at her audacity.

"Which way are you going?" he asked the girl.

"Whichever way *you're* going," she responded.

"But, in truth, I'm lost."

"Wonderful!" she giggled. "Then we shall *both* be lost together!" And she giggled again spontaneously.

On and on the pair walked until they had left the city and gone far out into the countryside. And they talked about everything imaginable — as it is said, of 'cabbages and kings and many things'. The Tramp Prince explained why he had started upon his travels and also tried to tell his new friend about Road Toad.

"I think," she said, "if I were around him long enough or tried hard enough, I could talk to him too." And she giggled again...as she always seemed to do when she finished talking.

"Tell me something about Pfantassiland, will you?" asked the Tramp Prince.

"Sure — what is it you want to know?" responded the Girl With Long, Curly, Brown Hair.

"Just...what it's like there; what the people are like...that sort of thing."

"Well...first...there aren't any police or courts or lawyers. Nobody wants to hurt anyone else. I guess mainly because we don't have some oppressive government leaning on us — or a few rich people taking most of the value of our labor like you have here. Our first law is love, not greed. And people don't waste their lives enslaving animals so that they can dine on their decomposing cadavers, the way almost everybody here does.

" And everyone in Pfantassiland can be an artist if he wants to be. So the Streets are paved with colorful mosaic tiles that depict beautiful scenes; the houses are decorated with delicate architectural designs. Everyone has plenty of *time* to express himself or herself because we don't have to be economic slaves to an exploitive system."

"I'm sorry," said the Tramp Prince shaking his head in disbelief, "but I can't even fathom a place like that existing anywhere — knowing as much as I do of what the people I've met and have heard about are like...just human nature."

"Oh, you poor boy..." the Girl With Long, Curly, Brown Hair looked deeply into the eyes of the Tramp Prince with an expression of great sadness to her face, "You really don't belong here. I do so wish you could come with me."

Her voice had an imploring softness that made the Tramp Prince feel like holding onto her and never letting go.

By now, the Tramp Prince and the Girl With Long, Curly, Brown Hair were walking hand in hand, enjoying the late afternoon sun as it highlighted the clouds in a frosty peach and purple icing.

"Look," said the Girl With Long, Curly, Brown Hair, "those clouds are really peach and grape ice cream! All we need are some cones and I will stand up high on your shoulders so that I can reach out and scoop some of it off for us."

And so that is exactly what she did. When she stood high on the Tramp Prince's shoulders, the Girl With Long, Curly, Brown Hair scooped two imaginary cones toward the clouds and handed them to the Tramp Prince, who then lowered the girl to the ground.

"There!" she exclaimed, "That's one of our favorite foods in Pfantassiland."

They both quickly devoured their make-believe cloud-cream cones.

"Oooo... that was *good*!" said the Girl With Long, Curly, Brown Hair.

"Yes, it was!" agreed the Tramp Prince. And then he laughed.

"But I didn't get a chance to taste your grape flavor." The Girl With Long, Curly, Brown Hair had a slight tone of disappointment in her voice. "The only way I can taste it now is on your lips!" And she giggled like a little child as she stood on her tiptoes and put her lips against his.

"Mmm... that tasted so wonderful!" she asserted as she dropped back down.

"Well," interjected the Tramp Prince, "you know that I didn't have a chance to taste your peach flavor either." So he bent over and put his lips against hers.

"That taste was so nice that we should do it again!" the Girl With Long, Curly, Brown Hair giggled.

And so they did.

As the pair walked along the country lane, a brightly colored butterfly flitted across their path.

"Look!" exclaimed the Tramp Prince pointing to the unseasonable insect. "It's so late in the year to see one of these!"

The Girl With Long, Curly, Brown Hair stood still and held out her arm; the butterfly circled, alighting on the back of her hand.

"I asked him if he'd like to say hello." The Girl With Long, Curly, Brown Hair giggled again.

"That's amazing! I've never seen anyone else who could get a butterfly to land on their arm."

"Oooh...well, Hawthorne wrote that:

Happiness is as a butterfly, which when pursued,

is always just beyond your grasp, but which,

if you will sit down quietly, may alight upon you.

"So you see, he must have known..."

"Hmm... perhaps..." responded the Tramp Prince.

The face of the Girl With Long, Curly, Brown Hair took on a serious expression: "All of life, from the tiniest amoeba to the greatest whale, all have a connection of some kind — like an enormous psychic web, each strand touching all of the others, perhaps with only the tip of a separated tentacle.

"But even plants are part of that connection... they have spirits too, you see. I like talking to plants. Of course, they don't really talk, they *sing*. You can hear them in the woods in the evening."

"Yes, I think I know what you're trying to tell me."

"I talk to them all the time. Maybe it's like you talking to your little toad... well — I guess it's not *exactly* like that, but somewhat the same. It may be that we could communicate in some psychic manner with any life form if we just concentrated long and hard enough. Anyway, that's what *I* think."

They walked along silently for a few minutes, the Tramp Prince mulling over what his companion had said. Then she gave another quick laugh.

"Have you ever heard Judy's song?" she asked.

"Why...I wouldn't think so..."

"Well, it goes:

Where the streets are paved in golden bricks

and the roses bloom in December

And the snow is sweet as sugar licks

Ah, your love I will remember."

"That's strange — rather strange...." And the boy smiled questioningly at his beautiful companion.

The Girl With Long, Curly, Brown Hair looked up at the Tramp Prince: "What color are my eyes?" she asked.

"Why...they're...green? That's unusual."

"There's nothing wrong with being unusual. Why should I want to be usual? Let me see *your* eyes. Yours are... sort of a greenish brown."

"Does that make *me* unusual?"

"I don't know...perhaps." And she laughed her musical little giggle.

"Everything in Pfantassiland is unusual," she said very seriously. "But everything eventually ends up in Pfantassiland anyway...if you know what I mean."

"No, I really *don't* know what you mean," came the Tramp Princes' response.

There was a sudden weightless feeling in the air — as though the bottom had fallen out of the afternoon and the weightiness of evening had still not caught up with it.

"Listen to how *hollow* our voices sound," observed the Girl With Long, Curly, Brown Hair. "There's something very *odd* about it."

"What does it matter?" asked the Tramp Prince, "as long as *we're* odd enough to go along with it?"

The Girl With Long, Curly, Brown Hair grasped the Tramp Princes' hand and swung their arms as high as she could swing them as they walked along. She laughed so long and loud, that it seemed as though she were trying to frighten away the ghosts of an unfriendly end to afternoons.

Suddenly, a brisk wind picked up as an unseen storm approached, sending dry leaves flying about and birds and animals scurrying for shelter.

"We should try to get over to that old barn on the far hillside as quickly as we can," the Tramp Prince advised.

The Tramp Prince and the Girl With Long, Curly, Brown Hair both ran hand in hand toward the old barn, with Road Toad bouncing around in the jacket pocket.

"Easy there!" Road Toad tried to shout.

"Sorry, Road Toad," the Tramp Prince told him, "but if we don't hurry we're going to get soaked."

When they had reached the barn's entrance, they sat down in a pile of straw somewhat back from the open doorway. Lightening flashed and thunderclaps exploded so close that it sounded like the end of the world was at hand. Darkness fell rapidly as the storm continued, the distant sky lighting up bright with Nature's fireworks.

"Come on!" said the Girl With Long, Curly, Brown Hair as she pulled the Tramp Prince up and out to the edge of the barn door. "Look — it's *so* beautiful...and exciting!"

They stood there watching until the rain began blowing heavily through the open barn door. Then they moved back into a warmer part of the barn where the straw was still piled up high, and they laid back into a golden bed of it. The Girl With Long, Curly, Brown Hair cuddled up in the Tramp Prince's arms as they watched and listened to a storm that seemed to be there to stay for the night.

"What will your family think if you don't return tonight?" asked the Tramp Prince.

"Oh, my family knows I can take care of myself."

"But...I'm just curious about something," said the Tramp Prince with a certain degree of seriousness. "How do you *get to* Pfantassiland?"

"Well, there are lots of ways you can get to it," the girl began. "Some people just imagine their way to it. Others are able to travel there through a mirror. Sometimes one can just go to sleep and suddenly you wake up there!"

The Tramp Prince looked over into the face of the Girl With Long, Curly, Brown Hair. She was exceedingly beautiful, he thought — but at the same time, very fragile — like a delicate china doll.

"I'm afraid I can never get to Pfantassiland," he told her and a tear began to form in one of his eyes. The Girl With Long, Curly, Brown Hair noticed it and put the tip of her finger up to collect the tear. Then she kissed the Tramp Prince's cheek and snuggled closer into his arms.

"Of course you can find Pfantassiland;" she encouraged, "you just have to try *very* hard!"

The Tramp Prince looked again at his lovely companion. Her wide face fairly beamed out a smile from well placed features and eyes that sparkled like a pair of precious jewels.

"You have a truly beautiful smile," he told her.

"That's because I think beautiful thoughts."

"Such as...?"

"Oh...all kinds of things!"

"That's no answer...well, *hardly* an answer. Alright, I'll just accept that you think beautiful thoughts. So *how* do you do it?"

"It's simple. I just turn all *negative* input that I get into positive frivolity. Then I paint pictures in my mind of hazy pink castles and maidens dancing on the floating mist with their partners to harmonies that are like those of melodious flocks of dawn-birds. Now, isn't that easy?"

"Hmm," thought the Tramp Prince out loud, "perhaps for you..."

The girls' face formed a half smile, half frown. "Why should the world be filled with ugliness when all we have to do is smile and turn everything around in our minds? That's what *everyone* does in Pfantassiland!"

The girl with Long, Curly, Brown Hair smiled again and closed her smile with another giggle, thoroughly confounding the already confused Tramp Prince. He shook his head slightly with a look of bewilderment that took over his face.

"And, so is *that* what you think really *matters* in life?" he asked her.

The Girl With Long, Curly, Brown Hair laughed a long, intense titter that trailed off into one of her silly giggles. "Why, *nothing* really matters!"

"Nothing? Nothing at all?"

She laughed and giggled again as the Tramp Prince straightened up with another totally mystified expression.

"You'll understand when you're dead," She asserted.

"How will I understand *anything* when I'm dead? You...I mean..."

"Oh, don't worry; it will all be as clear and fresh as the morning antelope!"

"As clear as..." the Tramp Prince began to repeat her words to himself. Then he stopped, wondering if he had heard her correctly...maybe she had said 'cantaloupe'? No — he was positive he had heard it right.

The inscrutable young protagonist reached up and grabbed the Tramp Prince's face, putting a quick tempestuous kiss on his lips. "See — *nothing* really matters!"

The Tramp Prince was afraid to say, "No, I don't see" — the thought pounding in his head. He merely gave the girl another hug — then the two of them lay back in the straw and quickly fell asleep.

When daylight returned again, the Tramp Prince awoke and realized that the Girl With Long, Curly, Brown Hair was no longer next to him. He called out to her and walked around in the barn, finding no one.

"Road Toad — hey, Road Toad! Wake up!" The Tramp Prince sent the thought to his small friend.

"What?" answered Road Toad.

"Did you see where the Girl With Long, Curly, Brown Hair went?"

"No, I've been sound asleep in your pocket all night; I have no idea."

The Tramp Prince grabbed his bindle sack and stick and quickly walked around the hillside on which the barn was built, really expecting to see the Girl With Long, Curly, Brown Hair anxiously waiting somewhere outside.

"She's gone!" he said, with agonizing despair. "The most beautiful girl I've ever met."

After walking off the hillside back to the road, it was only a few feet along before the Tramp Prince came upon a large persimmon tree loaded with ripe fruit. The storm had brought down many of the ripest persimmons and he breakfasted on the little orange sugar balls until he could hold no more.

"I wonder," the Tramp Prince thought aloud to Road Toad, "…I wonder if that girl was just the product of my own imagination?"

"Oh, I don't think so," replied Road Toad, "I saw her too and I don't see how the two of us could have shared the same hallucination — but then, I can't be absolutely certain, either."

The Tramp Prince walked on in a stunned and thoughtful silence.

Chapter 6: The Woman With A Face Like An Angel

Many miles and hours later, after examining several disappointing lanes, the Tramp Prince stumbled upon an old farmhouse perched on the edge of a hillside, yet nearly hidden in a maze of brush and tall trees. It was barely visible from the road, and as the Tramp Prince approached that decrepit domicile, he sent a thought to his amphibian friend.

"I would guess that no one has lived here for at least several decades. What do you think Road Toad?"

The little animal returned a thought: "It's hard to tell. The way it's so overgrown, one would think so. But the house seems to be almost completely intact... Who knows?"

"Maybe the door's unlocked. We could tell more from looking at the inside," replied the Tramp Prince.

Finding the door ajar, they entered the front hall of the two-story farmhouse.

"Not even much ceiling plaster on the floor, Road Toad. Apparently the roof must still be reasonably sound. I didn't see any shakes missing when I looked at it outside. A lot of moss on the roof, though."

"Could be that helped protect it."

"Yes, I think you're right."

The only piece of furniture they found in the house was a very rough kitchen table and an equally crude chair. On the floor in a corner of the room was a badly silverfish-eaten page of a newspaper with the date still visible.

"That paper is dated 1882, Road Toad. Maybe that's the last year anyone lived here."

"Yes, it's certainly possible."

As they left the old house, the Tramp Prince attempted to find the homestead's orchard. Off to the rear of the house, a dense tangle of tall, young trees amid the remains of numerous apple stumps covered the hillside below.

"Just look at that orchard! There's nothing left of it! Those maple trees growing in between the apple stumps must be thirty years old by now."

"Yes, ...not even anything left to work with, I'm afraid," Road Toad telepathized back.

The Tramp Prince took out his note pad and pencil: "I'm going to write down the location and make some brief notes about this place. It's certainly better than much of what we found."

"But there's no water — no spring nearby."

"You're right, Road Toad, but it probably has a cistern, even though all of the house's gutters seem to be gone."

"The cistern's walls have probably collapsed by now," Road Toad replied with cynicism.

"Well, anything can be repaired — if one really wants to do it.

On, the Tramp Prince walked, not even stopping for a mid-day snack. Eventually, he reached a fork in the road where he was forced to make a decision as to which branch to take.

"Road Toad — I'm not sure whether to go to the left or the right."

"Well...what does it matter? All roads seem to lead *somewhere* don't they?"

"Yes, yes...but..." the Tramp Prince frowned as he pondered. "So far, we've been heading largely in a northwesterly direction as I see it. If we take the right fork, we'll be going almost due north. The left one would take us more toward the west. But I can see what looks like a tall church steeple quite a distance along the right fork. That would mean there's a town ahead and probably more habitation. Lets take that road. What do *you* think?"

"Suits me. *You're* the one doing the walking!"

About three fourths of an hour later, they entered another typical small town. An early afternoon mist began to turn into a drizzle as the Tramp Prince reached the town square.

"I'm going to inquire where the town's library is located. We can wait out the rain in a dry place that way."

"Yes," thought back Road Toad, "do indeed, find the library!"

They stayed in the reading room of that small town library until nearly closing time, when the Tramp Prince inquired as to whether the librarian knew of a youth hostel in town. She replied that she thought that there was still such a place and looked up the location, writing down directions for the Tramp Prince to follow.

Leaving the high ceilings and warm, polished interior of the library, the Tramp Prince pulled out his flute and began to play a lively Italian tarantella that reminded him of his afternoon's reading. Outside, on a bench by the door, he sat down, trying to regain his sense of direction as he played.

Road Toad telepathized a message: "With all these people coming by, why don't you put your cap down and see if they'll put some money in it?"

"Sure...why not?" replied the Tramp Prince.

Since the hour was late, people were leaving the library and parents were coming to pick up their children. The Tramp Prince removed his cap and placed it in front of him with the few coins and a single bill in it from his pocket. He played three spirited tunes over and over as people passed by, and soon the cap contained enough money to pay for his night's lodging with a good bit left over.

As he stepped out into the now nearly deserted street, the evening chill seemed to be accentuated by the harsh humidity in the air. Although the rain had, by now, completely stopped, there were low clouds of foggy mist beginning to form almost everywhere. Darkness was falling as the Tramp Prince walked rapidly in the direction of the hostel.

In the block ahead, a rather tall, slender woman was walking away from him at a very rapid pace, only slightly less fast than that of his own. It was not until three blocks later of his very fast paced walk that the Tramp Prince came alongside the woman. Her long graying hair, tied behind her head, bobbed and bounced with her every step. As she became aware of the Tramp Prince's presence, she turned slightly and smiled.

"My! You're certainly a fast walker, young man!"

"You're an extremely fast walker yourself, ma'am — you see, I normally wouldn't walk this fast. It would wear me out too early in the day. But I'm trying to get to a hostel before it closes its doors at seven."

"Where is it?" the woman asked as she stopped in front of a gate leading to a small bungalow. "I haven't heard of any hostel in town — of course, I have no reason to inquire about something of that kind."

The Tramp Prince took out the piece of paper from the librarian and handed it to the woman.

"Hmm...on Hickory Street? Why, that address is only another couple of blocks from here. It must be in one of the residences because there aren't any more store fronts or apartment buildings this far from downtown."

Pulling out her watch, she opened the gold case.

"It's six forty. You have plenty of time to get there. Actually, though, I'll have to say goodbye to you here anyway; you see, this is as far as I go. My niece lives in this little bungalow." And she pointed to the modest brick home on her right. "I'm going to visit her to try to cheer her up a bit. She's not been well for the last week."

"Oh," said the Tramp Prince, "I'm sure you'll succeed in cheering her. I don't want to seem abrupt, but I'm very tired from having walked so many miles today — and also hiking through some very rough terrain...see...I'm looking for some sort of abandoned farmstead or garden where my family can move into it. It's too long a story for me to go into now."

"Of course," the woman replied.

"Ma'am..." the Tramp Prince seemed to be thinking aloud. "I hope you don't think I'm too strange for saying this...but your face...well, it just looks so much like those pictures of angels I've seen in religious books and painted on walls of churches; more than anyone else I've ever encountered. You know what I mean?"

The Woman With A Face Like An Angel blushed slightly and smiled. Then she gave an embarrassed laugh: "If I took my coat off, you'd be disappointed; you'd see that I don't have wings."

"It's just the expression on your face...it seems so angelic," the Tramp Prince offered.

"Well...I don't quite know what to say. I'm flattered, but I suspect that if you knew me better, my dear, you wouldn't think I'm so angelic." And she laughed again.

"Oh, I don't know..." said the Tramp Prince, "don't people begin to look like what they really are inside? Or maybe it's the other way around — someone becoming like the way they look. Do you think so?"

The Woman With A Face Like An Angel said nothing as she stood there in reflective silence.

A brisk chill wind swept along the street, spinning a few yellow leaves up onto and then off of the nearby lawns.

"Brrr...*that* was cold!" said the Woman With A Face Like An Angel.

The Tramp Prince shivered slightly and buttoned the top of his jacket.

"Yes, it really *was* cold."

"Here," said the woman, pulling off her purple wool scarf and wrapping it around the Tramp Prince's neck with a motherly gesture. You *need* this right now much more than I do."

"Why…thank you, ma'am…but…what will *you* use for a scarf?"

"Oh, don't worry — I have more at home. I knit them. And from here on, you can believe that you have part of an angel going along with you."

"But, I don't have anything to give you in return…"

"Dear boy…you've already given me a wonderful gift — a compliment which I know I don't deserve, but which I will now, *always* try to live up to."

The Tramp Prince shrugged, with a questioning aspect to his countenance. "Just one more thing before we part company," he uttered with great sincerity, "Can you please tell me what *really* matters in life?"

"Ummm…you know that you've *really* caught me off guard with *that* one. Let's see…"

"Just whatever comes into your head, ma'am — anything!"

"Well, taking care of my family. Certainly that. And doing things to help even strangers; *you're* an example of that. Five minutes ago I didn't even know you existed — now I'm *very* concerned about you."

With intense emotion, the Tramp Prince stood there for a few more seconds gazing deeply into the eyes of the Woman Who Looked Like an Angel.

"I wonder if I really have met a living angel," he murmured. Then he lifted her hand to his face and kissed it and began walking again very rapidly toward the hostel.

Halfway down the next block, the Tramp Prince sent a thought message to Road Toad.

"Road Toad…?"

"Yes."

"What do you think of my encounter with that woman back there?"

"I don't know what to think…well, you certainly put her on the spot with your blunt, uncompromising questions."

"I know — but she seemed to answer them very well. Maybe she really *is* an angel in disguise — an angel among us — and doesn't even realize it."

The little amphibian hesitated momentarily.

"Maybe *everyone* has some degree of angel to their makeup and some just have more than others. Anyway, no matter how well you might get to know someone like that, it still comes down to believing whatever you *want* to believe."

"Yes…perhaps so…"

As the Tramp Prince approached the street on which the hostel was located, Road Toad sent out another thought. "Do you realize…the scarf that woman gave you is *purple* — the color of *royalty*. Now if you ever become king of the road…"

"Yes…" anticipated the Tramp Prince, "I shall indeed make you court jester."

"Fair enough," replied Road Toad. "But I think tomorrow you're going to have to buy your jester some mealworms for dinner; it's getting too cold for me to find any bugs now. Otherwise I'll have to hibernate until spring and then you won't have anyone with whom to jest."

"Ah, that would truly be a pity," agreed the Tramp Prince.

Chapter 7: The Hermit

Brother Beano's polished, bald pate almost popped out of the door at the Tramp Prince's first knock. A beatific smile covered the elderly man's face as he warmly welcomed his newly arrived guest.

"You are a hiker — am I right, son?"

"Why…yes. I guess that would be accurate enough."

The Tramp Prince then paid the hostel keeper the very modest night's lodging fee and proceeded to explain all about his reason for being on the road. With his hand under his chin, Brother Beano listened intently, murmuring "mmhmm" and nodding frequently. When the Tramp Prince had finished his story, Brother Beano squinted in contemplation and raised his finger, as if to test the direction of the wind.

"Ah, yes…now I remember." He smiled again beatifically. "A couple of my guests have told me about a hermit who lives in the woods not terribly far from town. Since he lives in the woods, it may be that he can tell you about the farmsteads and homesteads that have become abandoned in this area."

"Oh, good!" said the Tramp Prince, "Tomorrow I'll attempt to find the fellow and see whether he has any ideas."

Leaning over slightly and raising his eyebrows, Brother Beano spoke softly; "You know...that you're much too late to avail yourself of our evening meal here...but I *can* take you into the kitchen and we'll see if there's something that you can find to eat that doesn't require cooking."

The Tramp Prince gave a light chuckle. "That's great! It's the way I'm used to eating, anyway. Simple fare for a simpleton. Isn't that what they say?" he joked.

Brother Beano's laugh rang throughout the building.

"Well, that's hardly correct — in your case," the hostel keeper laughed stumbling through his words.

In the morning, the Tramp Prince was up and ready to go almost the instant the door was unlocked. He thanked his host and then asked: "What is it, sir, that you think really matters in life?"

"Oh my...huh! Well...bringing good cheer to the hikers of the world. How's that for an answer to your question?"

"Wonderful!" the Tramp Prince laughed as he gave his hosts hand a very quick but vigorous shake, then nearly flew through the doorway.

Outside, the Tramp Prince sent Road Toad a thought message: I hate to backtrack, but if I'm going to get you some mealworms, I'll have to return to the business section and try to find a pet shop.

"Well, let's do it. I *am* quite hungry, even if I'm *not* quite starved yet."

After losing nearly a couple of hours procuring Road Toad's future meals, the Tramp Prince again found himself on the road north out of town. He made many unsuccessful inquiries in his attempt to find the local hermit and after exploring several possible lanes and field roads, finally, at the end of a narrow lane that led into some rocky hills, he came upon a tiny, strange-looking stone hut, half built into the hillside. In the remains of a very small summer garden, working away in it piling leaves over beds of carrots and turnips, was an unkempt middle-age man wearing a tattered suit jacket and unmatched trousers held up by suspenders.

"Why did you come here!" the man asked the Tramp Prince with an almost aggressive snarl. "Can't you see I'm a *hermit*?"

"Well...I...ah...you see, I didn't know whether I'd find somebody living at the end of this lane, quite frankly...and..." the Tramp Prince stumbled over his thoughts, trying to put them into words.

"Actually," he continued, "I'm looking for an abandoned garden for my family, and someone thought you might know where I could look."

"Why would they want an *abandoned* garden?" asked the hermit, dropping some of his hostility.

"Because," the Tramp Prince answered, "we are being evicted from the garden where we live and we don't have enough money to *buy* another one."

"Ah well, I'm certainly familiar with *that*! I've been thrown off a couple of other places where I've lived," the Hermit commiserated, but I just find a different likely-looking spot nearby and build myself another hut like this one."

"So, why do you want to live like a hermit?" asked the Tramp Prince with rather naïve directness.

"Why does *anyone* want to become a hermit?" responded the Hermit, his voice again taking on a more hostile tone. "I'm a hermit because I hate *people*! And I hate people because of how *they* have treated *me*!"

"I'm sorry," said the Tramp Prince, "I'm really sorry to learn that you've been treated badly."

"You see, it started out when I was a fairly young man," the Hermit volunteered. "My business partner kept the books for our company and he entered false figures in it. In the end, he milked the company dry and pulled out leaving me with all the bills to pay and no capital with which to pay them. Then that thief ran off with my wife! After that, no bank would lend me any money because of my bad business record. I couldn't find a decent job and finally had to take the only work I could get — pushing a broom as a night janitor in a factory. Then the factory closed during a business consolidation and I ended up out on the street looking through garbage cans for something to eat."

"That's just *awful*!" the Tramp Prince said, conciliatorily.

"But you haven't heard the worst of it," the Hermit continued. "When I was sleeping on park benches and digging through garbage cans, a kindly minister of a church befriended me and took me into his parsonage to give me a decent meal. While I was sitting in the kitchen, a woman came in, one of the parishioners, and pointed me out as the man who had sexually assaulted her young daughter. Although the minister knew that it was a case of mistaken identity, since I had never lived in that section of the city — had virtually never even gone there before — the woman was so convinced that I was the culprit she had seen assaulting her daughter, that she had me arrested and prosecuted. And the juries believe eyewitnesses — especially when you don't have any money to employ a private attorney and have to rely on a public defender. As you probably already know, they're all grossly overburdened with a plethora of cases. I didn't blame the public defender for the outcome. He was a nice, talented, young attorney. But he was already working on two murder cases to which he understandably gave priority."

"What happened then?" asked the Tramp Prince.

"After I was convicted amid my loud protests, they sentenced me to five years in the penitentiary. I served my time and when I got out, vowed that I would never have anything to do with humanity again. It's not that every person is always cruel or disagreeable, but some of them who are, seem to control the 'system'...and when you get caught up in it, if you have no money, it is designed to swallow you up!"

"Oh, your experience is *so* horrible!" said the Tramp Prince with great compassion. "I wish I could do something to right all the wrongs that have been done to you."

"You know something," said the Hermit, "you are one of the very few human beings I've met in the last twenty years that I didn't feel like throwing rocks at."

"Well, I'm at least glad for that," the Tramp Prince told the Hermit lightheartedly. Then, taking out the sack of dried fruit and vegetables, he took a piece for himself. "Here, take a piece of fruit if you'd like. We dry these at home from our own trees and garden plants."

"Why, thank you!" said the Hermit. "You know, I dry food myself from the garden — when I can. And I really wish I could help you and your family find another home — but I don't range very far from here. Usually, I just work my garden or walk in the nearby woods to see the animals and plants. Sometimes I sit in the grass and watch the beautiful cloud formations or the glorious colors of the sunset. In the cold weather, I sit in the hut and read. That may not seem like a very interesting or exciting life, but the kind of excitement I've had in the past, I just don't need."

The Tramp Prince nodded. "Yes, I understand what you mean. Actually, my own family lives much the way you do; but we're just a little more on the margins of society. We do have some contact with other local people, but it's minimal. Even living on the margins of society, it's very easy to be seriously affected by the whims of a few other people — so much so that it can change your whole life."

"You're right," said the Hermit, "and if it weren't for the fact that occasionally I need a few things I can't make — like a hoe and a rake and a shovel...except for that, I wouldn't even want to have anything to do with humans — or their technology. Other than my books and a few kitchen utensils, the garden tools and a saw and an axe — that's about all the worldly technology I own. It's not much, but it means I'm not exactly a Luddite."

"What's that...a Luddite?" asked the Tramp Prince.

"It's someone who believes or behaves like a person named Ludd — from the eighteenth century who supposedly hated machinery; and broke it up. The story is badly distorted and rather fictionalized. Anyway, you see, I don't hate machinery — technology; I just hate the people who make it — and who use it. That's why I live here as simply as I can."

"Ah," the Tramp Prince replied, "simple living..."

"I'm sorry I can't help you in your search," the Hermit told the Tramp Prince, "but I do know of someone who might be able to." They call him the Woodsman, and I'm sure he lives somewhere fairly nearby in the woods, because I've had him stumble upon me a couple of times during my walks in the surrounding woods. We've talked a bit. He's a friendly, agreeable chap. I know that he tramps through large areas of the backwoods. Someone else along the road may be able to tell you where to find him."

Then, after thanking the Hermit, the Tramp Prince just stood there for a few moments as if in anticipation of some grand finale. The Hermit looked at the Tramp Prince with a sad and soulful expression to his eyes.

"You really want to ask me how I can stand it being a hermit, don't you?"

"No, I'd just like to ask you what you think really *matters* in life."

"Agh…what really matters is after we *leave* this life. And I don't pretend to have any idea what that might be…whether it's angels, devils, spirits — Gods or Goddesses…or nothing. Just plain nothing. There's my answer."

The Hermit turned and looked off into the distance, so preoccupied with thought that he did not seem to notice as the Tramp Prince waved him farewell and began walking again down the narrow lane to the road.

"The world is full of strange people," Road Toad telepathized.

"Oh, I don't think that hermit is so strange," the Tramp Prince said aloud. "But he has certainly had more than his share of bad luck."

Chapter 8: The Woodsman

At several business establishments, as well as houses, that he came to along the road, the Tramp Prince inquired about the location of the Woodsman's home; but no one seemed to be certain of where to find the man. Finally in the one-room post office of a tiny village, the postmaster told the Tramp Prince that the Woodsman did, indeed, receive his mail at that office.

"We have no way to deliver it to him, because he lives so far up that old logging road at the edge of the village. And he won't put up a mailbox with his name on it — says the kids will just keep knocking it down. So we hold his mail until he comes in for it."

The Tramp Prince quickly found the logging road, and began a trek which lasted nearly half an hour, through mud holes, across creeks and then halfway up a virtual mountainside. At the end of the logging road was a rough cabin, built of logs and shake shingles split from the local pines. The Woodsman was not home, but the Tramp Prince sat down in a grassy spot awaiting the man's return.

It was still early in the afternoon when the huge shaggy figure of the Woodsman came clomp-clomping into the clearing by the house. His great size and the dark brown, furry coat that he wore, along with his uncut, unkempt black hair and beard, made him appear more like a massive bear than a human.

"Yes, yes...it is I, the Woodsman! And who, pray tell, are you...you who look to be a vagabond, but are too young to be one?"

"I am called the Tramp Prince, and I'm searching for an abandoned garden home where my mother, father, sister and I can move into and live. I've searched for weeks now since leaving home and I have not found any place suitable. The Hermit over on the next mountain told me that if anyone would know of a place such as the one I'm seeking, it would be you."

The Woodsman stroked his bushy, black beard in contemplation.

"Yes, you came to the right person. I've walked these woods all over this part of the land for many years. You see, I work as a woodcutter, helping to remove dead trees and then get the logs to the sawmill. I refuse to cut down living trees because I have no wish to hurt them. It's my belief that a tree or a plant can feel discomfort — perhaps pain when we mutilate it or cut it down. I also act as a kind of game warden for several wealthy landowners, reporting trespassers and poachers; so I'm familiar with nearly every nook and cranny of the woods around here. But I must tell you, that as I reach through my memory, I can think of only one old stone home that might have fit your family's needs — and a landslide buried that place not long ago. Beyond that one place, I'm sorry to say, I cannot think of any others. It seems to me that the problem is that you've come too far into this land of very rough terrain. As you go farther north and west, the mountains become even steeper and more formidable. And the weather, as well, becomes less agreeable."

The Tramp Prince listened intently as the Woodsman talked; then the young man looked around at the steep, often barren, rocky slopes of the great hills behind them.

"So what do you think I should do?" he asked the Woodsman. The Woodsman again stroked his long beard.

"From what I can understand…from the way you've explained your travels to me, you've come about three or four hundred miles northwest. Now, you don't have to go back the way you came", the Woodsman advised, "but I would suggest that you turn and go south immediately."

The Woodsman looked around at the sky and listened to the wind. "We may very well get our first snowfall tonight. It would be best for you if you could find yourself as far away from here as possible before it hits."

The Tramp Prince's face took on an expression of great anxiety: "The Hermit spoke very highly of you and I can see why. I'm extremely grateful for your advise," said the Tramp Prince with appreciation.

"Ah yes, that poor hermit," began the Woodsman, "the world has not treated him well. Even here, the young hoodlums have tried to make his life unpleasant — Like the time they placed a large glob of mud on top of his chimney and literally smoked him out.

"But I think they've learned to leave him alone," the Woodsman continued. "One time when I was resting by a saw log I'd felled near his hut, I heard three young hooligans coming up the path nearby. They were talking about what they planned to do to the hermit. I quickly walked up around the path until I was ahead of them, and as the first one came along, I leaped out from behind a tree, picked the devil up over my head and spun him around, throwing him at the other two, and knocked them down like tenpins.

"They got up and went screaming back the way they came. I don't think they ever knew exactly what hit them. I had roared when I picked up the first man and everything happened to them so fast that I'm certain they thought they'd been attacked by a grizzly. They've never been back since."

The Woodsman made a loud, throaty guffaw.

"That's quite a story," the Tramp Prince commented. "But I just can't understand why anyone would want to harass someone who is so peaceful — just because he *is* different from most other people."

"But they do," the Woodsman responded. "And that just seems to be the way the world is."

After a few moments of silence, listening to the sound of the wind whining and crying sadly through the pines, the Tramp Prince spoke softly: "It's so isolated up here — so lonely. I don't see how you and the Hermit can live up here in such isolation. Although, for the Hermit I know that he just doesn't like *people*. But what about you?"

"I like most people well enough," replied the Woodsman, "but there is something that I like more about the peace and solitude here with the mountain slopes and the trees. The trees are my *friends*! When you have lived with the trees long enough, you learn to speak to them," he smiled knowingly. "Their language, though, is not one of sound; it is a language of spirit. Many of them are much older than we will ever be — and much wiser."

"What an odd way of thinking about it," the Tramp Prince commented.

"Oh, not so odd — not really so odd at all..." reflected the Woodsman.

The Tramp Prince thought deeply again. "You know...I'm not sure how long I could keep my sanity if I had to live here."

"You see, my young friend, each of us has different needs. I understand what you're saying. But, this place works for me. It wouldn't be right for everybody — probably not even very many. People lose their sanity usually from not being able to cope with an extreme, irreplaceable loss in life or from being overwhelmed by frustration...where they're blocked in every effort they make to achieve some goal. There are other reasons, of course. I could be swept away too if I let myself get caught up in the same kind of make-believe adopted by so many who lose touch with reality. But up here, I can minimize my contact with the undesirable elements of society; that is my saving grace. You will understand this better when you become older."

"So, sir...is communicating with trees and trying to live with minimal human contact what you think is important in life?"

"Well...yes...yes, that's just about the way I would put it..."

The Woodsman lapsed into a reverie that the Tramp Prince could tell was closing their conversation. He took the Woodsman's huge hand, gave it a hearty shake, nodded with a smile and quickly began his descent down the mountainside.

Chapter 9: The Railroad Bum

Later that afternoon, the temperature began to drop precipitously. Purple-gray clouds were building up to an ominous, angry-looking frown in that late November sky. All through the Northern and Western realms, as far as could be seen over the horizon, were the gray and purple, and black plumes that drifted like a celestial ocean of some nightmare of doom.

With an exaggerated breadth of step that sped him along at a very commendable pace, the Tramp Prince walked south along the road. Once on that lonely road, a huge log truck rumbled by, going upgrade — and though the Tramp Prince put out his thumb in solicitation of a ride, the driver did not stop.

"Ah...I really didn't expect him to stop — not going up this steep hill," the Tramp Prince told Road Toad.

"Maybe you'll be luckier next time and catch someone going downhill," Road Toad suggested.

"But there's been no other traffic on this road..." the Tramp Prince replied with more than a touch of disgust to the tone of his voice. He buttoned his jacket up higher. "It seems to be getting colder by the second!"

"You mean that your scarf from an angel isn't keeping you warm?"

"Ha! Even the love of an angel couldn't warm the body — or perhaps even the heart — of someone caught in the frigid blasts of this pending storm."

But somehow...I think that fate may have been smiling just a bit on the Tramp Prince and Road Toad, for at the bottom of the hill there was a shabby, unpainted, clapboard building with a sign advertising that the owner sold gasoline and food. Parked out front, next to a rusty, red cast iron pump was the log truck that had passed the Tramp Prince as he walked up the hill.

The outside of the building was plastered with signs promoting every imaginable type of soft drink, chewing gum, razor blade, antacid and tobacco product. Inside, the dingy lunch counter was brightened only by a couple of softly glowing oil lamps at each end, and a candle stuck in a bottle on the table occupied by the log truck driver. The driver recognized the Tramp Prince immediately as he walked in.

"Hey kiddo, I woulda' stopped for you if I hadn't been goin' up that steep hill. Sorry."

"Oh that's alright," the Tramp Prince told him, "I actually didn't expect you to be able to stop. I don't even know why I stuck my thumb out. Maybe just so desperately cold," and he gave a simulated shiver.

"Yeah — it's cold alright, kid. Ha! You c'n ride up there with me if you want but that damn truck cab don't have no heater. The curtains seal it up pretty good — that keeps most a' the wind out. But it's still mighty cold inside there. Warmin' up's as much the reason I stopped here as fer buyin' gas."

The driver held his hands around a hot bowl of soup as he waited for it to cool down enough to eat.

"So where you headed, kiddo?" The log truck driver began to slurp his soup, speaking between spoonfuls.

"Probably going at least as far as you are — then a lot farther," the Tramp Prince told him, "as long, that is, as you stay headed *south*!"

"I'm just takin' this here load a' logs t' the sawmill in the next town — that's about an hour's drive from here. But there's a railroad goes through town — takes the lumber on out. I think the track goes south — maybe east too. You could probably hop one a' them lumber cars an' get pretty far that way."

The Tramp Prince nodded and sat down at the table.

"I'll buy yuh sumpthin' hot if yuh want, kiddo," the driver offered.

Again nodding, the Tramp Prince then ordered a bowl of vegetable soup. The hot, steaming soup came in a thick, crockery, restaurant bowl on which the boy warmed his hands before eating the contents.

"Listen kid, I got an extra pair a' gloves out there in the truck cab. They ain't much — got a few holes in 'em. You're welcome to 'em. Better than nuthin'."

"Sure, thanks," the Tramp Prince answered.

When they had both finished their soup, the driver pulled out his large pocket watch, and popped open the case.

"Oops...gotta go, kiddo. Just enough time left t' get this load in before the saw mill closes."

The driver put on his jacket and grabbed his leather cap with earflaps, pulling it down over his bristly, short-cut hair. It made the man look like a racecar driver without the goggles. The driver went to the cashier's counter and paid the bill, smiling at the café owner.

"Wish me luck," he joked, "that we don't have three foot snow drifts 'fore I get there!"

"Good luck and come back," the middle aged, pasty-faced owner called after the pair as they walked out the door.

After retarding the spark lever and raising the throttle a bit, the log truck driver cranked up the big slope-nosed Mack's engine and climbed up into the cab from the passenger's side.

"Driver's side curtain's too hard to hook," he explained. "Just stow yer sack on yer lap; that'll help keep yuh warm."

The Tramp Prince sat down on the lightly padded board of the truck seat, feeling a jolting thump with every bump in the road that the truck's solid rubber tires encountered.

"It's like riding on a washboard," the Tramp Prince laughed.

"Yeah — you'll get used to it." Came the reply.

On and on the truck rattled and rumbled its way over some of the roughest dirt road that the Tramp Prince had ever seen. The constant unmuffled roar of the truck's engine and the growl of the transmission gears made a cacophony of mechanical dissonance that progressed into a veritable symphony from hell.

A few times snowflakes began to dance around in the frigid air in front of the truck.

"We're just gonna get there in time; I mean before the snow starts." The shivering driver made his comment as they rolled into the edge of town. "That sawmills right next to the railroad tracks; you can ask someone at the mill when the next train goes through, they'll probably know."

The massive Mack with its long trailer of huge logs pulled near the mill's loading dock where the driver and his passenger left the cab. Thanking the driver again, the Tramp Prince walked over to where the gigantic saw blade was still whirring, as the final cuts were made on the logs for that day.

Screeches from the cutting made a deafening sound and the Tramp Prince was forced to wait until the operator threw the switch, shutting down the enormous electric motor that drove the blade. He walked over to the operator, a young man about his own age, who offered a friendly smile. The fellow looked at the Tramp Prince's rather ragged clothes and his bindle sack.

"Bet you're gonna ask me when the next freight leaves outta here — right?"

"You're very perceptive," the Tramp Prince told him.

"Nah," said the young man, "you're just very *obvious*!" And he laughed, the steam condensing from his breath as he spoke. "Let's see, it's almost six now...won't be nothin' through 'til maybe one or two in the mornin' — I think. But this is Friday...you might have to wait 'til tomorrow when they send out the cars with this week's load. I'm just not real sure about it."

The Tramp Prince offered his thanks and walked around to the rear of the mill, where tracks had been laid in a long siding and where several loaded lumber cars sat in the dismal evening gloom. In a brush-hidden clearing just past the far end of the siding, a faint, flickering glow became visible whenever the wind shifted the weeds that largely screened the firelight.

He continued toward the hobo jungle and, entering the clearing, found no one. As the Tramp Prince crouched close to the warmth from the blazing sticks, a large man entered the clearing with what seemed like an equally large armload of trimming slabs from the mill. The man dropped his load at the feet of the Tramp Prince.

"Sure didn't 'spect t' see someone here when I got back!" he chuckled, his heavy breath condensing in long plumes.

"Here," said the Tramp Prince, "I'll help you build this fire up a bit more." And he began adding slabs where they would have the best chance of igniting.

"They calls me 'Artie Top-rider,' the older man said as an introduction.

"And they call me 'the Tramp Prince'," was the reply.

"Glad ter meet yer, Tramp Prince. See, m' real name is Richard Theobold an' so th' initials is R.T. — an' them two letters is jest got sorta run t'gether so now everbody calls me Artie — like short fer Arthur. Yuh see?"

"Yes!" laughed the Tramp Prince. "That's funny!"

"Well, it ain't always funny," said Artie Top-rider. "Oncet when a couple railroad bulls had me in front of a kangaroo court jedge, he thought I wuz givin' him a phony name, 'cause the name Artie didn't match the name on a couple letters to me that I wuz carryin'."

"Uh…what's a railroad bull?" asked the Tramp Prince with some trepidation. Artie Top-rider laughed and laughed.

"I'm sorry, kid, but it's mighty clear that you're jest as green as grass," and he laughed again. "You ain't never even hopped a freight train, have yuh kid?"

"No," admitted the Tramp Prince, "I haven't."

"Ok — now railroad bulls is the cops that the railroad company hires t' try t' keep us hoboes from ridin' the freight cars. Most times they ain't smart enough t' cetch us, but oncet in a while they will — 'specially if there's two of 'em workin' the tracks together. The bulls is pretty bad aroun' this here town, so tomorrow, when we tries t' cetch out on one a' them lumber cars, we'll wait 'til they're already movin' an' cetch one on the fly."

The Tramp Prince looked around at the hobo jungle. A makeshift lean-to shelter had been erected from old sheets of corrugated steel and Artie's fire was made as close to the entrance of that shelter as it seemed safe to make it. Inside the shelter, was a very large, cardboard box that had been smashed down on one end so that it would fit the angle of the roof steel. He could see a blanket roll inside the box.

"Listen here, Tramp Prince", Artie began, "it's gonna be too cold out t' try t' sleep t'night without havin' some kinda pertection. I think there wuz 'nother one a' them big cardboard boxes over where I got this one — by the back wall a' the lumber shed. You go over there n' get you one a' them big boxes an' then smash it down like I done mine. Cardboard ain't the best insulator in the world, but it'll keep yuh warm enough, no colder 'n it's gonna be t'night.

The Tramp Prince retrieved a box, finding one that still had the lid intact and after crushing the closed end, he turned the box so that the lid hinged down like a door flap. Artie looked at the Tramp Princes handiwork.

"Yer a smart kid y'are. Don't know why I didn't try that trick with the flap for a door...! Listen kid, I hate t' tell yuh, but there ain't no easy food that we're gonna be able t' snag aroun' here. These people in this here town don't care nuthin' fer hoboes. I doubts we're gonna have any luck knockin' on doors — 'specially this late. But we kin try."

"If what you said is true", the Tramp Prince told his new friend, "We may just end up burning more energy walking around in this cold than we'll get back from any handouts. I had a bowl of hot soup just before I got here, so I guess I'll be okay until morning."

"Suit yerself", Artie Top-rider said to the Tramp Prince, "but I'm gonna try a couple houses anyway. Maybe I'll get lucky."

As the Tramp Prince crawled into his cardboard cocoon, Artie placed two more slabs on the glowing orange coals of the fire. When he returned a half hour later, the Tramp Prince was sleeping soundly.

"I really saved this here one ham sanrich fer the kid", Artie thought to himself, "but I'd hate t' wake him; guess I'll jest hafta eat it myself." And he crawled into his own blanket roll still munching the sandwich.

It was still early in the night when the Tramp Prince was awakened by the low, melancholy whistle of a freight train, somewhere on another track off in the distance. He pushed up the flap on his box and tried to look up at the moon. The air was crisp and exquisitely clear...and the moon, still well within the first quadrant of its arc, was so bright that it hurt his eyes to continue to look at it. He tried to remember what he had been dreaming, but could recall only that it had something to do with searching for Pfantassiland. He shut the box's flap and removed the sleeping Road Toad from his pocket, placing the little fellow in a warm fold of blanket near his head.

By the time daylight finally arrived, the fire had burned down to a small pile of white-gray ashes. Frost was visible on the dry grass of the surrounding fields. The icy crust invaded right to the edge of the jungle clearing. Artie was the first to awaken.

"Ooo! No wonder I didn't sleep too good. Look kid — a real heavy frost!"

The Tramp Prince pushed up his box lid and gazed out at the sunlight that made the icy fields look like a sea of diamonds.

"Well at least the snow never materialized. I'm thankful for that and I stayed warm enough last night in that box. But if we have to catch out early today, I hate to think what it's going to be like riding on an open flat car in this kind of temperature."

"Yeah, kid", Artie said, recalling many agonizing memories of similar rides, "We'll freeze our butts off!"

The Tramp Prince closed the box lid and lay in the warm blanket roll, pondering how he was going to tolerate the cold air rushing by on the lumber car's open surface.

"Hey Artie," the Tramp Prince called out, "What about each of us taking our boxes down there and getting back in them on top of a stack of lumber?"

"Good idea, kid, but it won't work — cause the lumber's gonna have frost on top of it too — an' the first little bit a' wind 'll slide the box with you in it, right off an' back down between the cars — right under the wheels, an' it'll grind yuh up like a pile a' hamburger!"

The Tramp Prince shuddered at the thought.

"Maybe we'll be lucky and the load won't go out early."

"Maybe," said Artie, "but I don't count on it."

The two hoboes put away their bedding and quickly walked down to the siding, staying hidden in the deep trench on the side of the tracks away from the mill. They crept along, examining each of the several cars in an effort to determine which ones might be the best to ride on.

"Look, Artie, this one has a space up in front of its stack. I think one of those big boxes would fit right up in there."

"Yeah, you're right, kid. Quick — before the workers get here, go up there an' grab another one a' them boxes an' we'll tie it on an' both of us get inta it.

After retrieving another box, the Tramp Prince placed it in the open area in front of the lumber.

"These stacks of lumber," Artie observed, "they got 'em all strapped down tight so they can't move around like they could in a closed car. We can tie off the box right to the boards."

"How?" asked the Tramp Prince.

Artie pulled out a length of strong tie rope.

"I use this to tie myself on whenever I have to — like if I'm ridin' the tops an maybe I think I might fall asleep. An' I use these here big nails t' drive inta a board if there's nothin' else t' use fer a tie-down."

He then reached into another pocket and took out a rusty railroad spike, using it as a hammer.

"Here," he told the Tramp Prince "tie this end of the rope t' one a' the nails on the other side, then take it around the box a couple times an' hand it t' me so's I kin tie it off on the other nail."

That having been completed, the two hoboes crawled into the large box along with their bindle sacks and pulled the lid down only far enough to allow space for air circulation.

"Sure is cramped in here." Artie observed. "Listen now —when the train crew gets here, drop this flap all the way down. They'll only take a few minutes to do the hookup."

In a surprisingly short time, the sound of a locomotive's chuff-chuff could be heard approaching.

"Don't make no noise, kid," Artie whispered.

Soon, two brakies began walking along the track to inspect the cars. The boxed railroad bums could hear one brakie say to the other: "What t' hell they shippin' out now in cardboard boxes?"

"Damned if I know," said the other.

"Must be pretty heavy," the first brakie replied. He pushed on the box, but it didn't budge.

"Hell, it's heavy machinery of some kind! Lotta weight there."

"Yep," agreed the other.

Their voices dimmed as they walked away.

All morning long, the two boxed up railroad bums rode along in their cramped, crouched positions.

"Kid, I can't take another minute a' bein' scrunched up like this; I gotta get outta here!"

"Me too!" agreed the Tramp Prince.

Slowly, they eased themselves and their bindle sacks out of the box and stretched out on the small area of the floor that was left beside the box.

"Let's get rid of this thing." Artie suggested, taking down the rope and the nails and then kicking the box off the lumber car. They watched the box bounce alongside the track and break up.

"Maybe we got rid of that box too quick," the Tramp Prince told Artie. What if there's a bull at the next place we stop?"

"We can probably outsmart 'em — jump off an' hide — then get back on when he's gone. Don't always work, but I tell yuh, kid, I couldn't a' taken another minute stuffed inside that durn box!"

"Agh...me neither," the Tramp Prince agreed.

Artie watched as the power line poles whizzed by. He timed between each, counting the seconds off in his mind.

"This train's movin' along at a pretty good clip — 'bout forty five miles an hour I'd guess. We been ridin' about three hours, so that's what...'bout a hundred thirty five miles more or less? The air's not 'zactly warm, but it's a whole lot warmer 'n' it was when we got on this mornin'.""

The old railroad bum then took out a cigarette and tried to light it, but the rush of air was so intense that it put out every match he struck.

"I don't know about you, kid, but I'm fer gettin' off fer good, soon as the train stops somewhere. What d' you think?"

"Yeah," the Tramp Prince replied. "There's no snow down here and we need to try to get something to eat, anyway."

It was nearly another hour before the freight train slowed and began moving off the main track onto a small siding. When the train's speed had reduced to little more than a fast walking pace, both hoboes threw their bindle sacks off and leaped out and away from the moving cars. They tumbled into cinders and dry brambles left from the summer's growth.

"Damn!" Artie exclaimed as he got up and brushed off dirt and cinders. "Look at this; I caught that little tear in m' pants an' now it's three inches long. Gotta stitch that one up 'fore it rips all the way down t' my knee."

"I've got a needle and some thread down in the bottom of my sack," offered the Tramp Prince.

"Yeah, thanks, kid. I've got one someplace myself, if I can ever find it."

Artie waited until the last lumber car had passed, then he motioned to the Tramp Prince to cross the track with him. The two then went over to an unpaved road that led toward the town, still some distance away.

Artie looked up at two huge commercial grain silos by the track. Winter birds clung to the steel bands that wound around the silo's sides, some of the birds flying off and others landing in the grayness of the midday haze.

"Looka' them birds — 'Free as a bird', they say. Now ain't that the truth? Think how easy it'd be t' get away from a railroad bull if he wuz chasin' yuh — jus' flap yer wings!" Artie chuckled.

As they approached the center of town Artie pointed to the courthouse. "I think I remember this town, kid. Those towers on the courthouse — an' if this is the town I'm thinkin' about, there's a pretty good café right in the north edge a' the town square. An there's this waitress, got the biggest pair of knockers y' ever seen on a woman that small. I like t' kid around with her. You got any money? I ain't got much left, but its enough t' get us a little somethin' t' eat."

"Oh…I still have a little change left from the last time I played the flute. That was quite a while back, though. I really need to find some kind of work here if I can."

They walked into the town square and Artie found the café he had described to the Tramp Prince. Soon, the two were seated at one of the tables in the center of the café. Pungent odors of frying onions and garlic permeated the entire room.

"Hey Maggie!" Artie called out, "eggs n' bacon!"

A smiling, plain-faced little woman came to the table.

"So — you got money, honey?"

"Yeah, sure — see…I worked a few days ago," and he held up a couple of bills.

"Ok…now what about your friend here?" and she pointed to the Tramp Prince.

"I dunno what he wants. He'll tell yuh."

The Tramp Prince looked at the menu on the table and saw little that was appealing — or affordable.

"I'll just have a baked potato," he told the woman.

She laughed, "You won't never get t' be a big, strong man like Artie, here, just eatin' somethin' like that!"

Then she grabbed Artie's long, graying beard and gave it a playful tug. "Look at this pile a' brush — yuh gotta eat lots a' bacon n' eggs n' sausage t' raise one like this! Let's see yours, kid."

Maggie bent over, her buxom bust almost bumping the Tramp Prince.

"Hey, looka here — he's startin' t' grow a little goatee! She stuck her finger under the Tramp Prince's lower lip and laughed again uproariously.

"Well, you're startin' t' get there kid. Maybe in a few years…bet he'll be a handsome dude when this fills out and darkens some. Look at that peach fuzz moustache!"

The waitress grabbed a pocket mirror from behind the counter and held it in front of the Tramp Prince's face. He looked at himself in amazement, not having seen his own face in a mirror for several weeks. He did, indeed, have a half-inch growth of fine beard hair forming on his chin area and the barely visible moustache would look quite nice when it darkened, he thought.

Maggie soon brought the plates of food over and clanked them down on the table. Artie began eating away hungrily as the Tramp Prince split his potato to let the steam out and allow it to cool down.

Across the street, a few doors down along the square, a commotion could be heard — even inside the café. Maggie went to the door and looked out.

"There's a cop poundin' on some guy sittin' on that bench over there. Looks like he's a tramp," she called to the people inside. "Oh my god, the guy grabbed the night stick an' hit the cop with it. Now the tramp's runnin' off!"

The policeman lay on the sidewalk motionless. With her apron flying behind her, Maggie ran over to where a crowd had already gathered. Someone checked the pulse of the man's prostrate form.

"I think he's dead," said the pulse checker.

"Damn!" said another bystander, "Look at the side of his head; look how it's smashed in!"

As fast as she could run, Maggie sprinted back to the café and grabbed Artie's arm: "That was a tramp — killed a cop! You guys gotta get out of town. They'll round up every hobo they can find! Quick, now!"

Artie hurriedly shoveled the last of his plate of food into his mouth and reached into his pocket to pay for the meal.

"Go on!" Maggie pleaded. "It's on the house today — you guys need to get the hell out of here!"

The Tramp Prince picked up his still intact potato and slipped it into his pocket. He followed Artie out into the street where the two quickly stepped into an alley in which they would be less easily observed.

"What will we do now?" asked the Tramp Prince. "They'll be watching the tracks and every road out of here."

"I know, kid. We better find some place t' hide out for a few hours an' try t' sneak outta town when it starts gettin' dark. Otherwise we might jus' end up in a jail cell for God knows how long."

"Maybe they'll catch the guy soon and then we won't be bothered."

"Nah. I know what these small town cops is like, kid; even when they catch up with that guy, they're still gonna round up every tramp an' hobo aroun' here an' put all of us in the clink."

Artie was looking around, thinking as he made his comments, trying to remember where he had seen a boarded up building once before.

"Come on, kid."

They began walking rapidly toward the far end of the alley where it came out on another street that formed the courthouse square. Very cautiously approaching the end of the alley, they waited until no one could be seen within the nearby area, then they crossed into the next alley.

"I think this is the one," Artie whispered. He walked slowly now, looking up at the back windows of the old brick stores whose back walls lined the alley.

"Here! See them boarded up winders? Maybe we kin slip in through a basement winder."

They did, indeed, find a basement window where someone had pulled the board off; and when they pushed the window, it swung open to the inside.

"It's just wide enough t' get through," Artie remarked as he pushed his sack in and slid inside after it.

The Tramp Prince quickly did the same, but was barely able to push his larger diameter sack though. Groping their way in the nearly pitch black of the cellar along the rough, trash strewn floor, they made their way toward a front basement window that had been boarded up with two wide slats that allowed a sliver of light to enter.

Standing near the window there appeared to be a man, whose figure they could barely make out. He was looking out through the narrow slit.

"Who are you?" the man asked in an unfriendly tone of voice.

Artie identified himself: "And who's yerself?"

"Flatcar Fred," was the answer.

"This here light's s' dim I can't see yuh well enough t' know if I recognizes yuh but ain't you from out west someplace? I think I met yuh somewhere — long time ago.

"Yeah, I 'member yah. We wuz both a lot younger."

"This here kid is the Tramp Prince. We're travelin' buddies."

"Oh…yuh got yerself a road brat?"

"Nah, he's older'n that."

"This is a helluva way t' have t' meet up again. Did you guys see what happened out on the square a few minutes ago?"

"We wuz in the café when it happened."

Flatcar Fred diverted his attention again to the square as the crowd began to increase.

"I didn't see it myself neither, but some guy that wuz there said t' me a cop told a tramp t' get off a public bench where he wuz jus' settin' peaceful-like. He wouldn't move an' the cop started beatin' him with his club. Then the tramp grabbed the cop's stick and whacked the cop's head with it. Killed the son'abitch!"

"Yeah, well we figured that they'd be roundin' up every hobo aroun', so we're gonna hide out 'til it gets almost dark an' then hightail it."

As the trio looked through the slit in the window, they could see that, by now, a group of citizens had caught up with the tramp as he tried to run through the town. They had walked him back into the town square with his hands tied behind him. An angry mob was already milling around the courthouse, one man swinging a rope with a hangman's noose at the end.

"Lets string the bastard up!" called out the man with the rope.

"Yeah, string him up echoed several others.

A deputy sheriff appeared from the courthouse and approached the cadre of people holding the shivering tramp.

"Alright folks — nobody's stringin' nobody up aroun' here in this town. I don't happen t' care *what* you think, this man's entitled to a fair trial!"

The deputy took charge of the cringing wretch and walked with him back into the section of the courthouse where the cells were located.

"Damn!" Artie exploded. "That poor son'abitch ain't got a chance! You know with all them eyewitnesses the jury'll convict him an' the jedge'll sentence him t' hang.   What t' hell's the difference if the government does it or the crowd does?"

"Well," said the Tramp Prince, "at least he'll have had due process of law."

"Due process, my foot," Artie responded, "They'll give him some half-drunk old sop of a lawyer for his defense — a guy that don't care if the poor fool lives or dies 'cause he'll get his pay from the gov'ment either way.

"Extenuating circumstances could make a difference, though," the Tramp Prince stated. "But it seems that wherever there's capital punishment, people just like to see it used. It's kind of an 'eye for an eye, tooth for a tooth' mentality. Really brutal! Actually, it's retributive murder!"

"But that's just the way most folks is," Artie returned.

The Tramp Prince went on: "You know that there are murders that occur where there aren't any eyewitnesses — everything's circumstantial. If you have capital punishment and hang a person on the basis of circumstantial evidence, then later other evidence turns up proving him innocent...how are you going to give him his life back?"

"Well," said Flatcar Fred, "life ain't perfect."

"I know," replied the Tramp Prince, "and most people don't care — don't even think about this unless their unlucky enough to have it happen to them — or someone in their family. Then it's too late to do anything about it. You know that, 'two wrongs don't make a *right*.'"

"Bud," said Flatcar Fred, "I think we ought t' try t' get you 'lected hobo president!"

The Tramp Prince chuckled with cynicism.

All afternoon the three men remained in their cellar hideaway. Finally, as the sun began to sink low, Artie nudged the Tramp Prince.

"Time t' go, kid. I don't know how we're gonna scoot up high enough t' get out that winder. Guess we could stand on our sacks an' then reach down an' pull 'em back up."

"That would be really hard to do," the Tramp Prince commented. Then he took out a match, and shielding it with his hand, looked around the trash-strewn floor, hoping to spot an old crate to stand on. There were several boards, but nothing comparable to a crate. Then an idea came to him. He took a short piece of thin board and tried scraping against the mortar between the foundation stones about halfway up the wall below the window. The mortar was very rotten and fell out in large chunks. Then he scraped the mortar out far enough back to be able to wedge the board solidly between the large stones. He propped the window open with another board and shoved his bindle sack out onto the alley bricks. Then he placed his left foot on the board that protruded from the wall and by standing on it, was high enough to pull himself through the window and crawl out into the alley. The other two men used the same procedure.

"Pretty smart," Flatcar Fred complemented.

"Yeah, the kids' got brains!" Artie added.

"I don't have any more brains than anyone else," the Tramp Prince reflected modestly. "I've just learned how to *use* what I have."

The three vagabonds moved quietly down the alley and away from the center of town.

"I think," Artie began, "that if we can keep on followin' this alley far enough, it'll end up at the edge a' town an' then we can take t' the woods 'til we're far enough away from town to go back t' a road. If anything happens — some cop sees us — everybody split up — go a different direction. That way he can't chase but one of us. Okay?"

The other two agreed.

Since it was now suppertime and with the falling temperatures, it seemed that the entire town had retired to their kitchens and dining rooms to eat. An occasional dog woofed as the hoboes passed along the alley.

The trio could see what appeared to be the end of the alley just two blocks ahead, and beyond that, the darkened silhouettes of distant forest trees. As they emerged from the second to last block, they were spotted by a policeman patrolling that residential area of impressively large homes. The patrolman blew his whistle and called, demanding that the men halt, just as they reached the last alley.

"Run for it!" Artie commanded.

All ran to the middle of the alley block where another alley intersected. At that point Artie ran to the left, the Tramp Prince ran to the right and Flatcar Fred continued straight ahead. The cop soon reached the middle where the alleys intersected. He hesitated a few moments, not knowing which man to follow. By then he had lost all chance of pursuing even one of them.

With a huge pounding pace, the Tramp Prince bounded up one alley and down another, now crossing the town again at a right angle to his previous direction. Dogs barked as the young tramp's footsteps echoed along the empty, often cavernous confines between the buildings. At the eastern end of the little town, in exhaustion, the Tramp Prince slowed his run to a trot and headed out into the first open field he encountered. Reaching the hedgerow, he fell face first into a slight trench filled with leaves and dry grass. Several large poke plants, only recently frosted, formed a sheltering cover over the grassy trench.

Instantly, his mind began to churn in phantasmagoric gyrations of wild colors and brilliant lights of weird surrealism. When he opened his eyes, he realized that he was in a tiny, cramped house, no larger than a child's playhouse. The ceiling was so low that he could reach up, even from a kneeling position and touch the varnished, beaded ceiling boards. There were tiny wooden framed windows on each side of the single room — and when he placed his hand to a window, it covered more than two of the diminutive panes. A minute bed spanned one end wall and the Tramp Prince knew it was useless to attempt to crawl into it; so he lay scrunched with knees to chest on the empty floor.

After what seemed to be a passage of several hours, he was abruptly awakened by a low-pitched voice that fairly bristled with anger. The boy could not understand the words — only the angry tone.

In a half-sleeping response he barely mumbled: "I'm sorry, I'm sorry," not knowing why he was saying it or to whom the apology was directed. Vaguely, he could make out a tiny figure standing next to him, furiously beating on his head with a large turkey feather.

There was no pain, only the strange brushing feel against his forehead.

The light of dawn had begun to push away the darkness and the Tramp Prince opened one eye, just far enough to notice that a small, dry leaf, still attached to a branch from a low, limber sapling, was continually touching his forehead in the morning breeze. The open trench into which he had fallen the night before was slightly sheltered from the early chill by the hunched over poke plants, but the cold air pervaded everywhere with a biting vengeance.

"Road Toad," said the Tramp Prince with an anxious hesitance, "are you alright?"

There was no response. The Tramp Prince reached into his pocket and pulled the cold, motionless form of the small amphibian out, trying to warm it in both hands. Almost imperceptibly, after several minutes in the warmth of the Tramp Prince's hands, the little animal began to move again. Then, as the toad's body temperature increased, he sent a telepathic thought to the Tramp Prince.

"It got so cold yesterday — and last night, that I had to start hibernating."

"I know," said the Tramp Prince. "I'm sorry I didn't realize what was happening. But there was so much excitement and turmoil going on yesterday, that I have to admit that I completely forgot about you."

"Ugh!" said Road Toad trying to regain a little more warmth by jumping up and down. "Just don't let it happen again or I might be unavailable for the rest of the winter."

Later, back on the road heading south, the Tramp Prince sent a thought to Road Toad.

"Things happened so fast and furiously yesterday that I completely forgot to ask those two other hoboes what they thought really mattered in life."

"They probably would have told you something like: 'Not seeing any cops around' — or 'Getting a sumptuous meal as a handout'."

"Yes, possibly," the Tramp Prince laughed.

Chapter 10: The Lady With The Fancy Chair

For nearly a day and a half, the Tramp Prince continued his walk southward, investigating every possible lane and field road that he came upon. The piles of orange and yellow leaves in the ditches along the roads, where sugar maples and hickories overhung, had by now lost most of their delicate brilliance. Leaves on top of the piles were a crispy brown and only here and there a tinge of the flaming fall colors peeked through as an almost forgotten reminder. Oaks still held their leaves, but their dark red had faded to a dingy brown as well.

As had usually been the case, the Tramp Prince found only a couple abandoned homes and neither one, he thought, might have much potential for rehabilitation. He then began walking down a very woodsy side road, which seemed to end at a quiet river bottom.

Having walked so far off the main road already, he decided not to backtrack, but to try to cross the stream and continue on a grassy road which followed along the bank on the other side. But there was no bridge of any kind in sight in either direction.

"I'm going to try to pole vault across!" he telepathized to Road Toad. "Hang On!"

After first testing the bottom of the creek bed with his walking stick and feeling solid rock only a short distance down, the Tramp Prince went far enough back up the dirt road to be able to come at the stream with a very fast run. When he reached the edge of the water, he took a huge leap and jammed the long walking stick into the bed, then pushed off, effectively hitting the ground on the other side. The walking stick remained stuck in the creek bed, though — and it was too far out to grasp from the water's edge.

"Now what?" asked Road Toad.

"Well…maybe I can pull it down with another stick."

"Maybe…I don't know about that."

Just as the Tramp Prince turned to begin looking for a branch, so as to retrieve his walking stick, the top of the stick began to ease its way lazily over toward the bank. By placing a couple of large rocks at the edge of the stream, he was able to barley touch the end of his pole and carefully pull it toward him.

"Ha! I did it, Road Toad. What do you think of that?"

"Well...very good."

"Yes," He laughed. "I wasn't sure I'd ever be able to retrieve that one!"

Once they had passed out of the valley bottom, the old logging road turned into a field road and then suddenly they found themselves at the end of a street that led into what eventually became a fairly large city.

The Tramp Prince wandered about, looking at buildings and monuments, parks and palatial homes, until he finally came to a slum area with a number of storefronts and a mission home sandwiched between two of the stores.

The hour now being rather late, the Tramp Prince decided to sleep at the mission. A large sign out front scaled almost a full two stories of the building, where the name, South Side Mission blazed in small incandescent bulbs and the words "Jesus Saves" flashed on and off in a green neon glow.

The building appeared to have once been a hotel and the front lobby still retained much of the appearance of its former use. As the Tramp Prince walked in, an older man greeted him.

"It's ten cents for the bed," the mission manager told him gruffly, "and another ten cents for the shower...and another ten cents for a plate of grub tonight...and another ten cents for oatmeal tomorrow morning."

"Whew...so how much altogether?"

"Forty cents, if you want it all."

"Alright...I guess I'll go for the package."

After digging through his pockets, the Tramp Prince pulled out two quarters from his last few coins, then handed them to the man.

"Be right back with your change," he told the young traveler.

When the Tramp Prince had received his change, they proceeded to the dining hall. The room was a dingy time-eroded remnant — a relic of its former glory days of bustling business and bright conversations — rollicking laughter...and waiters clinking dishes and the pallet-tempting aromas of delicacies and delectable meals.

There was a low murmur as each man either complained to his neighbor about the food...or about the economy...or about life in general. The Tramp Prince picked at his plate of beans and shaved cabbage. He pushed a thin, almost disgusting-looking sausage to the outer edge of the plate.

During the meal, the men were subjected to a half-hour religious sermon on 'The Sinfulness of Sin', the preacher never explaining exactly what that was, but only exhorting everyone to avoid being caught up in it.

"What did you think of the sermon?" asked the Tramp Prince in a telepathic thought message to Road Toad.

"I didn't understand much of it — but what I think I understood makes me want to get down and clean up all the bugs on the floor. Aren't they sinners?"

"Oh I don't know!" laughed the Tramp Prince. "I can hardly believe an answer like that!"

Later, in the sleeping quarters, he found the cots crammed almost next to each other with barely enough space left to walk between them. The bedding was clean, but ragged, having been washed so often, that the patterns in the blankets were no longer visible. On the cot next to him, an older man with a nearly white mutton chop beard raised his long eyebrows as the Tramp Prince sat and removed his shoes.

"Better tie yer shoes t'gether n' stuff 'em in yer bindle sack; put yer wallet under yer pillow. That's what I do — jus t' be safe, see?"

"Yes, thanks for the tip."

Snores, grunts, coughs and mumbling conversation could be heard nearly the entire night. In the morning, the Tramp Prince was anxious to be on his way and to resume his search.

As he left the mission, the boy could see, a couple blocks ahead, the dome of a large building, which when he arrived close to it, was marked with the words 'Public Library'. The doors had just been unlocked and he found himself to be the first person in the building that day.

The warm, welcome atmosphere of books and paper and early sunshine streaming through the windows was an odor and a sight, if not pleasant to the nostrils and the eyes, at least to the imagination.

Gray skies and the brisk wind he had encountered outside tempted the boy to spend some time there.

All morning, the Tramp Prince busied himself with books on esoteric subjects that he discovered on obscure shelves. There were tantalizing treatises on the nature of man and the universe — fantastic formulas for pursuing everything from the Holy Grail to the unholy trail. And when the midday arrived, he had become so absorbed in thought that he hardly noticed that his stomach was asking for food.

But physical needs eventually have a way of making their presence known to us, so I think that the Tramp Prince could no longer repress the growl of peristalsis; nor could he afford to ignore the nudging of his tiny pocket occupant.

"Let's get out of here — I need to find some bugs — or you need to buy me some more meal worms — I'm out, you know." Road Toad's thoughts conveyed both an urgency and an irritation. "I really got tired of reading Schopenhauer," he told the Tramp Prince. "What a bunch of crusty rot!"

"Oh now...we need to study the classics in literature and philosophy if we're ever going to be able to make sense of this culture, don't you think?"

"No," Road Toad replied acidly, "I don't think at all, when I haven't eaten since the day before yesterday."

With the little money that he still had, the Tramp Prince was able to buy a few items at a green grocer, which they came to on their way through town. Not far from the grocery, they passed a vacant lot where the Tramp Prince was able to kick over several rocks and old boards, exposing plenty of insects for a sumptuous repast for Road Toad.

Their food needs having been satisfied, they began again going toward the far end of the town. After traveling only a few blocks, the Tramp Prince had to move to the side to avoid an older lady sitting in a very fancy chair right in the middle of the sidewalk.

As he passed, the woman called out to him, "Do you want to buy this chair?"

"No," he replied, "I'm traveling — what could I possibly do with a chair?"

"Well...you could sit in it whenever you got tired of walking."

"Yes, it looks very comfortable. And I would be sitting in it almost constantly after having had to carry the weight of the thing around with me!"

"It's also very beautifully carved, don't you think?"

"I agree…why don't you carry the chair with *you*?"

"But, I have been carrying it — about the last five blocks from where I found it in the alley."

"I'm sorry," the Tramp Prince chuckled, "I don't want to seem like I'm just laughing at you…but wouldn't it make a lot more sense if I were to help you carry that chair to your house? Then you could make use of it and enjoy it."

"I don't have a house," the Lady With The Fancy Chair said in almost a hushed undertone.

"You…just live out here…on the street?"

She nodded.

"Oh, I'm so sorry," said the Tramp Prince.

"You don't have to be sorry," the Lady told him. "Life simply *is* the way it *is*."

The Lady With The Fancy Chair looked off into the distance, tears welling up in her eyes.

"I had a home once — a very nice home. But I had to leave it several years ago."

"Why?" asked the Tramp Prince with great compassion in his voice.

"Well, you see, my husband was a skilled cabinet maker and he provided a beautiful house — and he made an excellent living. But he was mean; he was cruel. I don't want to make you think that he ever hit me, because that never happened. It was just what he would *say* to me."

"He didn't like you? Why, you have a lovely personality and you're still an attractive woman, even now."

The Tramp Prince saw a profound, enduring sadness in the woman's deep-set eyes. Her black hair was tinged with silvery streaks as it passed under her tattered headscarf. Yet there was an ageless beauty to her finely chiseled features that reminded the boy of the carved cameos of nineteenth century women one often sees in jewelry displays. The enormous coat, which the woman wore, however, made her look as though she carried a body of extreme corpulence on her obviously thin legs.

"When I was living with my husband," she continued, "I had very little to do, so I took to going on long walks around the streets of the city where we lived. One day, I was taking a short cut through an alley, and I came upon the most beautiful lamp I had ever seen. It was extremely dirty from having probably been in someone's attic for decades, but I saw great potential in it after it had been cleaned. I took the lamp home and before I could walk into the house with it, my husband came charging out in anger, refusing to let me bring that 'horrible, filthy thing' as he called it, into the house. He grabbed it away from me and hurled it at the pavement, where it broke into a thousand pieces.

"After that, every time I would find something else nice on one of my walks, he would have a fit of anger if I tried to bring it home. I became so lonely and felt so unloved that I began befriending the 'street people' that I would see where I walked never thinking that I would become one of them myself.

"One cold day, I found a ragged young woman, still in her early twenties, slumped down in the doorway of a vacant store. She was a very sick young lady, but I managed, by engaging some help, to get her to my house. It was during a day when my husband was not home, so I hid her in a basement room that my husband almost never entered. Then I brought her some hot tea and blankets to try to bring up her circulation. She began reviving quickly and I told her that I thought she might be well enough to leave by the next morning and that I could not allow my husband to know that she was there.

"That evening, when my husband returned home, I said nothing about the girl, knowing what his response would probably be if he found out about her. Actually, by that point, we hardly talked anymore anyway. But for some reason —and I could never understand why — my husband suddenly got up from the dinner table and went into the basement and then into the little back room where I had hidden the girl. I cannot imagine what possessed him to do that — perhaps some unusual noise. Of course, once he found her, I had to confront the issue. He came to the basement steps dragging the girl and screamed up at me: 'What is this ragged whore doing in my house? She is going out of here *now*! Do you understand?'

"But she's very sick," I told him, "She needs to be someplace where it's warm and dry."

"Then let the bitch go to the charity ward of a hospital!" he shouted.

"At that, I simply went over and got my heavy wool coat, slipped the girl's arms into it and I took her thin jacket and put it on myself. We walked out of the house into the street and then we slowly made our way to a nearby hospital.

"I sat with her until they admitted her, then I went back out into the street again and began to cry. I walked and walked aimlessly, crying uncontrollably until I could no longer see where I was going. I had to sit down in the doorway of a store next to me. It was the same doorway where I had found that girl. I huddled in a heap by the door and slept until morning. I never went back to my home again."

The Tramp Prince reached over and hugged The Lady With The Fancy Chair — splattering her with his tears.

"Come on," he told her, "Let's take this chair to a furniture refinisher somewhere and see if we can get you some money for it."

The Tramp Prince picked up one end of the chair and the woman took the other and they began carrying it down the street, inquiring as they went, about a suitable shop to which they could take it.

"I guess we never got introduced," said the Tramp Prince. "They call me the Tramp Prince — that's my road name. My family at home doesn't call me that, but all my brothers and sisters of the road do."

"I'm Rosita," the Lady With The Fancy Chair told the Tramp Prince. "Just plain 'Rosita'. I no longer use a last name. I want no connection to my husband anymore.

"You need a *hobo* moniker," the Tramp Prince suggested, "How about 'Bonita Rosita'?"

"Oh, I *like* that!" she responded. "I know that you have lots of road brothers and sisters, but would you like to have a 'road mother'? I could be your 'road mother' — for a while at least. I know I can't follow you on your travels, but I can be with you in spirit."

The Tramp Prince then went over and hugged his new 'Road Mother'.

As they continued along, attempting to find someplace to sell the chair, they passed a street of large, well-constructed homes. When they came to the alley behind the homes, Bonita Rosita stopped, pulling the Tramp Prince to a halt.

"Wait here for a minute," she told him. "You sit down in the chair and I'll be right back."

Bonita Rosita walked into the alley and began lifting trash can lids and looking into ash pits. Every so often as she walked the cobblestone pavement she would open up her large coat and drop a piece of copper or brass or some small, still useful item into one of several cloth bags sewn to the inside of her coat.

When Bonita Rosita returned, the Tramp Prince laughed.

"So that's why you looked so fat! All those bags under your coat."

"Sure — I do it because this way, no one can see that I have any scrap to take to the junkyard. Once, before I started doing things this way, a young thug watched me collecting copper from the cans and when he saw that I had the bag filled, he pushed me down and grabbed the bag and ran off with it. So, 'out of sight, out of mind'."

The Tramp Prince shook his head sadly.

"*This* is the only way you have to get money?"

"Yes, you see, I was never trained in anything…and besides, I actually *like* doing this. It's really just a form of treasure hunting. The rewards are not great, but the risk is small."

When they finally found the furniture refinisher that one of the shopkeepers had told them about, the Tramp Prince asked the man if he might be interested in restoring the chair.

"We can't pay you to do it," he said, "but thought possibly you might be willing to buy it and then whatever you sold it for would give you a profit."

The furniture restorer looked the chair over very carefully, finding the maker's name stamped into the underside of the frame.

"Look," he told the chair's finder, "this chair is extremely valuable — *after* it's been re-glued, some of the springs replaced and retied, the finish stripped and the surfaces sanded, then several coats of new finish applied…*and*, when all the chipped off corners of the carvings have been remade and glued in. And then, of course, it has to be reupholstered with a high quality fabric. There's a *tremendous* amount of work to put this chair back into top condition. I can't give you more than a small fraction of what it will bring when it's finished. I don't want you to think that I'm trying to cheat you, but in order for me to put all my labor and materials into it, I simply can't give you more than that. I can't cheat myself either."

"I understand," said the Tramp Prince. "Just give us whatever you think will allow you to pay yourself for your labor and materials and your trouble to resell it."

The man reached into his pocket and counted out a pile of bills that was more money than the Tramp Prince had ever seen at one time.

"Here," he told them, "This is really a little more than I probably ought to pay for it, but I can see that you folks need the money badly."

"Give it to her," and the Tramp Prince pointed to Bonita Rosita.

When they had left the refinisher's shop, Bonita Rosita tried to give half of the money to the Tramp Prince.

"No, just give me a small commission." He pulled out enough money to pay for lodging and food for a few days.

"You know what I would do with this money, Rosita? You have enough here that you could pay for a couple month's rent on a small store in the less expensive part of town…then you could go out each morning and make your treasure hunt finds and bring them to the shop and open the door to customers in the afternoon. I'm sure you could sell even unrestored items to collectors for more than a restorer would pay you. Then let the collectors employ the restorer. And you could sleep in the back of the store."

"Hmmm…I'll have to give that some serious thought." Bonita Rosita looked at the Tramp Prince and smiled so wide that most of the sadness in her eyes seemed to evaporate into the sunlight. "But you know what I would *really* like to do? I think it would be so much fun to have you walk the alleys with me, so we could make finds together. Sharing the excitement of making a great find would be fantastic!"

"It *would* be fun," the Tramp Prince nodded in agreement, "but I can't do it for very long. I need to continue looking for a new home for my father, mother and little sister."

"I guess it wouldn't work — their moving into the back of a store that I'd rent, would it? Of course not," she corrected herself, "that's silly. I just wish you could stay around — you've brought me such good luck."

"Why don't we go out and try to rent you a store? There's still enough time today to look at some."

The Tramp Prince and his road mother walked all around the business area where there were small shops of tradesmen and those selling used merchandise. Where red brick dust from a decaying wall had sifted onto the cobblestones at an alley's entrance, Bonita Rosita hesitated — watching two scrawny mongrel dogs as they sniffed at trashcans. One of the dogs lifted the edge of a can's lid with his nose, flipping it off; and he began hungrily digging into the contents, growling as he devoured a few chicken bones.

"There," she said bitterly, as she pointed up the alley, "we're a lot like that. The dogs, I mean…those of us who are street people. We're forgotten and abandoned; perhaps not helpless — but fighting over society's scraps merely for a pathetic existence."

The Tramp Prince grasped Bonita Rosita's hand and looked sternly into her eyes.

"Not now…not now — come on. Things will change."

At one block of low buildings, there were two vacant stores close to each other. Both stores had the same "for rent" sign posted in the window with the name "Max Ginzberg Properties" and an address in the same block as the empty stores. They found the address at the corner on a door between two storefronts. The door opened onto a steep stairway that led to a second floor office. Creaking up the narrow stairway, the Tramp Prince dodged the peeling wallpaper draping off the stairwell walls, and even a few strips dangling from the ceiling. At the top of the stairs there was a short hallway ending at a door with the words 'Ginzberg Properties' written on the frosted glass in peeling black letters.

Bonita Rosita opened the door into an office space so small, there was room only for a desk and a filing cabinet. The single window toward the front of the building was fogged with dust and cobwebs that had obviously not been cleaned for years. The room gave the impression, the Tramp Prince thought, of an overgrown rat's nest.

Behind the desk sat a little man wearing a brown fedora over his bald pate. His clean-shaven face brightened when he saw two potential customers.

"Hallo, hallo! I am Mex Ginzboig! Vell, vot can I'm doink for you dees fine day? Ain't it?"

"We might be interested in renting one of your stores up the block." Bonita Rosita smiled as she spoke.

"Sure! Vait a minute. I got to put avay some very himportant pepers."

The Tramp Prince watched the man make a notation on the paper and slip it into the desk. The paper tilted slightly as it went into the drawer and the boy could see that it was a crossword puzzle. He turned away so as not to be seen smiling.

As Max Ginzberg pulled a pad of contract forms out of another drawer, he looked in vain for a place on top of the desk to lay the pad. The entire desktop was piled with papers and magazines, empty pop bottles and a miscellany of pens, pencils, rubber bands and unidentifiable accumulations. The floor around the desk was heaped with books, newspapers and magazines and the paper flood even flowed over onto the top of the filing cabinet. The cabinet itself was crammed so full that the drawers would no longer close.

'Meester' Ginzberg smiled. "You can having either store — feefti fife a month. How's dot zound?"

"Is that the cheapest you have available?" asked the Tramp Prince.

"Oi, oi yoie! Dot ain't *cheap* enough? So vot d'y' vant from me — I should *gif* it avay?"

"We're not asking for a gift, really. It's just that we're trying to get a business started selling used merchandise and you know how the first couple of months are — well, it takes a little time to become known — get customers to realize that you're there." The Tramp Prince spoke with all the sincerity he could muster. "We don't have a lot of money."

"Awride...leesen, sonny boy. I tell you vot. I rent to your mama for thirti-fife a month, first two months. After dat, fifti. Hokay?"

"Yes," Bonita Rosita answered him, "I think we can do that. Let's go look at the stores."

Back down the stairs they went, boards creaking and cracking, sounding as though the entire staircase would fall at any second. When they reached the first store, Max Ginzberg unlocked the door and motioned for his potential renters to come in. After they had walked through the store and looked at the shabby paint on the walls and a deep brown stain on the ceiling from a roof leak, Max pointed to the stain.

"Dot leak been feexed. Hokay now. See, dees store ess *beeger* dan d' otter von. More space for d' money. Ain't it?" The store ran straight through to the back door, with no partition in the rear.

Two doors down was the other store. The owner unlocked it and went over to a ceiling gaslight fixture and lit it. Immediately the room lost some of its dismal aura that had been cast by the dirty pea soup green of the walls. There was a tiny cubical in the rear which had served as living quarters for a previous tenant. An old couch still hugged the floor.

"You could clean that couch off and sleep on it — temporarily at least," the Tramp Prince told Rosita.

"Yes, I think we'll take this one," the Road Mother told the landlord as she handed him the first month's rent.

For three days, the Tramp Prince and Bonita Rosita hunted through the alleys and carried back nearly a store full of items, most requiring minor repairs. During the afternoons, the Tramp Prince would first fix those needing the least amount of work, using his multi-bladed hobo knife and a few borrowed tools.

"These things that need the most work, I'll do last," he told his Road Mother. "That way, you'll have the greatest amount of repaired merchandise to offer for sale. I think there's already enough that we can put a sign in the window and open your door to customers tomorrow. And...tomorrow I must be on my way again."

Later that evening, the Tramp Prince consulted with Road Toad:

"I'm concerned about whether Rosita can actually make a go of the shop on her own."

"Yes, that is truly a question. Perhaps you should stay an extra day — just to see how things go when she opens her door to the public. And you could make her some sort of sign that would be more permanent than the one on that piece of cardboard in the window."

The next morning, the Tramp Prince delayed leaving.

"I think I should make you a better sign than the one on that piece of cardboard," he told Rosita. "When we scout the alleys this morning, I'll see if I can find a sheet of plywood and some whitewash. We already have some black paint — and those paint brushes we found a couple of days ago. Maybe I can mount the sign on that old coaster wagon frame with no bed. Then you could easily move it out each day onto the side walk."

"Oh, you have such *great* ideas! I'd give anything if you were my *real* son."

The woman smiled sadly and placed her arms around the Tramp Prince. She closed her eyes and held tightly onto the boy. He looked at her fading hair and shoulders beginning to round just a bit and realized where time leads nearly all of us.

"Did you ever have any children?" the Tramp Prince asked her quite directly.

"No..." replied Bonita Rosita, "I had always wanted children...but I was never so blessed. But actually — now, I realize that it would have been a terrible burden to have had to bring children along with me like this — very unfair to a child. And if I had had children and left them behind for my husband to raise...well, god knows how they would have turned out...possibly like him, heaven forbid!"

"That...that is *really* sad, Road Mother. It makes me *very* unhappy for you."

"But dear Tramp Prince...we do *not* always get in this life that which we want — or even *need*. Life is always a compromise, isn't it? And for some of us, it's just much more of a compromise than it is for others. Some things in life can be changed. But we need to learn what can *not* be changed and then simply *accept* those things."

"That," said the Tramp Prince, "has to be probably the most difficult of all lessons in life."

The morning sky was dreary with early clouds—and did not presage a profitable day. Bonita Rosita picked up an antique formal dress and began stitching an open seam.

"I'd like to finish this before we go out, so that I can get it hung up, if you don't mind."

"That's alright," the boy answered, looking at the sky through the shop's front window. He stood for several minutes watching and thinking.

"Bonita Rosita..." the Tramp Prince's words trailed off into a questioning sigh as he smiled warmly at the preoccupied woman.

"Um hum." She looked up and raised her eyebrows with a hint of a smile catching his gaze.

"What do you think really matters in life — to you. I know this might seem a bit silly, or at least out of place to ask you right now, but I'm asking while I'm thinking about it."

Rosita reached over and tried to give the Tramp Prince an off-the-cuff hug.

"Oh, *you* really matter to me! Don't you already know that? Silly young boy! Just like you were my own flesh and blood son. And I worry about you; and I'll worry a lot more about you when you leave."

The Tramp Prince said nothing more, but stood there holding the arm of the seated woman. A long wordless interim ensued. The Tramp Prince broke it.

"I was going to leave this afternoon...but perhaps I'll wait 'til tomorrow..."

"Whatever will I do when you're gone? You've become such an integral part of my life."

"You'll do everything you did before we met — and I think a whole lot more. And you'll be meeting so many new people through the store, you might not even miss me!"

Bonita Rosita wiped a tear from an eye and shook her head "no", then laid her head on the Tramp Prince's arm.

When the pair searched the alleys most of that morning, they fortunately found a suitable piece of material for a permanent sign. Upon their return, the Tramp Prince hurriedly whitewashed a thin coat over the board. In a few minutes, when it had dried, he painted the black letters over it, and mounted the sign on the wagon frame.

"Well...are you ready to open your door to the public? It's almost afternoon now. The sky has cleared; it's a nice, sunny day. I'm really anxious to see how everything goes. I'll roll out the wagon with the sign on it."

"Alright, go ahead. But I'm a little worried about those prices we put on everything."

"Why...what do you mean?"

"Well, we didn't really know what a lot of these items sell for new. Neither of us has bought merchandise at retail stores...me, for so long, I can't even remember. And you...probably never."

The Tramp Prince just laughed and shook his head slightly.

"Oh, I don't think it really makes any difference if we've been accurate or not. If a price on an item is too high — the customers will let you know — they'll complain. I'm just sure of *that*. And if the price we put on an item is too low...your customers will snap it up. Then they'll tell their friends about what bargains they bought here. You know that later on you can go into department stores and dime stores and look at the prices on items similar to what you have. Then you can price yours at about half of new. Anyway, your investment is so minimal — all you have in any of this is a little wear on your shoe soles and a few calories of food and some soap and water cleaning the dirt and grime off things...and perhaps a new nut or bolt or screw to replace one that's missing."

"You're just *so* convincing!" Bonita Rosita chuckled, forgetting all of her fears. "Isn't it sad, though, how wasteful people are? Most of this should never have been thrown out."

"That's what happens with an affluent society," the Tramp Prince responded. "The greater the affluence, the greater the waste."

"But another thing that worries me is having so much of this in cardboard boxes on the floor," Rosita told the Tramp Prince. "I just wish the store had more than that one wall of shelves. But maybe later I can get someone to build some more."

"You'll find a lot more apple boxes like the few we set up with boards across them. They're not the best shelving—but they work. And you'll find tables that can be used as well. It will all work out eventually. I'm sure of it."

That evening, as they took count of the sales, Bonita Rosita's face was rather glum.

"We had only about six sales all day," she complained. "I was hoping for a lot more."

"But you're not known yet. And anyway, you took in almost seven dollars. Think of it this way: If you were open twenty-four days a month and took in only seven dollars a day, that's a hundred sixty-eight dollars. I think that would be considered successful. And I'm certain you'll have a lot of days when you'll do much better — when people know that you have some antiques."

The next morning, when the time came for the Tramp Prince to depart, he hugged his Road Mother goodbye and she placed a kiss on his cheek.

"I won't be washing my face for a long time," he laughed.

"And *I* will miss you terribly," Bonita Rosita told him again, closing her eyes and clutching his arm.

"Oh, now that this shop is opened, your whole life will change — everything will change for the better."

"Perhaps," she answered, hesitantly "...perhaps it will."

Then the woman looked off into the distance as if in a misty reverie.

"You know that if I had had a son, I would have wanted him to be just like you. Please…come back some day and visit me."

"I will," said the Tramp Prince. But he had a dreadful, sinking feeling in his heart that if he did someday return, he would find the shop deserted and no trace of his Road Mother.

"You will always be with me in spirit," he told her, and quickly kissed away a tear that was spilling down her cheek. Then he turned and walked out the door before she would be able to see his own tears. But she watched him through the front window of the shop…and saw him wipe his eyes with his jacket sleeve…and then she smiled.

Chapter 11: The Organ Grinder

Many blocks away, toward the edge of the city, the Tramp Prince came upon an organ grinder with a small monkey on a string. The morning had already become quite warm for that time of the year and so the monkey went bounding around, holding a tin cup out, as the Organ Grinder cranked away on the hurdy-gurdy. The Organ Grinder smiled and nodded to the Tramp Prince.

"Buddy, do you think you could crank this for me for a few minutes; my arm is getting very tired."

"Sure," said the Tramp Prince, "looks like fun."

After having cranked the hurdy-gurdy organ for several minutes, the Tramp Prince admitted to the man: "This is harder work than it looks like it would be. I see why your arm got tired."

The man emptied a few coins from the monkey's cup.

"They tell me it shouldn't crank that hard…like it needs lubrication. Another thing is, it only plays two tunes. The lever that shifts to other rolls is stuck. But I've just had this outfit a couple of weeks. I got it from a friend. He's an elderly tramp who's gotten too feeble to carry it around or crank it any more. I promised him I'd take good care of the monkey for him. The little guy's name is Bunko. I don't know whose idea *that* was!" And the man laughed.

"Have you ever thought of having someone sing to the music?" the Tramp Prince asked the Organ Grinder.

"Why? Can you sing?" the man asked in response.

"I'm not a professional, but I do know those two tunes. I just thought it might attract a little more attention and more contributions if I sang along with the music."

"Yeah," agreed the hurdy-gurdy man, "let's try it!"

So, the two musical tramps wandered around the city streets for the rest of the day, the Organ Grinder cranking his hurdy-gurdy, the monkey bouncing about and the Tramp Prince either singing or playing his small hand-carved flute. As evening arrived, they stopped and counted up the money.

"My goodness!" exclaimed the Organ Grinder. "That's far more than I *ever* collected in such a short time! Here," he said to the Tramp Prince, "I'll give you half. You certainly deserve it."

They then walked to the cheapest hotel they could find in the slum area of the town. The Tramp Prince paid for their room and the Organ Grinder left to go to a café where he knew that he could prevail upon the owner for a very cheap meal. While the Organ Grinder was still eating at the café, the Tramp Prince went outside to a nearby park and hunted several bugs for Road Toad's dinner. He then found a grocery where he was able to purchase enough fresh food for that night. Even the monkey feasted on some of the pieces of fruit.

"Seems like a very satisfactory day," Road Toad commented with a telepathic thought.

"Yes, it was," the Tramp Prince reassured him. "Maybe we'll do it again tomorrow."

The next morning, the Tramp Prince and the Organ Grinder decided to stay together for a while and proceed on to the next town, which was only a short distance away. Before they left their room, the Tramp Prince disassembled part of the hurdy-gurdy and found the reason for it's stiffness. He lubricated the parts with the graphite from a soft lead pencil and unlocked the lever that switched to other song rolls, lubricating it with some soap.

"Oh, that's wonderful!" exclaimed the Organ Grinder when he had tried the repaired hurdy-gurdy. "I think we'll do even better today than we did yesterday!"

"One problem," the Tramp Prince told him, "is that I don't know the words to those other songs. I'll have to sing to 'The Sidewalks of New York' and 'My Wild Irish Rose' — the ones we did yesterday. But I can play the flute along with the others."

"I just have a feeling we'll make a hit wherever we go!" the hurdy-gurdy man replied.

Part of that day, the musical team spent traveling to the other town, and, in walking around the town, collected far more money than the Tramp Prince had imagined they would.

"I guess a lot of people would call us beggars," the Organ Grinder observed, "but I think of us as street musicians giving entertaining performances. And since we don't charge an admission, we have a right to seek donations from people if they enjoyed our show."

"That makes sense," the Tramp Prince agreed. "But actually, I don't see anything wrong with someone being a beggar if he has no other way to survive. When society makes it impossible for someone to make a living, then society ought to either at least provide the minimum needs for the person, or somehow make it possible for that person to become a useful, productive member of society."

The Organ Grinder looked down at the ground. "Them durn politicians don't see it that way. Neither do lots of church leaders. They think that we poor are responsible for our *own* poverty. And they *really* have nothing good to say about hoboes."

"I bet if that monkey could talk," the Tramp Prince philosophized, "He'd say 'That's just the way the world is!' and let it go at that!"

When night fell, the musical team again found a cheap slum room and an inexpensive meal. In the morning, the Tramp Prince told the hurdy-gurdy man that it was time for him to say goodbye.

"Ah, I wish you could stay longer — we do so well together...but, I guess you have to do whatever you have to do." The Organ Grinder held out his hand.

"Perhaps someday we'll get together again — when I'm not under the kind of time pressure that drives me now."

The Tramp Prince grabbed the Organ Grinder's hand and shook it vigorously.

"At least you've got a lot more songs to play now and the hurdy-gurdy is much easier to crank."

"That won't make up for the loss of you," the man advised him, "but you know you're welcome back anytime — if you can find me. I've really enjoyed your company."

"Please forgive my waiting so long to ask this, but there *is* a question I have for you," the Tramp Prince responded, with a steady gaze. "It's just: What is it that really matters to you in life?"

The hurdy-gurdy man merely stood there. He thought for a long time before he spoke.

"I don't have a ready answer for you. No one has ever asked me anything like that before. Maybe if I thought about it for a day or two... You know — I'm tempted to say, just off the top of my head, something like: 'A warm dry place to sleep and a decent meal at night.' But I'm sure that's not what you want. You're looking for a deeper meaning to life; but right now my life doesn't have any deeper meaning. Maybe it has one, but I just can't grasp it. Let me think about it. The next time I see you, I might have a better answer."

The Tramp Prince smiled warmly, tipped his cap and went walking briskly down the street — whistling and singing to himself until he was soon far out onto a country road.

Chapter 12: The Religious Woman

Several more fruitless days had passed, when the Tramp Prince awoke and crawled out of a warm haystack into a bright, but chilly morning. After having spent the first couple of hours searching along more field roads, as usual to no avail, the boy then walked on, to a nearby small town. Upon reaching the town's center, he found that all of the streets converged at a small park surrounded by shops. A large church with a dirty brownstone exterior loomed almost menacingly at one end of the park.

He plodded into the park and dropped lightly onto one of the benches, placing his bindle sack on the bench next to him.

"Today must be Sunday," thought the Tramp Prince to Road Toad. "This crowd of people must be waiting for the church service to begin."

The Tramp Prince began picking off the stick-tights and other kinds of burrs that had collected on his clothes earlier during his morning hike. As he sat busily picking burrs, a thin, middle-aged woman with pursed lips sat down at the other end of the short bench. She was attired in a long coat and a high-collar, conservative dress of the eighteen-nineties style.

"I'm sorry, ma'am," apologized the Tramp Prince. "I'll move this sack off the bench so that you'll have more room."

The woman nodded politely. Then she looked more closely at the boy and spoke in a rather high-pitched, cracking voice. "I assume that you are a tramp."

"*However* would she know *that*?!" telepathized Road Toad with more than just a note of sarcasm.

"Yes, ma'am," the Tramp Prince replied.

"Well, even a tramp needs religion; I hope you are here for the church service, which starts in a few minutes."

"Frankly, ma'am, I was tired from a long walk, and just sat down here to rest."

The woman gave the Tramp Prince a fierce look.

"If you don't accept the lord Jesus Christ as your personal savior, you will roast in hell for all eternity! All of you tramps will suffer the same fate for your sinful ways if you don't repent and believe in the Lord. There is only one true God and you must come to him through his only begotten son, Jesus Christ!" The woman's voice had by now become frosted with a tone that almost reached into hysterics.

The Tramp Prince stopped picking burrs off his clothes. "Now look ma'am — you know just as well as I do that there are millions of people in this world who believe in their own religions just as strongly as you believe in yours. Are they all doomed to that fate because their idea of God differs from yours?"

"Yes!" replied the Religious Woman emphatically. "There is only one true God and all must come to him through his only begotten son, Jesus Christ!"

"I think you said that once before," snickered Road Toad with more sarcasm.

"Quiet!" thought back the Tramp Prince.

"Oh, she can't hear me," returned Road Toad.

"What religion are you?" asked the Religious Woman.

"Ah...you see, *my* family professes no formalized religious belief," answered the Tramp Prince. "But a religion is — or ought to be — a way of life. So, if I wanted to assign a name to my beliefs I would have to say something like 'a religion of love and kindness' or of 'living and letting live', or of 'trying to live as helpfully and as hurtlessly as possible'."

"That's *not* a religion!" said the Religious Woman in almost a shout.

"Well, it doesn't have a name like Methodist or Catholic or Baptist — not something recognizable, but it's equally valid."

"Not to *me*!"

"Ma'am…listen…I have no desire to offend you, but if I go into this church during the service, it will be as much to warm my body as to warm my spirit."

The Religious Woman gave the Tramp Prince a glaring look and skitted away as the church bells tolled. Looking back over her shoulder; she called to the Tramp Prince: "Repent and be saved! Lest you die in the dungeons of Hell! You," said the woman almost savagely, "are one of the multitude referred to in the Bible as being of little faith."

"Well, I have a *lot* of faith in certain things," the Tramp Prince shouted back. "I have great faith in humanity's ability to often make the most destructive moral and ethical choices that can be taken. I have great faith in people to be as obnoxious and as self-righteously unrealistic as it is possible to be. But, on the brighter side, I do have great faith in the basic dynamics of human and even animal love for each other of our own kind. If I didn't have that type of faith, it wouldn't be possible for me to carry on my life."

But the Tramp Prince did decide to go into the church service and found a seat in one of the very back pews. Everyone else was dressed in their Sunday finery and the young man felt rather embarrassed to be seen in his increasingly tattered clothing. I think he would have immediately fallen completely asleep had the sermon been just a little bit more boring. He, however, like most of the parishioners, managed to fight off drowsiness for a while by hanging his thoughts onto an occasionally meaningful word. The chanting voice of the darkly robed dispenser of the faith droned on and on, drawing many of the listeners into a mesmerized state of semi-sleep. It took very little more to push the Tramp Prince over the edge into a blissful slumber.

When the service ended, the Tramp Prince stood near the isle in the church entrance, curious to see what the people there were like as they filed out. Finally he walked out and sent a thought to Road Toad.

"Well, what did you think of the sermon?"

"I'm sure I've heard better...at some point...in one of my past lives. But I thought even less of the part of the message that was in Latin."

"What?!" exclaimed the Tramp Prince. "You understand *Latin*?"

"Oh...probably it's somewhat more like *pig*-latin. From one of my past incarnations as a pig...of course."

"Yeah, yeah...of course!" the Tramp Prince shuddered. "You know something, Road Toad?" the Tramp Prince continued. "You're sometimes even better at being a toad than you are at being a comedian."

"Hum, hum," Road Toad countered, "I didn't think I was particularly good at being either!"

Throughout the rest of that chilly morning, the Tramp Prince and his small companion traveled a major road that headed west from the town, turning them at a right angle to their previous direction. He found only one empty field road to explore and he afterward sat down on the trunk of a fallen tree to rest.

"There's something that bothers me about that church, today," he told Road Toad. "I was rather shocked that not even one of the regular church-goers came up to me after the service to try to welcome me — my being an obvious stranger. It's not like that in the small town churches that I've been to around my home."

"Maybe," returned Road Toad, "everyone was so concerned with trying to get out of that oppressively dark religious dungeon that they just couldn't spend any more time in the place greeting strangers."

"They weren't even half as friendly as people I've seen in other places," said the Tramp Prince.

"Mathematical proportions are rather peculiar," Road Toad then responded. "If only one person in another church shook your hand and introduced himself, then it would be one infinity more friendly. If four people did the same, it would be four infinities more friendly — and so on."

"But it seems to me," the Tramp Prince reflected, "that to be considered really friendly, nearly *everyone* would want to get to know a stranger in their midst. Am I expecting too much to think of it that way?"

"Knowing humans in this culture," responded Road Toad, " I would have to answer that, 'Yes — *definitely*!'"

Chapter 13: The Christmas Gift

Several days later, after the boy had explored up and down many weed-grown trails and farm lanes, walking all day long in a cold, dreary drizzle, he found only one farm that held any possibility. He then made a note of it on his pad.

Luckily, he found himself near the outskirts of a city as the day drew to a close. Making his way toward the glow of lights from a street with many shops, he found one place still open. When he entered the warm building, they told him that the late-night café would close in only another hour, since it was Christmas Eve.

As the Tramp Prince sat in a booth, soaking up the warmth of the air and the cheer of the last few patrons, he was filled with a great longing for his own family. A deep, agonizing frustration overcame the boy's usually unperturbed mental state, as he realized that he would not even be able to speak to them this holiday season. The knowledge that so many of those away from home would be traveling back to be with family and friends stirred ideas in the Tramp Prince's mind of attempting to do the same himself. But he realize that even if he had known the correct freight lines to ride back home, there would have certainly been too little time to get there quickly enough… and he had no money for a passenger ticket.

Road Toad slowly absorbed the warmth of the inside air and the Tramp Prince sat there with the little fellow still tucked away in the jacket pocket. The boy tried sending a thought message to Road Toad:

"Can you get this message?"

"Yes," was the reply. "I can *think* more easily than I can *move*."

"It makes me so sad, Road Toad, not to be able to see my family at this season."

"Yes, I know — but think about me. I wouldn't even have any idea where to begin to *look* for mine...not that it would make any difference if I found them, anyway."

"I guess it seems a bit odd to say this, but you, Road Toad — you're the only connection I have with my family right now. Although you're not exactly a family member, you're the closest thing I have to family here."

"Ha!" responded the little fellow. "Just be happy none of the rest of your family *looks* like me!"

"Oh...I'm sure my little sister thought you were cute!"

"Hum, hum...it's all a matter of scale. Just think of how 'cute' I'd look if I were *your* size!"

The Tramp Prince was forced to laugh. But just then, an older woman entered the café and she trudged over near the booth where the Tramp Prince sat. She plopped herself down in the booth right next to his and began sobbing gently, dropping her head over the ragged arm of her coat. The boy waited several minutes before he went to her booth and slid in next to her. The woman's head was still slumped down on her arm and her soft sobs were like the gentle murmur of rustling leaves in the forest.

"It's possible," the Tramp Prince began carefully, "that I might be able to help..."

The woman raised her head with a strange 'other world' expression.

"He's dying."

She said nothing else and the Tramp Prince did not press her for more.

A few seconds later, he asked, "Your...?"

"My friend. A dear friend."

"Where?"

"Nearby — just a couple of blocks. I came here to try to get this jug filled with hot water. He's *so* cold."

She pulled a small crockery jug out from under her coat and placed it on the tabletop.

"Can't we take him to a hospital?"

The Tramp Prince's young face took on an agonized look to it.

"He was in the charity ward for terminal consumption patients...a sanatorium in town. But he had been in there long past their limit. They have such little space. They kept him because he was so sick they thought he would surely die each day. But for some reason, he didn't. He was still able to hold some water down then and so that's all he took for, I dunno, maybe a week or more. Then he seemed to get stronger for a little while. So they decided he had to leave. I'm sure it was a difficult choice for them, but I understand how things are. There's just not enough room for everyone who needs to be there."

"But to turn him out on Christmas Eve?"

"Actually, it was several days ago. And they even offered to buy him a train ticket to another city that has a hospital with a charity death ward where he could have been warm and dry. But he refused. I don't know why. Perhaps some kind of misguided pride. Maybe he felt too weak..."

"Look, I've been learning about proper nutrition — maybe if we could get him into some warm, comfortable place and I could take over his feeding program, then..."

"It's too late. His lungs are all eaten up inside. And he can't keep any food down — not even water now." She began sobbing again.

The Tramp Prince grabbed the jug from the tabletop and went over to the short order cook.

"Would you be kind enough to fill this with hot water for us?" he asked.

The cook obliged the request without even a question, having observed the intense drama being played out in the booth. After he had walked back to the booth, the Tramp Prince tugged the woman's arm: "Come on...let's go. Let's see if we can do anything for this guy."

As they were walking, the Tramp Prince questioned the woman about her friend.

"There isn't a lot to tell you about him. He's just an old hobo — a tramp — you'd probably call him a bum; at least a railroad bum. I met him years ago...and we didn't see each other often. We traveled a little together. He was like my big brother. See, I don't have any other family now, other than my road brothers and sisters. My mother died when I was still very young and my father, they tell me, drank himself to death grieving. So I was tossed around from one aunt to another as I grew up. None of them could afford to keep me fed and clothed. I never had any training so I'd be able to get a

decent job. I just drifted from one waitress job to another —
until…well, there's a point where you sort of give up. All my
relatives are dead now — but I was never close to any of them
anyway."

"I'm sorry," the Tramp Prince empathized. "I'm really sorry to
hear that."

They had walked only about a block and a half when the woman
led the way into the cellar of a darkened, vacant building. Though
the temperature inside was considerably warmer than the outside air,
the Tramp Prince began to sneeze almost uncontrollably from the
presence of large amounts of mold and dust.

"That you, Wilma?" a voice called out form the darkened cellar.

"Yeah, it's me, Billie," she replied. "Got someone with me —a
kid. Says he wants t' help you."

"Nuthin' gonna help me…" Billie's voice was gentle — but not
even sad…just resigned.

Wilma lit a candle that had been jammed into a hole in a brick.
The Tramp Prince could see the emaciated face of the elderly man
lying on a makeshift bed constructed of two wooden crates with a
large door over them and padded with cardboard. The man was
covered with several layers of blankets.

"At least," said Wilma, "they gave him some blankets when they
sent him away."

The Tramp Prince shook his head in amazement: "I don't see
how he made it this far — how he ever found this place."

"Oh, he already knew it was here. The street people and hoboes
all use it. That's how I found him. I was just trying to get
somewhere warm for the night myself."

Wilma had placed the jug of hot water under the blankets next to
Billie's feet.

"Hey, honey — you're feet gettin' warm yet?"

"Naw. Listen — I can't feel nuthin'. Wilma, I'm jus' so tired —
but I don't want t' sleep. I jus' wanna know you're still here with
me."

His words drifted off as he closed his eyes. Billie's breathing
seemed very rapid and shallow, the Tramp Prince thought; and he
wondered if the man could last even another hour.

Previously, Wilma had dragged the remains of a large
overstuffed chair close to where Billie lay. She dropped heavily

down into the chair and put her hand to her forehead. The Tramp Prince sat on one of the large overstuffed arms of the chair. Every few minutes, Wilma would get up and check Billie's breathing, sometimes feeling his pulse.

Billie was in and out of consciousness for what seemed like an interminable amount of time. Wilma had fallen asleep and the candle had long ago burnt out, when finally a church bell tolled twelve times off in the distance.

Wilma awoke: "Midnight mass, I guess."

She struck a match and lit another candle, bending over Billie to see the rise and fall of his chest. She looked and listened, then tried to feel his pulse.

"He's gone! Oh, my God, he's gone!" Wilma wailed and sobbed uncontrollably. She looked at the Tramp Prince. "We never had any kind of romance — but he was my big brother — as much my brother as any real-life brother could ever have been. Sometimes years would go by and we wouldn't see each other —but it was always the same when we met again. Some people can be like anchors in this life. He was my anchor. Now that he's gone, there's suddenly less holding *me* here."

She threw herself down, crying on the dead man's body. "My road brother — he's gone. Why? Why on Christmas Eve?"

Wilma looked up at the Tramp Prince, her large dark eyes were like two question marks of the soul — reaching for an answer that she already knew, but did not want to accept. The Tramp Prince tried to comfort her.

"Everyone has a time that he or she has to leave here — and I guess this was just his time. If I could have met him a year ago — and knew what I know now, perhaps I could have helped him find a better lifestyle. But it didn't happen that way."

He took Wilma's hands and looked directly into her eyes: "I know that it hurts that you've lost someone so dear to you, but please try to think of it this way: At least for him, Billie had the most wonderful Christmas present he could have hoped for — at least the way things were. He received the gift of blessed relief from his suffering with you there at his side. And *you* are receiving a gift also. What could be more fitting than, when you lose one road brother, you immediately gain another? I will always be your 'little road brother'."

Wilma buried her head in the Tramp Prince's arms, crying, he thought, not as much for herself as for the strange inscrutability of life itself.

"Wilma," he said to her softly.

"Yes?"

"Don't you think there must be some kind of connection that remains between us after death...like an invisible wire that keeps us sort of plugged into each other's mind? I mean with all of those we've known and loved — maybe even with our dogs and cats?"

"I don't know — not now. But someday I'm sure I *will* know."

There was nothing more that either of them could say.

For a time, the Tramp Prince stood there in a silent vigil over Billie's motionless form. Then he slipped his blanket roll out of the bindle sack. Wilma sat again in the remains of the chair and the Tramp Prince sat back on one of the huge arms, wrapping the blankets around both the woman and himself.

When daylight began to filter its way into the basement, the Tramp Prince very quickly got up and put away his blanket roll. He then covered the still sleeping Wilma with two of the blankets from Billie's body. It had been an unreal experience, that night before, and the Tramp Prince wanted it to remain in the realm of the indefinable, as he walked out of the musty cellar.

Chapter 14: The Accident

The dusk-gray of evening quickly gave way to the desperate-dark of night. Road Toad pushed his head up out of the Tramp Prince's jacket pocket only to be spattered by several large raindrops.

"Whew! This weather is too cold... It's god-awful! I'm freezing. I think I'm just going to hibernate for the next few weeks!"

"You're lucky!" the Tramp Prince shot back an answering thought. "Hey, I'd do the same thing if I could! But *I'm* the one who has to get us somewhere south."

Ahead, on the track, the Tramp Prince could see dim lights from a switchyard and the misty blobs of the outlines of boxcars. The rain that had slapped his face seemed to be slowing, a blessing in itself, since the water had already soaked part way through the boy's jacket. Now, however, everything was becoming glazed with a thin coating of almost invisible ice. The Tramp Prince's every step had to be carefully calculated to avoid a fall.

As he approached the train yard, he could hear the familiar crashing of coupler against coupler as an engine far ahead slowly yanked a line of cars into motion. The engineer screamed the whistles into a triple high-balling shriek that penetrated in spite of the deadening mist.

With the thought that it would be good just to leave the area, no matter where the train was headed, the Tramp Prince ran gingerly over toward the moving boxcars. When he was no more than fifty feet away from the track, he could see from the rain and mist-obscured yard light, that another man was running beside the boxcars, trying to catch out on the fly. The man slipped and gyrated wildly on the ice, but suddenly grabbed a car's ladder rails, trying desperately to pull himself up. His feet danced on and off the bottom rung as the train gained speed. Then he completely lost his footing and his legs went flailing and flapping out to the side like some limber rag doll.

In a flashing instant, the hobo's foot and pants leg caught on a partly raised switch handle by the track, and he was yanked off the boxcar with a searing scream.

By the time the Tramp Prince reached the man, the hobo was moaning what sounded almost like a melody of intense agony. After he touched the shoulder of the prostrate hobo, the man turned his head, giving an open-mouthed, wide-eyed grimace of horrific pain.

"Oh my God! Oh my God! Pray for me bud... I'm gonna *die!*"

"Maybe not. I'll try to get help."

Ice was starting to form on the clothes of both the injured man and the Tramp Prince. Immediately, the boy took out his knife and cut away the bottom of the ragged, blood soaked pants leg, trying not to jar the leg or cut more than necessary.

Finally, with most of the cuff trimmed away, he ripped the pants leg to the man's knee twice, making two equal strips. Then he loosened the victim's belt and pulled one side of the pants down enough to allow a tourniquet to be fashioned from the cloth strips.

"Aghhhh...the pain! My God...I can't stand it! The pain —the *paaain*!"

He grabbed the Tramp Prince's hand and squeezed it so hard that the boy thought his fingers would break. With a long, low moan, the injured hobo fell into unconsciousness.

The Tramp Prince began running carefully toward a light that appeared to be coming from a switchman's shack. Twice, as he ran, his feet shot out from under him as he slid on icy ties. Breathless, he fell against the door of the shack.

"Who's that? Wha...!"

The switchman reached over and pulled the door open, allowing the Tramp Prince to stumble into the tiny room, almost burning himself on the coal stove as he reached out to break his fall.

"Injured man down the tracks! Hooked his foot trying to catch out. Almost tore his foot off! I gotta go get help quick. He'll die of exposure out there."

The switchman's initial frown melted into a look of amazed concern.

"Exposure, fer sure — if he don't bleed t' death first."

"He won't. I put a tourniquet on below the calf. Which way should I go to get help?"

"Depot's about a hundred yards thataway." And the switchman pointed toward another speck of light. "First, though, guy, you gotta show me 'bout where he's layin' so's I kin direct the rescue crew."

They walked only far enough that the Tramp Prince could point out the prostrate figure. When they returned to the shack, the switchman grabbed a ragged quilt from a hook on the wall.

"I'm goin' down there an' cover him with this here ol' quilt; it might help keep him alive."

"Yes — that's really a good idea!"

"Listen, kid, before y' go to the depot, I want ya' t' take one a' these here lanterns with ya'."

The switchman lit the coal oil wick in an ancient-looking lantern with a fluted top.

"I'm givin' ya' this here old one 'cause its got a clear glass in front so's ya' can see straight ahead of ya'. But when ya' get up there by the depot, ya' gotta switch the red lens in front an' set the lantern at the edge a' the track facin' south. There's a train due through here in about another half hour — it'll pass right next t' the guy. Just in case the engineer don't get a signal t' stop, this'll tell him not t' go through.

"Now, see this here little knob on the side? Well, ya' just slide the knob forward and that changes the lens." The switchman demonstrated the procedure, then rubbed a drip off the bottom of his nose before it could hit his bushy mustache. "The red's on the right and the green's on the left. Jus' be sure t' switch t' the red. Okay?"

"Yeah, sure — I got it!"

The boy then opened the shack door and began moving toward the depot light. In a heavy-footed, pounding trot, the Tramp Prince started a slow, careful run toward the depot. Before he arrived at the steps to the mostly darkened building, he set the lantern out as he had been instructed to do. He entered the depot and literally fell across the stationmaster's counter in complete exhaustion. It took several seconds for the dozing, elderly man to shake himself awake enough to confront his nocturnal interloper.

"No trains goin' out from here t'night, kid — have t' wait 'till eight-fifteen tomara."

"Not that...not that! Man had his foot almost torn off...down by the switchman's shack. I put a tourniquet on it, but he's got to get to a hospital — quick. Please, can you help?"

"The guy a buddy a' yers?"

"No — don't know him. I was just nearby when it happened."

"Okay, let me call for some help."

The Tramp Prince sat on a bench, glad to be warming himself and he hardly paid attention to the several telephone calls that were being made to get together a crew. He had nearly fallen into a sleep of exhaustion by the end of the final phone call. The station master walked over to where the Tramp Prince was sitting and gently shook him awake.

"Do me a favor, bud — please don't go out there again an' try t' catch out tonight on one a' those through freights. One accident is enough. I'll give you a key t' a caboose on the siding just a little ways down on the right. You can unlock it an' sleep in there tonight. Just leave the key in the padlock in the mornin'. It's strictly against the rules, but I don't think anybody'll bother yuh. If the stove's burned down, there oughtta be plenty a' coal an' kindlin' inside."

The old fellow pushed a shock of white hair off of his brow and shook his head: "Always sumpthin', aint' it? Guess that's just life."

"Well," responded the Tramp Prince, "I hope they can save that poor guy."

"I dunno — we ain't got much of a hospital in this here town. Oh, they'll try alright. But they never was much on surgery; probably hafta amputate his foot..."

The Tramp Prince shuddered at the thought and grimaced. Then he picked up the key from the counter.

"Thanks for your kindness, I really appreciate it."

"Okay, kid. Stay outta trouble — hear?"

The Tramp Prince had just entered the caboose when he heard the crunching sounds of many boots on the ice and men's voices. As he looked out the fogged window, he could barely make out the forms of several moving figures.

"At least they were quick to get here," the boy thought to himself. Road Toad was too cold by now to catch the thought.

The inside of the caboose still retained a cozy warmth and the Tramp Prince shoveled several more scoops of coal into the small potbellied caboose stove, stirring the contents with a poker. Then he looked for the bunk, first against one wall, then the other. He even tried pulling on the benches, but finally decided that for some reason, this particular caboose had no bunks. Too tired now to return to the depot and sleep on a bench, the boy laid his blanket roll on a short table and soon fell asleep with his feet supported by the back of a chair.

The uncomfortable sleeping conditions added to the unsettling experience of the evening and he kept reliving that terrifying horror in his dreams. He awakened at daylight, still badly shaken.

Later, walking along the ice-encrusted tracks toward the depot, his mind kept posing the same question over and over: What really matters — at a time like this?

As he entered the depot again, the Tramp Prince found the nighttime stationmaster gone, and a younger man in his place, busily pouring over piles of routing papers. The stationmaster was so engrossed in his work, that he paid no attention when the boy sat on a bench near the blazing coal stove. After several morning passengers had gathered on the benches, the Tramp Prince asked a man next to him the location of the city's hospital.

"Jest go on down this road in front of the depot; go to the right. It's...I'd say, about a half mile. It's on the left. Big group of yellow brick buildings. What's the matter, boy, you sick or something?"

"No...someone I saw was taken there last night. Accident victim. I just wondered if he survived."

"Didn't hear nuthin' about it," said the man. "The 'mergency room office is in the first building yuh come to...I think. Bet they can tell yuh."

"Yes, thanks."

The Tramp Prince sat with his feet on the stove's foot rails. He sent a thought message to Road Toad: "I'd like to find out if the guy made it. What do you think, Road Toad — should I go there?"

The small amphibian, now sufficiently warmed, returned the telepathic thought: "Well, if he survived, it will make you feel good about it; but if he didn't — then...I don't know. I don't know what to tell you."

The Tramp Prince got up and went out the depot door. When he reached the road, he turned right and started briskly walking.

"I'm going to the hospital," he said in another thought message to Road Toad. "Maybe I can comfort the poor guy in some small way. That's reason enough to go, isn't it?"

"Yes," replied Road Toad, "*if* he's still alive."

There was no problem for the Tramp Prince to get information about the hobo accident victim. Nearly everyone he talked to at the hospital had already heard about the man. But it did take some time to locate the man's room in the charity ward and for the boy to get there. It was already mid-morning when he walked into the room. The surgeon was just leaving to continue his rounds. He looked the Tramp Prince over critically.

"Is this your friend?" he asked the boy, pointing to the hobo's bed.

"No, sir, but I did see the accident and reported it."

"Then you must have been the one who put the tourniquet on his leg."

"Yes, that's right."

"Good thinking — you may have saved his life."

"Saving his life was a team effort."

"Yes...but we might not have had anything to save without your initial quick foresight."

"But, what about his foot?"

The surgeon began speaking quite slowly: "I...I would say...that I'm cautiously optimistic. At this stage, however, we can't really tell yet much about it. The surgery last night was extremely long and difficult. I'm only the regular staff surgeon here. I'm not a specialist in reconstructive surgery. We should have had a whole team of surgeons on him. I was *very* careful... and I did the best I could possibly do reconnecting tendons and severed blood vessels. Right now, his circulation in that foot looks alright. But even if we can keep it good enough to prevent gangrene from setting in, and if we can avoid any bacterial infection from developing, there's still a question as to how much function he's going to have there.

"If these tendons develop adhesions to surrounding tissue, there might be only a limited amount of movement. Physical therapy could help prevent serious adhesions, but they won't be able to keep him here long enough for him to be able to take advantage of that."

"What if he just started walking around again? You know, if a tramp can't walk, well, he isn't going to ever be much of a tramp."

"We'll try to get him up and walking just as soon as he can put weight on the foot again — but you must understand that there was a *lot* of damage there. It could be weeks before that happens."

The injured hobo, who had been listening in spite of his heavy sedation, spoke up weakly: "Kid...thanks. Never be able t' thank yuh enough...thanks!"

"It's okay," the Tramp Prince assured him, "I just did what I would have wanted someone to have done for me — if I'd been in that situation."

As the surgeon turned to leave, the Tramp Prince accosted him.

"Sir, isn't there any way we could provide this man with better quality food than is usually available as hospital fare? I mean — if anyone ever *needed* high quality nutrition to prevent infection, it's this poor guy."

"Well, son, I've always thought the food here at this hospital was alright — certainly no worse than the food at most other hospitals."

"But I *saw* some of the food they were serving today — and I would have to call it typical hospital 'gloop'. Of couse, I didn't taste it, but it *looked* terrible! Overcooked, probably heavily salted and sugared. Just *terrible*."

"Listen...as doctors, we have only one short course in medical school on nutrition. We leave our patients' diets up to the professional nutritional consultant. If you want to talk to our staff dietitian, I'll arrange for you to speak to her."

"Yes," said the Tramp Prince, "I really would like to."

Some time later, the Tramp Prince met with the nutritional consultant in her office. The plump, middle-aged woman sat at a small desk. She looked up at the boy seeming very professional-appearing in her facial expression. She introduced herself and then asked, "What sort of problem do you have with our hospital food? The staff surgeon told me that you had some objection to it."

"Well, ma'am, it's just that...I'm not quite sure how to begin this...see, when a person is debilitated, whether it's from bad living habits or from an injury, they're really desperately in need of optimum nutrition — so that their bodies can have the necessary building blocks — all the nutrients they need to rebuild their bodies quickly and efficiently...and to prevent micro-organisms from establishing any kind of foothold."

"Young man, I don't think *anybody* could argue with you about *that*. So what are you trying to say?"

"Just that the food you're offering the patients here — it doesn't give them the optimum nutrition they so desperately need! I can't think of food that's further from optimum nutrition than the typical hospital fare I've seen here. Now, I didn't taste the food; but the looks of it, at least what I've seen, are about as far from nutritional excellence as I can possibly imagine."

"Those are awfully strong words, young man! I personally oversee every food item we serve, and I assure you we obtain the best quality of whatever is on the market."

"Oh...ma'am, I'm sure you do...it's just that what you do — especially to the fresh foods — the way you cook and overcook it — the way you smash it and boil it and fry it and bake it — the additives that are in it either before you get it or that you put in it...that's what destroys the greatest nutritional value of it. When you cook it the life force is gone. You probably bake it with baking soda and salt it. Then you've added toxic non-nutritional chemicals."

"So what's wrong with salt?" she asked. "People have been using it for...forever!"

"I know," the Tramp Prince replied. "Salt was undoubtedly the first food preservative, and it's still being used that way. But it's *not* a food. At least I've never seen any salt growing on a sodium chloride bush or tree anywhere, have you?"

The woman shook her head negatively. "So what's wrong with it?"

"Oh...it's just that I don't think it's a smart idea to be eating ground up rocks. Even plants don't normally absorb the soluble inorganic minerals. They wait for the bacteria and fungi in the soil to convert the minerals into an organic soluble form."

With a perplexed look, the nutritionist rubbed her pudgy nose and wrinkled her brow. Then she spotted the bindle sack and walking stick.

"I don't understand...are you some kind of field geologist? Or a chemist...or, or...you're so young to have a degree in one of those disciplines."

"No...no," ma'am. I've just spent a lot of time reading books in libraries — studying a great variety of subjects, actually."

Then the Tramp Prince briefly explained why he was traveling the roads, and that during days of inclement weather, he sometimes found a library where he could spend the day.

"Often, when I study in a library, I find books whose authors are not bound by conventional thoughts or ideas...such as the ideas one would get if he were studying the same subject in a college or university. But...returning to the subject of salt, you see, the way salt is used today, as a flavor accentuator, undoubtedly began because of the loss of fresh flavor caused by the cooking process. And now, salt is dumped indiscriminately into almost every kind of food — cooked or uncooked. It seems like everyone's become a 'salt addict'."

"Well, young man... I guess I really don't know exactly what to say to all of that. I've never studied what you're telling me. But all I know, is that if we left out the salt in our food, the patients probably wouldn't eat it."

"Hmmm..." the Tramp Prince pondered, "It's sad, but you may be right. Of course, you *could* serve the same foods raw — then they wouldn't need salt to accentuate the flavor. But then, your patients might not eat the foods...just *because* they were raw!"

"It *is* a complex problem," the nutritionist responded.

"I hate to make it seem even more complex than it obviously is," the Tramp Prince began again, "but when you mash the food and smash it, instead of allowing the person's own chewing process to predigest starches and other substances, you..."

The woman raised her head to stop the Tramp Prince from continuing his tirade. "I do understand what you're saying, young man. And in some ways I agree with you. But what *you* don't understand is this: There are certain limitations that prevent us from providing food that might be a lot more nutritionally desirable. First of all, a lot of our patients are elderly. And they have to chew their food with often poorly-fitting dentures. And some of them don't even have *any* teeth. So we have to cook the food well in order for them to be able to eat it at all."

"Couldn't you grind tough foods in a food grinder?" asked the Tramp Prince. "That would retain the nutrients and the patients wouldn't have to do the chewing, just masticate the food."

"Yes, I suppose we could grind some things...but I do want to say to you that in school, we learn a lot more about good nutrition than we end up being able to put into practice. You see, we have a serious problem, because if we were to provide our patients with these foods only in the highest nutritional form — they wouldn't *eat* them! We're dealing here with deeply ingrained cultural preferences. And these cultural preferences — patterns — attitudes — have been going on for centuries. You can't change something like that overnight.

The Tramp Prince thought for a moment.

"No," he replied, "but if you began teaching good nutrition to children at school, then you'd slowly start to break that pattern."

"Even that approach wouldn't be easy or very quickly effective," the nutritionist replied. "It's because those children, no matter what you try to teach them in school — they have to go home at night and eat whatever their mothers put on the table for them; and its going to be the same kind of nutritionally compromised food that the parent's culture has taught them to use for centuries. And then the children will pass along a lot of that culture.

"Another thing," continued the woman, "is that we have such limited access to fresh foods here at this time of year. Everything fresh has to be shipped in and what few kinds of fresh foods are shipped here — they're very expensive. So we generally don't buy them, because if our patients won't eat them anyway, that's very expensive waste."Youths like you, who are already enlightened — who see a better way to eat — perhaps a better way to live...you want to change the world overnight. But it doesn't happen that way. A change may come — but its going to be just a little at a time. And that means many people will suffer because of the lack of change. But there's nothing that you can do to expedite it. Not that I can see, anyway. Maybe in a hundred years from now there might be some significant changes. When and if that happens, it's going to be a *long* way off."

"Well," said the Tramp Prince, "I hope you're not right. It would just be so sad if you are."

The boy then sat staring in front of himself in a deep, momentary reverie. As a hospital orderly wheeled a tall, multi-tiered table of food trays past the open door, a wheel dropped into a slight dip in the wooden floor, causing a loud rattling that brought the Tramp Prince back into reality.

"I know we've already talked about an awful lot of things," the boy told the dietitian, "but my primary concern — the reason I came here was because of that hobo accident victim they brought in last night."

"Yes, I heard about him," the woman responded. "They said that another tramp found him."

"Well...that was me... See, ma'am someone like that really needs optimum nutrition to give his body the best chance of fighting infection. If he loses his foot — well, that'd be terrible. I can't think of anything worse than a hobo without one foot trying to catch out on a freight train."

The woman shuddered and grimaced.

"Alright," she told him, "I'll personally supervise that fellow's diet...for whatever good it will do. But you know that tramps — hobos — they have so little access to food of any kind, that they're probably not going to be very particular about *what* they eat. But I'll do the best I can."

"Oh, that's wonderful, ma'am. I appreciate it — even if *he* doesn't!"

When the Tramp Prince got up to leave, the dietitian gave him a warm, motherly smile — then patted his hand:

"Keep trying to educate us," she told the boy, "even when we act like we don't want to be educated."

The Tramp Prince chuckled and walked out.

Chapter 15: The Attorney With The Pencil-line Moustache

After several more days of walking southward, the Tramp Prince reached a fairly large southern city. Although the climate was far from tropical, it was truly many degrees warmer than the cold temperatures that the boy had been enduring for the past couple of weeks. Even in the south, though, night descended rapidly during the winter months, and the Tramp Prince found himself in an area of the city with a bewilderingly confusing array of intersecting streets and imposing, forbidding-looking buildings.

He walked past an alley where he could still see in the dim light a gathering of several unseemly-looking men as they stood on a huge steel grating set in the edge of the pavement. Joining them, the Tramp Prince nodded to one of the men. The man nodded back.

"Yeah...yuh wanna join us, Junior? It'll stay pretty warm here all night — less someone closes that basement winder in the factory here." And he pointed to the carriage factory next to them.

"I guess this place is better than just trying to sleep on the pavement or in a store front," the Tramp Prince agreed.

"Sure — go find a piece of cardboard to lie down on," suggested the bum.

After setting himself up for the night\, the Tramp Prince nibbled on the last few pieces of dried food that he had left in his bindle sack. Then he fell asleep and did not awaken until it was already light, when one of the bums sleeping on the grate rolled over with a loud groan. The boy stored his blanket roll back in its sack and walked out of the alley.

Shopkeepers along the street were just beginning to place their wares out in front on the sidewalk and a few early customers trickled up and down in front of the shops. A couple of panhandlers were already actively soliciting among their potential donors. As the Tramp Prince walked up to where one of the panhandlers was accosting a woman, the angry shop owner came charging out.

"Get out of here, you bum!" he yelled at the panhandler.

"Agh, I didn't hurtin' nuthin'," returned the bum. "You don't own the sidewalk, anyhow."

At that, the shop owner threw a vicious blow that caught the panhandler squarely on the side of the head. A fistfight then ensued in which the panhandler came out very much on the losing end.

"Now — get out of here!" screamed the still irate shop owner with self-righteous indignation.

The badly beaten panhandler moved slowly down the street and the Tramp Prince followed, offering the man his handkerchief to wipe the blood from his forehead.

"That's mighty kind of yuh, bud," said the battered bum. "I guess I shouldn't a' messed wit' dat guy...but it jus' ticked me off; him tryin t' stop me from beggin' a few pennies from people...when I got nothin', an he's got plenty."

"I know," said the Tramp Prince. "I'm sorry it happened to you. Why don't you go report it to the police?"

"Dat would be useless!" explained the bum, bitterly. "Dey'd jus' tell me I got what I had comin'. I know what dem cops is like."

In the next block across the street could be seen a sign indicating the services of an attorney. The bum looked over at it with his one eye still not swollen shut. "Hey, kid, would youse come wit' me over to dat lawyer's office an' tell him you wuz a witness t' what happened? He might take my case so I could sue dat guy an maybe git some money outta it."

"Sure," said the Tramp Prince, "I'll do that."

When the panhandler had told his story to the attorney, the Tramp Prince added: "It's true, sir. I witnessed all of it, and the shop owner did, indeed, hit this fellow first."

The attorney drew his hand across his pencil-line moustache, thinking. Then he said to the panhandler: "It's too bad you chose to hit the shop owner back; you would have had a *much* stronger case if you hadn't. But there's another factor that I'll have to consider before I can take your case. Since I'd have to take this case on a contingency basis — it's obvious you have no money for a retainer — I must be at least relatively well convinced that we can win something, in order for me to tie up my time. The way that this city's panhandling statures are written may well influence the decision a jury will make as to whether or not to award damages — if this case would go to a jury trial. I'll have to look this up in the stature books since I'm not completely familiar with the way that aspect of the law is written. Come back tomorrow about this time and I'll be able to tell you if I can take your case.

"In the meantime," continued the Attorney With The Pencil-line Moustache, "You need to go to the police and have them make out a report of the assault, then go to a hospital or a doctor who can write up a medical evaluation of your injuries. Now, do you understand everything?"

"Uh...yeah...I guess so," replied the panhandling bum with an uncertain tone.

"It's all right, sir," the Tramp Prince interjected. "I can explain to him later, anything that's not clear."

"Young man," said the Attorney With The Pencil-line Moustache, "would you mind staying for a couple more minutes. I need to speak to you in private."

The panhandling bum walked out, leaving the Tramp Prince sitting in the law office.

"I'm curious," inquired the Attorney With The Pencil-line Moustache, as he eyed the Tramp Prince's bindle sack and by now, somewhat ragged clothes, "It's clear that you're a bright, young fellow — so what on earth are you doing on the street, hanging around with a bunch of old panhandlers and bums? You look to me like you can't be more than seventeen or eighteen years old. With your intelligence, you should be in some kind of college studying to be an engineer or a doctor...or even a lawyer like myself."

The Tramp Prince very briefly explained the situation into which he and his family had been thrust and his purpose in traveling about — then how he happened to end up sleeping in the alley.

"Well," mused the Attorney With The Pencil-line Moustache, " you seem to have quite an analytical mind. You just might make a very good lawyer. When you've completed your search, I think it would be worth your while to consider obtaining higher education, with a view toward going to law school. I do quite well as an attorney; I haven't won every case I've taken, but I've won a great number of them. And, you see, I get a third of the amount of my client's damage settlements when we win — plus a retainer in those cases which I didn't win."

" Good lord!" exclaimed the Tramp Prince. "A third of your client's damage settlement — that seems like so much!"

"It's not," the Attorney With The Pencil-line Moustache assured him. "It's a standard of the profession — except in cases where the settlement might be in the hundreds of thousands — as with a case against a large corporation. Then we would expect to reduce our percentage."

The Tramp Prince shook his head in bewilderment. "But it's the little guy — the poor person who really needs as much of the settlement money as he can get. Why cut the percentage only in cases where a client gets a very large amount?"

"I don't make the laws, my friend, and I don't make the rules either. I just follow them, and that's the way the rules have been worked out since long, long before I entered the profession."

The Tramp Prince simply sat there for a few seconds thinking. "You know... I guess it's not clear to me why people even need to settle their disputes in civil cases using lawyers and courts and juries — all this litigation stuff," he asserted.

The Attorney With The Pencil-line Moustache then smiled with half-closed eyes like a cat having just finished swallowing a canary. "It's because most people are not mature enough —emotionally, intellectually, rationally...in any or every way — for them to be able to realize that they would be better off to make a relatively small, voluntary mutual compromise with someone they have a dispute with, than to have to engage the services of an attorney and then go to court — where they will probably be forced to accept a far less acceptable compromise. But, if the people weren't the way they are, we attorneys couldn't make much of a living."

With a loud sigh and an indecisive shake of his head, the Tramp Prince looked off into the distance out the window of the office. "I suppose I'm not even sure I could ever be a good attorney. I care too much about people and too little about their money."

The Tramp Prince got up to leave. "Sir, would you mind answering a question for me before I go?"

"I guess not — I don't have a lot of time, so ask away!"

"I ask this question of anyone I have a prolonged or important conversation with. It's just: 'What do you feel really matters in life?'"

The Attorney With The Pencil-line Moustache sat back in his chair, with a nonplussed expression on his face. "Ah...well...hmmm. You've caught me off guard with a question like that. A trial lawyer always likes to be prepared to answer questions adequately, you know. I haven't had time to think about this..."

"But sir, this isn't a courtroom. Just tell me whatever comes into your head. I prefer that kind of answer."

"Well...as an attorney...obviously winning as many of my cases as possible matters. And getting paid well by my clients — that matters so that I can take care of myself and my family with a satisfactory lifestyle. Yes, that certainly matters. And then, I suppose building a good reputation in the community — in case sometime in the future I might decide to enter politics. I'm sure there's more, but I'm running out of time."

The Attorney With The Pencil-line Moustache pulled his briefcase across the desk and closed the clasp, and got out of his chair.

"I need to leave now, but I'd like to say again, that with your quick mind and strong, articulate personality, you could easily become an attorney yourself. Why, if you were to attend law school and graduate...there might even be a position here for you as a junior partner!"

Drawing another long sad sigh, the Tramp Prince looked straight into the eyes of the Attorney With The Pencil-line Moustache. "Oh...I think not, sir. You see, I've begun to believe that I should focus my life on trying to help those who need help the most — not necessarily on those who can *pay* me for my help...focus on *their* needs rather than my own."

"But we all help ourselves — at least to some extent, when we help others."

"Yes, that's true... I suppose a lot depends on how one concentrates one's time and energy."

"Well, if you ever change your mind, come back and see me. I can probably help you get into law school."

"That's very kind of you sir, but I think not — not the way I see the world right now, at least."

The Attorney With The Pencil-line Moustache grinned with a wide smile. "You may change your ideas in a year or two." He smiled even wider and gave a self-satisfied chuckle that made the Tramp Prince think that the man looked a lot like a polished carnival barker.

"Goodbye," said the Tramp Prince as he turned and walked out the attorney's door into the bustling street.

"Well, what did you think of that lawyer?" he asked Road Toad in a telepathized thought.

"I think he looked a lot like a wicked, polished carnival barker," laughed Road Toad.

As soon as the Tramp Prince was back out on the street, he looked around for the injured panhandler, but the man was nowhere in sight.

"I can't understand why he didn't wait here for me," the Tramp Prince thought.

"Without you for a witness, he really doesn't have much of a case," Road Toad observed. "Maybe he changed his mind about suing the shop owner."

"I can't afford to wait around for him... And I wouldn't know where to look for him, either," the Tramp Prince advised Road Toad. "I'll just have to walk on."

A couple of blocks further down, the Tramp Prince came upon two other panhandlers, and as he walked past, he overheard part of their conversation:

"Did you see poor Bennie?" one of the panhandlers asked the other.

"Yeah...someone sure beat d' shit outta him! But I notice he's out beggin' again an' people is handin' him *foldin'* money — even fives 'n' tens — dey feels so sorry for him!"

"Did you hear that?" the Tramp Prince asked Road Toad.

"Yes, and I'll bet that guy takes in more money looking the way he does than he would *ever* get out of a lawsuit."

Chapter 16: The Fat Lady, The Smoker With The Big Cigar And Pre-Pre, The Boy Motorman

Concrete pavement is not the easiest surface on which to walk. That is the conclusion the Tramp Prince came to, as he attempted to make his way from one edge of the city to the other.

"Right now, I'd like some nice, soft grass to walk on," he told Road Toad with a thought message.

"Yes, I'm sure you would," the little animal returned telepathically. "But perhaps you could catch one of those streetcars that are always clanging past us. It would be a lot faster and easier than trying to walk all the way through town."

"I'm trying to save every penny I can right now, with my funds as low as they are. But...perhaps you're right. For only a nickel, I'll save a lot of unpleasant walking."

He approached one of the streetcars, just as an enormous fat woman was trying to get on. She had her feet on the first step and was attempting to move up one more step into the car. As she tried to take the step, her body became wedged within the doorframe's sides. The streetcar motorman clanged the bell for everyone to enter if they intended to go.

"Come on, lady — get in," the motorman commanded.

"I can't! ... I *can't*, I tell yuh. I'm stuck! *Stuck* — can'tcha see, yuh god-damned idiot? I'm stuck!"

"Oh, gimmie yer hand; I'll try t' pull yuh up."

The driver pulled and pulled, but to no avail.

"Hey!" he called out to the Tramp Prince. "Try pushin' against this woman's back while I pull, will yuh, bud?"

The Tramp Prince pushed and the motorman pulled, but the Fat Lady remained solidly stuck in the door frame. More passengers collected behind the Tramp Prince, waiting to enter.

"We gotta get this circus fat lady outta here and get movin'! The next trolley'll be here in only another eight minutes! An' it can't get through 'til my car is gone."

The motorman then braced himself against the side of his seat and put his feet up against what he thought were the woman's shoulders.

"I'm gonna try t' push yuh out this time with my feet on yer shoulders," he told the woman.

"Hey, them ain't my shoulders, man. *Raise* yer feet!"

"Oh — sorry. Well, here we go!"

After great straining and puffing, the motorman finally stopped, not having moved the woman out.

"Hey, bud," he called out to the Tramp Prince, "was you pullin' or pushin'?"

"I was pushing — just like you told me to do."

"Well, *pull* this time. Got it?"

"Yes — sure."

Again, the motorman positioned himself and tried to shove the Fat Lady back down. Suddenly, her coat ripped, releasing the woman and she virtually exploded out of the streetcar door, narrowly missing the Tramp Prince as she slammed down to the pavement on her more-than-ample derriere.

"Oh, my God!" she cried out. "How am I gonna get up now?"

"I dunno," came the motorman's reply through the open door. "That's your problem, lady. Call a tow truck! They deal with wrecks, don't they?"

"Awright, you sarcastic S.O.B." And the fat lady shook her fist at the motorman as he drove off. Then she began to cry in great resounding sobs.

Since the Tramp Prince had not entered the streetcar, he stooped down and attempted to comfort the Fat Lady.

"Maybe I can find two or three husky men to help lift under your arms and get you up. Then you could go over to that park bench and at least sit down properly."

"Oh thank you, young fella. But if I sat on that bench, it'd probably break under my weight. concrete or heavy steel — that's about the only thing I'm able to sit on now. I'm so, soo *fat*!"

The Fat Lady began to wail and sob again — finally, she spoke to the Tramp Prince once more: "My doctor says if I don't lose weight, the strain on my heart and vital organs is gonna *kill* me."

"Well, he's right, of course. That's just plain common sense. You don't have to be an M.D. to see that."

"Yeah, but no matter what I eat, I never lose. All I do is gain more."

The Tramp Prince smiled compassionately. "Actually, it ought to be simple to lose. It's all just a matter of calories. You have to take in fewer calories than your body burns each day; then you begin to use up stored fat to produce the rest of the calories that you need."

"I *know* that—but how?"

"Well, you might want to try eating what I eat — fresh, raw fruits, vegetables, nuts and seeds. Then you'd begin to lose — and continue until you reach your ideal weight. A person who eats that way *can't* get fat."

"Oh yeah — well I'll bet *I* could! Anyway, I ain't no damned rabbit or squirrel!"

"Maybe you have some glandular disorder."

"Naagh," said the Fat Lady. "My doctor already checked me for that. I just eat an' eat. I can't stop. An' I like the taste of good food."

The Tramp Prince's face took on a serious expression.

"I suppose that's a problem for a 'head doctor' — I can't help with that. You may have had some sort of childhood trauma that's affecting you emotionally. Anyway, I'll go try to get you some help so that you can get up."

It took only a few minutes for the Tramp Prince to round up several strong men, who lifted the Fat Lady to a standing position.

"I think I see a concrete bench down at the end of this walk, ma'am — if you'd like to go there. I can try to steady you, if you want."

"Oh, I'll be okay. I can make it. Thanks."

The tramp Prince walked with the Fat Lady as she waddled to the concrete bench where the woman sat with a great sigh of relief.

"Whew! Boy, life is such an effort when you're this fat."

"Yes, I can see how it would be. So you never had any childhood trauma?"

"Nope!"

The Fat Lady opened up her purse and unsnapped a small pocket from which she removed a photograph.

"I just had a real normal family — a normal childhood. See -this is me when I was eighteen years old! I keep this here to remind myself of how I used to look."

"Oh wow! My god — you were *beautiful!*"

Tears began to well up in the woman's eyes.

"Yeah — an' I was slim — nice an' *slim*... That was twenty-five years ago. Look what I done t' myself in twenty-five years. You can't even see any resemblance to me in that photograph, can yuh?"

"No," admitted the Tramp Prince, "you're right. I really can't."

"Well, it started when I broke up with my boyfriend; I got real nervous an' that made me overeat."

"And then..."

"I dunno...seems like I always got these jobs that made me nervous. Everything just got worse a little at a time. Figure it out; if I only gained a quarter of a pound a day — that's ninety pounds a year. Then in ten years?"

"I know what you're saying — but you could reverse the process."

"Not with the kind of job I got now, I couldn't. I'm so nervous...I'm sittin there eight hours a day screwin' little pieces onto handles of gigidigs. I gotta keep up with the assembly line an' if I drop one a' them tiny screws, the belt just moves the gigidig along to the next person an' then they can't assemble their part on it. It messes up the whole line when that happens. That's why I gotta be so careful... an' it makes me nervous as hell!"

"That's terrible!" said the Tramp Prince. "I'm sorry, what's a 'gigidig?'"

"What — don't you really know what a gigidig is?" asked the Fat Lady.

"No, I've never heard of one."

"Well...it's one a' them little...uh...it's kinda like...oh, you know what a gigidig is — it's one a' them things you use to put on a, a...aw, whatda they call that thing...a...a... Anyway they got 'em all over the place. They're about so long an' they're usually painted green...that is, the part that ain't plated. Oh hell. I guess I don't know what the damn things are for."

"But you *make* them."

"Yeah, I make 'em — an' makin' 'em makes *me* nervous!"

"And when you're nervous, you try to calm your nerves with food — right?" asked the Tramp Prince.

"You *got* it!" the Fat Lady replied with finality.

"It seems to me," said the Tramp Prince, "that if I had a job that was making me nervous, I'd try to find some other less nerve-wracking line of work. Have you ever thought about maybe opening a flower shop?"

"Hey, that's a great idea! I *love* flowers! But where would I get the money to do something like that? I don't make enough on my job at the gigidig factory to be able to save anything."

"If you didn't buy the huge amounts of food you're eating, you could save *that* money and in a fairly short time you *would* have enough," the Tramp Prince offered.

"Yeah, an' if I did that, kid, in a short time I'd either be dead from my nerves blowin' the top of my head off — or I'd be in the loonytic asylum."

Just then, another streetcar arrived and the Tramp Prince waved goodbye and ran over and leapt on board.

Before dropping his nickel into the till, the Tramp Prince asked the motorman how far his trolley went.

"More'n half way to the edge of the city — but if you want to go farther than I go, you'll have to transfer to another line." And he held up a transfer slip. "I take it you're not from around here, so just sit up in the seat behind me and I'll tell you where to get off."

"Thanks," said the Tramp Prince as he dropped his nickel into the till and watched the motorman crank the handle around several times.

As the old rolling wooden barn rumbled down the tracks, it screeched and creaked as it lurched into every curve and turn. The Tramp Prince looked around at the car's interior, which contrasted sharply with the peeling yellow-orange paint on the exterior wood. All of the interior wood trim still retained most of its original varnish, and the bright colors of the advertising placards overhead gave the streetcar a welcome, rather cheerful image inside.

Even the seats' small square and oblong pattern cane coverings were largely intact and the Tramp Prince wondered if that caning could have taken the extreme weight of the enormous woman they had just left at the last stop.

"I think not," reflected Road Toad, who had picked up the boy's thought. "But luckily for the seats, people that fat seem to be very few and far between."

"I wonder how long things will continue this way," thought back the Tramp Prince. Right now almost everyone you see is normal weight; but just look at all those advertising placards for candy and soda pop and confections of every type. If they buy into that, it can't do anything less than make everyone extremely fat."

"I know it," returned Road Toad. "But if the people change that badly, at least we won't be around to see it."

"Speak for yourself," said the Tramp Prince. "Anyway, you might even reincarnate back as a human someday."

"Ugh... I don't know if I'd ever want to be a human again. Tell me now, which are more absurd, toads or humans?"

"Well, you certainly win that one," admitted the Tramp Prince. "Of course, you could reincarnate as a pig... Then you'd look like all the rest of the people."

"Sorry, no thanks! And it's not just because I don't speak pig Latin very well, either."

At the next stop, a sportily dressed, middle-aged gentleman boarded the trolley car. He was smoking a big cigar. Sitting down in the empty seat next to the Tramp Prince, he immediately began blowing thick clouds of cigar smoke almost directly into the boy's face.

"I beg your pardon, sir, but could you please try to blow your cigar smoke in some other direction — away from my face?"

"Why?" asked the Smoker With The Big Cigar. "No one else seems to mind my cigar smoke."

"Well, I find it highly *obnoxious*."

"Humpf!" said the Smoker With The Big Cigar. "Why doesn't it offend anyone else?"

"It probably does. Maybe they're just too polite to say anything about it. Or perhaps there's something about your appearance that intimidates them."

"Nonsense!" said the Smoker With The Big Cigar. "People tell me they *like* the cigar odor. Why...when I've carried around a box of fresh cigars, as soon as I open it, people comment on how nice the cigar odor is."

"But that's different. Those are the cured, *unburned* leaves. It changes radically when they turn to smoke. Also there's an odor that a person's body emits into the smoke that makes it even more offensive."

"Hey, kid, if you don't like being around my smoke—just move into the back of the car."

"I would if I could, but since I'm not from this city and don't know where to get off to transfer, the motorman told me to sit right behind him and he'd let me know when we get to the proper stop."

"Well, I'd move, but it doesn't look like there are any seats left in the back."

"I'm curious," said the Tramp Prince, "Just *why* do you smoke that cigar, anyway?"

"What!? I... I *like* it. Isn't that reason enough?"

The Tramp Prince shook his head and blinked his eyes. "I suppose so. It just seems odd that anyone would want to smoke something that has such a permeating *stench* to it. And after you've smoked a box of cigars, it's really just the same as having burned up a bunch of dollar bills. All you've got left is a pile of ashes.

"Also, I find it equally odd that you'd want to do something that obviously hurts your lungs."

"It doesn't hurt my lungs!" said the Smoker With The Big Cigar, "Not now, anyway."

"All I know," said the Tramp Prince, "is that when I tried to smoke once, it hurt my lungs so badly, I could hardly breathe for a while."

The Smoker With The Big Cigar sneered. "Humpf...it hurts everyone's lungs the first few times they do it. Then you get used to it. It becomes something pleasant."

"That makes no sense to me, sir. If something hurts once — it *always* hurts. What happens is that your lungs toughen — so that they can stand the smoke. Then the smoke coats your lungs and that means also, that your lungs are less capable of extracting oxygen from the air you breathe."

"That's not what my doctor told me."

"Hmm...yes—and I'll bet *he* smokes."

"Well — he does. So what of it?"

"I guess you don't get the connection. Anyway, your cigar smoke stinks."

"Now see here, kid, I don't appreciate having to listen to your insults."

"But I'm not insulting *you*, sir, just your terrible cigar smoke stink."

"Agh...well, that seems to me like saying the same thing."

"No...no, it's not really. Why, someday they'll even have laws against smoking in public."

The Smoker With The Big Cigar just laughed. "Not in *my* lifetime they won't! Why, most men you see out on the street smoke."

"I know...but just because most people do something or believe something — or act a certain way toward certain people —that doesn't make it right...or good — that is, *beneficial* to our lives."

"Now look, I'm not going to continue to argue with you, kid. It's..."

"Please," said the Tramp Prince, "your smoke is about to suffocate me!"

"What?!...suffocating from a little cigar smoke? Why, that's about the most stupid thing I've ever heard!"

"Well, if we're going to talk about stupidity — you certainly don't have to be very smart to smoke. Even a moron can do it. Even a complete idiot can take a lit cigar or cigarette, stick it in his mouth and puff away on it."

"Alright, now!"

"Sir, it's just that you're being highly disrespectful of your fellow passengers by blowing all that smoke around. Couldn't you please just put the cigar out until I get off? I'm sure it can't be very far."

At that, the Smoker With The Big Cigar took his stogie and stepped it into the floor, crushing it and putting out the glowing coals.

"There!" he said angrily. "Is that what you wanted?"

"No," the Tramp Prince told him, "I just wanted you to put it out temporarily. I didn't want you to *destroy* your cigar. I know you enjoy smoking it."

"Well," the man said sadly, "it's gone now."

"See, I don't have anything against you enjoying your cigar smoke; I just didn't want to have to (ugh!) 'enjoy' it along with you.

I hope you understand that," the Tramp Prince told the Smoker With The Big Cigar as apologetically as he could.

"Actually, I feel really bad about your cigar. I'd buy you another equal quality cigar if I could afford it. But I have an idea. Maybe at my stop, we can get off and I'll go into a shop and see if I can borrow enough glue to put your cigar back together."

"*Glue* it? Talk about something that would *stink* when I smoked it!"

"Well, I don't really know about something like that, I've never tried smoking glue, myself. I haven't been around anyone else who has, either."

"How *ridiculous*!" said the Smoker With The Big Cigar.

"I'm sorry, sir — it was just a suggestion; just an idea…"

The Smoker With The Big Cigar walked angrily out of the streetcar at the next stop.

"Hmm. Wonder what got into him," said the motorman. "He always gets off at the next stop *after* this one."

"Didn't you hear our conversation?"

"Mmm…well, not a lot of it. The traffic was heavy and I had to pay attention to it."

"Well, I didn't like his cigar smoke…and I'm afraid he didn't like the *fact* that I didn't like it."

After the Tramp Prince had left the trolley, Road Toad sent a thought message:

"You forgot to tell that cigar smoker that his stinking smoke also bothers any toad that someone may be carrying around in their pocket."

"Yes," laughed the Tramp Prince, "that certainly is another very important consideration. Yes, *indeed*!"

For the first few minutes, the Tramp Prince stood alone in silence at the isolated trolley stop. Then he sent out another thought message to Road Toad:

"You know — I just can't seem to get that poor fat lady off of my mind; her situation was *so* sad."

"Ah well," Road Toad replied, "life just doesn't seem to give some people a chance, does it?"

"No," returned the Tramp Prince, "and what you might have said is that it's some *people* — those in a position of great power — who don't give most of us a chance. Or at least we're not smart enough to figure out a way to get around the obstacles they put in our paths."

There was a wait of only a few more minutes until the small, rickety, old trolley car rolled up to the stop where the Tramp Prince was standing. He thought that the car looked more like some kind of dilapidated rolling woodshed than a real streetcar. The sign above the trolley's front glass read "Crows Nest — End of the Line".

After he had entered the trolley car and handed the transfer slip to the motorman, the Tramp Prince asked the young driver what the meaning was of "Crows Nest".

"Hee, hee...why I'm not sure — hee, hee! Maybe 'cause it's really brushy out there — lots of sticks an' sticker bushes; like a crows nest. I didn't name it — so I don't know!" he replied, with a melodic lilt to his final sentence.

The Tramp Prince then looked more closely at the driver. He was just a boy — probably no older than himself. The motorman's jacket and cap that the young fellow wore were clean and well-fitting. His unlined, boyish features, though clean-shaven, indicated a dark, substantial beard.

"I'm trying to figure out how old you are," he said to the youthful motorman. "Your face looks *very* young — except for your beard. It's a lot darker than mine, and I'm eighteen."

"I'm Pre-Pre the Motorman, hee, hee!" the driver laughed with a silly vacant look. Again, he ended his words in a musical note. "I'm the world's only fourteen year old motorman — hee, hee! Look, I can open the transom!" And the boy lifted the transom rod up and down. He then clanged the trolley bell several times more than necessary — obviously for the enjoyment of the sound — and closed the door, the Tramp Prince being the only passenger.

As the trolley car swayed along on the poorly maintained track, the Tramp Prince sat down on a wicker-covered bench just behind the motorman's seat.

"How did you get to be a motorman?" he asked the boy driver.

"My uncle owns the line," the boy laughed. "I can play motorman any day after school. Hee, hee...I'm Pre-Pre the Motorman. Hot sticky stew!"

"What's that name mean, Pre-Pre?"

"That's what they call me in school. I have a toy trolley n' I push it aroun' on the banisters. When I go around curves, I make a noise like a trolley! Cree, cree — 'cept they think I'm sayin' Pre-Pre!"

"Now I get it," the Tramp Prince laughed. "And your uncle pays you, yes? No?"

The boy shook his head negatively. "No."

"So he gets a free driver whenever you want to work?"

The boy motorman nodded "yes" and kept the silly vacant expression to his face.

At that point the Tramp Prince sent another telepathic thought to Road Toad:

"What do you think of all this?"

"I guess they get around the child-labor laws by the fact that they don't pay him anything."

"Maybe so. But I'm just glad *this* is the *end* of the line!"

Road Toad sent another telepathic thought:

"See if you can find a name bar on his jacket. That might tell us something. Perhaps he 'borrowed' the clothes from someone. His uncle maybe? The whole thing seems somehow wrong."

"Yes — there *is* a name on the coat…with a photo of *him*! The name is 'E. Hanley Lavender'. What an *odd* name!"

"Well, not so odd when you consider everything. An odd name for an odd young man. It fits!"

Just then, the trolley entered a long curve.

"Listen," exclaimed the young motorman, "It goes 'Creee, Creee'!"

"Yes," the Tramp Prince replied, "just as you said."

With a glaring, gleeful expression, Pre-Pre the boy motorman took the trolley fast into the curve. It made a loud screeching noise as the wheels scraped against the rails.

"Oh, hot sticky *stew*!" he shouted in delight.

"What?!…Say aren't you going a bit *fast*? This old top-heavy car could flop over!"

The gleeful expression remained on the young motorman's face. Then he suddenly brought the streetcar to a halt at a trolley stop that seemed to be in the middle of nowhere.

"End of the line!" he shouted. "It's the *Crow's* Nest!" And, again with an exhilaratedly animated, though vacant expression, he melodically shouted: "Oh, hot sticky *stew*!"

"Let me ask you something...if you don't mind," the Tramp Prince inquired of the boy motorman. "Just what do you think really matters in life?"

The young man raised his eyebrows and with a completely silly expression quickly answered: *"Hot sticky stew!"*

The Tramp Prince then departed from the car with great alacrity, making his way up a narrow cinder path to the country road.

"I'm just glad to be out of there with that young oddball! Road Toad, are you getting my thought?"

"Oh yes," replied Road Toad, "and I think your noun describing him is very modest, indeed. Yes, indeed!"

Chapter 17: The Bell Museum

It is seldom that one merely happens by a bell museum — particularly a museum that is selling out. When the Tramp Prince found himself standing in front of Lauritz Oldman's 'Bedlam of Bells,' he was intrigued and at the same time somewhat confounded.

"Now why," he said to himself aloud, "would anyone ever want to create a bell *museum*?"

Road Toad answered his thought:

"For the same reason people create *other* kinds of museums. They collect certain types of things — until they have a large representation of that category of item. Then they try to capitalize on their collection by opening a museum to the public... and charging admission."

"But this museum doesn't charge admission, Road Toad. There's the sign; it says, 'Lauritz Oldman's Bedlam of Bells. I have bells in my batfry. Free admission.'

As the Tramp Prince entered the museum, he saw shelves with rows and rows of bells. Large bells sat next to small bells. The bells were made of every material imaginable, in every shape one could think of. They were made of brass, steel, aluminum, glass, silver, ceramic, wood — even gold. There were train locomotive bells, tramcar bells, huge church bells, ship's bells –- the list went on and on.

"This is incredible!" said the amazed Tramp Prince.

"Yes, I'm glad you like it," returned the museum owner.

The owner sat on a chair near the door as he greeted his visitor.

"Look around, young man — buy one bell or a thousand; they're all for sale. You want to buy me out?"

"Well, not exactly," replied the Tramp Prince, laughing. "But I did see something in the window that I might be interested in. There was no price on it, though."

"What was it?" asked the owner.

"It looked like an alcohol stove of some kind."

"Oh...yes. I know the one you mean. It folds into a flat unit. It's for camping...I suppose."

"Yes... you see, it might be just what I need on cold or wet nights. So, how much do you want for it?"

Lauritz Oldman's face beamed in anticipation of a sale.

"Why... if my dear old mother wanted to buy that little stove... I'd have to charge her *ten* dollars for it!"

His face took on a sad grimace as he continued:

"But I wouldn't want to dig her up just sell her a stove. So you can have it for only two."

The Tramp Prince gave a loud laugh. Then he stood there and fidgeted — thinking and feeling around in his pockets.

"I'm sorry, sir ... I just don't think I have that much."

"Well," said the bell collector, "I can't wave my magic wand and put money in your pocket."

"Why not?" asked the Tramp Prince with another laugh, "You must have been some kind of wizard to have collected all these thousands of different kinds of bells."

"No, no — just an avid... a very *determined* collector. Hmm...so exactly how much *do* you have?"

"Just a little over a dollar." The boy replied with honesty. I have to save some for food until I can get more work to do."

"Alright...well, since its not a bell — I'll sell it to you for a dollar. How's that?"

The boy reached into his pocket and withdrew the correct amount, placing it on the Bell Museum's counter.

"Hurray!" yelled the museum owner. "We eat *tonight!*"

Then he ran around the large museum room ringing every type and size of bell with a small mallet.

"Bells, bells bells — I have bells in my batfry!" he screamed.

"Yes, I... know that..." The Tramp Prince acknowledged. "Listen", the boy said calmly, "I can understand why you might have wanted to *start* a bell museum, but I just can't fathom why you would suddenly try to *sell* it out."

"The decision wasn't quick — or easy," said Lauritz Oldman. "But I've been pondering just what might happen to all of this soon when I'm in my old age. You see, I have no family to leave it to."

"I'm really sorry to hear that," the Tramp Prince told him. "But you actually don't look to be very old. So your old age must be a long way off."

"Don't let appearances deceive you. I'm a *lot* older than I look. What you don't realize is that by not having the responsibility of taking care of a family, I'm not under nearly as much stress as most folks. I don't have a wife to nag me -- I don't have children to have to worry and fret over. I never have to argue with my bells. They do exactly as I command; they ring when I tap them." And he laughed loud and long and tinged a tiny bell with his mallet. "I'm almost at retirement age. Maybe, when the museum is gone, I'll take the money and start traveling; I've never been able to do that before."

As the Tramp Prince slipped the little alcohol stove into his bindle sack, he turned once more to the young–looking museum owner.

"Sir...what do you think really matters in life — besides bells?"

"Ah well ... good food...good rest...good sex... good friends...good thoughts and good... good..."

"And goodbye!" said the Tramp Prince as he began walking toward the door.

"I agree with everything you mentioned, but the only thing you left out was 'a good family'."

"Oh ho!" said Lauritz Oldman, "that last one might negate *all* the others! Because there probably *is* no such thing as a *good* family. When siblings are young, they're always fighting with each other. The mother and father fight with each other — and with the children. Then when the parents die, the children fight over the inheritance. Even aunts and uncles enter into the fray."

"But not *every* family is like that!"

"Maybe not *every* family; but enough are -- at least of the ones I see."

"Not mine! said the Tramp Prince as he walked out the door. Then he stuck his head back in again. "And a lot depends on the attitude of each person in your family - particularly what you, yourself give to that relationship."

Lauritz Oldman shrugged and drooped his lower lip.

When the Tramp Prince had gone about a half block from the museum, Road Toad blinked one of his bright eyes and reached out of the jacket pocket, tapping the boy hard on his ribs and sending out a thought:

"That man in the bell museum really was a little bit crazy, don't you think?"

"Oh, I don't think so... he seemed pretty rational to me. He, no doubt has had some very different experiences in life from those that I've had - maybe even from the experiences that almost anyone else has had..."

"Anyway, he seems kind of crazy to me."

"I hope you're not equating lunacy with eccentricity."

"Oh no," clarified Road Toad, "he's just a little of *both*!"

Chapter 18: The Artist With The Red Beret

Back out on the street, the Tramp Prince began walking toward some tall buildings in the distance, which he assumed was the city's downtown area. After a walk of many, many blocks, the boy finally arrived at the tall buildings ... and an extensive wharf, on a waterfront that, when he looked out upon it, seemed to go on forever. This would certainly be as far south as the Tramp Prince could go; as far, at least, as he would be able to walk.

After having wandered around the docks, looking at freighters and smaller ships - wondering what their cargoes might be and their possibly exotic destinations, the Tramp Prince come upon an artist with a red beret, dabbing furiously away on a canvas clamped to a lightweight easel.

The daylight was fast fading as the sun slipped low behind buildings near the western edge of the waterfront. A beautiful pastel haze seemed to engulf everything in the distance. The painter suddenly turned and with a bit of surprise in his voice, addressed the Tramp Prince:

"Ha! You see, I must huree; zee light, eet weel be soon gone, and zee color, eet ees extraordinaree! *Oui, mon ami?*"

"Oh yes!" replied the Tramp Prince, "but you have so much area to cover and so little time to cover it."

The Artist With The Red Beret was placing small dabs of color upon the canvas with such rapidity that his hand appeared almost as a blur. Every few seconds, he would reach down to the palette and scoop up more paint onto the small brush.

"I weel get only zee base colors tonight," he explained, "tomorrow, I weel return and paint een whatever detail I weesh, when zere ees again more light."

"This is really interesting, watching you paint." The Tramp Prince then added an apology:"I hope you don't mind my watching – – hope it doesn't make you nervous."

"Oh no - eet ees not bother me; I am used to eet. People watch me paint every day. I have do thees for manee years."

The Artist With The Red Beret worked with such great speed, that by the time the last rays of sun had faded, the canvas was entirely covered with a transition of tones ranging from pink and blue to purplish-gray with fringes of a frosty orange highlight.

"Ha, ha," he said. "On tomorrow I weel put een zee ships and zee buildings."

"Is this — what you're doing - a certain school of painting?" The Tramp Prince asked, hoping that he did not display too much of his ignorance on the subject.

"Some say zat I am zee eempresionist... but I do not alwazees paint zee same way. I have study art een zee best academee een France and Etaly — and zee wealthy collectors, zey buy my work."

"So do you come here often to paint?" asked the Tramp Prince, now genuinely intrigued.

"No... I love to paint zee beautiful landscape — anywhere een zee world, but most of zee time, I find enough nice subject where I leeve — een Pfantassiland."

"Pfantassiland! You live in Pfantassiland?"

"*Oui!*" replied the Artist With The Red Beret. "I have leeve there many year now!

The Tramp Prince stood in amazement at that revelation.

"I met someone else not too long ago who said she lived in Pfantassiland - but I never got her name. She just refered to herself as 'the Girl With Long, Curly, Brown Hair'," The Tramp Prince awaited the artist's reply with intense anticipation.

"Oh, of course, of course. I know zees Girl Weeth Long, Curly, Brown Hair. Everyone een Pfantassiland know her; she ees varee beauteeful."

Just at that point, a huge steam locomotive pulling a half mile long line of freight cars, came crashing along the track that ran just back from the water's edge and along-side the warehouses. The intense noise from the locomotive's massive engine and wheels was punctuated only by the screaming blast from its whistle, as the horrendous sounds reverberated in hellish echoes from the hollow waterfront.

The Tramp Prince put his fingers into his ears, hunched his shoulders and squinted his eyes in a futile effort to block out the hideous mechanical thunder. It took the train several minutes to finally pass by and when the Tramp Prince looked around him, the Artist With The Red Beret had disappeared.

"Oh, no!" The Tramp Prince cried out "The painter is gone... and I had so much I wanted to ask him. Road Toad, did you see where he went?"

The small amphibian immediately heard the question and shot back his thought answer:

"No, how could I see anything? I was slumped down as low as I could get in your pocket, trying to get away from that horrible noise!"

For a few minutes in the dim evening dusk, the Tramp Prince wandered around the nearly deserted wharf, wondering what to do. He knew that the Artist With The Red Beret must return in the morning to finish his painting and that when the artist returned, it might be the only opportunity there would ever be to ask him about Pfantassiland.

The industrial buildings along the wharf were all closed down for the night, but in a narrow walkway going back alongside one building, there came a whooshing noise. The sound seemed to emanate from that same area every minute or two, lasting only a few seconds. The Tramp Prince walked back to investigate.

Near the concrete walk toward the back of the building was a stairway that led down to a basement area with windows almost at the ground level. Lights glowed from within and the Tramp Prince could see workers pressing clothes that had probably been made in the factory above

"Look, Road Toad." The Tramp Prince pulled his little companion out of the pocket and held him up where he could see the interior of the building, "they must be behind schedule to be working at night like this."

"*We* don't have to work at night — why can't you find someplace where we can sleep?" Road Toad responded irritably.

"I'm thinking, said the Tramp Prince," that if we could get next to the building where the steam from the presser is coming out, we'd at least stay warm.

The periodic cloud of steam and warm air rushed from a pipe near the walk. In between spurts, the Tramp Prince located the rusted end of the tube.

"I'll see if I can find some cardboard to put down on the walkway and another piece to direct the warm air out toward us instead of letting it go straight up."

"Better get with it," Road Toad advised. "There's almost no light left."

After having hunted through several piles of trash nearby, The Tramp Prince had found enough cardboard to at least make himself moderately comfortable for the night. He could tell that the periodic noise, and the peculiar odor from the steamed fabrics would not make for a restful sleep. Before slipping into his blanket roll, He took out the last bit of food he had left, one apple and a few pecans he had found beneath trees. He broke the pecan shells against each other in the palm of his hand and offered a piece of the nut meat to Road Toad.

"These are very good quality pecans," the Tramp Prince told Road Toad. "See if you like them."

Road Toad chomped on the piece of nut and then spat it out.

"That's terrible!" he told the boy. "How can you eat that stuff?"

"Oh, I manage." Replied the Tramp Prince, who said nothing further.

It was a fitful night of sleep for the Tramp Prince. The whooshing noise kept him from sleeping soundly, but then, when the workers had completed their pressing shortly after midnight, even though there was no longer any noise, there was also no longer any warmth.

In the chill of the early morning, dock workers were assembling to load and unload cargos, factory workers entered the large many-storied brick and steel "gehennas of toil', and the Tramp Prince again began wandering. up and down the wharf. He walked until late in the morning, never certain of the exact location where he had seen the Artist With The Red Beret. But the painter never appeared.

"I wonder if he's ever going to return." The Tramp Prince stated with concern.

"Who knows?" Road Toad responded. "You know that an artist with as much skill as he has could easily add in the buildings and other detail right from his own memory."

"True." Said the Tramp Prince with dejection in his voice. "Maybe we'd just better try to go somewhere and find something to eat."

"Good idea! Now you're starting to make some sense." Road Toad agreed.

Chapter 19 The Jewelry Merchant (*aqua caliente*)

As he walked along the narrow streets of the city's downtown business area, The Tramp Prince came to a series of merchants selling their wares from tiny stalls along the sidewalk. At one stall there was a loud altercation going on and the Tramp Prince walked near so that he could listen to the exchange.

"How'm I gonna get this ring off my finger?" shouted a woman customer.

"I do not know, ladee. But eef you no can get eet off, then you got to pay for eet, *si*?"

"Listen - I ain't payin' fer the ring. I don't like it enough t'buy it."

The jewelry merchant then grabbed the ring and pulled as hard as he could, but was not able to get it off the woman's finger.

"You can't get off dee reeng - you got to buy eet."

"I don't want it! I won't buy it! she screamed and stamped her foot down so hard the heel broke off her shoe.

"Ladee!" shouted the merchant. "You take off dee reeng and geeve back or you buy eet. Or I call police."

The poor woman was by now simply livid with rage. But she reached into her purse and handed the merchant enough money to pay for the ring.

"I'm gonna get a lawyer and sue you in court - yuh hear me!" yelled the woman in a continued fury. I'll get a tin snips an' cut the damn ring off an' you'll get it back an' a lot more. An I'll get my money back –- an' a lot more!"

The Tramp Prince walked on past the jewelry stall:

"Boy, was she *mad*!" said the Tramp Prince to Road Toad in a telepathic message.

"Yes," replied Road Toad, "she's just one of many, many adult children."

The Tramp Prince watched the woman as she went limping away down the street in her broken shoe.

"The seller must not have had any soap and water - that probably would have gotten the ring off, don't you think?"

"Yes, but it's so cold now in these outdoor stalls that no one would want to put their hand in icy cold water, anyway," Road Toad shot back.

"Of course," continued the Tramp Prince, "The woman could have gone to one of those larger shops across the street for some soap and hot water."

"The vendor probably wouldn't have trusted her to return." Road Toad reminded him.

"What a shame... so much suspicion and so little trust." The Tramp Prince shrugged and shook his head in disgust. "I guess that's why we need lawyers to protect us."

"Oh... I don't know about that..." Road Toad responded. "We probably need lawyers to protect us from *lawyers*!"

And they both laughed.

Chapter 20: Figmund Trickaday

A short distance away, the Tramp Prince came to a small, roofed open-air market. He stopped to view the fruit at a vendor's stall. All of the fruit appeared so delicious, that he was having a difficult time deciding which to buy. You see, he had only about twenty cents left in his pocket.

As the boy was standing there, a tall, well-dressed gentleman stepped up to him:

"Hello there, young man. Here is my card. As you can see from the card, I am Figmund Trickaday. And how are you on this fine morning?"

" I'm well, sir. Thank you for asking."

"Oh...why it's nothing... nothing at all, my boy. So, as you can see from my card, I represent the Diamond-Star Coffee Company. Ha, ha - a diamond with a star in it, of course... of course. And what brand of coffee do you drink, young man?"

"Um... as a matter of fact, I don't have any particular brand that I drink."

"Oh - why not?"

"Well, mainly because I don't even like the taste of the stuff."

"Don't like coffee?"

"No."

"Why not?"

"Just...just... because I *don't*!"

"Well, have you ever tasted Diamond-Star?"

"No."

"Then you should. It's different! Come to my shop - just inside the door of the market building. I'll sell you a cup for a dime. You'll like it. I guarantee!"

"But...sir...I really don't like the taste of coffee - any kind of coffee. Besides, I have only twenty cents in my pocket and I was planning to spend that on fruit of some kind."

"Ah, then, I shall open up a fruit stand and sell you some fruit. Oh, I will have the most delicious looking and tasting ripe fruit in the market."

"Yes, but when?"

"Oh, tomorrow perhaps. What difference does it make which day you eat?"

"What! How ridiculous!"

"I know …" And Figmund Trickaday gave a loud laugh, The Tramp Prince did not laugh: "So, just who are you, anyway?"

"I already told you my name."

"That's not what I mean, what's your game?"

"Oh, putting people on – you know what I mean?"

"Yes - but that's cruel.''

"No, it's not.. Most people laugh when they find they've been spoofed, Follow me around. Just watch."

The Tramp Prince followed Figmund Trickaday as he moved through the market. The gentleman first stopped at a stall selling drinks and sandwiches. An older woman wearing an apron stepped up to Figmund from behind a cheese stand.

"Whatcha need Sir? We got some nice ham 'n' cheese on rye wit dill pickles."

The woman's comment was made with enthusiasm.

"Uh …ahh b-b-b be-be-be-be e bu-bu be-be e-e-e be-be-be-be…"

The Tramp Prince began to laugh, but held it back as the woman stood there with a look of amazement on her face.

"Whater'yuh tryin' T' say, mister? Spit it out!"

"Ah...I e-e-e-e-e be-be-be-be be, be-be-be-be."

"Try talkin' slower-than maybe you won't stutter so bad."

Figmund Trickaday stood silently, his pleasant features enhanced with a smile and half-closed eyes like a Cheshire cat.

"Oh, just give me a ham and cheese on rye. You can leave out the pickles."

The vendor woman immediately burst into uncontrollable laughter, and continued laughing as she fixed the sandwich.

Figmund smiled at the Tramp Prince: "What do you want, kid? It's on me. Want one like mine?"

"Yes. Sir - the same. But leave out the ham."

As Figmund Trickaday paid for the sandwiches, he handed the woman a card.

"Here's my card; I'm C. V. Ebee. I give lessons in stuttering. Know anybody who wants to learn to stutter? Have them look me up,. I have very reasonable rates."

The woman again burst into almost uncontrollable laughter as did some of the other customers standing nearby.

"Well, kid," said Figmund, "what do you think now?"

"Oh, you're funny – definitely funny. But what do you do for a living?"

"This"

"What! …spoofing people? Why that's insane!"

"No it's not."

Just then a man who had been listening walked over to Figmund Trickaday, and handed him two dollar bills.

"Here my friend; thank you for making me laugh – you've made my day a pleasant surprise."

After the man had left, Figmund confided to the Tramp Prince:

"Now, are you convinced? You see, sometimes a wealthy person will hand me a sizable amount of money, I'm an entertainer. . .not a conventional one, but an entertainer none-the-less."

The Tramp Prince stared at his companion in disbelief.

"I just can't see how this would work all the time."

"It does!"

"And you're bound to run out of characters."

"Oh, no. . .I have hundreds of them."

After they had finished eating their sandwiches, Figmund Trickaday beckoned for the Tramp Prince to follow him. They walked out of the market onto the sidewalk. Across the street was a shop offering sheet metal work and boiler construction. The huge brick building loomed like some ancient repository for pre-constructed dungeons, thought the Tramp Prince as he walked toward the clanging and banging of the dimly lit interior. When the pair had entered the office of the boiler company, Figmund

Trickaday then laid the briefcase he had been carrying on a desk. He opened the lid and rummaged through the papers with which the case had been stuffed, pulling out a strange-looking pen and ink rendering of what could have passed for any number of different iron or steel objects.

"Hallo!" said Figmund to a man sitting at the desk. "Here is card with mine name." The man seemed perplexed as he read the card."You not can say name? I say for you. It: Ignatz Faugheit! Good Slavic name, yes? ...You can make boiler? I vant chu to make boiler –- Gothic type. Maybe like one in picture...yes?"

The man looked at the picture.

"Hmm. Well... I don't know. What's this for?"

"To making soup for army. You know vhare is Balkans?"

The man behind the desk nodded and wrinkled his nose.

"See," Ignatz continued,"in Balkans is always fighting vars. Armies must have soup; need boiler to make. But must be Gothic-style. Hokay? You can make?"

"I suppose so," the man replied, "but I'm not sure about the thickness of the metal you'd want to use."

"Oh, *heavy*! Armor plate! So vhen get hit by cannon ball – just vill bounce off."

"Well," said the man, "that might be awfully heavy to try to move around, don't you think?"

"No, no, no! Must be on iron vheels. Pull behind tank. But need to have Gothic look."

"Sir," the boiler engineer responded, "if we were to add all those gee-gaws and decorations like the picture shows – all that excessive iron probably couldn't even be pulled by a *pair* of military tanks!"

"Harumpf!" growled Ignatz Faugheit, "you vont make – I find place dat vill!"

He closed his briefcase and walked out, the Tramp Prince following, leaving the bewildered boiler engineer scratching his head.

Outside, they began to laugh.

"That *was* funny," the Tramp Prince admitted, "but the engineer didn't seem to think so."

"Oh, sometimes it takes them a day or two to realize they've been spoofed. Then they laugh. Anyway, that was just a demonstration to show you how I can go anywhere and do this. I have better characters, but they require costumes – and make-up: A Japanese Army general, an Eskimo – an old woman Irish fishmonger. I do an Arabian rug seller, a Congolese tribesman … I haven't figured out a way yet to do and African Pygmy – but I'm working on it!"

At that, the Tramp Prince laughed so hard he could barely contain himself.

"This really sounds like fun," said the boy. "I might like to try it myself sometime!"

Figmund Trickaday smiled directly at the Tramp Prince with an almost child-like expression of gleefulness."

"A caveat for you, my boy; if you try this … it takes a *lot* of practice!"

"How would I get practice?"

"By doing accents every time you talk to someone."

"But…but…who would think I could be an older Bulgarian man?"

"Just choose a character that doesn't have an age requirement."

"Mister Trickaday… do you mind if I ask you a question? It's not exactly related to any of this, I suppose."

"No, go ahead –- ask away."

"Well, I just wonder what you think is most important in life."

"Whimsy!" said Figmund Trickaday without hesitation. "And making people laugh with that whimsy. Now, watch this…"

He then immediately accosted an elderly woman walking along the street, and, using a thick cockney accent, attempted to sell her some phony 'snake oil'.

"Oi soi there loidy, Oi've got 'ere the world's most won'erful cure fer everything!"

From his pocket, he then pulled a tiny bottle of greenish liquid labeled: Doctor Gumbah's Genuine Snake Oil. As Figmund was exalting the virtues of his imaginary 'snake oil', the Tramp Prince slipped into the milling street crowd and began working his way back to the fruit stand.

When the boy was walking toward the fruit stand, Road Toad pushed up out of the pocket.

"You certainly seem to attract some weird characters," the little fellow commented in a thought message.

"Yes, you're right; look at the one I'm carrying around in my pocket!"

"Alright!"

"Yes, it is!" And the Tramp Prince laughed.

Chapter 21: The Carnival - The Wild Man

When they reached the center of the city, they came to a large park that must have been a half mile wide and two or three miles in length.

"I almost feel like I'm back out in the country." The Tramp Prince exclaimed. "But what do you suppose that group of yellow tents is up ahead, Road Toad?

Road Toad looked out of the pocket:

"I don't know... but it certainly doesn't look like anything to eat, and *that's* what concerns me. Humpf! Trying to get me to eat bits of your pecans last night...and I didn't like that fruit, either!"

The Tramp Prince walked over to where there was a wooded nature trail and searched under some fallen tree trucks until he had found plenty of insects to satisfy Road Toad's hunger. Then they went on to the group of yellow and red tents. A carnival had been set up there the day before and customers were already beginning to flow into the grounds.

As the Tramp Prince passed a popcorn vendor, there was a sudden burst of a white, fluffy foam of popcorn that almost exploded out of the top of the popper. The dark-haired woman behind the counter quickly jumped up and shut off the flows to the machine. But the white flow continued pouring out of the open top onto the counter and then the floor — until everything had a layer of several inches of popcorn on it.

"That idiot husban' mine!" The dark-haired woman almost screamed. "I tell him not overfill da machine — but he not listen!"

The Tramp Prince thought her accent sounded Hungarian or Roumanian.

"Boy!" she called out to the Tramp Prince." I pay you help me clean up t'is mess. You do it? Yes?"

"Sure," said the Tramp Prince, "I'll help you, but you don't have to pay me. Just give me some of that popcorn."

The first popcorn on the surface, the Tramp Prince scooped into bags and set off to one side. The rest he swept into other large bags which he then emptied into trash barrels. When he had finished, the dark-haired woman came over and put a few coins in his hand:

"Here," she said, "you work good! You need money... I can tell!"

The Tramp Prince dropped the coins in his pocket, thanked the woman and carried away the two huge bags of popcorn.

"Won't have to starve now," he told Road Toad. "This will last a couple of days.

"Well, don't save me any!" Road Toad replied. "That dry stuff has to be even worse than nuts!"

Someone had placed a couple of folding chairs behind one of the large tents, and the Tramp Prince decided that this would be a good place to sit and eat some of his popcorn. When he had been sitting there for a time, the back flap of the tent opened and there appeared in the opening, a barefoot man dressed only in a loincloth. His face was painted with streaks of green and blue greasepaint and his long hair stood out from his head in spikes that had been waxed into points

"Phew! It's *hot* inside there with all those lights turned on you!"

He walked over to where the Tramp Prince was sitting and sat down in the empty chair.

"Here, want some popcorn?" offered the Tramp Prince.

"Nagh – I'm not supposed to be seen eating anything but *raw* food," the man advised him. "I'm the 'Wild Man From Tasmania', see – so I gotta act the part. They tell the crowd that I've never had use of fire, so I eat everything raw — and I never wash and I can't talk; never heard language. My 'trainer' brings me in on a chain leash attached to this collar on my neck. I'm real wild, — jumpin' around and throwin' my arms out like this." And he raised his arms high, flailing the air and snarled with a throaty growl.

"My 'trainer' cracks a whip several times and I calm down, then he takes off my leash and I go to the edge of the waist high divider wall between me and the audience. I get curious about the people out there and I pretend to try to grab at 'em, then I growl and scream and my 'trainer' runs over and puts the leash back on my collar. I scare the hell out of the audience!"

The Tramp Prince laughed and laughed: "You're really pretty good; you've got *quite* an act!"

"You should come in and see it. Only costs twenty cents."

"Oh, I wish I could... but I don't have a lot more than that in my pocket. I'll have to settle for your description. But, you know, I thought that wild men were always supposed to be from Borneo."

"Well... Tasmania, Borneo... so what's the difference — a few thousand miles between friends?" And the Wild Man chuckled, then he continued. "Those suckers all believe I'm really a wild man when they see me grab a turnip or a pineapple or anything that's in the bowl of food they put there for me and then watch me bite a big chunk out of it. I've got pretty strong teeth."

"How about raw meat?" asked the Tramp Prince.

"I tried eatin' some once," said the Wild Man From Tasmania, "but it didn't taste very good — not to me, anyway. "Besides, everybody would know you can't just go up to a cow and bite a chunk out of it."

"Good point," the Tramp Prince laughed.

"You know something," said the Wild Man thoughtfully, "there must have actually been a time — somewhere way back in history when *everyone* was a 'wild man' — just eating raw stuff and looking a lot like I do. Makes you wonder what happened. Well, I gotta get back in there. This is all the break I get."

"Good luck!" offered the Tramp Prince. "Don't try to bite into too many raw coconuts!"

Road Toad gave a thought–laugh: "You can be pretty funny sometimes, yourself," he commented.

Dagger Don

Midafternoon customers were beginning to swell the carnival attendance as the Tramp Prince edged his way through the crowds of laughing children with their parents.

From behind another tent came and almost constant sound: whooshsschnk... whooshsschnk. It intrigued the Tramp Prince and he carefully stepped over some crisscrossing tie ropes through a narrow space between two tents in order to reach the source of the sounds.

A young man with long, shaggy black hair was throwing specially designed knives at a target board. The short, powerfully built fellow barely nodded his head as he maintained his concentration on hurling the daggers at the target. The dagger thrower had a red bandana tied around his forehead to hold his hair from falling in front of his eyes and the Tramp Prince remembered that in books, he had seen pictures of pirates who looked a lot like this knife throwing chap. The fellow's small, rather deep set eyes, together with his strong chin and hooked nose, gave him an appearance of a swarthy storybook character.

The man walked over to the target and retrieved several knives. He nodded again and gave the Tramp Prince a grim smile as he returned to the throwing position.

"I'm 'Dagger Don'," the young man asserted.

"They call me 'The Tramp Prince'! This is really fascinating — watching you pitch those knives. How on earth did you ever learn to do it?"

"Practice... just *lots* of practice. That's why I'm practicing now. You have to keep practicing in this business. My show doesn't start for another couple hours, but I want to be completely confident."

Whooshsschnk, Whooshsschnk, the two knives flashed, one immediately after the other. The first knife sliced through a narrow ribbon holding a small gas-filled balloon to the board, and the next knife punctured the balloon against the board before the small red gas bag had reached the top edge of the target board.

"Wow! That's amazing! Some *really* skillful throwing," exclaimed the Tramp Prince.

"Thanks – well, I guess that's enough practice for a while. So tell me, what is a tramp doing at a carnival?" asked The knife thrower.

"I was cutting through the park on my way out of town and ... here I am!"

"Well," replied Dagger Don, I don't travel with this carnival. I just take advantage of an opportunity like this when it comes along – – just to pick up a little extra money. Actually, I'm in my third year in the art school at the university here,"

"And the knives?"

"I just started throwing a couple of bowie knives at logs when I was a thirteen year old kid. Kept doing it. Finally progressed to these specially designed knives made for throwing. They have a certain balance of weight between the handle and the blade. Come on... let's get out of this human zoo for a few minutes."

The two young men walked out of the carnival area to a less open part of the park where the trees were close enough together that they formed almost a canopy. There they came upon a boy with a bb gun shooting at birds in a tree. Just as they came near the boy, he shot at a small song bird which fell to the ground mortally wounded.

Dagger Don went over to the boy, who appeared to be about thirteen years old, but who was nearly as tall as Don. Narrowing his eyes as he stood directly in front of the boy, Dagger Don spoke in an intimidating tone:

"What makes you think that you have the right to take that inoffensive little bird's life away from it?"

The boy shrugged his shoulders and smiled an embarrassed, silly smirk, looking aside.

"I'm just having fun," he replied. "Birds make great targets."

"How would you like it if there was some giant walking around, tall as a ten story building and he shot a cannon ball through *your* head? Think *that'd* be fun?"

"I dunno... maybe..." countered the boy in an effort to justify his outrageous behavior.

Dagger Don then grabbed the bb gun away from the boy, put his foot on it in the center and held the end of the stock and barrel with each hand. He pulled hard with the enormous strength of his powerful arms and handed the gun, with its now almost u-shaped barrel back to the already crying boy.

"When your father asks you what happened to your gun, be sure you tell him that some mean man took it away from you right after you killed a little bird with it. And this is what the gun looked like when he gave it back to you. Bet you'll never shoot another bird with this one!"

The boy ran off still crying, carrying the mutilated bb gun.

"My God... that irritates the hell out of me when I see something like that!" Dagger Don shook his head and spat on the ground. "See, I specialize in doing watercolors of birds. I'm hoping someday to do one of every species."

"I can understand why something like that boy's shooting the bird would really get to you." The Tramp Prince responded.

"But there's really a lot more to it than just that kid shooting a bird," continued Dagger Don. "Shooting bb guns teaches these kids to become the nimrods that dominate our world everywhere — destroying all the wildlife — killing off even the predators — just disrupting the entire balance of nature... even more than we humans have already done with our massive cutting off of the forests to make cropland. It provides a huge food supply for just a very limited number of wild species of animals. Eventually, the world is going to pay a terrible price for all this destructive imbalance. And having a few National Parks as wildlife preserves is simply not nearly enough."

"Well," the Tramp Prince told Dagger Don, "I haven't studied this anything like the way you have, but trying to live in some kind of ... some semblance of balance is part of why my family and I don't eat animals; we don't raise them and we don't hurt them... in spite of the fact that almost everyone else around seems to think killing and eating animals is a great thing to do."

They walked along in silence for another few minutes.

"I wish I weren't addicted to eating meat," said Dagger Don, "But it's the way I was raised."

"When you discover enough high quality plant foods," suggested the Tramp Prince, "Perhaps then you can learn to lose the taste for meat."

"Hope you're right ... but you know... if this country gets drawn into another one of those damn wars, I'll probably get drafted into the army, and then what choice would I have but to eat the slop they give you?"

"I know... I've wondered about that myself," the Tramp Prince mused. "And wars are so stupid. Started by stupid, egotistical, often tyrannical leaders – really they're *rulers* — and they haven't sense enough to employ diplomacy when there's dispute with one of their neighboring countries. Then the rulers drag – or I guess you'd have to say *force* all the rest of the average citizens into an armed conflict. Maybe there are actually some 'just' wars, but I, personally, can't imagine anything that justifies wanton killing and mutilating and the random cruelty and destruction of war."

The Tramp Prince continued: "I just don't know what I would do if we were to get into a widespread conflict where I'd be drafted. I mean... I wouldn't be afraid to fight to protect my family from physical harm, but from what I've been able to read and study on the subject, it seems to me that wars are usually fought to protect the wealth of the wealthy and the power of the powerful. And, of course the military-industrial complex *needs* war so that it can sell its guns and bombs and related products.

"At my age, I just know I'd be drafted; the military needs lots of able-bodied young guys like me for cannon-fodder. I'm not sure what I'd do."

Dagger Don stopped walking and looked thoughtfully into the distance:

"Henry David Thoreau once wrote something that I read on civil disobedience. I don't know if it would apply – or if I could do it. Conscientious objectors often receive prison terms. You could go to a different country – but what if *they* got dragged into the conflict?"

"Yes... well, war *is* insanity," the Tramp Prince stated emphatically, "and I think it might just be partially an extension of the mentality that people have that lets them kill the birds and animals they think we need for food."

"Ah..." Dagger Don emitted a long, dolorous sigh, "You and I can talk about this forever, but we aren't going to change a thing. Maybe no one ever will – until there aren't any more animals left to hunt and eat."

"Or maybe any humans left to eat them!" laughed the Tramp Prince, cynically.

"Hey, it's been great talking to you," Dagger Don told the Tramp Prince, "But I gotta go back to the carnival."

He smiled grimly again and shook the Tramp Prince's hand:

"Look me up at the art school if you ever get back this way."

As the Tramp Prince began walking again toward the edge of the park, Road Toad popped up from the jacket pocket:

"Boy, you sure can meet the odd balls! Not that I mind... but I do mind your grabbing my acid remarks. Why, I was just about to say the exact same thing about there not being any humans left to eat the animals!"

"Sorry!" laughed the Tramp Prince.

Chapter 22: The Golden Goblet

Walking toward the western side of the city, the Tramp Prince soon passed through a small Chinatown which was still somewhat near the waterfront area. The boy looked in amazement at the strangely shaped buildings and shops with their distinct, orientally decorated roofs and trim. He went past one shop which particularly caught his eye.

There was a multitude of strikingly beautiful oriental porcelains that stood in the window of the Chinese merchant's small shop and they scintillated with all the colors of the rainbow... and silver and gold glazes. Delicate patterns in geometric designs, scenes of the Chinese countryside and finely drawn, tiny portraits and figures of ancient Chinese men and women in costumes from the past... all swept through the Tramp Prince's imagination as he looked at the large vases and plates and other porcelain wares exhibited behind the front glass.

He was so intrigued by the dazzling display of merchandise, that without having enough money in his pocket to buy even one small piece, he felt compelled to walk into the shop.

A tinkling little brass bell sounded as he opened the door. Immediately, a smiling, elderly, inscrutable-looking Chinese man came forward from the rear of the store.

"Ah yes — you see something you like?" asked the Chinese man.

"*Everything* I've seen in here I like!" the Tramp Prince laughingly replied.

"You look all place here – see much more," the shop owner told him.

"It's all so beautiful!" said the Tramp Prince, looking around in amazement. "And," he added sadly, "I haven't any money to buy anything."

"Ah... you rilly poor boy, yes?" The Chinese merchant looked over the Tramp Prince's ragged clothing. "I give you something worth rilly much sometime; not now, but later."

The Tramp Prince, much confused by the Chinaman's statement, stood in rapt anticipation. The man reached down and slid open the door on a glass case with a glass countertop. Bringing forth a gold-colored goblet, he then took a glass container from a shelf behind the case, and after unscrewing the top, poured a cupful of water-clear liquid into the golden goblet.

"You drink this from magic golden Chinese goblet – you have great wisdom!" The Chinese man told him.

The Tramp Prince picked up the golden goblet and raised it to his lips. Frigid thoughts suddenly raced through his mind — of being drugged and shanghaied to work as a sailor on a ship going to some foreign port. He smelled the contents of the golden goblet carefully, but could detect no odor at all. Then he drank a few swallows — and finished the contents.

"Ah, now you are very wise boy," said the Chinese merchant.

The Tramp Prince smiled at the Chinese man and turned, walking out of the store, still quite confused.

"Road Toad... hey, Road Toad, do you think that man was just playing some kind of crazy game with me... or what?" I'm sure that liquid I drank was nothing but plain *water*!

"Yes," replied Road Toad, "and I can tell you with complete certainty that there was nothing special about that 'golden' goblet, either. I looked down from my lower position in your pocket and could see that where he put the goblet back into the case, there were several rows of them — all exactly alike."

"It probably wasn't even real gold!" The Tramp Prince observed cynically.

"Of course not!" Road Toad agreed. "I doubt if they were even gold plated - just polished brass."

The Tramp Prince laughed at his having been duped by the man's appearance of inscrutability.

"But why... what was he trying to say? I don't get it!"

"Well, I'm not sure I really know, either," Road Toad remarked, "unless he was trying to show you that wisdom does not always come from where you think it might — or in a time that you might expect it."

"The Tramp Prince stopped and looked at more of the strangely beautiful architecture in Chinatown. He shrugged and smiled slightly. "I guess I just don't get it. Wisdom can't come without both knowledge and experience — and I don't have much of either."

"But when you *do* have them," Road Toad reminded him, "Then you will have already drunk from the Chinaman's magic golden goblet of wisdom — and you will certainly be *very* wise."

"Oh, *absolutely!*" laughed the Tramp Prince, chuckling at his own gullibility.

Chapter 23: The Orphan

The road out of the city began to veer away from the coastline as the Tramp Prince walked westward. It was already midday before the slightly northern direction the road had taken, revealed an almost continuous series of low hills ahead. The costal plain had been left far behind, the Tramp Prince realized, and he wondered just what sort of terrain might lie ahead beyond the hills.

As he plodded along the rutted, partly graveled highway, occasional trucks and horse drawn wagons raised their signature dust clouds, that left a covering of micro-fine detritus on everything within a dozen feet of the road. There was no way to avoid the choking dust as it penetrated into the clothes and onto the skin of any road traveler.

As the Tramp Prince sat on his bindle sack taking a brief rest, a rather young boy appeared over the crest of the hill. The boy walked leisurely on past.

"Hello there!" The Tramp Prince called out to the boy.

"Hallo — yes?" answered the boy. "You are going same way?"

The boy, who appeared to be about thirteen years old, was dressed in only a pair of filthy, ragged pants and an equally dirty striped 'T' shirt. He carried no bindle or luggage case. His skin, where his neck come through the shirt, was caked with a black crust, the result of not having washed for many days. What, thought the

Tramp Prince, could have caused the boy not to avail himself of the many sources of water suitable for washing — at least that he had seen along the way.

"I'm just resting for a few minutes," the Tramp Prince told the boy," and when I start walking again, I'll be heading northwest — the same way you're going. We can walk together for a while, if you want to."

"Sure — for me is good."

As the two youngsters made their way along the increasingly trafficed road, The Tramp Prince began a friendly inquiry into the other boy's origin.

"I don't recognize your accent," he began. Could you be from Poland?"

"Ho, ho, no! I from Hungary. I talk few Polish word, but not Poland is my home." I talk German, French, yes? Walk all Europe countries. I learn!"

The Tramp Prince spoke slowly and clearly, so that the Hungarian boy would have time to grasp the meaning of each word.

"Then, how did you get here? And why?"

"When I fourteen, year ago, run away orphan home. Ladee there, mean ladee, she scream. Teach mathematic. If we not understand, she *very* mad! Throw on floor, chalk. Scream, Oh, really mad! Shake head, long red hair go in face. So mad, I not like it there. Bad food. No good! I start to walk. Get to France. Hide on sheip. *Beeg* sheip."

"An ocean liner?"

"Yes — yes, liner! Captain make me work. Cabin boy. I talk people. Learn to speak English. Pretty good, huh?"

"Yes." The Tramp Prince gave a laugh. "That is good, for such a short time."

"We come to beeg city. They want send me back. I jump off sheip. Walk, hitch hike. Now I meet you."

"You must have been traveling on land now for weeks; is that right?"

"Oh sure, yes. I go California. Be in movies, yes? I be beeg movie star! Can be actor, yes?"

The Tramp Prince looked very critically at the boy, his scrawny, stunted stature made him look to be two years younger than his age. He did not have handsome facial features and the dirt on his face accentuated his homeliness.

"What sorts of parts do you think you could play in movies?"

"Oh... I will be love-boy! You think, yes?"

"Well... I don't know... you look awfully young for that kind of role."

"Sure — I can be love-boy. Make love, ladees!"

The Tramp Prince sighed. Then he decided not to try to discourage the boy.

"I'll just let him find out reality for himself," he thought.

Road Toad caught the Tramp Prince's thought:

"He'll be in for a rude awakening!"

"But maybe he'll land some kind of bit part. The guy certainly has plenty of determination — you can't deny that!"

"Yes... who knows? Perhaps someday we'll see him playing a major role in some movie. Who are we to say he can't do it."

The two youths walked along together for most of the rest of the day. Leaving his young companion outside, the Tramp Prince went in a roadside cafe to wash off some of the road dirt. When he came back to where he had left the boy, he could see the fellow riding off in the back of a customer's motor car as it quickly moved away down the road.

The Tramp Prince sent a thought message to Road Toad:

"I would have liked to have wished him good luck in his travels through life. He's going to need it."

"Yes, indeed" replied Road Toad. "Yes, *indeed*!"

Chapter 24: Doctor Salvage

Another fork appeared in the road, and this time the Tramp Prince made no hesitation in choosing the road which veered off slightly toward the south — even though it did not appear to be the more well-traveled route. As he walked along, the road seemed to become rougher and narrower the further the boy traveled on it. Large stones pushed out in the middle, as though the road had once been a high-wheel wagon trail from a hundred years in the past.

"This *can't* be the main road any longer," the Tramp Prince called out to Road Toad. "It was a mistake to have taken this fork! I don't know if we should backtrack or keep on going straight ahead. What do you think?"

"Well..." thought back Road Toad, "I don't see much point in backtracking. That's just a waste of time and energy. Anyway, this road certainly leads to someplace; it might even widen and smooth out again somewhere ahead... if it doesn't and simply stops... you know that you don't *have* to walk a road; I mean that you could just walk over the land, whatever the terrain is like and eventually there'll be another road that you'll come to. There are roads everywhere. Just keep headed generally southwest."

The Tramp Prince kept hiking the narrow wagon track until it finally seemed to end in a flat clearing, a bit small to be called a field. He was now noticeably high in a group of wooded hills that swept for miles... as far as the eye could see. Down slightly from the end of the flat area, a rustic-looking clapboard farmhouse protruded from the brown ridge like a dead mushroom on the end of a log.

The boards of the house were weathered gray... and if any white paint had ever adorned the dismal sides, not one speck of it was still in evidence.

Before the Tramp Prince had traveled even half way across the length of the clearing, he could hear the slamming of a door. Soon there appeared a tall man with flowing white hair and a white, trimmed goatee. His ancient black suit jacket and string tie contrasted sharply with his faded denim overalls that seemed to try to hide beneath the coat.

The two met near the farmhouse:

"Hello, hello! They call me Doctor Salvage — I'm not really a doctor, don't you know — but they call me that because I try to resuscitate sick soils."

"They call me the Tramp Prince," the young tramp told Doctor Salvage "that's because I'm a tramp."

"Ha!" laughed Doctor Salvage. "Well, welcome to the University! How did you find out about it? Did someone tell you about it?"

After looking all around and seeing nothing that could pass for a university building — or even a campus, the Tramp Prince remained silent — not wishing to be viewed as perverse or ignorant in case there actually were buildings hidden well back in the timber.

"Did you perhaps, just walk back in here?" Doctor Salvage smiled with a warmth that could surely have melted the ice of any awkward introduction.

"I was just walking along a well-traveled road and it slowly narrowed and turned into... this!" And the Tramp Prince gestured in the direction of the clearing.

"Ah, perhaps I should explain all of this to you better. The University was established here by my grandfather in seventeen eighty-five as a land-grant college. You see, the buildings all caught fire and burned down about eighty years ago when I was still a rather young man. I had just completed my master's degree in agronomy and was about to begin work on a PHD. I was only twenty-four at the time of the fire and thus had no money to continue my education at another school. My family could not help me, they having lost everything and so I had to give up on obtaining my doctorate. But now... it doesn't really matter."

The Tramp Prince did some quick mental calculation.

"You're a hundred and four?"

"Well, yes — more or less. I think so. You see, by the time you get into your nineties, it becomes rather easy to lose track, don't you know?"

The Tramp Prince could scarcely begin to believe the fantastic story he was being told. The tall man who stood before him had the face and skin of someone still in his sixties; and he stood with the erect posture of a youngster of his own age.

"I'm totally amazed and confused." The Tramp Prince responded.

"Yes, I can understand that."

Doctor Salvage then looked out at the sky with sadness showing in his eyes.

"I hardly ever have anyone come to the University any more to study. My family was forced to place all of the instructors on administrative leave. I don't suppose that even one of them is still alive today. I hope none of them waited thinking we would be able to hire them back right away."

Walking a few paces into the clearing, Doctor Salvage pointed down.

"Here... you see? This is where the stone steps to the largest building were. They're almost covered with wind-blown dirt now.

"Many of my family members were instructors at the university and resided in one of the buildings which burned." Doctor Salvage continued: "Others of the family lived in the old house which I still occupy. Of course, it was much larger then than it is now. There were additions, which, after the University staff was gone from there, I never used, and which deteriorated and finally fell to the ground."

"What an unbelievable story!" the Tramp Prince exclaimed with sincere amazement. "So, what is it you were teaching — that is, the last time you had a student to teach?"

"Agricultural and nutritional philosophy through mineralized soil techniques... and practical garden management. I still raise a minimum mineral standard garden and keep a large herd of goats for manure. The goats, of course have to be fenced out of the garden areas, don't you know?"

Then he gestured toward a herd of goats nibbling away in the distance.

"Local people often call me 'The Goat Man' and they refer to this place as: Billy Goat Hill'."

"But I don't much care. At my age, I no longer care what anyone thinks of me. I've learned that you can't force enlightenment on the world. It will come about... but in its own good time. And if someone seeks out my knowledge, then its worth giving it... but only then."

The wind began slamming the old screen door on the house — so viciously that it could easily be heard above the baahing of the goat herd, which had moved much closer.

"Soon it will be even more windy and cold up here on Billy Goat Hill." Doctor Salvage told the Tramp Prince. "It's late in the day, and if you would like to spend the night here you're welcome to, don't you know? During the colder months, I live only in the kitchen. It's easier to heat just one room. That's where my bed is, but there's a couch you can sleep on in the living room and we can leave the door open into there so that you get a little heat."

The Tramp Prince followed the elderly man to the ramshackle house. There, Doctor Salvage took an old wooden frame bucksaw hanging on the porch and went to an x frame which held several small logs. He deftly cut through the stack and carried back an armload of stove wood while the Tramp Prince returned the saw to the nail on the porch wall.

"I enjoy cutting wood and splitting logs in the winter," the old man said. "It gives me something to keep me occupied – and a little exercise. It's lonely here now that my wife is gone. She passed away a few years ago. She was still a youngster — only ninety-seven. It's a shame. But she got so that she couldn't take the winters here; the house has fallen apart so badly — and as you'll see, it *is* drafty.

"My wife moved into town with our daughter and the food there wasn't the quality of what we ate here from our mineralized garden. She didn't last long there. She became ill a few weeks after leaving here and never recovered."

The old man sat down in a battered wooden chair and bent over with his elbows on his legs and his hands under his chin in deep thought.

"I think that the doctors may have tried to give her some kind of new vaccine against the flu. Oh... I guess I'm not really certain. The doctors said no... but one knows how they are; they tell you only what they want you to know."

"But you really aren't sure?"

"No, it's just what I suspect. You see, I wasn't there, so I'm merely guessing from her symptoms."

"But sir,.. what would have been wrong with the vaccine, *if* what you suspect *were*, in fact, true?"

The old doctor of sick soils looked up with deep sadness in his eyes:

"Ah, it's just this: you see, vaccines and serums are prepared from dried sterilized filth, don't you know?"

"Filth?"

"Yes... that is the whole theory of immunization. They take dried pus or infected tissue serum and deactivate it. Then they inject or incise a fairly large amount of the material into someone's body. Immediately, the person's systems of natural defense go to work, building up large amounts of antibodies in the blood, just as if they had been exposed to the actual live microorganisms of the disease."

"So what's wrong with this? So far, it sounds like it's the body mimicking the same process that would happen naturally if one were to become exposed to some pathogens just floating around out there in the air."

"Yes, however, it's the *quantity* of the foreign protein substance that is injected or incised. A tiny amount, your body is well-equipped to handle. But not such large quantities. At least not for some persons who react violently — allergically to such foreign protein substances. Some extremely sensitive individuals may have the equivalent of an almost anaphylactic shock and actually die from it. In any event, it is a poor excuse for not having a healthy body to start with, which has sufficient strength to handle the tiny quantities of pathological microorganisms that one might encounter."

"Our bodies create antibodies every day to all sorts of pathogens and we do not get the disease — if, that is, we have had an adequate diet and have not been physically weakened by lack of rest, or exercise, or fresh air, or sunshine, or pure water... or some intense psychological trauma –- or by exposure to toxic chemicals."

"But sir, it seems to me that almost *everyone* has been weakened in one way or another."

"Oh yes, young mister Tramp Prince... you are correct. That is precisely why the doctors look to these immunology panaceas. They may save some who could get sick and perhaps die, but many, many others may be made ill by the very vaccine designed to protect them from illness. In fact, it is well known that many have died from the vaccines."

"The entire concept of immunology is fundamentally flawed, don't you see? It's the idea of forcing the body to do what it should be naturally doing every day of our lives when we encounter microorganisms in the air or in our food. You simply can't get away from microbes. They're everywhere –- by the billions, floating around on every speck of dust. We inhale them; we eat them; we get them into cuts. But our bodies' self-defense systems are able to handle those tiny quantities. That is to say *if* we have healthy bodies!

"There is another factor as well, which further complicates the picture. That is the transmutation of some microorganisms. Some of these microbes have the amazing ability to transmute from one form into another, depending upon the environment in which they find themselves. Simply put, they change form to suit the conditions of any particular body in which they find themselves; or their location within that body. So, you see, immunology is not a logical, reasonable approach to good health."

"Yes, I guess I understand now the logic of what you're saying, sir, but would you ever *really* expect most people to live sensible, healthful lifestyles?"

The old doctor of sick soils thoughtfully stroked his goatee.

"No,… I suppose not. At least, I probably wouldn't expect them to as long as their access to education as children and to their influences as adults continues to come from the vested interests of the processed food and the drug industries. This the sad state of the human world."

The old doctor of sick soils sat back in his ancient creaking wooden chair. He closed his eyes and withdrew from further conversation and the Tramp Prince sat in deep contemplation.

When the logs that had been added to the wood stove in the kitchen had burned down, Doctor Salvage got up and slipped another two small logs into the stove, as well as some to the old fashioned cooking range, which he kept fired up as well. The wood cracked and popped as it caught and the glow of the warmth soon filled the room. A large pot of vegetable soup sat on the kitchen range off to the side, where it slowly simmered.

"You might like some of this vegetable soup," Doctor Salvage offered. "It's made from some of the mineralized vegetables I raised here last summer. Some had to be canned, of course, but it's quite good, don't you know?"

Doctor Salvage pushed a small throw rug up against the bottom edge of the kitchen door and then dragged a pair of battered wooden chairs close to the wood stove. He ladled out two large bowls of vegetable soup and handed one to the Tramp Prince. They sat down — and the good doctor put his boots up on the stove's foot rail.

"Keeps your feet warm, don't you know?" was Doctor Salvage's comment. And the Tramp Prince did likewise.

"Ugh! The Tramp Prince exclaimed, "It's too cold! This weather makes me wish I were living in the tropics."

"If you were in the tropics, you'd be warm, alright, but so would all the billions of mosquitoes, flies, roaches and ants — all gnawing away at you and your food supply. Every place has its problems. Some are just worse than others."

"But surely, the human animal originated in the warmer regions — otherwise we'd grow fur like a dog or a cat."

"You're very perceptive, my young friend... but because of the nature of who we are, and where we are at the time of our birth, we may not ever be able to have or do everything we'd like, or to live where we think we ought to.

"Fate does not always give us everything that we need. We may be smart, but poor; we may be talented, but be of a race that is plagued by intolerance. Or we may be burdened early in life by family commitments. Life is not perfect."

"Well, then... just what is the purpose of life? What really matters?"

Doctor Salvage smiled and looked at the Tramp Prince as he shook his head: "I can't tell you that."

The Tramp Prince squinted as he returned his elderly host's gaze. "Do you mean... that you don't know?"

"I didn't say that." Doctor Salvage merely continued eating his soup.

"Then, you *won't* tell me." The Tramp Prince could see that his question had reached a snag.

"In time," said Doctor Salvage, "you will come to know the answer to your question on your own. No one will have to tell you."

"I guess I just want answers now." The Tramp Prince explained.

"Everyone wants everything *now*. Immediate gratification — like little children. Perhaps, because they've never really grown up. Patience is one of the greatest virtues, don't you see... you need it to obtain wisdom."

"I guess because I'm still young, I have a right to be impatient."

"Ha, ha, ha!" laughed the old soup eating doctor of sick soils, "you have a *need*, not a *right!*"

For several minutes, silence ensued as the doctor and his guest finished their food.

"There is one very important subject about which I'll tell you anything you wish to know." The old man told the Tramp Prince.

"What subject?"

"Ah... it is soil mineralization. The Bible, tells us that 'from dust thou were made, and to dust thou shalt return... but the dust from which most peoples' bodies are made does not have the full range of minerals that are necessary for good health and long life — thus, they return to dust prematurely. And this is part of the reason we grovel in ignorant dismay and huddle in wretched slums in fear of the next onslaught of nature or some human predator."

"These minerals you're talking about — they don't occur naturally?"

"Oh yes, they are or were in many soils — until we mined them out by our destructive farming practices. Largely, it amounts to the fact that we don't return to the soil what we remove from it."

"That," replied the Tramp Prince, "sounds like such a completely logical and reasonable concept that everybody should know it already."

"Ignorance is consummately pervasive," said Doctor Salvage. "And those in power, if they know the truth themselves, will never permit it to get out to the public. An uneducated mass is much more easily controlled and exploited!"

"It makes this a very difficult world to live in," the Tramp Prince commented.

"And if the powers that be don't change their repressive ways," Doctor Salvage continued, "the world may become a very difficult place in which we all may be forced to die."

The old gentleman walked over to a heavy oak bookcase with glass drop-doors. He pulled out a copy of Victor Hugo's 'Les Miserables. "Here, read the chapter 'The Earth Impoverished By the Sea'. The message of that chapter transcends Jean Valjean's adventures. It stood as a clear warning to the deaf ears and blind eyes of an indifferent world. I think that everyone skips that chapter, or if they read it, have no idea of the meaning."

Then the doctor pulled out several other small volumes, among them Hensel's 'Bread From Stone'. "When you've finished that chapter, then read these."

The Tramp Prince read through all of the materials that Doctor Salvage placed before him. The old man then pulled up a chair next to where the Tramp Prince sat and opened up a black case jammed with various technical papers, letters and analysis sheets.

"This is my work — The soil analyses, the recommendations and the crop results and analyses. It would take you all night to read through and digest everything in here. Perhaps you can start on it tomorrow morning. But first, I'll explain very quickly how the salvage system of soil mineralization works.

"You see, we use four different rock types, each containing major elements and a complement of minor and trace elements. As you can see from the analyses sheets, there is what we call 'black rock', a shale containing lots of iron and sulphur, plus the greatest list of trace elements of the four. Then there is a form of limestone I call 'cave rock' with fossil trilobites visible. That contains not just the necessary calcium and magnesium, but a long list of other elements on the printed sheet. Completing the rocks are what I call 'potash marl', a greenish clay, its main element potassium and with another long list of minor and trace elements, and finally, rock phosphate with its own minor and trace elements. And that finishes out all of the necessary minerals.

"First we analyze the farmer's soil and then blend the ground-up rocks to try to provide the soil's missing or low elements. The analytical averages are based on chemical analyses of both crop plants and of thousands of human remains. That way we give the plants the correct minerals they need to not only produce their own good growth, but also to provide all the minerals needed for optimum human health.

"When we have finished mixing the powdered and granulated rocks, we then compost them with aerobic and anaerobic bacteria by adding plant residues and pond scrapings — so that as the bacteria consume the organic matter, the carbonic acid which they produce breaks down the minerals into soluble organic forms that mycorrhiza soil bacteria can turn into plant food."

"There is a technicality beyond this which I'll try to explain: Each of us has differences in our hereditary makeup, don't you know — as well as possible differences in the soils that provided the foods our mothers ate as our bodies were being formed. These differences may have created mineral preponderances in us that demand being satisfied for us to achieve optimal health. For this reason, I recommend composting each of the rocks separately and using only a single mineral rock type in small plots next to each other in the garden.

" Then the rows are planted straight through all of the plots so that each row of vegetable variety will have been raised on all four of the rock types. After that one uses his own taste buds to determine which type is best for him. Then that rock compost should predominate in the soil for that person's particular garden. Now — is that clear?"

"Frankly...no." The Tramp Prince responded.

"Well then, think about it for a while, Doctor Salvage told the boy. "It will be a long time before you're ready to begin a program of soil mineralization for yourself, anyway. Until then, just be sure to eat plenty of as many varieties of seaweed as you can get."

"Seaweed?"

"Yes, certainly — seaweed! Sea water has the full range of soluble minerals that have been leached out of the land, and though sodium chloride is nine tenths of the mineral content of sea water, the plants that grow in it pick what they need from those minerals available to them and form those minerals into their tissues. Sodium and chlorine are only a tiny part of what they take."

"So where do I get seaweed?" asked the Tramp Prince.

"Go to the sea shore — or buy it from Oriental merchants. The peoples of the orient use many varieties of seaweeds — kelps, lavers and the like. Go to Nova Scotia in the early summer and harvest Dulse off the rocks along the shore. You can dry enough to last you for a year, don't you know?"

The Tramp Prince sat in a fog of bewilderment.

Doctor Salvage returned his attention to the case with its papers:

"I know you are not going to grasp all of this in one sitting, but just take your time looking through the printed materials and ask me questions whenever you need to."

The Tramp Prince was by now, truly overwhelmed by the volume of instructive information that Doctor Salvage had provided him, but he began immediately making notes on his pad of paper. After a few more minutes, he because too drowsy to continue and turned the wick on the oil lantern down until it extinguished the flame. Then he curled up in his blanket roll on the couch.

The next morning, Doctor Salvage had arisen early and gone to his root cellar that was dug into the hillside below the house. When the Tramp Prince awoke and entered the kitchen, he was greeted by a large bowl on the kitchen table filled with strange looking, aromatic apples. Next to the large bowl was another slightly smaller one with two varieties of cabbage and some root vegetables. Between the two bowls sat a small wheel of goat cheese.

"When you get hungry," Doctor Salvage told the Tramp Prince, "Just take whatever you want. I have plenty more in my two root cellars. Of course, you know you can't keep apples with cabbage...or they'll taste like cabbage!"

"That's interesting," the boy replied, "we use a root cellar at my home also."

"Well, there's nothing unusual about a family having that kind of food storage, Doctor Salvage interjected, "Every family had one before so many moved to the cities to work in the factories. The human world is rapidly losing touch with its natural roots — which are connected so firmly to the soil."

When Doctor Salvage left the kitchen to bring in more fire wood, the Tramp Prince reached into his pocket and touched the cold skin of Road Toad. The little fellow was in a state of deep hibernation.

"No point in trying to awaken him now," thought the boy as he watched his breath condense in clouds of steam only two feet away from the wood stove.

Since the Tramp Prince was hungrier for knowledge than for physical food, he immediately began looking again at the file of papers that he had started on the night before. Doctor Salvage returned and dropped a pile of small logs on the floor. He looked over at the boy and smiled:

"What I would suggest," he told the boy, "is that when you find something of interest to you, that you look behind the paper to see if there might be a carbon copy of it. You may take any of those copies that you find. Until a few years ago, I had a secretary who would ride out here in a donkey cart, bringing her typewriter once or twice a month. She organized my files and did all my typing for me — and she always made two or three carbon copies of everything she typed. That, of course, was when there was a much more active interest in my mineralization work by the farmers around here, don't you know? Over the years, some of the carbon copies have been taken out, but many remain. If you take those copies, then you'll have just a minimum of material that you will have to hand copy."

"Yes," replied the young tramp, "that will certainly speed things up."

"Ah, I do miss having a secretary," Doctor Salvage reminisced. "I'm not able to type myself, so I have to hand-write everything now. What a shame my secretary had to die so young; she was only eighty-eight, don't you know?"

As the Tramp Prince sat looking through the piles of papers, Doctor Salvage raised one finger and cocked his eyebrows with a half-smile:

"You haven't seen my laboratory yet have you, young tramp?"

"No, I guess not. I didn't realize that you even had one."

"Oh yes, oh, yes... come along and I'll show it to you ."

The boy then followed Doctor Salvage to the far end of the room, where the old fellow opened a door leading to a narrow staircase to the second floor. Expecting to see a traditionally pictured, brightly lit room filled with glass vials and twisted coils of glass tubes dripping strange liquids into an endless array of more glass coils and beakers, he was shocked to see only a small group of enamel trays on the floor with what appeared to be green stalks of grass growing from them.

"These are my latest experiments!" said Doctor Salvage. "I'm trying out a new type of rock that someone sent me from a place in Mexico — a place whose name I can't quite pronounce. But my laboratory mice are going to show me how the rock compares to the rocks I have been in the habit of using for all these years, don't you know?"

"Where do you keep the mice?" asked the Tramp Prince, not seeing any cages anywhere in the dim light coming from the two end windows of the unfinished attic room.

"Why... I don't *keep* them at all!" the soil doctor laughed. "They keep themselves... wherever it is that they want to live, don't you know?"

"But... but... how can *that* be a lab? I mean — so what do the mice test?... or I guess what I'm trying to say, is: How do they test it?"

"Well, you see, my friend, first I place different types of composted powdered rock into these trays that you see on the floor. Then I put wheat seeds over the rock and water them down, then cover the trays to hold in the moisture. I wait for the seed to sprout. When the wheat grass has grown to a height of about two inches, I change the dark covers to glass and allow the light to turn the sprouts green. Then I allow the mice to have access to the experimental trays. Whichever grass they prefer to eat the most of, tells me how well that particular type of rock will sustain life. You see, the seed sprouts will pick up whatever soluble minerals are available from the rocks."

The Tramp Prince laughed: "that's not exactly what I had expected to see as a laboratory experiment. But I'm very glad to know that there's no animal cruelty inflicted on the mice — as one would usually expect to see in conventional laboratory experiments."

"Ah well," Doctor Salvage replied. "It's not necessary to have animal cruelty in an experiment. All you have to do is design the experiment in the proper way, don't you know?"

"Then, why can't regular labs avoid all their animal cruelty?" asked the boy.

"Um... I don't know," Doctor Salvage replied thoughtfully. "Perhaps they're not testing for the right things perhaps – not at the right time... or... perhaps the experimenters are not actually a great deal more intelligent than their laboratory animals." And he smiled affably.

When he had spent fully three days thoroughly reading books in the case and looking through the hundreds of papers in Doctor Salvage's file, the Tramp Prince reluctantly bade the old 'Goat Man' farewell.

"I could stay here studying this work for weeks," he told Doctor Salvage, "but I simply must return to my family very soon. Hopefully, I'll be able to come back sometime and continue where I've left off — when I have more time to spend; until then, I can't thank you enough for your hospitality and the access to your great knowledge and wisdom."

"Ah, you are most welcome," said Doctor Salvage, "and when you return, we can begin to explore the theories of cosmogony and the globular theory."

He shook the Tramp Prince's hand:

"I would be most grateful if you *could* return and continue studying this work. You see", he said rather sadly, "I haven't anyone to continue my work when I'm gone. Of course," Doctor Salvage added in a happier tone, "that shouldn't be for another thirty-five years, don't you know? That is, if I live the normal lifespan for a human being — about a hundred and forty years."

The Tramp Prince smiled and chuckled at the amazing person grasping his hand. Then in a wistful, somber tone he spoke once more:

"I'm so sorry that your wife and secretary will no longer be able to be with you in the next thirty-five years."

"Yes," said Doctor Salvage, "and the sad thing is that they possibly *could* have been, had the allopathic physicians not gotten hold of them. You see, I believe they fell victim to the toxic drugs of the allopaths and that's against the very nature of our body's own system of health. Our bodies are self-regulating and self-rebuilding so long as we haven't taken our debilitating lifestyles to the point of no return.

"We can rebuild our systems only with correct nutrients and rest. The toxic drugs of the allopathic physicians rebuild nothing — except the deep and unfilled pockets of the doctors and the drug companies. Drugs are an added burden for an already overburdened, toxic body to have to handle. A drug never cures anything. The most it can do is to cover up the symptoms of our illness and its own side-effects. When the drug is gone from the body, the symptom returns -- if you stay alive that long. Drugging is not curing. Well... be warned... and go in peace, and in good health — and good luck.

As he walked out onto the battered porch, the Tramp Prince asked Doctor Salvage whether the trail continued on beyond his 'university'.

"Yes, it did, at one time," the ancient fellow replied. "But I haven't traveled it in years. There is probably nothing left now, but an overgrown foot path. But you can probably follow it if there are still any remains of the old rail fences left. Many farms had stone fences all around them and those would still be visible no matter how dense the woods have become."

With that, the Tramp Prince again grasped his elderly friend's hand and looked directly into his sparkling blue eyes.

"One can never tell what is in store for us around any bend in the road of Life," the old man mused. "If for some reason, we fail to meet again, my wish for you is for a long and productive and meaningful life, my young friend."

"Goodbye..." said the Tramp Prince with more than a touch of sadness.

Dense forest trees covered the hillside below the old university. There was no sign of a foot trail or even a field fence when the Tramp Prince reached the narrow, wooded valley below. He followed the small creek for what seemed like miles over some of the roughest, rockiest ground he had ever encountered.

Finally, as the day wore on and the temperature began to rise somewhat, Road Toad awakened.

"My goodness — where *are* we?" he thought out.

"I guess I don't really know, myself." The Tramp Prince answered. "All I do know is that we've left Doctor Salvage's 'university' and we're walking in a southerly direction over some of the worst land I've yet seen."

Chapter 25 The Native Man

As the Tramp Prince moved ever farther away from Doctor Salvage's 'university' it seemed that the more he walked, the rougher and steeper the land became. Hills turned into low mountains; the terrain was so rocky that the trees had very little soil in which to grow. They were scrawny and low, twisted and gnarled by the incessant wind. Plants clung into crevices where pockets of soil had accumulated. An occasional rabbit or squirrel scampered away as the boy passed.

Traversing the narrow foot trail, the Tramp Prince could see, a short distance up the side of one of the hills, a small clearing with a crude building constructed on it. He climbed the path to the clearing, and as he reached the top, he was greeted by a man dressed in a buckskin jacket and pants.

"Ho!... Who are you? You... who travel into... this godforsaken... all-but-forgotten... crevice of the earth?"

"I am called the Tramp Prince," he replied, somewhat dubious of the intent of the Native Man's fierce countenance.

"Welcome... to my...village," said the Native Man , who spoke in often halting, disconnected words, making his sentences difficult to follow.

"You... must pardon... the way... I speak. Sometimes... I almost forget how to talk. Months... years go by... and I speak... to no one."

"So you live here alone?" asked the Tramp Prince.

"Yes," said the Native Man. "All the rest... of my family... this part of my tribe ... now is gone... died or moved to the cities of... you European invaders."

There was a great deal of bitterness in the words of the Native Man, the Tramp Prince thought, and he was unsure of what he should say next.

"I cannot adequately apologize for what my ancestors did to your ancestors," said the Tramp Prince with a wistful expression.

"Do not try... it would do no good... anyway. Europeans have been... the scourge of the earth! Everywhere... they have gone in this world... they have enslaved the native peoples... stolen their lands... and pillaged and destroyed the resources. When I was... a child, the descendants... of the European authorities... Took all of us children away...to be educated in the white man's schools. Perhaps this was because... they had some genuine remorse... after two centuries... of constantly pushing... my people further... and further... into the worst land imaginable. They said... they wanted us... to integrate... into their culture. Some of the children did. But a few... like myself refused. We would not allow... our culture... to be denigrated and destroyed.

"But now... there is very little left for us. Even now... the cultural destruction continues. I have learned the Europeans' language well... but I have never learned... Their greedy ways of destruction... to natural beauty and to the human spirit... and to the animals of the forest."

"It worries me very much," responded the Tramp Prince, "that someday all of the cruelty and destruction perpetrated by my people may come back upon them in unforeseen ways — some kind of global catastrophic retribution. Even if it is long after I am gone from this planet, it still worries me. I can only hope, that I never develop the insensitivity of so many of the Europeans and their descendants.

"You may find this hard to understand," the Tramp Prince continued, but if I owned a piece of property, I would try to give it back to the Native people from whom my ancestors took it — whether by outright theft, or by deceit."

"You... are not like most... of the people... of your race... so be advised... they may well revile... and punish you... as a nonconformist."

"Yes, I can see that," the Tramp Prince responded with sadness. "But now, I must be on my way. Before I go,...I'm wondering what you think really matters?" the Tramp Prince asked his usual question with some hesitation.

The Native Man did not answer quickly. He thought for several minutes, until the Tramp Prince was afraid that he did not intend to answer at all. "What matters most...is that the white man... must come to realize ... how he has injured the *Native* peoples; how he has destroyed... and stolen the land... that sustained my people... for thousands of years... since my ancestors... first came to this land. What maters ... is... that the white men ...make amends for their cruelty and destruction... and stop continuing to carry on those practices. But I know... it will not happen in my lifetime. Perhaps... not even in many lifetimes. I am confident, though ... someday it will happen... someday the Native human beings... men and women of darker color... will be compensated ...for at least some of the outrages against the Native nations."

The Tramp Prince bowed his head slightly and tipped his cap, not knowing how else to show his respect to the Native Man.

"I give you... this thought to remember," The Native Man responded, "wherever you go, take the spirit of life... and plant it over the dismay of death and destruction...For only then... will you achieve real meaning... to your life."

The Native Man stood there, erect and unmoving — without a change of emotion showing on his stoic features.

Chapter 26: The Lady Who Loved Animals

For many hours, The Tramp Prince hiked over hill and vale —
across rocky rivulets and alongside massive forested hills, until at
last, the path suddenly opened upon a steep, narrow hollow with a
fence that went all around the central area of the valley bottom and
halfway up the hillside.

Inside the fence, there were animals of every size, shape and
description — milling about: grunting, mooing, braying, whinnying,
barking, meowing and baaing. It was a cacophony of sound and a
comedy of sight.

The fence was so tall that the Tramp Prince could not cross it and
he followed it until he found himself in the front of the property
where it faced a road. Above a large gate was a sign which read:
'White Elephant Animal Sanctuary'. He looked around inside the
compound, but could not see even one ordinary elephant, let alone a
white variety. A woman was near the gate as she threw hay to a
horse inside its own small fenced division. The woman noticed the
Tramp Prince looking in.

"High thayah, y'all. C'mon in ef y'all want," she drawled.

There was a small entrance gate at the end of the main gate; the
Tramp Prince lifted the latch and walked in.

"Well ah declah! exclaimed The Lady Who Loved Animals.
"Y'all look so young an' strong... y'all must be a Godsend!"

The Tramp Prince looked around himself to make certain that
someone else hadn't followed him in. The Lady Who Loved
Animals laughed. "That's just the way mah folks talks whah ah was
raised." She laughed again. "But what ah meant," she went on in a
more serious vein, "is that since mah workeh nevah showed up
today, maybe y'all could he'p me — an ah'll pay y'all."

The Tramp Prince was out of money and so he gladly accepted
the offer of employment.

He followed The Lady Who Loved Animals around as she instructed him what to feed to which animal and how to clean out their straw bedding.

"I guess I really don't understand something," The Tramp Prince finally said to the Lady Who Loved Animals. "I don't see why you have so *many* animals here. Why would anyone need an animal sanctuary like this?"

"Well Ah declah! Y'all must surely not have been livin' out in the world very much; wheah y'all from, anyhow?"

The Tramp Prince explained his circumstances.

"The reason ah hayuve so many animals is just 'cause people breed these pooah thangs an' then cain't take cayuh of them, or don't want them — so Ah just feel like Ah hayave to give them a home. Otheahwise, people would jest shoot them or ship them off to be killed at some slaughterhouse. Ah just couldn't staund t' see thayut."

"Well, why do people even *breed* them?" asked the Tramp Prince.

"Cause they hayeven't learned yet to do without eatin' thayah fellow creatures," she replied sadly. "Animals hayuv rights too, y'know, but most folks don't b'lieve it."

"I know... I know what you mean," said the Tramp Prince. "We don't raise animals at my home, and I know our lives are much simpler and our health is better for it."

"The worst thang," continued The Lady Who Loved Animals, "is thayt all the forests in the world are bein' cut down t' make fields t' grow food for animals t' eat. Then folks eat the animals. Thayt's a awful inefficient way t' get our protein. Ef we would just eat the plants ourselfs, we could hayve protein betteh suited to our own bodies an' get it from one tenth the acreage!"

"Ah yes," replied the Tramp Prince, "the world has become a sad place, indeed."

"Well, y'all are an unusual young man! Seems like most men jest scoff at what Ah'm, doin' heah. Ah think women are a little more sympathetic... d'yall think?"

The Tramp Prince agreed.

"Y'all know sympthin'," reflected the Lady Who Loved Animals," it's the men in this world who've made such a mess of things. And mean... 'now look how they'eh always fightin' wars an' destroyin' eventhin' they touch. Why, the men has kept us women at best as second class citizens... an' at <u>wuhst</u> as vertual *slaves*! One of these days, women all ovah the world gonna get the right t'vote, an we gonna vote *women* into office!

"Ah do b'lieve this world gon' be run someday by us women. An it'll be a bettah place, too! Not that some women can't be as stupid an' cruel as men, but theyah, jus' not as many women like that... Ah mean, we women gotta beah an' raise the child'en. Wasn't for us — wouldn't be a human race. We women gotta be the mothes an' teachehs of those child'ren. Wereh the ones who nurcher an' instruct. Ha! Maybe we didn't do too good a job teachin' ouah sons. Ah don't know...

"Anyway, theyah were matriarchys in the past an theyah gonna be a worldwide matriarchy someday in the future — might even be in this century. Mark mah words!"

At midday, The Tramp Prince sat down on a bale of hay to rest. He began contemplating — Looking off in the distance with a vacant expression to his stare. The Lady Who Loved Animals walked over to him:

"What y'all thinkin about, honeychile?"

"A place I've never been to, but wish I could go to."

"Ah bet its Japan or India or China, huh?"

"No," laughed the Tramp Prince, "nothing like that... though maybe it's even more exotic than any of those places... in its own way".

"Well, where is this?" asked The Lady Who Loved Animals.

"A place called... 'Pfantassiland'." The Tramp Prince seemed embarrassed to even say the word. Almost everyone he had told about the place had never heard of it.

"Why ah go theyah most eveh night! Ah jus' fall asleep an... pow! Ah'm in Pfantassiland; then, in the mornin' when ah wake up... here ah am back with mah animals."

"Someone else told me that once — that you can go there when you fall asleep", said The Tramp Prince sadly, "but I've tried and tried for months and I can't do it. I guess I never will be able to."

The Lady Who Loved Animals patted the Tramp Prince on the head:

"Oh, honeychile, ah think y'all *will* find a way t' get theyah someday; but maybe it won't be the way y'all expect."

All the rest of the day, the Tramp Prince helped the Lady Who Loved Animals. When evening arrived, he bedded down in the barn on some straw bales. He took Road Toad out of his pocket and let the little fellow jump about catching bugs of all sorts that wiggled and crawled around on the barn floor.

The next morning he could hear that the regular worker had returned. The Lady Who Loved Animals was talking to him:

"Oh senorita," began the worker, "'*Lo siento*! I try to do mucho better — be here now on."

The Tramp Prince went up to The Lady Who Loved Animals:

"I hope that your worker becomes more reliable... because you understand that I cannot stay any longer," he told her.

"Yes... Ah know... so heah is youah pay. And please... hep the animals wheaheveh you can. Goodbye... and good luck, y'all."

Chapter 27: The Tall Man Who Lived In A Tall Tower

As the Tramp Prince left the animal sanctuary, the narrow hollow in which it was located widened into a broad fertile plain. The slender creek became a small river and warmer breezes drifted across the more open landscape. At one point the stream emptied into an even larger river, which the Tramp Prince would not be able to cross. He was then forced to change direction and follow the river bank to where there might be a bridge.

Miles and miles he walked, until late in the day, he came to a small town, built along the river's edge. Just before entering the town, the boy saw what had once been a large farm with fields that lay along the edge of the river. The foundation of the farmhouse was all that remained where it had been built too close to the flood plain. A large ramshackle barn still stood a little higher up on the sloping ground, and nearby was a towering four story round residence that had once been the barn's silo. It had windows in all four of the single, round, twelve foot diameter rooms that comprised each level. A tall, thin man was just walking out of the door when the Tramp Prince passed by.

"Hello there," called out the man. "You look like a tramp!"

"Yes," the Tramp Prince replied, "I've heard it said before that I look like one. So, indeed, I must *be* one!"

"Are you headed to town?" the Tall Man Who Lived In A Tall Tower asked. If you are, you won't find much. It's almost all been washed away with the last few floods. That's why someone built this silo into a house. You can see the foundation where the farmhouse once was."

The Tramp Prince went over to the tower house and looked at it carefully. It had been nothing but a common concrete sided silo banded by steel, however, the entire exterior had been covered with small, round river stones stuccoed into varying color patterns.

"This is truly an amazing architectural gem!" the Tramp Prince commented.

"Oh yes, I certainly agree with you; that's why I bought the place. But the inside is just as interesting. It's been decorated with wood carvings and plaster embellishments from the inside of an old church. If you'd like to see it, I'll be happy to show it to you."

The Tall Man Who Lived In A Tall Tower then invited the Tramp Prince inside. As they walked in the door, the boy could see a narrow, steel spiral stairway that led from floor to floor.

"Apparently, this stairway was in here before they made the floors," said the Tall Man Who Lived In A Tall Tower, "possibly so that the roof could be accessed for repairs."

As they climbed the stairway, The Tramp Prince looked in amazement at the series of fluted wooden columns with their highly ornate, painted plaster Corinthian capitals that circled each of the rooms. The top floor had less architectural decoration, but a wide expanse of windows all around the interior.

"I just love this place, and I have my winter bedroom on the fourth level so that I can look out on the countryside and contemplate." The owner told the Tramp Prince.

"Contemplate what?" the boy asked him.

"Oh... Many things, but mainly, I'm concerned with trying to determine why we humans have drifted so far from our natural state.

Why we seem to prefer artificiality to the beauty and truth of Nature."

"I've met others who are perplexed by that problem — or at least areas of thought somewhat connected to it," the Tramp Prince commented, as he gazed in awe out of the panoramic view afforded by the windows.

"Where are you staying tonight?" the Tall Man Who Lived In A Tall Tower suddenly asked his guest.

"Why — wherever I can find a barn or a shed with a little straw for a bed."

"Well, you're welcome to stay in one of the downstairs rooms if you'd like. They're warmer and more comfortable than a barn, I should imagine."

"Why, thank you, I'll just do that," replied the Tramp Prince.

"The upper room is the warmest in winter and, of course, that's why I live up here," continued the Tall Man. "You see, there's a wood furnace in the first level and the heat rises through the stairwell and the floors, so its quite comfortable up here. The entire building is insulated with six inch cork from old refrigerated boxcars that had been left to rot down when they pulled up the rails from the train track that used to go through town."

"Oh yes," the Tramp Prince laughed, "we hoboes call those freight cars 'reefers."

The Tall man continued:

"If you look out the window, you can see that the railroad bridge is still there across the river. Local farmers paved it so that they could drive their farm products to the big city that's about thirty-five miles south of here."

The Tramp Prince looked out the window and spotted the bridge: "I'm glad to know that I'll have a real road to travel on again after all the miles I had to hike through brush. But as to my sleeping, I think I'd probably be most comfortable on the second level where its cooler. I'm so used to sleeping in cool temperatures."

The Tall Man Who Lived In A Tall Tower laughed: "I live on the first level myself in the summer; it's like a refrigerator down there then."

For the next several minutes, they sat watching the birds fly by and the distant pastoral picture afforded by the extraordinary view from the tower's high windows. With his eyes sparkling into a smile, the Tall Man Who Lived In A Tall Tower spoke:

"You know... I may never find the answers to my questions up here, high above most treetops, but at least I'll have had an enjoyable time trying."

"Yes, it is strangely attractive to be in a room like this — so high up," the Tramp Prince pulled his chair closer to a window as he watched the birds dart across the spaces from tree to tree. "You almost feel like God looking down on the world."

The Tall Man Who Lived In A Tall Tower smiled again: "Even if I were to go into a tall building in the city... it would not be the same. I know this, for you see, I had a business office in a city skyscraper. But I sold my business so that I could buy this place and live here. It may be a much more simple life, but simple values can often far outweigh any fascination we may find with industrial complexity."

"Those simple values you speak of... they could also be the most intellectual values," the Tramp Prince reflected.

"Yes, and you can't force intellectuality on people. Most of them will never see beyond the baseballs on the fronts of their faces — you know...? Where their noses ought to be? Or maybe it's *inside* their heads — where their *brains* ought to be. "

"So, is that what you think really matters in life? Intellectual values?" asked the Tramp Prince.

"Ah... well, perhaps not exactly that. In a word, it's *thought*. After all, that's what we are — just fluffs of thought... in a brief spark — a minute flash in eternity."

"I suppose I'll have to give some of my *own* serious *thought* to that one," was the Tramp Prince's reply.

"But there's more — more to it than that, said the Tall Man. To me — and this is only me, of course, I would have to say that equally important is being able to look out this window at the world — watch the beautiful sunrises and sunsets — see the birds fly from branch to branch — seeing them as they see themselves, up here isolated from the din and travail of human absurdity. It's the quiet and relaxed, restful peace."

"And the sunlight on the clouds — that too?"

"Yes, yes — I had forgotten — that too."

The Tramp Prince stood silently at the window for several minutes, looking out and contemplating.

"It's almost like an awake, out-of-body experience up her; the way we look out on everything –- far above it; and the silence."

"Yes," said the Tall Man, "You're quite right. I'd never thought of it that way, but you're quite right. You know –- you're welcome to stay here as long as you wish. I like your company. You're not at all intrusive like most people."

"Thank you," said the Tramp Prince. "That's a high compliment. I really wish I could stay; I like this tower... but I have no choice in the matter. Tomorrow, I must go."

The next day, the Tramp Prince bade the Tall Man Who Lived In A Tall Tower goodbye and thanked him for his hospitality. The 'town' when the Tramp Prince walked into it, was nothing more than a few houses on stilts and a few stores built up on high earth-filled platforms.

"I wonder why anyone would want to build their home or business right here in a flood plain."

"Oh, you know why," Road Toad sent out an acid thought comment. "It's because there really isn't much improvement in the cerebral ability of the human brain over that of the monkey.",

"Stop insulting monkeys, the Tramp Prince joked."

Chapter 28: A Biting Remark and A Bite of Food

On southward the Tramp Prince headed, but each abandoned farm house that he investigated seemed to be even more rotted away than the last.

"Road Toad" the boy called out to his amphibian friend, "this must be on extremely humid area where we are now. Its flat land and we may be at the confluence of rivers. There has to be some reason for the severe rotting of the farm houses."

"Yes," Road Toad sent back a thought. "I can feel the moisture in my skin. It's not nearly so dry anymore."

As they progressed further south, the dust-brown trees were just starting to sprout tiny flecks of yellowish bud-fuzz. The Tramp Prince encountered a welcome-looking farm house with shutters painted bright pink, and with an early spring garden already planted in rows of earth-toned loam. He went to the back door and asked the woman who answered his knock, if she had some work that he might do for a meal.

"You may straighten the yard..." and after thinking a moment she said: "then dig that small last part of the garden for me. How's that sound?"

"Great!" The Tramp Prince told the woman. "I'll start right now."

After he had completed the work that the woman had asked him to do, the lady came out and looked approvingly at the Tramp Prince's efforts.

"What would you like to eat?" she asked.

"That's unusual — to have you offer, I mean."

"Well," The woman replied, "I have guests coming over tonight, so I have quite a lot of variety — and more than we'll need."

"If you could just give me a plate of raw vegetables, that would be fine." The boy responded.

As the woman opened the kitchen door to go back in and prepare a plate of food, her cat came dashing through the door, out onto the porch and up the porch post as it spotted the stranger.

"Oh, that cat is *so* absurd!" the woman commented.

"Really, I can't imagine *any* animal as absurd as the human animal," the Tramp Prince said to the woman.

"People are *not* animals!" the woman replied with emphatic finality.

"Well if we're not animals, what are we?"

"We're *people*; we're different."

"Yes, I'd agree with you on one point; we're certainly different, alright." The Tramp Prince told her bitterly, "I don't know of any so-called 'lower' animal that can be as cruel, as vicious, as destructive, as stupid, as absurd, as egotistical, as capricious, as...

"Oh, stop it; just *stop* it!" the woman nearly screamed. "Why are you telling me how *bad* people are; there are some very 'good' people out there too."

"Yes, there are good people in this world. In fact, I'd say that they're probably vastly in the majority. But the bad ones have a strangle hold on the systems that control everyone; the good folks out there are so cowed with fear of the system's 'man with the gun', that they just go along with all the cruelty and absurdity of the conventional systems."

"You make me want to cry," the woman almost sobbed over her own words.

"It deserves crying about." The Tramp Prince interjected with great sadness in his voice. "Solutions and answers to the pressing problems of both individuals and society at large are out there within grasp. But it's an unwillingness to even look at these answers that makes them so arcane — so remote.

"With our great inventive, problem solving powers, we're found solutions to all sorts of mechanical obstacles — but we've never been able as a society, at least, to apply the same kind of reasoning to spiritual and inter-personal relationships. Social disputes are still settled by the violence of war; personal disagreements by hatred and cultural differences by intolerance. The more I travel the world, the more of this I see."

"Well for land sakes — I don't need to hear a college professor's lecture on social morality — especially from a young tramp. Just *who* are you," the woman asked, "a prophet of doom? Are you some kind of anarchist?"

"I don't know what I am yet," said the Tramp Prince closing his eyes in serious contemplation. "Nor do I know yet what I will become."

"One thing that you are," said the woman petulantly," is a *very* upsetting young tramp."

She went back into the house, returning with a plate containing the raw vegetables that the Tramp Prince requested.

"Here, just take your food and leave!"

The Tramp Prince pulled a brown paper bag from the top of his bindle sack and emptied the plate into it.

"I'm sorry if I upset you ma'am," the Tramp Prince apologized, but your comments led me to my criticism."

"I don't wish to seem harsh and cruel; "the woman advised, "but I simply cannot take any more of you telling me how worthless and stupid the world is — these are my neighbors and friends and family that you described."

"Yes," the Tramp Prince returned, "I am well aware of that," and he walked on out through the gate.

Chapter 29 :The Rockhouse Gang

Just a little farther down the road, the Tramp Prince came to and quickly walked through, the little town of Mudford. He crossed a bridge over a 'river', understandably called the 'Mud River'. Its brown swirl of churning early March rainwater was only a few feet across and it was more suitable to have received the appellation creek, he thought. The term 'river' was just a way of attempting to add some dignity that the word 'mud' did not have.

The road out of town led over the well-polished steel of an interurban track but the station was a quarter mile past town where another gravel road intersected. The Tramp Prince walked on through the edge of town and up a steep hill that looked down upon the interurban station. Near the top of the hill, a graveled foot path led off on the left side. Thinking that he might find some peaceful spot in the woods where he could eat, the boy followed the path to where it appeared to end in a thicket. The growth of small trees and brush was so densely tangled in wild grape and poison ivy vines, that they formed a veritable screen that hid the end of a large stone building with its tile roof.

Skirting the part of the thicket that blocked the path, the Tramp Prince then climbed a short stone stairway to the door of the building. He sat down on the door step-stone and took out the bag with his food, eating all that the woman had given him.

As he ate, he looked around at the rockhouse, which had been built rather long and narrow, with half of its length devoted to what had once served as an open pavilion-like porch with a fireplace and chimney in the central end. When he walked to the far end of the building, he could see that another chimney graced the opposite side of the rockhouse's end wall. The place appeared to have been unused for years, the Tramp Prince observed, from the accumulation of leaves on the flagstone floor of the open portion of the house.

All of the windows of the rockhouse had been boarded up, and the pale gray color of the wood indicated that those boards had been installed far back in the distant past. The red tile roof of the house appeared to still be intact, as it swooped far out over the walls with a slight curve toward the horizontal — a trick to avoid the need for gutters. The walls, themselves had been constructed from multitudes of small round stones as well as jagged flat pieces of limestone — a rock that protruded everywhere along the rocky hillside. With careful scrutiny, the Tramp Prince was able to tell that the very thick walls had been actually poured, using a concrete 'rubble wall' method with slip-forms. He made a mental note to record this place as a possibility for a new home.

In spite of the obvious years of disuse, there was a slight whiff of smoke that drifted from the chimney and the Tramp Prince decided that it would be best to knock on the door. The heavy, rough oak of the door resisted the soft knuckle–tap of the boy's hand. He picked up a stone and knocked harder.

Receiving no response, he tried the thumb-latch and found that it moved. The door swung open easily and the interior was slightly visible from the light emitted by one exposed window at the far end of the large, undivided room.

By the glowing fireplace, there stood three people as they attempted to warm themselves. They were still almost shivering — though now, more in anticipation of some dire intruder.

"We thought you might be a cop!"

The first to speak was a tall, dark-haired man with attractive features and a winning smile. He looked to be only a few years older than the Tramp Prince.

"I'm 'Brains' McKinnon," and pointing to his left, he introduced a tall, portly, rather shapeless man with a silly grin. "This here is 'Looie the Barber.'" Looie's silly grin proceeded into a silly laugh.

Then 'Brains' McKinnon reached out and playfully grabbed the arm of a thin, leggy young woman on his right.

"Now this is the best lookin' hobo anywhere on the circuit — 'Sleazy Jane'."

"Oh let me go, you big jerk," she laughed and then tickled Brains until he crumpled in paroxysms of laughter.

Brains held Sleazy Jane by the shoulder and put his right hand under her chin: "Just look at this face — prettier than any movie queen you'll ever see! Classic nose! Voluptuous mouth!"

"Aw, stop it, Brains," the girl told him with an embarrassed tone, "I'm just an average gal who knows how to use my make up."

"Don't agree, baby... you're special! Hey, bud, what do *you* think? Hey, what's your moniker, anyhow?"

"They call me the Tramp Prince — and yes, I do agree with you."

Everyone exchanged handshakes and squatted down around the fire.

"Damn, it feels colder inside here than it does outside!"

Brains McKinnon made his comment with all of them nodding their heads in agreement.

"It's the thick stone walls; they take a long time to heat up," the Tramp Prince suggested. "But once the walls do, they'll hold the heat and release a lot of it back into the room like a thermal flywheel. Apparently you haven't been staying here very long."

"Yeah, you're right," Brains responded. "Hey — that's pretty smart... but we better get our beds set up now while we can still see. There's plenty of cardboard over on the floor. Lay some down by the fireplace," he told the Tramp Prince.

After they had all arranged their bedding, Looie the Barber sat on his blankets with his head in his hands.

"Whatcha thinkin' about, Looie?" Brains asked him.

"Hey Brains, you know there's a movie house down in that town? I seen it when we wuz walkin' through there."

"Yeah?"

"Yeah, an' they got a John Bunny picture playin' — 'Her Crowning Glory', supposed to be really funny. I missed seein' it last year."

Brains nodded: "Yeah, I heard it's supposed to be good. But if I can't think of some way t' get us in, you might just miss it again this year."

"Hey, Brains — how 'bout if we pool our money an' buy one ticket, then keep passin' it out to the rest of us?"

"I don't think that'd work, Looie. The usher usually tears the ticket in half when you enter. Anyway, how would we get the ticket back out?"

"Hmmm," Brains put on his thinking cap. 'So how much money we got among us? Probably not enough for even one of us to get in... right?"

"I'm broke," Looie told him.

"Yeah, an' I'm close to it, honey," Sleazy Jane reached into her jacket pocket and held up a nickel. "See!"

"How 'bout you?" Brains turned to the Tramp Prince.

"I don't know... I might be able to come up with a dime. No more than that."

"Humpf! Bunch of paupers. And I'm no better off than the rest of you!"

Brains gave the matter more thought, "This is Thursday night... right? If they're runnin' that film tonight, there's gonna be hardly anyone there. They're gonna be showin' it to a bunch of empty seats. There probably won't be ten people in there on a Thursday. They really ought to be <u>givin'</u> those empty seats away to us poor folk."

"But they can't do that," the Tramp Prince responded, "you know that if they did that, everyone would wait until there was a free night and no one would pay."

"Well, it's still not right to waste those seats. You wouldn't let food go to waste if someone were just lettin' it stand around, would you?" Brains snickered.

"Food is different — it's a necessity. A seat in a movie house is a luxury. We don't *need* to watch that film."

"Well, maybe its food for the soul — yuh think?"

Brains began again: "Okay... this is a democracy, right? So, let's take a vote. Who says we should try to get in free? Everyone who says 'yes' raise their hands."

All but the Tramp Prince voted 'yes'.

"You're out voted, pal," Brains laughed. "Are you comin' with us?"

The Tramp Prince reluctantly agreed to go along, if for no other reason, he told himself, just to see what kind of crazy scheme Brains had in mind.

"Now listen you guys," Brains confided as they were walking into town, "I'm goin' to the front of the theater and the rest of you wait near the side exit door. That door opens only from the inside, so when you see it open, just slip in no matter who comes out. We need to wait 'til the movie is goin' for about five minutes before I'll get us in."

"Aw, Brains, "Looie the Barber complained, "I don't want t' miss the first five minutes of it. I like t' see a film from the start."

"Yeah, well you go get some money some place and then you can see it from the start. I'm gettin' yuh in *free*, jerk!"

Brains stood in the lobby of the theater and waited a few minutes until everyone had been seated and the usher had gone in to sit in one of the many empty seats. Standing in the doorway of the darkened theater, Brains screamed at the top of his lungs: "Fire! Fire! Fire!", so as to be heard easily above the piano player's music.

Immediately, everyone came pouring out of the theater into the street. The side door opened and as the patrons flowed out of it, the three tramps made their way in. Brains slipped into the back of the theater and sat down in a seat next to the wall. In just a few moments the theater owner flipped on the house lights, saw no fire and was out in the front telling people that it had been a false alarm. He encouraged them to return and promised to show a couple of extra 'shorts' as compensation for their trouble.

In another few minutes, The John Bunny film was again in progress and four of the empty seats were now filled.

Later that night, after returning from the movie, the Rockhouse Gang built up the fire with sticks from around the hillside and dragged in a somewhat wet stump, which they had pulled out of the ground earlier.

"This ought to burn through the night." Brains told Looie the Barber who had helped carry the stump in.

When they threw the stump onto the blazing sticks, the fire cracked and popped, throwing glowing coals out on the hearth.

"Don't anybody put your bedding too close," Brains advised. "There's no water to throw on you if you catch fire!"

Late into the evening, the four Tramps lay on their cardboard beds, exchanging stories of their adventures and misadventures. Finally, Looie the Barber grabbed up the rest of the sticks and threw them into the fireplace.

"G'night, all you tramps, hoboes an' bums — see yuh in the mornin'."

The rest of the night was broken only by the sound of a late interurban as the train's wheels echoed along the track at the bottom of the hill.

Early the next morning, Brains McKinnon was up trying to rekindle the fire by adding some new sticks to the still glowing coals in the fireplace. The Tramp Prince began to help him.

"We're movin' on," Brains told him. "There's no food to be had anywhere around here. We're goin' to go down to that interurban station and use their washrooms. You can come along... or stay here. Whatever you want."

Looie the Barber went up to the Tramp Prince. "Yuh want me t' give yuh a haircut, huh?" He sounded almost gleeful. "I went through barber college an' I worked for a couple years in a shop in a train station in a big city. But I got tired of the pressure. Too many customers for even five of us to handle. You could never do artistic cutting. That train station is where I met Brains. Now I'm his personal barber. I give him a shave an' trim his moustache. Right Brains?"

"Yeah," Brains responded "Bet even old Rockyfeller can't afford to bring his personal barber around with him when he travels."

Everyone laughed.

Opening a small, black leather kit showing the tools of his trade, Looie the Barber offered the Tramp Prince a trim:

"Let me shape up the back of your hair. The front looks okay, but the back is pretty ragged. Like you tried to cut it yourself."

"That's right," advised the Tramp Prince.

Looie trimmed away for a few minutes and stepped back nodding in approval of his work.

"Thanks," the Tramp Prince told him. "Maybe someday I'll be able to return the favor."

The Tramp Prince was the first to pack his blanket roll and he went rapidly down the long flights of terraced stone stairs toward the interurban station. Each flight of stairs was connected by wide flagstone terraces, some of which were still adorned by concrete urns and stone banisters with decorative posts and an occasional short colonnade. The massive stairway system suggested that the

Rockhouse had at one time been part of a resort or perhaps a Chautauqua, now long gone in history.

When he reached the station, the Tramp Prince found the entrance blocked by a large four wheel baggage wagon being pushed through the barely accommodating width of the doorway. As the baggage wagon suddenly popped through the door, it bumped a gentleman, who fell to the floor. The Tramp Prince followed the wagon inside and immediately spotted a man's wallet on the floor near the wall.

After picking up the wallet and looking around, he saw no one searching the floor. Then he went over to the huge cast iron potbellied stove to warm his hands. The stove's warmth revived Road Toad who conveyed a thought message to the Tramp Prince.

"What's been going on the last few hours? You let me get too cold again, so I hibernated."

"Oh nothing worth mentioning happened — except that I just found a man's wallet on the floor."

Road Toad looked out at the inside of the station:

"Well, what are you going to do with the wallet? What's in it, anyway?"

"I don't know."

"Why don't you look?"

"I don't want to be placed in a position of being tempted not to take it up to the station master — if, say there were a hundred dollars in it."

"You wouldn't keep it, would you?"

"I don't want to let myself even be tempted, so I'm not going to look in it — just return it."

After taking the wallet to the station master, the Tramp Prince used the restroom facilities to clean up, and as he was about to leave the station, the man who had been bumped to the floor by the baggage cart walked up to him.

"You're the one who found my wallet, right? They described you to me at the ticket office."

"Yes, sir." The Tramp Prince replied.

"Well, I'd like to do something for you. How far were you planning to take the train?" asked the man.

"I really wasn't planning to take it — I just came in here to wash up; I'm tramping."

"Heading South?"

"Yes."

"How far?"

"Possibly further than this line goes."

The man scratched his chin

"Well, If I were to buy you a ticket for as far south as this line goes, would that help you?"

"It certainly would," replied the Tramp Prince. By now, he had decided that he must soon begin his return trip home and that the most direct route would be by finding some freight train that would leave from the large city to the south.

The man whose wallet the Tramp Prince had found, went over to the ticket window and bought a ticket to the end of the interurban line. He handed it to the Tramp Prince.

"Good luck, son..,. and Thank you. There wasn't a lot of money in my wallet, but it had a great many important personal papers. Thanks again."

The boy put the ticket into his pocket and went out to the waiting train. He got on, letting the conductor punch his ticket. Then he found a seat near the center of the coach.

The motorman called the conductor up front and made an announcement to the passengers:

"Folks," he told the dozen or so people , "we're over ten minutes ahead of schedule, so we'll wait a few more minutes before we start."

The motorman and the conductor left the train car and went into the station. They took the blue and white coffee pot from a table near the stove and placed it on the stove's top lid to rewarm it. Both men took off their coats and caps, hanging them on hooks in the station's entrance hall. The two were speaking loudly about the time difference for their train when Brains, Looie and Jane walked past.

Brains immediately grabbed the arms of his two companions, walking them quickly back to the entrance hall. He pulled down the motorman's coat and cap and told Looie to take the conductor's as well.

The three hoboes ran laughing out to the waiting train with its motor still rumbling away. Brains sat in the motorman's seat while Looie The Barber went to the center door and Sleazy Jane plopped down in a passenger seat.

From where he was in the center of the car, The Tramp Prince had been gazing out the window next to him, completely preoccupied with watching the touch of sun on the still brown trees – – and with the thoughts of home and his family, thoughts that kept rushing in a torrent through his mind. He paid no attention as a few more passengers entered during the last three minutes before the scheduled departure.

In a sudden motion, Brains pulled the door control lever and closed the doors. Instantly, he swung the motor control to the right and the car quickly moved out of the station. The train car was rapidly gaining speed as the real motorman and conductor came racing out of the station in a rage. They arrived at the track just in time to see their interurban go speeding away.

"Wha... it's not just our coats and caps they stole — they got the *train*!"

"Geeze... what'er we gonna do?!"

"Common — quick! The sheriff's office is across the street, Hurry up... *quick*!"

The pair ran over to the office, bursting into the room breathless and agitated. Sheriff, I. Will Doolittle, sat at his desk with his feet up on it, leaning back in his desk chair; his eyes were slitted. He was only half-awake.

"They stole the interurban!" shouted the motorman.

"They?.. huh? wha...wha'd they steal?"

"The interurban — the... train!"

"The train... the *train*? Holy pickled herring! Well I'll be danged! Com'on — let's try t' intercept 'em at the next station! Get in m' car. I'll ketch them rascals or m' name ain't Ichabod William Doolittle!"

The sheriff's Model T Ford touring sat at the curb in front of the office. For a change, Sheriff Doolittle spared no alacrity in turning on the key, setting the spark and gas levers and running to the front of the car, where he gave the crank a sharp spin. The engine caught with an almost ferocious growl to life, and in mere seconds, the three men were racing down the street away from town.

"How fast does that streetcar a' yers go?"

"About thirty-five miles an hour, the way I drive it."

The motorman clung to the windshield post with his right hand, his knuckles turning white — every chuck hole and bump shaking his entire body. The rotund conductor sat hunched in the back, shivering in the chill morning air.

"I've got the throttle wide open — must be doin' forty-five. Ain't no speedometer, but that's my guess, we ought to get to the next station just a little ahead of 'em. I'll block the track with the car — up there where the road crosses the track again!"

The sheriff shouted above the clanking screech of the screaming engine: "I'm makin' you two my deputies. Ain't got no extra gun, but you two kin use my billie club. Take the back door a' that train an' I'll take the front, okay?"

The motorman's "Yeah" almost drowned away in the swiftness of the wind.

As the interurban moved leisurely along the track, none of the passengers seemed to be aware of the change in motorman or conductor. The Tramp Prince turned his attention away from the bucolic landscape and instead, for some unknown reason began to scrutinize the motorman. Something seemed peculiar about the man, he thought, though he could see only the man's back from where he sat. Then, moving up to one of the empty seats near the front of the car, he could easily observe that the motorman's blue jacket and cap did not match his pants. The Tramp Prince moved again to the seat immediately behind the motorman. Suddenly it become obvious to him who was driving the train car.

"Say, don't I know you from someplace?" "The Tramp Prince asked playfully. Brains turned his head and whispered behind his hand.

"Yeah, you know me alright — I just hope nobody *else* does! Hey, it's okay, bud... I always wanted to drive one of these big things — an' now I'm *doin'* it!" Brains McKinnon almost choked on his giggled laugh.

"But, Brains — you know what they're going to do to you when they catch up with you?" The Tramp Prince still spoke in a whisper.

"Sure," Brains whispered back, "cept they aren't *gonna* catch up with me," he laughed again.

"If you wanted to run a train so bad, why didn't you just get a job as a motorman?"

"What! A *job*! Why would I want a job? A tramp doesn't need a job!"

"Oh man... when they find you, you'll spend the next few months behind bars."

"Don't count on it," Brains giggled again. "Now listen, I'm gonna stop about a half mile from the next station. Looie'n' Jane'n' me — we'll get off an' run for the woods. You need to move this thing a few hundred feet up the track so the passengers don't see where we run to. Then wait about three minutes or so and drive it to the station. That should give us enough time to get away. From there, though, you're on your own."

"How do you run this car?" The Tramp Prince asked.

"Simple — you move this control lever to the right. There's nothing to it."

As the train approached the next station, Brains stopped the car and motioned for Looie to come up front.

"Why we stoppin'" asked Looie the Barber.

"Cause we're gettin' off here." Brains told him.

"Aw, Brains, can't we stay a little longer? I didn't even get to punch many tickets yet. That's fun!"

"Listen, dummy, if we stay on into the next station, you'n' me'll be punchin' rocks with a sledge hammer for the next few months. Think *that'd* be fun? C'mon!" Brains grabbed Looie's arm. "Now keep up with me, y' hear?"

"Aw, Brains — you know I can't run as fast as you."

"Yeah, well y'er gonna do it *this* time!"

At that moment, Brains pulled the lever and opened the doors. As he got up and took off the motormans jacket and cap, the Tramp Prince tugged his arm:

"Before you go, there's one thing I forgot to ask you."

"What's that?"

"Well... it's just... what do you think really matters in life?"

Brains' face clouded in a grimace of bitter exasperation — he was about to tell the Tramp Prince that he couldn't be bothered with such nonsense at a time like this... but then, almost immediately, he burst from the seat with an explosive laugh.

"Its havin' *fun*! Yeah — for sure! Its havin' *fun*!"

Then he dashed out the open door of the car, quickly followed by Looie the Barber and Sleazy Jane. Jane stopped only long enough to plant a quick kiss on the Tramp Prince's cheek.

"Bye, bye, honey — see yuh in the funny papers!"

With a loud laugh, the Tramp Prince closed the doors and moved the train forward a few hundred feet as Brains had requested. He took off his own cap and plopped the motorman's cap on to his head, then almost shook it off laughing to himself. "What a bunch of characters," he thought.

Road Toad perked up from the jacket pocket.

"Hey, Road Toad — you awake?" The Tramp Prince sent the thought to his pocket companion.

"Yes, I've revived, thanks to the warmer temperature now."

"Then you heard Sleazy Jane — what do you think she meant? Do you think she was trying to tell me that I look like someone out of a comic strip?"

"No, what she meant is that we're *all* a bunch of cartoon characters."

"Well... maybe so. Yes, maybe so..."

After waiting about three more minutes, the Tramp Prince moved the interurban on, slowly into the station. He left the motorman's cap on the driver's seat and opened the doors. Then he walked to the back of the car and sat down. Only three other passengers remained, whose destination was farther than this station.

From where he sat in the right hand side of the coach, the Tramp Prince had a clear view of the depot and the road that fronted it. He had been looking out the windows only a few seconds when the county sheriff came speeding up to the depot station's entrance in his model "T" police car. The train's motorman and conductor leapt out of the car and ran toward the train.

Just as the sheriff shut off the car's engine, a hiss of steam began to emerge from under the hood. There was an abrupt pop, loud enough to be heard a block away. Clouds of steam engulfed the car and everyone around it. Sheriff Doolittle threw open the hood and could see a four inch tear in the upper radiator hose. By then, the motorman and the conductor had returned to the sheriff's car.

"Just look at that hose," screamed the sheriff. *Now* what the hell am I gonna do?"

He turned to the two Train Men: "That's what I get fer lettin' you guys have me run the thing wide open like that. This engine ain't got no water pump on it!"

The train men looked apologetic. "I'll buy you a roll of tape". One of them said meekly.

"Yeah," said a bystander, "wrap it tight enough with tape. That'll at least get you back."

"Well I ain't headin' back... not 'til I catch that gang that stole the train. Anybody see which way they went? Hell, maybe they're still in there!"

"Oh, don't be ridiculous," the conductor told the sheriff. "Why, if they were still on there, they'd have tried to take the train right on through here. Don't you realize, they got here first?"

"Well, then, let's look for 'em. They gotta still be right aroun' here. We hafta catch them criminals. God knows where they'll go with the next train they steal."

"Yeah," said the motorman. "Now where would they take something the size of a train? Maybe move it off the track and take it somewhere and hide it!"

"You ain't funny today!" shouted the sheriff, still fuming with frustration. "You want to be helpful come with me an' try t' find the gang."

"Sorry sheriff, we have to try to get the train back on schedule. But thanks for the buggy ride."

The motorman and the conductor pushed the sheriff's Model T off the track and went to their train. It then proceeded along southward, the Tramp Prince riding on uneventfully until the train reached the interurban terminal.

Chapter 30: The Prophet

After leaving the interurban terminal, The Tramp Prince found that he was at the edge of another very large port city. This metropolis, he thought, seemed to be sprawled over many miles from the distant appearance of tall buildings in three different directions. He immediately inquired where the main train station was located and began walking toward it.

In one area that he passed, of back streets and small shops with second floor garret rooms, there was a crowd of people gathered around a gaunt figure standing on a stool near a busy corner. The orator wore a flamboyant, but yellowed white robe spangled with sparkling metallic red stars. On his head, he attempted to balance an extremely tall, spiked hat, similarly colored and decorated. His hat tilted precariously to one side as his oratory became punctuated by wild gesticulations and an almost windmill movement of his arms.

"Oh beware, ye children of sinful fathers – ye sons and daughters of reprehensible mothers... ye perpetrators of depravity and debauchery! The time will soon be upon us when we shall all pay a retribution for our wicked ways and our negligent decadence."

On and on the Prophet of Doom raved, intoning his tirade with seemingly artificial squeeks and squawks from what was actually a cracking characteristic to his voice. The Tramp Prince stood there utterly fascinated by the Prophet's fanciful and facile oratory. The man was so inventively articulate, that hardly ever did he repeat his words or phrases.

Although the boy understood only part of what he was hearing, he moved in as close as he possibly could so as to be able to observe the Prophet's subtle, but highly expressive facial features, he listened carefully to the Prophet's message to determine whether there might be some elements of truth to the wild and often exaggerated words.

The Prophet carried on with his seemingly unending prophetic utterances for another eight or ten minutes. Standing directly in front of the Prophet, the Tramp Prince did not even notice that he was, by then, the only one left listening. But the Prophet, seeing that the crowd had dissipated, finally decided that it was no longer reasonable to preach to one listener. He stepped down from the stool and looked into the box that he had placed out for donations. Only a few coins graced the bottom.

"Humph!" said the Prophet in bitter dismay. "That won't even pay for my dinner, let alone the week's room rent."

"Where did you learn so many expressive words and phrases?" the Tramp Prince asked the Prophet.

"Humph! Why I just bought a dictionary a long time ago. I still read it every day. You get so, after many years of preaching, that you automatically begin to put these words together in very forceful ways. If you want to follow me up to my garret room, we can talk about how I do it."

So, the Tramp Prince accompanied the Prophet to his room on the third floor of an old tenement building. What intrigued the boy most about the Prophet was the man's total lack of self-consciousness, even as he was in the process of making a complete spectacle of himself.

"How do you do it?" asked the Tramp Prince.

"Do what?" the Prophet responded, frankly confused.

"I mean... you have so much self-confidence when you're speaking out on the street."

"Uh... well, it's because I...uh... I truly believe everything I'm saying."

"I guess I don't fully *understand* everything you're saying."

"Oh... it's the message that's been given to me. That's all it is."

The Prophet sat down on his bed and the Tramp Prince opened up the Prophets' folding stool and also sat down.

"This is fascinating," said the Tramp Prince. "I just might like to *be* a Prophet. How does one go about getting into the prophet business?"

"You can't simply *become* a prophet, said the Prophet. "You must be *born* with the ability. If you are, then you can channel it, perhaps enhance it — direct it... but it isn't something you can learn."

"But how do you know if you *are* born with the ability?"

"You are born with the knowledge that you possess the ability. What else can I say?"

The Tramp Prince shook his head in confusion.

"But you wouldn't want to be a prophet, anyway," the Prophet told the Tramp Prince. "Believe me, there's very little profit in being a prophet. Just look at where I'm forced to live. This room is very cold and drafty in the winter. And I don't even have a stove in here. Sometimes I have to either starve or try to find scraps of food that people have thrown out in the trash."

"Like a hobo — or a tramp... a bum?" asked the Tramp Prince.

"Yes, exactly. It doesn't matter how much one knows of the future, or how important it could be to people. They don't want to hear the truth, even when you tell them."

The Prophet closing his eyes, then continued in prophetic oratory:

"I see a future... where the world will be filled with motor cars, racing over great concrete highways — through the hills and valleys, billowing huge clouds of their fumes all over everything. And aeroships flying thither and yon — millions of them doing the same. And the trucks and trains and trams we already have — multiplied by the tens of thousands. Talking machines, telephones, movie houses; and there will be great factories everywhere belching out thick clouds of black smoke; and those factories will produce great multitudes of products not yet invented — not even thought of!

"I see great aeroships that roar like the blast of thunder rolling down a mountainside. And there will be people whose mouths explode a sound as piercing and loud as a train whistle. Horns and other musical sounds will shake the earth until church steeples fall. There will be those who scream out the news of the day around the world — and whose unending babble and blather are consumed by the people just like pabulum fed to a babe. Noise will be the order of the day and silence will be looked upon as suspect.

"The human population will be exploded many times what it is now and everyone will be using all the world's resources until there is nothing left for anyone. And then there will be great natural disasters — fires, floods, droughts, cyclones, volcanoes erupting, covering huge areas of the earth with hot lava. I see people dropping great bombs on each other's cities; I see cruel dictators and abominable tyrants ruling all the countries — industry strangled by giant corporations; I see workers everywhere grasping to try to break the chains of their economic slavery; I see wildly erratic temperatures freezing the tropics and melting the arctics; I see ocean waves that sweep away whole cities; I see earthquakes that swallow up continents.

"The brains of the peoples of all nations will be stupefied by the potions of the alchemists and the libations of the brewers and by the toxicants of the great and gigantic industrial agro-barbarians who will spew their ghastly, deathly spoor across the entire world. Millions will follow blindly the leaders and rulers to engage in grim and senseless combat for obscure and meaningless ends.

"World disasters will fall like a torrent of great behemoths. Global calamities will overpower the weight of the continents and seas — and the sky will fall into the bowels of the earth... and forever there will be fire and brimstone hailing down in a boiling, brutal drench of calamitous catastrophes."

"Hmm," said the Tramp Prince, laughing. "Sounds like it might get kind of bad. So when's all this supposed to happen?"

"Ah, listen to what I have to say, young man... when any animal breeds far beyond its habitat's ability to sustain it... it is destroyed by natural forces, or the population starves — or it is decimated by disease with everyone's weakened state, or if not these, then the people will be cut down by the millions in the insanity of senseless wars for whatever resources are still left.

"I will not live to see this — sometime in the next century. But *you* could; though you would be a *very* old man, indeed."

"Yes, in your lifetime, religious madness that has infected the minds of millions for centuries will explode into massive military lunacy and the unspeakable cruelties that will arise from that madness will tear asunder cultures and countries alike. It will spread from one continent to another, pitting Catholics against Jews as 'Christ killers,' Protestants against Catholics for 'Papal outrages', Hindus against Muslims for real or imagined improprieties — a planet gone totally berserk with the lunacy of pogroms and wars of religious hatreds incited by evil armaments manufacturers and their political allies."

"Now *that*," responded the Tramp Prince, "sounds almost like an 'end of the world' scenario."

"Oh... the world will not end, though millions will perish in the conflicts; but neither will there be an end to evil intent. The peoples of the world's cultures have learned civility only in the most rudimentary manner and only over vast eons of generations. Lessons are quickly forgotten, even when written into widely read histories."

The Tramp Prince pondered, then slowly commented:

"Yes, that is certainly true — though I haven't even the slightest idea why. Why do you suppose this always happens?"

"Ah," said the Prophet, "it is because there needs to be a further development of the human brain. I suppose there is no other explanation."

"But isn't there any way to avert these calamities that you've described?" asked the Tramp Prince.

"Yes, if the worlds human population were to be reduced by three-fourths of its highest number — to a sustainable level. But then, the nation states will need to cease to exist and the concept of coercive government, itself with even the policy of majority rule will have to disappear. That form of coercion will be replaced by a system of voluntary association."

"Just tell me," said the Tramp Prince, "what the world will be like in... say 1992. I could still be alive then."

"Why do you think I can tell you something that specific? I prophesy only in generalities. All I can tell you is that the technology of the world will have increased exponentially and it will bring about terrible destruction on Earth. Human populations will have doubled, perhaps tripled, but the morals and ethics of humanity will not have.

"Ah, you see," said the Prophet, rubbing his hands together as though he were trying to wash away the sins of all humanity, "The atoms of infinity could shatter the structure of the cosmos — render it into wreck and rubble like a crumpled sandcastle splattered across the empty vacuum of the universe... sending into the darkness of forever the...

"What!!" exploded the Tramp Prince. "I'm sorry... but, I don't get it!... I mean... well, could you please repeat all that last again?"

"Oh... my goodness... I don't know if I can. Many of these prophesies of mine are inspirations, you know? Let me see... now just *what* did I say? My goodness, gracious. I've forgotten. But I don't suppose it matters. Perhaps a little later I'll have another inspired revelation. You don't mind waiting do you?"

"I suppose not." The Tramp Prince seemed a bit dejected, if resigned.

They sat in silence for the next few minutes until the ringing of distant church bells brought both the boy and the Prophet back into the reality of the present.

"Aha... now I have something!" said the Prophet with a quick burst of loquacious energy. "I predict that there will be a great army — perhaps even an *armada* of hoboes and tramps that will descend upon the powers of the world and...and...and...

"And *what*?" asked the Tramp Prince in amazement.

"Ah...I'm not sure. The fine print is a bit fuzzy here."

"You're... you're *reading* this?"

"Well... yes. You see, sometimes I can get predictions out of the 'Prophet Weekly."

"What's *that*?"

"It's a publication for prophets. I have to concentrate very hard; then it just pops up in my mind."

"How ridiculous!" laughed the Tramp Prince.

"Well, I guess it's really a little hard to explain," the Prophet admitted, scratching his head. "But don't worry, none of this will be in your lifetime, anyway."

"A great army of hoboes — why, almost everyone would have to *be* a hobo!"

"Yes, I suppose so. But you know that there *will* be widespread hard times. I didn't write the article, but that's what it says."

The Tramp Prince walked around the garret room laughing and shaking his head. The Prophet began speaking again:

"Humans — humanity for the most part is really rather absurd a large part of the time — don't you agree?"

With a deft grasp of his hand, the Tramp Prince lifted his cap and smoothed down his long brown hair — allowing him a few moments for contemplation.

"You know... I probably would have said the same thing myself until recently. I've met a few people who seemed pretty sensible. I guess I'd have to qualify my agreement by saying that I think ... there could be lots of times in human life which are not at all absurd."

"Ah," replied the Prophet with a tone of great sadness in his voice, "sometimes... I might agree with you. But for someone like me, at least, those meaningful times in life are like finding a single, ripe, sweet wild plum at the edge of a forest. It is a rare treat. But once you've tasted it, you search again, perhaps for the rest of your life to find another. And some people may live a long life, never even having tasted that plum."

"I understand exactly what you mean, though perhaps I've been luckier than most people — at least so far in my life," the Tramp Prince responded.

"Well, I don't expect to be understood or appreciated by many — — if any people," the Prophet concluded. "But you know," he then added, "I just might be like Nostradamus. No one has proven or disproven his prophesies. Most of them are yet to come. And perhaps no one will ever even realize it when they take place."

The Tramp Prince thought to himself: "This man has got to be a little crazy. But... nothing he says is absolutely beyond possibility. And the world *is* such a crazy place anyway. So — who knows?"

"Well, *I* know *one* thing," Road Toad popped out a thought to the Tramp Prince, "I'm getting hungry and I'm tired of listening to a man who may not be completely crazy, but who *is* completely ridiculous! Let's *go!*"

"Actually, I think it's time I should leave." The Tramp Prince looked over at the Prophet, who nodded and smiled sadly.

"Yes, it always happens like this;   no one stays long. I understand."

"Could you please answer a question for me, though, before I leave?"

"Yes, of course."

"What really matters?"

"Oh my... what really matters? Why... being able to foresee the future is what really matters! If one can predict the future, then one can avoid making the mistakes of the past."

"But can't we do that anyway by just looking at our history and applying a little common sense to our future actions?"

The Tramp Prince smiled and gave his head a slight affirmative nod, a bit amazed at his own simple realization.

"Ah, what you say is true enough, but *who* ever uses common sense in making decisions? People are largely ruled by emotion rather than reason. You know that it's always that way. That is why the human world is always in such a turmoil."

"You make it sound so *hopeless!*"

"Yes, yes, indeed. It *is* hopeless! I predict that the giants of industry will swallow up the resources of the earth and destroy everything they touch until there is nothing left to destroy."

"And I predict," said the Tramp Prince as he looked out the dingy garret windows into the bustling crowds in the street — "I predict that we will soon go out to obtain something to eat." Then he laughed a light spontaneous chuckle.

"There,: said the Prophet, "You see, you're getting the hang of it. Someday you may be a great prophet."

"I doubt it," the boy told him, "I'm not even sure I'd want to be a great anything — at least in *this* kind of a world. But let me shake your hand. Then I can say that I've shaken the hand of a living prophet."

He shook the Prophet's hand and walked out of the garret room, down the steps and out again into the bright sunlight of the street.

Chapter 31: The Twoliver Brothers

As he began walking down the street, the Tramp Prince started searching vacant lots for old boards and rocks to look under in an effort to find insects that Road Toad could eat. After satisfying his small friend's food needs, he realized that he hadn't enough money left to buy himself a meal.

"Play your flute, why don't you!" Road Toad telepathized."

"There just doesn't seem to be enough foot traffic out here in this residential area — certainly not at this time of day. But maybe I could find some copper or brass scrap in the alleys around here and take it to a scrap yard."

Approximately halfway down the first alley, the Tramp Prince came upon two young men about his own age. Both were tall and slender with shabby clothing, the face of one of the boys, the Tramp Prince thought, had a rather fiendish appearance, while the other boy looked almost sleepy with a perpetual slight smile that made his face look like a cartoon character.

"Hi, said the first boy as the Tramp Prince walked past. "We're d' Twoliver Brovers."

"Glad to meet you," the Tramp Prince replied.

The Twoliver boys had been attempting to remove a very long, coiled fire hose from a trash can into which it had been jammed.

"Wook," said the first Twoliver brother, "if we can get dis hose out, we can make it into owah own pwivute tewaphone!"

"B-b-b-but its t-t-too stiff." The second Twoliver Brother replied.

"We'll just put it out in da sun fowa a wiwle. Pull hawd on it wiwle I howd d' can."

The boys got the fire hose loose and unrolled it as much as possible. But the sides stayed flattened from having been rolled up for so many years. The hose still looked to be new, other than for its stiffness.

The Tramp Prince walked on past the Twoliver Brothers and their hose, continuing to look for scrap in every can and ash pit that he came to. By the time he had reached the end of the alley, the Tramp Prince was passed by the first Twoliver Brother pulling on the fire-hose.

"Hey, can you heaw me?" he asked his brother, calling into the hose. The second Twoliver Brother answered from the middle of the alley. The boys carried on their firehose telephone conversation until a patrolling policeman confronted the first Twoliver Brother.

"Hey, kid, where'd yuh steal that hose from, huh?"

"No pwace!" the first Twoliver Brother answered.

"Come on, kid, that hose looks t'me like it's brand new. Now where'd yuh get it? A school or a hospital?"

"We got it wite outta duh awey. In a twash can. Dats d' twooth!"

The second Twoliver Brother had come to where his brother was being confronted by the cop.

"B-b-b-but that's wh-wh-wh-where we g-g-g-got it!"

"I think I'm gonna run you two guys in an' charge yuh with theft," the cop told them.

The Tramp Prince stepped up to the policeman. "Officer, I saw where they got the hose — out of a trash can. It was thrown out because it was stiff as a board. They laid it out in the sun, and that's what softened it up slightly. I'll testify to that."

"Who are you?" The cop asked the Tramp Prince. You just look like a young tramp t' me."

"Uh... officer, may I ask you something?"

"Yeah, what's that?"

"Well... I'm just wondering if there's some new ordinance now against walking on the street — that is, against tramping. If there is, I'd really like to have you show me a copy of that ordinance. Do you mind?"

"Alright, you smart-ass kid. Listen, I got half a mind t'run all three a' yuhs in fer...fer... I guess I can't think of anything t' charge yuhs with... Well... go on — get on outta here!"

The Tramp Prince followed the Twoliver Brothers down the block as they dragged their fire hose.

Dat thupid cop, " said the first Twoliver Brother," he gave me twouble onth befowa."

"W-w-w-we don't h-h-have t' l-l-l-listen t' that j-j- jerk. L-l-let's go home." As the trio walked away from the alley, the Tramp Prince offered a comment, attempting to soothe the injured pride of his two companions:

"You know, sometimes these big city cops act like they think they own the world; like everybody should bow down to them because they're carrying a gun. Some of them just have a dictator complex."

"Yeah," agreed the first Twoliver Brother, "You got that right, Hey yuh wanna come wit us? We're goin hom et' get thumthin' t' eat."

The Tramp Prince followed the Twoliver Brothers, helping them carry their fire hose. After a few blocks, they entered another alley and walked down it half way, to a gate leading into the back yard of a small bungalow. As they went into the yard, the Tramp Prince was inundated by a collection of every imaginable kind of item, many defying description and all of which the two brothers had dragged home from the surrounding alleys. There was a look of shocked disbelief on the Tramp Prince's face.

"Hey — dis ain't all! We put the betta stuff in duh gawage."

Laughing, the first Twoliver Brother pointed to a ramshackle, gray, clapboard building in the corner of the yard. "You can't even get in dewh t'thee anyting. Duh west is in duh celweh. Wanna thee it?"

"Sure," said the Tramp Prince, nodding affirmatively.

The three boys then went down a few steps leading to the basement of the house. There, they first opened a screen door missing the screen. Small nails had been driven all around the edge where the screen was supposed to fit. Strings of various colors and thicknesses had been tied in random directions from one nail to another, forming a crude net with openings that ranged in size from a half inch to as much as an inch and a half.

The Tramp Prince stood in amazement looking at the door.

"Now, how can this screen possibly keep out flies and mosquitoes." he asked.

"Well," the first Twoliver brother smiled with a gleeful expression, "It keeps out duh *big* ones!"

Inside the basement, there were shelves covering every wall from floor to ceiling. Each shelf had been crammed full of miscellaneous small appliances, lamps, toasters and other assorted items, all of which the brothers had found discarded in the alleys. When they turned on the basement lights, two roaches appeared on the floor.

"Quick," shouted the first Twoliver Brother to the other one, "Help me get out duh thweepas an'thweep up duh cweepas!"

The Tramp Prince roared with laughter as the two brothers ran around the cellar pushing vacuums and carpet sweepers in a vain attempt to catch the insects.

Soon, they all climbed the inside stair to the back hall and entered the kitchen. An older man sat dozing in an arm chair in the living room; he was barely visible from the kitchen. At first, he took no notice of the boys, but then roused slightly:

"That you, Sonnie?"

"Yeah."

"Your mother had to go out for a while. She left lunch for you boys in the icebox."

"Okay — we'll get it."

"Take anyting yuh thee dat yuh want t' eat." The first Twoliver Brother told the Tramp Prince .

"Thank you, I will."

But the Tramp Prince found very little that had not been heavily sugared or salted, and he was able to make only a very meager meal. He thanked the Twoliver Brothers for their hospitality and as he bade them goodbye, he told them: "I hope you can continue trying to help save the world from destroying itself by its waste, but those of us who do this seem to be like only a few grains of sand on the ocean's beach. I don't know how much good we'll ever do..."

"Well," said the first Twoliver Brother, "at weast we're makin thum new pwaces for duh bugth t'hide when dey taketh over duh world".

When the Tramp Prince began walking past the house next door, an older woman emerged and called out to the first Twoliver Brother, who was still standing by the gate.

"Sonnie! Oh Sonnie — do you think you and your brother could help me carry out the trash to the alley? My husband's got an attack of the gout and he can't do it; the bags are too heavy for me."

"Yeth, ma'am, we'll help." The first Twoliver Brother nudged his brother and the pair proceeded to the front porch of the neighbor's house. The Tramp Prince followed along, thinking that a third helper might quicken the process. After the three boys had taken a couple of loads of bags and boxes to the ash pit, they filed on back through the neighbor's house.

"Thank you, boys. Say, maybe you boys would like to take advantage of these Philharmonic concert tickets. They're for this afternoon and we can't go. There are three tickets. Our daughter was going to come in town and go with us, but she didn't want to bother if we can't go. If you don't want them, I'll just throw them away; the tickets didn't cost us anything, but you can't get in without them."

The first Twoliver Brother looked at the second Twoliver Brother, then both looked at the Tramp Prince. All three of the young men nodded in agreement.

"Yeth; we'll take 'em. Thauths, Ma'am."

A discussion then ensued among the three companions as to how to get to the concert hall.

"W-w-we n-n-never b-b-been t' the c-c-concert before," said the second Twoliver Brother.

"I haven't been to one before, myself." The Tramp Prince told the boys.

"Ith's tho far," commented the first Twoliver Brother, "We can't walk dere befow it stwats."

"L-l-lets t-t-ake a street car offered his brother, Uh-uh-uh-I got a n-n-nickel. How b-b-bout y-y-you?"

The first Twoliver Brother nodded 'yes'.

They both looked at the Tramp Prince: "How 'bout you?" The first brother asked.

After feeling in his pockets, the Tramp Prince determined that he had only twenty-five cents left. He debated momentarily whether he should spend a fifth of his remaining money on street car fare, but quickly answered in the affirmative.

"Sure, let's go."

The streetcar line was only a two-block walk away and luckily a trolley arrived minutes after the boys got to the car stop. Although the ride took less than twenty minutes, they arrived at the massive concert hall with just a few minutes to spare before the program began. After taking their tickets, an usher directed them to the only free seats left in the hall — high in the top row of the farthest tier. As the boys looked down on the stage, the performers appeared to be not much larger than small dots.

"Wewl, at weast it ain't cood up hewh dis high," commented the first Twoliver Brother

"Y-y-yeh — an' I'm g-g-glad I'm n-n-not scared of heights!" his brother answered.

The Tramp Prince took off his cap and placed it on his knee. He looked around studying the highly decorative architecture of the interior of the enormous concert hall.

In the next instant, spotlights beamed on the performing orchestra on stage, and the concert began.

After nearly three hours of the music of Beethoven, Bach, Brahms and Mozart, the concert ended, and the three young companions filed out of the hall with the rest of the crowd.

""Tho, wh'd'd' yuh think of it?" the first Twoliver Brother asked the Tramp Prince.

"Well, I'm not used to listening to something that long — but I enjoyed it."

"Yeah, said the second Twoliver Brother, "it s-s-s-sure was a-a-awful long."

"What did *you* think of it?" The Tramp Prince directed back to the first Twoliver Brother.

"Aw. I ain't crathy 'bout dat kinda muthic, but I tell yuh, I sure liked watchin' dem cute lil' monkies down dere, scratchin' 'emselfs wit sticks."

The Tramp Prince laughed so hard that he nearly fell over.

"S-s-say... maybe w-w-we could s-s-slip in at the b-b-ball park t-t-tonight an' w-w-w-watch a b-b-baseball game!"

"Nagh..." said the first Twoliver Brother, "we'd pwabab'y hafta be way up high again jus' watchin anuvh bunch a' lil' monkies runnin' aroun' tryin't' hit each oveh with dem bats!"

The Tramp Prince laughed again at the boy's outrageous comments.

"I really need to go now," he told his companions. "But before I leave, I wanted to ask you guys what you think really matters."

"He, he, ha, ha. I'll tell yuh what mattehs — what mattehs is finh' thu somethin' neat in duh twash — in duh alwey!"

"Like?"

"Like a owd fiwuh hose! Wight?" He looked over at his brother.

"R-r-right! Th-th-thats' w-w-what really matters!"

"It's been fun being with you guys — so long." And the Tramp Prince began walking away.

"Yeah... come back thum time an' we'll go to anoveh conthert. I weally like watching dem li'l monkies."

When he was a block away, the Tramp Prince sent a thought message to Road Toad;

"Well, what did you think of the concert?"

"I'm afraid I slept through most of it — except when they hit those big kettle drums and woke me up."

"And the Twoliver Brothers?"

"Don't make me say! But I will say this: Why didn't you grab those two big water bugs for me, that were on the floor of their basement?'

Chapter 32: Captain Lee and the African Man

By looking up at the skyline, the Tramp Prince soon realized that the concert hall was near the city's downtown area — probably not far from the waterfront. After walking only a few blocks, he could see, not far in the distance, the tangle of silhouetted freighters and loading cranes. He decided to walk to the dock, recalling that he had met the Artist With The Red Beret at another port city.

Upon arriving at the wharf, he found himself alongside huge ocean-going steamers, flying flags of every nation conceivable. With a delighted stride, he paced the wooden planking of the docks and listened to the unending slosh of the waves... waves that sighed in a lyrical chant as ancient as the sea itself.

When he reached the end of the wharf area, he realized that had he taken a step further, he would have had to have walked out onto the blue-green ocean that straddled one end of the horizon to the other. The great green sea swallowed his imagination — just as the sky had often done to his mind, when it had descended upon and totally enveloped the edges of everywhere.

Just at the end of the part of the wharf where the ocean-going steamers were moored, the harbor curved sharply into an indented cove where a great multitude of private yachts and sailboats lay at anchor. Long wooden docks extended out into the bay with ships tied on either side. Anchored and tied at the middle of the first dock was a large sailing vessel that impressed the Tramp Prince sufficiently that he walked out to look more closely at it.

"Hey, buddy-boy!" A man called out pleasantly to the Tramp Prince as he stood at the gang plank. "Come on up here; I have a favor to ask of you. And, I'll pay you a couple of bucks."

When he had walked up into the boat, the young man was handed a dollar bill by the ship's captain.

"Listen — my crew is late in showing up here and we were supposed to sail for Costa Rica. I need to go after 'em. Since I know their habits, 'it shouldn't take too long to find 'em. I should be back within a couple hours. I need to have you watch the boat until I return. Ok?"

"Yes, I guess that would be alright."

"Now, don't let anyone on board except the crew. One's a big, tall, black haired guy and the other's a short, kind of stocky little guy like me. There's not much on board that anyone would want to steal, but I'm a little concerned about someone trying to vandalize something."

The captain then wrote out a note on a pad, signed it and tore it out. He handed the note to the Tramp Prince. As the boy read it, he nodded, "Give this boy a dollar bill. I'll reimburse you. Captain Lee."

"Just hand it to one of the guys if they get back here first. Ok?

"Sure," said the Tramp Prince.

For over an hour, the Tramp Prince waited for the men to return Night was beginning to creep over the evening sky and the boy looked for and soon found a food pantry in the cabin. He appropriated a couple of apples and a few nuts that had been apparently long forgotten at the bottom of a drawer. After he had eaten his meager meal, he lay back on a bunk, listening to the night water-sounds.

The gentle washing of the waves intoned a soothing, if muted melodic refrain. When the Tramp Prince dropped his head down on the narrow bunk it required only a few seconds for him to slip into a ponderously profound sleep.

All through that night, the boy dreamed of being a crew member of the ship and traveling from one tropical island paradise to another, meeting exotic people and seeing extraordinary sights and touching and tasting the inordinately bizarre and wonderful fruits and vegetables of that unknown world.

During the night, no one entered the ship and the sun was already quite high when the boy awoke.

"Road Toad," the Tramp Prince thought out to his small friend," they've still not returned! I can't imagine what could possibly have happened to all of them!"

"Well," Road Toad replied, "The captain said that he thought he knew where his crew might be — perhaps he joined them in some 'spirited' revelries."

"Hmmm... I just don't know what I should do. But I simply can't afford to remain here any longer."

"Oh, leave them a note," the amphibian returned his thought, "and perhaps you could tie a rope across the access to the ship. Of course that won't keep out anyone who really wants to come on board, but it's at least a way of saying 'Keep Off'."

"Yes, that's true."

The boy then picked up another apple from the provision pantry and, as he dropped it into his pocket, he began looking around for a stout rope to tie across the entrance to the ship. Then he scribbled a note to the boat's owner: "Dear Sir, waited all night and into the morning for your return, but I can wait no longer. I'm sorry, but I must leave. You owe me nothing more, considering my nights lodging and a small amount of your food which I used. Sincerely, the Tramp Prince."

He then found a medical supply kit and tore a small piece of adhesive tape from a roll. With the tape, he stuck his note on the most prominent edge of the deck and tied a piece of rope across the ships entrance.

After leaving the dock area, the Tramp Prince inquired again and was given directions to the location of the large, inner city Railroad station. He began his robust walk with a resolute commitment not to allow himself to be sidetracked or delayed again by anything.

But after having walked some fifty or sixty blocks, the boy began to think that he had either received incorrect directions, or that he had followed them improperly, because directly ahead, his path was blocked by an enormous university campus.   The grounds and buildings seemed to proceed for several blocks, both to the left and to the right.

"I suppose I should I should inquire again about the Union Station." The Tramp Prince telepathized to Road Toad.

"Yes," Road Toad responded, "but perhaps you could take a rest-break on the campus... and give *me* an opportunity to look for insects to eat."

Only a short distance from the street, there was an inviting park bench along a walk with well maintained, but dormant flower beds beside it. The Tramp Prince placed Road Toad near one of the beds, then sat down to rest on the bench.

The morning sun had become bright and warming as the Tramp Prince sat there on the park bench in front of the great university buildings. Soon, a very nattily dressed dark-skinned man sat down in the middle of the bench.

"Hel-lo," he said, very musically and smiled. The Tramp Prince looked at the man's skin color, which was the darkest, almost blue-black he had ever seen.

"Hi," returned the Tramp Prince, "I'm not from around here; I'm just passing through — as you can probably see."

"Yes, I noticed your backpack. But I'm not from this country, myself, said the dark-skinned man. "I'm not even from this continent; I'm from Africa. And if I told you the name of my country of origin, you'd say that you had never heard of it. It's so tiny and so remote that hardly anyone has ever heard the name."

The African Man then gave a loud, infectious laugh.

"I'm guessing that you're in the university here," the Tramp Prince said.

"Yes," responded the African Man, "You see, I've actually lived around here the largest part of my life. My father has been in the diplomatic corps for years. He's now an ambassador from my country. So today, I know your language far better than I know my own native tongue."

"And you teach at the university?" asked the Tramp Prince.

"Only part time," answered The African Man, "I'm working on my doctoral thesis for a PHD in psychology."

"Wow! I'm impressed," the Tramp Prince told him.

As the Tramp Prince sat looking at the African Man's face, he realized that the features of this very dark-skinned person were not at all like the facial features of the other persons of color that he had seen previously. There was almost an oriental look to the man's face. Still, even that did not quite fit the man's appearance appropriately. "That African Man," the boy thought, "has truly an unusual set of facial features — pleasant-looking, but extraordinary by any definition."

The African Man smiled, then opened his large briefcase, removing several hand-written papers.

"I'm going to have to put these pages in the right order so that I can type them in the library this morning. I forgot to do this last night. I use the library's business typewriters because they're so much better than my own dinky little portable, you see."

"Um...sir... so, what is your thesis about? I mean, if you don't mine my being so curious," the Tramp Prince politely responded.

"Oh, no, I don't mind telling you about it." And The African Man laughed again, long and loud.

"It's rather complex... and involves a *very* unconventional theory concerned with how a culture's food choices may be affecting the psychological patterns that are prevalent in that culture. Now, I've been studying this for a number of years, and I'm convinced that most of the dark-skinned peoples in Africa today may have emigrated from some colder climate where they lived for many hundreds, possibly thousands of years, after having moved out, or been forced out of their native lands which they again occupy today.

"My own people," the African Man continued, "occupy a tiny kingdom in a mountainous section of central Africa. Although we have lived there for at least many hundreds of years, our written history is quite brief. There was another culture which occupied the same lands many thousands of years before us. The stone remains of some of their walls — probably their temples and homes, are still in evidence, but even our oral history tells us nothing about them. Teams of European archeologists have visited those ruins occasionally and even they can tell us nothing about the people who built them."

"That's truly astonishing!" was the Tramp Prince's response as he listened with increasing intensity to the African Man's story.

With another of his infectious laughs, the African Man carried on with his description:

"Ah, young man... this world is so large and so full of mysterious cultures and even more mysterious histories — often intensely inscrutable histories... when one begins to study these, it is often a frustrating object lesson in futility. You see, written records, even when they did exist, have sometimes been lost far back in the turmoil of wars and natural disasters. We can make only partly educated guesses about some of these cultures."

"But your own culture — your own people," asked The Tramp Prince, "where did they live before they came to your present lands?"

"Ah... I have no idea. Our oral history does not tell us that. Perhaps it is too far back in time. My own studies indicate that we lived in a colder climate. My people still do not fully utilize the tropical fruits native to our region. Confusing things is the very remoteness of our tiny kingdom. People in my culture, for example, had no substantial exposure to the matera medica of any other culture. We rely on simple herbs to treat physical disorders — which I must say are relatively infrequent compared to the disorders I have observed both here and in Europe. We are not caught up in the vast proliferation of synthetic drugs so commonly used here to try to treat disease — a method of treatment which, sad to say, attempts to suppress the symptoms rather than to remove the cause."

The Tramp Prince nodded his head in agreement. "Yes, I know exactly what you mean. My own family lives in such remote isolation that we simply must rely on having our own adequate nutrition to maintain our health. It never ceases to amaze me how great a quantity of patent medicines the average city dweller consumes every year. It's such a vast industry — and such an obviously erroneous concept!"

"Well," said the African Man, "that which is conventionally — and conveniently *accepted*, is not necessarily the same as that which is morally, ethically or intellectually *acceptable*.

"Industry is generally driven by two factors. The first is its' own avarice and the second is the public's indifference. Everyone, it seems; wants to swallow a 'miracle' pill to make up for their poor health habits."

The African Man looked off into the almost-spring distance, as if attempting to draw clarity from the hazy clouds and the brushy brown trees.

"So... you see, the reason that I believe there is such an unnatural food focus by many of the African peoples today — the reason that they attempt to subsist mainly on various non-indigenous root crops and tubers, using these as a mainstay of their diet with animal flesh, is because of their long history in a cold climate. In a cold climate, that was all that was available to them for food. But tropical fruits and vegetables will grow quite easily where they now reside. And these tropical fruits and vegetable sprouts are the mainstay of the diets of the apes which inhabit the forests there. Those apes are the closest relatives of humankind.

"Those apes possess the same long digestive tract as we humans have, with our same low acid content in their stomachs. Very different from the high acid content and short digestive tract of carnivores. Also, the apes have no way to cook or process their food, so what they eat has to be their natural diet. In addition, neither apes nor humans have claws or teeth suitable for tearing raw flesh from the bones of animals. Neither can we run down the larger swift-legged animals as can the big cats, for example."

"That's really interesting!" said the Tramp Prince, "But I don't quite see a psychological connection to this."

"Well," continued the African Man, "since some of these African people are almost constantly at war with one another, I'm trying to show a possible relationship between the unnatural diet and the war-like tendencies, since the family groups of great apes do not, for the most part seem to engage in corporate violence."

"So, what do you think... should *all* of us humans go back to living in small family units in the tropics?" The Tramp Prince tried to make his voice as respectful as inquisitive. "And, I guess everyone should be eating tropical fruit."

"Yes, certainly!" The African Man chuckled with a loud tone of sarcasm. "Even without paleontological evidence such as fossil bones, common sense will tell us that an animal without significant body hair, that is, fur, had to have originated in a very warm climate. Humans cannot survive in these colder climates without some kind of protective clothing — completely artificial, unnatural. Until our brains evolved to the point where we could make these adaptive inventions, that is, clothes, we were restricted to living only in the tropical or at least subtropical regions. All of the other animals that live in the north can grow their own fur coats."

"You know," said the Tramp Prince, "What you've said is so completely obvious, that you would think that it would already be just common knowledge."

"Or common sense," replied the African Man. "But you see, common sense is *not* very common."

The Tramp Prince thought silently for a few seconds...

"But if everyone in the world would go back to living in the tropics — how would there be room for all of us there?"

"I'm not sure if that would be a problem or not," said the African Man, who frowned a bit and put his hand under his chin." You see; there are vast uninhabited areas in the warmer regions of the earth — but, even if this becomes a problem, we humans need to begin the conscious restricting of our numbers, because no matter where we live, if we breed indiscriminately, eventually we will run out of space and resources for our population. That could cause a disaster of unparalleled intensity."

"Yes," agreed the Tramp Prince, "but if we humans continue to breed like a bunch of rabbits, how can we ever expect to reduce our numbers?"

The African Man hesitated, "Well... one obvious way would be for each couple to have only one child. In only the first generation, that policy would vastly reduce our population."

"So how would you get every family to agree to having only one child?"

"Ah," responded the African Man, "I have a lot of answers, but I do not have the answers to everything. That subject is beyond my area of expertise."

The Tramp Prince sat pondering these last words of the African Man.

"Well, going back to what we had been discussing," continued the African Man, "It's my personal opinion — and please understand, it's nothing more than this — that tropical fruit has a soothing effect on the psychological makeup of a person. Have you ever tasted the true tropical fruits?"

"Oh, I've eaten bananas and oranges." The Tramp Prince responded, "Even then, my family at home is seldom able to buy them."

The African Man then opened a large brown paper bag and brought out four different tropical fruits which the Tramp Prince had never seen.

"I'm going to make a present of these to you, young man, "the African Man told the boy, "It may be that tasting these could significantly affect your life. I buy these from an Oriental woman who has a small shop in the center of the city. I am not certain how or where she gets them. The names of these four fruits as they are called in the market here are: mango, sapota, cherimoya and papaya, "And he pointed out each as he said the name.

"In my country," he continued, "we have different names for these fruits, but it would be meaningless for me to tell you those names. You probably couldn't even pronounce some of them," the African Man laughed.

The Tramp Prince then ate all of the four tropical fruits, making facial expressions in sheer wonderment of their delightful flavors, He requested that the African Man write out the names of the fruits so that their characteristics could be recorded and thus allow the boy to better explain them to his family.

The African Man sat smiling and chuckling as he leaned leisurely back on the park bench. "I knew you would be amazed," he told the Tramp Prince."

After folding the paper with the names and notations about the tropical fruit, and carefully placing it in his bindle sack, the Tramp Prince then profusely thanked The African Man: "Well, I'm sorry to have taken up so much of your time," the boy apologized.

After saying nothing for a few seconds, the African professor began again hesitantly:

"I probably shouldn't even get into this because it's so marginally connected to my studies, but since you seem so interested in what I've been telling you, I suppose it wouldn't hurt to go into it a bit. You see, I'm not even sure there are any psychological implications involved in the matter and for that reason, I haven't included it in my thesis."

"Well... just what *is* this?" asked the Tramp Prince with great curiosity.

"It's concerned with the widespread dental deterioration of many — perhaps most — human cultures. I've given a great deal of thought to the reason for the existence of this problem. We humans are the only animals anywhere in the world — at least that I've been able to discover, who suffer serious dental caries and often total tooth loss long before the natural end of life occurs."

"Were you trained as a dentist too?" asked the Tramp Prince.

"Oh no, I've merely derived my theory from common sense — which is the reason that few, if any dentists or anyone else, for that matter, will probably ever come up with the same theory. That is to say, that there just isn't a lot of common sense around these days. Ha! Maybe there never was!

"At any rate, there are three factors at work here. First, and possibly foremost is poor heredity. And that, obviously cannot be changed. I believe that large portions of humanity have suffered a hereditary degradation — a 'devolution', the opposite of survival of the fittest, because of the fact that we have had, for so many thousands and thousands of years, no need to use our teeth in the way that nature intended for us to use them: that is, to chew often tough, hard raw foods.

" Because our ancestors moved to cold climates where tropical fruits and vegetables were not available, and humans had to subsist largely on roots and animal flesh, those foods were palatable only when cooked to a soft, sometimes mushy texture:

"You see, the fact that humans now almost universally cook their food, indicates that our ancestors, when they were forced out of or just left their natural tropical environment, did so only because they already were intelligent enough or became intelligent enough to have use of fire, be able to fabricate clothes of some kind and be able to forage for roots as well as to be able to make weapons sufficiently strong to kill large animals. In other words, they were able to become the hunter-gathers of antiquity.

"Having good quality tooth enamel no longer because a necessity. Those with poor quality enamel could live as well as those with good quality enamel. This did not mean that they could live very long, but long enough to at least reproduce themselves. You get the idea?"

"Yes," replied the Tramp Prince, "it's certainly unconventional, I must admit..."

"The other factors," continued the African Man, "are the use of large amounts of highly acid fruit — at least in our modern diets — and the loss of mineral content in the soils producing the bulk of our food stuffs.

" Inadequate nutrition meant that children often did not have enough minerals in their diets during the time that tooth enamel was forming. Therefore, we suffer enamel defects and porous enamel, which the high acid content of citrus fruit, apples and pineapples quickly erode away leaving holes, or dental caries as we call them. Then the bacteria which live on residues of sticky starches and sugars that collect in those holes, also produce small quantities of carbonic acid during their life processes and that adds to the problem. You can't do anything about the hereditary factor, but you certainly can change the other two factors."

"Well, what would most people eat, if not citrus fruit and apples?" The Tramp Prince asked.

"There's not a lot of choice in northern climates." was the answer, "Some sub-acid and sweet tropical fruits can be shipped in, but at great expense because they're delicate and have high loss in transit. The reason that oranges and grapefruit were developed from their small, sour wild progenitors, is because with the thick skins of citrus, they ship well and will ripen fairly well even when picked in a very unripe state. Also, the trees are not quite as subject to frost damage as most other tropicals, which means that they can be raised somewhat farther north, thus reducing shipping expense of the fruit."

"But what does this have to do with psychology in any sense," asked the Tramp Prince.

"Ah yes...well, the connection is tenuous at best. But I'm theorizing — and again, this is merely my theory — that the severe loss of teeth in a population, in addition to creating poorer food choices and then malnutrition, could affect the way in which these people are easily intimidated or manipulated by warlike rulers into following a philosophy of racial or ethnic hatred. That could contribute to the people supporting, or at least not opposing the wars in which the ruler's engage."

The Tramp Prince shook his head questioningly. "I don't know... I'm not sure I see the connection."

Yes... well, that's why I've not included any of this in my thesis. At least not at this point."

Again; the Tramp Prince apologized for having occupied so much of the African Man's time.

"Ho, ho!" laughed the African Man, "why, I have plenty of time! Now tell me about yourself."

The Tramp Prince then explained the circumstances which had started him on his journey and how, after months of searching, he had still not found a suitable abandoned garden for his family.

"Maybe you should be looking in a warmer part of the world, where plants grow longer and more rapidly and where shelter is not such a critical issue." The African Man had been listening very intently before offering his comment.

"Yes, you may very well be right. Perhaps I should relay this to the rest of my family as soon as I can."

In a moment when the African Man looked up, the Tramp Prince caught his eye, "There's one more thing — I'd like to know something, sir... just what is it that *really* matters?"

"What really matters? Ha!... what really matters is... the *truth*. Seeking the truth and speaking the truth; knowing the truth and acting upon the truth."

"Wow... it'd be pretty hard to argue with *that*!"

"Yes, I agree with you. You see, the world is so often dominated by the results of lies... and all of the destruction and suffering that follows in the wake of those lies. The reason that so many people don't tell the truth or seek after it is because often, the unvarnished truth hurts us to face it... people are seldom willing to give up economically destructive or even health destructive habits... even when they already know what the probable end results of those bad habits will very likely be."

The Tramp Prince nodded in agreement. "It's a strange world to try to understand."

The African Man smiled. "It's a strange world, alright"... whether we understand it or not. But if we *do* understand it — at least part of it, then we're in a better position to *act* upon our part of the world and *react* within it. I don't know what else I can say."

The Tramp Prince shook the hand of the African Man. "You've said an awful lot — really. And all I can say is that I'm glad to have met you."

With his back pack properly adjusted, the Tramp Prince bade farewell to the African Man.

"Goodbye and good luck in your search, young man," offered his new dark-skinned advocate. "You are quite an intelligent fellow and it may well be, that the next time I see you, you could be teaching some class here at the university yourself."

"Ah," said the Tramp Prince, "you probably have too high an opinion of me."

"No," returned the African Man, "I may be overestimating your ability to achieve, but not your ability to *think*!"

Chapter 33: The Wiry Haired Professor

As the Tramp Prince and the African Man began to walk away from the park bench, the boy soon realized that Road Toad was no longer in his pocket. His small amphibian friend had not been in evidence at any time during the hour that the conversation with the African Man had taken place. The Tramp Prince sent out a thought message to Road Toad:

"Where are you? Where are you? Do you hear me?"

"Yes," replied Road Toad, "I'm under some leaves in a flower bed. I've been asleep during your absurdly long conversation. What else did you expect me to do?"

"Well, you could have listened to us. That African Man was undoubtedly one of the most important people I've ever met!"

"Why...did he give you a lot of money?"

"Oh, of course not! But his ideas were worth far more than money."

"You can't eat ideas," Road Toad shot back with a caustic telepathic reply. Anyway, I thought you said that nothing was going to distract you again from reaching the train depot."

The Tramp Prince then put Road Toad back in his pocket and proceeded along the campus walk.

"Well, Road Toad, some personal contacts just take precedence over everything. So what else should I say?"

"Oh, nothing that would convince me. Anyway, its good to be moving again."

"I just realized — *I'm* getting hungry, Road Toad; I wonder if I can find the cafeteria on campus. You know, I still have that dollar bill Captain Lee gave me."

"Well, go ahead, I've had plenty of bugs for a while, so you won't have to buy me any nuts or raw vegetables. Ha!"

The Tramp Prince inquired as to the location of the campus cafeteria and began walking toward it. When he observed what appeared to be the cafeteria in the basement of one of the buildings, he entered it, knowing that it would be imperative that he spend as little of his remaining money as he could get by with spending. There had been no appropriate place — or the time on campus for him to play his flute and attempt to collect more money.

Students were carrying trays filled with steaming plates of everything from soup to... but not including nuts and the Tramp Prince sat down at a table to watch them. A cleanup crew walked past with a double tiered rolling cart. Here and there someone had left a plate or utensils that had to be cleared away and the tables wiped. The Tramp Prince went over to where a girl was just loading two plates on the cart. There was still an untouched raw vegetable salad in one of the compartmented plates.

"Are you just going to throw that salad out?" asked the Tramp Prince.

"Of course," the girl answered, "Why — do you want it?"

"Well... if it's just going to go to waste — sure."

"Here," she said "take it! This goes on all the time. I don't know why anybody even takes raw vegetables. Seems like they never eat them. Here, you can have an orange and an apple someone left too."

She scrutinized the Tramp Prince closely, noting his ragged, patched clothes, his bindle sack and walking stick.

"Say," she confided, "There's a lot more good food in the back on the trays -- it's just going to be pitched. You can have it all, if you want it. Come on back with me."

They proceeded through the swinging doors into the kitchen area, the girl pushing the cart and trying to avoid bumping other members of the lunch crew. In the next few moments, they entered a large corner section where carts and trays were cleaned and the dishes emptied and washed. The cleanup girl found a large brown bag and took some paper food cartons, filling each with whatever the Tramp Prince pointed out on the remaining plates.

With enough food to last him another three days, the Tramp Prince thanked the cleanup girl and headed back out the same way he had come in. As he moved now with a more jaunting step along the walk that divided the campus, he looked up with great inquisitiveness toward each of the large university buildings as he passed them. The massive two and three story edifices were styled like medieval palaces, one facing another across the central walkway. The names of the buildings on their facades gave only partial clues as to what was being taught inside.

He stood for a few moments, watching the students scurrying about in the late March burst of wind. In his thoughts, he could contemplate sitting in some classroom, listening to a lecture on arcane considerations of the mind — or on archaeological oddities -- or on obscure geologic formations. The list in his head seemed endless. The Tramp Prince was so caught up in his sudden reverie that he would not have even noticed the Wiry-haired Professor, had the man not tripped and stumbled almost into him, sending a briefcase flying off onto the walk.

The case burst open from the impact, and papers spilled out, caught by gusts of the wind and immediately scattered across the dry grass. Both the Tramp Prince and nearby students helped gather up the papers and returned them to the Wiry-haired Professor. When all the papers had been retrieved, the Wiry-haired Professor tried to rearrange them again.

"Drat!" he exclaimed so loud that the Tramp Prince could easily hear. "All of those student's mid-term exams I just graded were completely alphabetized so I could I could hand them back easily. Now look at this mess!"

"If you're in a hurry, I can help you re-alphabetize them," offered the Tramp Prince.

"Yes, I am *very* pressed for time. Will you really help? That would be very nice of you," said the Wiry-haired Professor.

The Tramp Prince followed the Wiry-haired Professor into one of the tall, granite faced, medieval-looking buildings where they found an open room with a desk. Each of them took half of the stack alphabetizing it by name; then they arranged the two stacks together.

"Well, that was quick," said the Wiry-haired Professor, smiling. He looked at the Tramp Prince more closely now. "Hmm... no wonder you had time — you're not a student here, are you? Class will begin in about three minutes. Mine is just down the hall. Sit in, if you'd like. We're discussing several of the seventeenth and eighteenth century philosophers today; you might get something out of it, who knows?"

"Yes," answered the Tramp Prince, "please lead the way."

As they walked toward the classroom, the Tramp Prince very briefly explained his tramping mission and his frustration after having been nearly six months on the road.

When they reached the classroom, the boy found an empty seat in the rear of the room, not wanting to allow his presence to be noticeable. He took out his small note pad and a pencil and sat in eager anticipation.

"Today, as I told you," the Wiry-haired Professor began, we will consider the works of some of the major seventeenth and eighteen century philosophers — and some from the nineteenth century as well, if we have time. We will begin with Descartes. Anyone who would care to pick a few paragraphs from Descartes' 'Discourse' that they think summarizes in part, the thought of Rene Descartes, please feel free to do so."

No one responded.

"Well!" the Wiry-haired Professor continued, his eyebrows lifted high in an almost silly-looking smile of surprise, "perhaps then, we can discuss Descartes' distinction between mental and physical behavior."

Again, there was silence.

"Yes... well, then..."

The Wiry-haired Professor began lecturing — on and on, so the Tramp Prince thought, and he like many of the regular students began taking voluminous notes, until it appeared as though he would run out of paper.

Quietly, the boy left his seat and found a trash basket in the rear of the room. Luckily, inside the basket was a pile of papers, most of which had been used only on one side. He grabbed out a large handful of sheets and returned to a seat.

During the three hour class, the Wiry-haired Professor continued on to Blaise Pascal, then to the writings of Baruch Spinoza, then to Gottfried Leipnitz and on to Jean Jacque Rousseau, spending a great deal of time on the philosopher's 'Social Contracts And Other Discourses'. The Tramp Prince was particularly intrigued by Rousseau's thoughts on slavery and political rights, as he thought about some of his own recent experiences.

Halfway through the afternoon, the Wiry-haired Professor called for a break and handed back the graded exams. Most of the students left the room for their ten minute reprieve from intellectual onslaught.

Since the Tramp Prince had been only vaguely familiar with a few of the names of the philosophers and not in the slightest with their works, his frantic note taking had left no time to organize the notes. He sat looking over his paper pile, trying to place each piece in some semblance of order.

The rest of the afternoon was a repeat of the first half, with the Tramp Prince writing notes frantically in the attempt to keep up. Starting with the Wiry-haired Professor's lecture on Imanual Kant's 'Critique of Pure Reason', the Tramp Prince fumbled and stumbled through Kant's considerations of space and time, as well as that of transcendental logic.

Then on the professor went, through a bewildering series of discussions of the works of Georg Wilhelm Friederich Hegel, Arthur Schopenhaur and Auguste Comte. But the Tramp Prince was not the only student who wrestled in vain to try to grasp Hegel's thought about the abstract characteristics of the nature of spirit. And he wondered if he understood anything at all about Schopenhaur's negativity in 'The World As An Idea'.

At least, though, when Auguste Comte's 'A General View Of Positivism' was reached, the Tramp Prince felt that he could relate to the idea of love in the positivism as it related to human religion. The Wiry-haired Professor ended with an almost brief reference to

Frederich Nietzsche and his belief in human super power. By that point, the boy felt like anything but a superman. He thought, in fact, that he almost might have to bend over and scoop up his poor spilled, macerated brains and pour them back inside his head.

The Wiry-haired Professor came over to him on the way out of the room. He looked at the large pile of notes on the desk in front of the Tramp Prince.

"Well, it looks as though you got *something* out of the class, eh?"

"Yes," replied the Tramp Prince, "but I would have gotten a lot more if I'd had some time to study all of this in advance."

"Why, of course," returned the Wiry-haired Professor. "My next class won't be until Thursday morning at eight, so if you want to stay around for that, you'd have two days to study for it. We'll be covering the social-political philosophers and activists of the mid and late nineteenth century — particularly those in the labor movement. We'll start with Pierre Joseph Proudhon, the father of Anarchism'. Also look up Kropotkin and Bakunin. There are several others you'll find when you do research in the library here."

The Wiry-haired Professor wrote the three names down on a scrap of paper as well as the directions to the university library.

After the Tramp Prince left the classroom, he began leisurely walking toward the university library. The large trees spotted around the campus buildings stood as leafless reminders that warm weather was soon to come. Squirrels playfully sped up and down the tree trunks and one furry fellow sat gnawing on a forgotten nut that had been hidden beneath the leaves.

As with the other buildings on the campus, the library stood like an impressively, massive granite monolith, somber and quite but at the same time placidly peaceful. The Tramp Prince went into the rather small checkout desk area, where a librarian sat reading. She wrapped a rubber band nervously around one finger then another as she read, so engrossed in her book that she did not even see the Tramp Prince as he entered.

The university library seemed low inside, the boy thought, compared to the usual impressively high ceilings of an average public library. All of the inside library space here was devoted to shelf after shelf of books of higher learning, with only one reading area of tables and chairs and a couple long benches.

A polished, golden oak card catalog cabinet was located near the librarian's desk, but far enough from it that, as the Tramp Prince looked through the drawers, he was still unnoticed.

There were very few books listed in the catalog that included references to any of the names which the Wiry-haired Professor had written on the scrap of paper. One notable exception was a 1908 English translation of Paul Eltzbacher's 'Anarchism'. The names the Tramp Prince sought were covered in the book.

After finding the few available books on the subject of anarchism, the Tramp Prince sat at one of the tables and began to read and take notes. Since there were still several unused backsides of the papers he had retrieved from the trash, the boy slipped them out of his bindle sack, writing on them this time, in a careful, organized manner.

Covered in Eltzbacher's book were not only Pierre Joseph Proudhon, Michale Bakunin and Peter Kropotkin, but also William Godwin, Max Stirner, Leo Tolstoy and Benjamin Tucker. That author's bibliography led the Tramp Prince to several other thinkers and commentators, and he spent the rest of the afternoon and early evening pursuing every source book he could locate.

Just before nine in the evening, the library's lights were dimmed to indicate closing time. The Tramp Prince was back in the 'stacks' attempting to find another title. He stepped into a partially hidden niche and waited until the librarian stuck her head through the doorway and called out: "Anyone back here? We're closing!"

The boy made no answer, but stood silently in the tiny alcove. Soon the lights were out and he could hear the door click shut and a key turning the lock bolt.

With the dim illumination from the lights along the walk outside, it was possible to see well enough to get to the reading area and for him to lay out his blanket roll on one of the padded benches. He nibbled at a few pieces of food in his bag and sat back contemplating the rather unusual ideas and beliefs of the various authors whose works had occupied so much of his day.

Before he could assemble any of his own thoughts into a meaningful conclusion, he had fallen asleep, and he lay there in the quiet of the library, until daylight began streaming again into the windows.

After having put away his blanket roll, the Tramp Prince went back again into the 'stacks' and retrieved the book he had been attempting to find the evening before. He carried the copy of William Bailie's 'Josiah Warren, The First American Anarchist' back down to the reading area and sat at a table critically perusing it. Knowing that it would be necessary for him to hide in an hour when the librarian came in, he looked around for a suitable place to easily conceal himself.

A rather small door in the long, oak paneled wall that faced the librarians' desk area just might lead into another room, the Tramp Prince thought. He went over to the door and opened it. There was no room on the other side, only a narrow coat closet with a woman's long raincoat hanging at the far end. The boy carried his bindle sack and walking stick over and pushed them to the end of the closet with the raincoat still hanging in front of his sack. Then he tried to slip behind the raincoat himself, straddling the bindle sack. By sitting on the sack, it allowed his head to clear the coat rod.

"If she just doesn't look down and see my feet, I'll be alright," he thought. Road Toad picked up his telepathic projection.

"Well! You certainly know how to get yourself into some pretty tight circumstances, don't you?" The warty little fellow commented with sarcasm.

"Yes, that's the fun in life!" the Tramp Prince responded, "the most they can do, anyway if they catch me is to kick me out. Right?"

"Right..." grumbled Road Toad.

The Tramp Prince watched the pendulum swinging back and forth in the big oak regulator clock on the library's wall behind the main desk. A few minutes before eight o'clock, he moved into the coat closet to hide behind the raincoat. Just as he pulled the closet door closed behind him, he could hear a woman's footsteps lightly tapping down the long hall from the outside door. Soon the key turned in the library door lock and the librarian propped the door open and walked to the coat closet, opening the door and placing her jacket on a hanger. Then she spotted the raincoat.

"Hmm," she said aloud to herself, "so that's where I left that raincoat."

The Tramp Prince's heart was pounding away, but the woman merely hung her jacket and closed the closet door. The boy then slid forward, twisted the inside door knob and opened the door just a crack. He watched as the librarian began dusting tables and chairs and then organizing her desk.

By squatting down and looking through the keyhole for a wider view of the library's interior, the youth was able to see when the librarian took a large armload of books and walked out into the next room containing the main shelves and the 'stacks'. Then he slipped quietly out of the closet with his bindle sack and stick and sat down at a table.

The librarian returned in a few minutes and spoke to the Tramp Prince:

"Good morning! I didn't even hear you come in," she offered pleasantly.

"Uh... I walk rather softly — I guess I speak that way too."

"Yes, and I see that you carry a big stick!" She laughed at her own joke.

All day long, again the Tramp Prince was in the library reading and taking notes, leaving only for brief intervals. At the end of the day, he again slipped into the alcove he had used the night before and repeated the previous night's system. Early the next morning, he unlocked and opened one of the library windows, dropped his bindle sack and stick to the ground and then pulled the window back down, balancing on the large stone sill. The seven foot drop to the ground was broken as he jumped into some low evergreen shrubs.

At exactly eight, he was already seated in the classroom when the Wiry-haired Professor came in.

"Well, I can see that you did some preparation," said the advocate of cerebral pedagogy as he viewed the pile of carefully organized notes on the Tramp Prince's desk.

"Oh... well... yes sir, a little," was the boy's reply. "This subject is so vast — so interconnected to other concepts, that a person could study it for years and never know all of it."

"Yes, and in years, there would probably just be much additional to have to study," the Wiry-haired Professor replied.

As the class proceeded, the Wiry-haired Professor writing names and dates on the blackboard, he would occasionally ask if anyone knew a pertinent fact in reference to famous incidents such as the Haymarket Affair.

The Tramp Prince remained in obscurity in the rear of the classroom until the instructor wrote on the blackboard the appellation: 'Father of Anarchism — Pierre Joseph Proudhon.'

The Tramp Prince raised his hand: "Excuse me, sir, but Eltzbacher calls William Godwin the Father of Anarchism. He does predate Prodhon, but Procedhon does seem to be the first to use the term 'Anarchism' and to refer to himself as an 'Anarchist'."

"Point well taken," said the Wiry-haired Professor as he raised his pointed eyebrows in a gleeful smile. "I stand corrected."

The professor then continued discussing the lives of each of the seven anarchists covered in Paul Eltzbacher's book 'Anarchism'. He considered each of those political philosophers and their writings, starting with William Godwin and carrying through to Pierre Joseph Proudhon, Max Stirner and then Michael Bakunin, Peter Kropotkin and finally Benjamin Tucker and Leo Tolstoy.

"Those seven anarchist thinkers," said the Wiry-haired Professor, "are the major writers and activists on the subject."

After having spent more than half of the class time on Eltzbacher's book, the Wiry-haired Professor's eyes lit up and his eyebrows shot up again, as if he had had a sudden revelation:

"One thing that Eltzbacher doesn't seem to discuss anywhere in his book is about the maligning of the word, Anarchy. The word Anarchy," the professor went on, "has managed by popular usage, to get a connotation equating it with and often using it as a synonym for the word *chaos*. Fortunately, the promoters of and controllers of governments have not yet had quite a similar effect on the word anarch*ism*. Both words meanings are derived from the roots 'an', that is, *not* or *without*, and... archi or again in Greek archos, meaning a chief or literally a *ruler*. When the suffix *ism* is hung onto the prefix anarch, it then takes on a meaning of the theory, if not the practice of the concept.

"Let's go a little further with this. You see, anarchism is a well-defined system of socio-economic interaction, where voluntary association replaces the coerced association demanded by the state. The state, that is, *government*, by whatever group or individual, no longer exists in a condition of anarchism.

"There are just two forms of social interaction: One is by *voluntary* association, and the other is by the *forced* association of *government*. And this includes *any* form of government, whether it be a monarchy, an oligarchy, a dictatorship or a so-called democracy.

"Now... am I making myself clear on all of this?"

No one responded, and it was not certain if the class actually understood, or if each one of the students was too embarrassed to admit that he or she did not.

"Alright!" said the Wiry-haired Professor with his eyebrows jumping up and down and a silly smirk inundating his face, "Let me ask, can anyone of you give us a *simple* definition of anarchism and how it relates to the thinking of modern theorists in the labor movement?"

Again, there was no reply. Finally the Tramp Prince raised his hand.

"Anarchism as defined in at least one dictionary is: the dissolution of government by mutual consent of parties controlled by that government, that is, the state, and as much as possible replacing the state's authority with voluntary association or cooperation.

"Since labor is forced to deal with the factory owners who also actually control the state, even in a so-called democracy, that would, at least in theory, make it possible for the workers to organize their own factories where they would also become the owners."

"Well!" said the Wiry-haired Professor, "that is not exactly what I had in mind in relating anarchism to the labor movement; you've gone a step farther. But you've certainly put a lot of food for thought on the table for discussion."

A student then raised his hand: "Something is not clear to me," he began. "If a group of people decide that they no longer wish to be governed by the laws and rules of society, that is, the state, then isn't that akin to secession? Won't that be forcefully put down by the government? Most countries have constitutions that everyone agrees to and that specify what actions can and cannot be taken."

The Tramp Prince did not wait to raise his hand:

"I don't know about the rest of you, but *I* did *not* sign a constitution; nor did I vote to ratify one. Therefore, I'm not bound by any of its concepts or dictates or their extensions as laws with which I may or may not agree."

"But," said the other student, "when you pledge your allegiance at a flag ceremony, you're agreeing to be bound by the constitution."

"I," replied the Tramp Prince, "pledge my allegiance only to my family... and to my extended family of tramps and hoboes... and, I suppose, to the 'Family of Man'. I do not pledge it to a particular country or to its various dictums. If I am a citizen of any place, it is of the planet earth, itself. The boundaries of nation states are highly arbitrary. Even a very cursory examination of history will tell you that. The boundaries have changed radically from time to time and are still in a state of constant flux."

A different student spoke up:

"If anarchism is completely voluntary, then how would society deal with criminal behavior?"

"You know that you can have all kinds of voluntary associations." The Tramp Prince responded. "They don't have to be only for economic or social reasons. There can be voluntary defense associations as well."

"Sure... but what if the head of that association — it's leader or coordinator decided to become a tyrant and forced the military arm to subject everyone to it by force?"

"Then you would no longer have voluntary association; it would again become suppressive government — the same thing we now 'enjoy' today. Today's democracies are democratic in name only. Democratic government is never government of the people. It is normally government by the majority over the minority... and usually to the detriment of the minority. Or it could be the reverse. It's not true of only a congressional system, it's also true of a parliamentary system as well!"

"But what about war?" asked another student.

"Again," replied the Tramp Prince, "you could have voluntary defense associations. And war, anyway, is mass insanity! Wars will cease only when the masses of citizens refuse to fight in them."

"So, what if a cop comes and holds a gun to your head if you don't?"

"Now listen... the rulers are cgomaniacs whose egos feed on the support of great masses – millions of people. If they shot or even imprisoned nearly everyone in the country, which they would have to do, then they would have nothing left to feed their faltering egos. They'll never let that happen!"

"I don't know about that!" replied the other student.

"Well, maybe we'll just have to wait and see..."

"Anyway," the other boy charged, "in *our* democracy we have the right to change things."

The Tramp Prince's face had a hint of a wince:

"But only if those who truly control the government will *allow* you to change things. I'm referring to the powers of 'big industry', 'big finance', 'big profession' and 'big politics'. *They* provide the candidates for offices and have the money to influence voters. It's just that simple."

"That's not what we're taught in school."

"What we're *taught* is not necessarily the same as what, in fact goes on in real life!"

The Wiry-haired Professor's eyebrows bounced up and down again.

"No one likes to see a lively debate more than I do!... unfortunately, there isn't time to allow this to turn into a college debating society, so we will have to continue with the assigned political philosophers."

During the proceeding time of the class, some of the students asked numerous questions, but the Tramp Prince remained silent until nearly the very end. Finally, in response to the professor's reference again to Eltzbacher's book, the boy raised his hand:

"Pardon me, sir, but I'm wondering why Eltzbacher didn't include Josiah Warren as one of the major early anarchist thinkers. In my estimation, he certainly belongs on that list... particularly because of his involvement with Robert Owen in the New Harmony project — but, if for no other reason because of his writing in 'Manifesto Regarding Individual Sovereignty and Disconnection'. Bailie describes Warren as the first American anarchist."

The Wiry-haired Professor bumped his head with his hand, as if to try to jar his memory into action:

"Of course... you are quite right. I had completely forgotten to mention Josiah Warren. And, you know, I've often wondered myself why Eltzbacher neglected to include Warren in his book."

Then the professor gave a loud laugh with his eyebrows jumping:

"Young man," he told the Tramp Prince, "if you don't stop embarrassing me, I'm going to have to have you come up here and instruct this class."

Everyone laughed, but the Tramp Prince slumped down into his seat. The last thing he wanted was to make a spectacle of himself.

At the end of the class session, the Wiry-haired Professor stopped at the desk in the back of the room where the Tramp Prince was gathering his papers into his bindle sack.

"Listen, my boy," said the Wiry-haired Professor, "I really think you should be a regular student in this school — and if you ever decide to return here, I will definitely be willing to intercede on your behalf to help you obtain a scholarship."

"That's very generous of you, sir," the boy replied, But right now, as I tried to explain earlier, I'm on a very important mission for my family. Someday, though, I'm hoping I'll complete my search and then I'll feel free to advance my own life. When and if that happens, perhaps I'll be able to return here... and I'll certainly take you up on your offer."

"Bon voyage!" the Wiry-haired Professor almost shouted, as the Tramp Prince walked away. "May the best of life follow you!"

Chapter 34: The Train Station

In his walk across the campus toward the streets leading to the train depot, the Tramp Prince began taking swift strides as if to try to make up for lost time. Road Toad gave the boy a kick in the ribs through the jacket.

"Well...! So its about time we started making some progress toward home!" The little fellow advised with obvious irritation.

The Tramp Prince responded to Road Toad's telepathic message:

"But don't you think it was worth the delay? I mean... what an opportunity for a really intense, unusual education! Didn't you listen to any of it?"

"Oh yes," responded Road Toad with another telepathic thought. "I guess I listened to about half of it."

"Pretty heavy stuff, huh?"

"I'll say! Even with what I heard, my brain feels like a lead weight. I don't know if I can even jump any more to catch a fly!"

"Oh, come now... why I think any person would have benefited from learning a true understanding of the forms of social relationships. Didn't you?"

"No!... *I'm* not a *person*."

"But you're smart."

"That may be... but I'm just a smart, warty, old toad! Nobody listens to toads."

"Yes, you've said that before. But remember, no one can *hear* you."

"Well... even if they could, nobody wants to hear the truth, anyway. Just look at the stupid decisions most people make."

"Now... I can't argue with you anymore."

"Don't try; you'll lose! See, I don't have anything to gain *or* lose by whatever I say! And I'm smart enough to know that people are too dumb, generally, to ever change the way they relate to each other."

"Ah, well..."

"Yes, another deep subject."

The Tramp Prince laughed and began a swift trot toward what he thought looked to be the station not far off in the distance. When he reached the massive building, he stood momentarily across the street from it, marveling at the towers and turrets. The contrast of the blue-green corroded copper tower roofs' colors against the white limestone walls and the red tile of the dozens of various gable and gambrel roof slopes, gave it the appearance of a monumental palace of some long-dead potentate.

Although the boy had hoped to find a large freight yard attached to the passenger depot, from the street, at least, there were no freight sidings or any evidence of the freight yard. He decided to inquire inside the station.

At the entrance doors, a couple of beggars stood seeking alms from the constant stream of travelers. The boy nodded to the pair, but knew he had only a few small coins left of his own. He stood next to the two ragged men and pulled out his coins. Then he dropped two pennies into each of the men's open palms. As he turned to go through the entrance doors, he hesitated momentarily, and before he could walk in, one of the beggars tapped his arm and handed the Tramp Prince back twice what the boy had given the two men.

After he had gone inside, he shook his head in amazement.

"Road Toad," he sent out a thought, "I must really look pathetically ragged and poor myself. "Do you think so?"

"Hmm... well, yes... I must say, you do look rather impoverished — even to me!"

Inside, the station stretched for two city blocks and was so tall, that it was difficult to see the huge rivets on the uppermost steel girders. Approaching an ornately framed window where a man was preparing routing schedules, the Tramp Prince inquired which track led directly north. The man, without raising his eyes said: You'll go to gate seven. What town? Let me see your ticket."

"I... I don't have a ticket — yet," the Tramp Prince said, rather embarrassed.

By then, the man finally looked up. "Go to one of the windows over near the arched entrance. They'll help you. They have the maps."

As the Tramp Prince walked back to the entrance, he noticed that the enormity of the main lobby of the station made every, sound echo, like a call from a mountain valley. Yet, there was a delicateness, a muted character that imparted a surreal, dream-like quality to the place.

The boy stood in a line at another window. When it was his turn, the worker asked him: "What's your destination?"

"I don't know what railroad town is near the place that I'm headed," said the Tramp Prince.

"Here's a railroad map of the region," the worker told him rather briskly, "Look it over and then, when you come back, I can help you."

The Tramp Prince went to the rear of the area with long benches. He sat down next to a woman sleeping with her body propped against a large bag of clothes. The boy tried not to disturb her as he unfolded the map, but he rustled the paper while positioning it and repositioning it to find the proper direction. The noise caused the rotund little black lady to awaken from her near-to-sound sleep. She rubbed her eyes and looked up at the clock above the huge arched entranceway.

"Mah goo'ness! Ah done slep' fo' most a *houah*!" she exclaimed, ending her sentence with a child-like chuckle. Her plump face beamed with a delightful smile that was highlighted by the gold rim on one of her front teeth. Suddenly, the black lady was ware of the color of the Tramp Prince's skin.

"Say, boy..." she said quietly," is you *passin'*?"

She quickly corrected herself:

"Now what d' mattah wid me. You ain't passin,' 'cause you'd be oveh deh wid d' white folks, if you wuz."

"I don't understand," said the Tramp Prince, genuinely puzzled.

"Chile... what is you doin' oveh heah in d' cul'ed section, sittin' next to a ol' cul'ed woman like me. Don't y'all see dem signs white an' cul'ed?"

"Frankly, until you pointed them out, ma'am, I hadn't really noticed."

"Why... dat's d' way it is evehwheh 'roun' heah. W-w-wheh y'all from?"

"A long way from here — hundreds and hundreds of miles. My family and I live back in the woods. We seldom see other people."

"Well, mah goo'ness!" said the black lady, "y'all betteh move y'self oveh wheh d' white folks settin' — 'fo' dey comes oveh heah an' *makes* y' move!"

"Why? said the Tramp Prince." Is a tramp like me too dirty to sit here?"

"Dat ain't d' point, chile, you is white an we is black."

"So a dirty tramp can sit with white people, but not with blacks? Why that's the craziest thing I've ever heard of! And an obviously clean black lady like yourself can't sit over with white people! Who thought up such a lunitic idea?"

"Ah do' know, chile... de worl' sho am full a' crazy ideas. Ah didn' make 'em up — but dat's d' way it is. An' ah gots t' live wid it dat way — or dey t'rows me in jail!"

"That's horrible... and stupid! said the Tramp Prince," I'm going to sit here right where I am. I can see the clock better from here."

Just then, a large, heavy-set guard walked over to where the Tramp Prince was sitting.

"Hey, bud, don't you know you're sittin' in the colored section? The seats for whites are over there," and he pointed in the direction.

"What's wrong with my sitting in the colored section?"

"You're not colored."

"Sure I am! You're just color-blind."

"I'm *not* color blind. Your skin doesn't look a bit colored!"

"Well... ok, I have a brown mole on my back."

"Oh, that's nothing — that doesn't count."

"Alright, just wait here for a minute, please, will you?"

The Tramp Prince walked a few feet over to a baggage express window and asked to borrow the stamp pad and stamp holder. He picked out a rubber stamp, inked it and put several black imprints all over his hands and face. Then he walked back to where the guard was still standing.

"Now — I'm at least partly black," chuckled the Tramp Prince, "be careful if you hit me, though, you can see I'm marked 'fragile'."

The guard began laughing in spite of himself and walked away shaking his head in thoroughly baffled wonderment.

"Chile," said the black lady, "you is bout d' funniest thing ah has eveh seen. Y'all ought t' be on d' stage makin' jokes!"

The Tramp Prince picked up his backpack and walking stick and tipped his cap to the black lady.

"I'd better wash this ink off quick or the joke will be on *me*!"

After considerable scrubbing with soap and water in the men's room, the boy returned, fairly ink free.

"Say, boy," asked the black lady, "wheh y'all headed?"

The Tramp Prince pointed out on the map, the town which he had determined was the closest to his nearby village.

"Chile, you is got to take d' same train Ah takes... an' dat ain't due in yeah fo' 'notheh six houhs. Ah be done wait three houhs awready 'tween trains. Ain't dat awful?" and she laughed again as though all life was something of a bad joke.

Not wanting to admit that he had no money for a ticket, the Tramp Prince told the woman: "Maybe I can find something else to do for a while."

"Dey tells me dat deys lotta nice shops 'bout three block down dis way," and she pointed in the direction. "But Ah ain' go' go deh – – walk dat three blocks an' den Ah gots t' walk three blocks back! Uh, uh! Ah gon' jes' set right yeah wheh Ah *is*!"

The Tramp Prince tipped his cap again to the dark-skinned lady and walked back out the front entrance.

"*Now* what are you going to do?" asked Road Toad in a thought message.

"There are so many people coming and going here," the Tramp Prince responded, "That I thought I'd get out my flute and play a few tunes. I was a little bit afraid to try to play inside, because I thought that the music might just get kind of lost in a cavernous place like that.

The boy found a spot to sit near one of the doors, where the large square base of a stone column protruded. He placed his cap down with his few remaining coins in it.

"You know, Road Toad," he telepathized, "I'm thinking of trying to ride the blinds of that northbound passenger train. I've never done that before, but it might not be too hard."

"Yeah... well, good luck!" responded Road Toad with one of his typically cynical thoughts.

For almost an hour, the Tramp Prince played lively tunes on the flute, and before long, he had emptied his cap three times with fairly large accumulations of coins. Tiring of the musical activity, the boy began walking toward the shops that the black lady had described. Near the edge of the shop area, he came upon a music store with a display of many musical instruments. On stands in the front window were several shiny new guitars and banjos, as well as fiddles and band instruments. Hanging by hooks in the walls inside were row upon row of other gleaming, polished guitars and mandolins.

On impulse, the Tramp Prince went into the store. No one seemed to notice his presence, as he stood before a row of stringed instruments. He looked in awe, not just at the quantity of the instruments, but also of their apparent quality. Then he reached up and plucked the strings of a guitar and afterward, a mandolin. The owner of the shop noticed the sounds and approached the boy.

"Do you play the guitar?" asked the store owner.

"No... but I love the sound."

The music store owner observed the Tramp Prince's ragged clothes and bindle sack. "You're a roadster, huh?"

"Yes, I guess you'd call me a tramp — a hobo."

"Some hoboes carry their guitars around with them — play and sing for a living — such as it is." the owner commented.

"They'd be awfully large to have to carry around with you," replied the Tramp Prince.

"Yes, they would be," the store owner agreed, "but not a mandolin — especially one of the flat types. "He pulled a flat mandolin off the wall and played a few chords on it. "I really don't play the instrument — just know enough to be able to demonstrate it."

"I like it," commented the Tramp Prince, "not as much as a guitar, but it *is* a whole lot smaller." He then tried fingering as the man had showed him and strummed across the strings.

"Do you play the fiddle?" the owner asked. "Mandolins are tuned the same way; so the chording would be the same. But usually a melody is picked, rather than only played as chords. Do you play any other instrument?"

"No," the Tramp Prince answered, "Just this little flute I made." And he slipped it from the bindle sack, playing a few brisk notes. The music store owner looked closely at the tiny flute, smiling in admiration at the innovative design and the beautiful, soft patina of the cherry wood.

"Why, I've never seen anything like it; and it does have a wonderful, delicate tonal quality to it. And you say you made this, right?"

"Yes," the boy responded, "I didn't have any kind of pattern to follow, so I had to make several others before this one in order to get the tone right and to get the holes in the correct places to be playable.

"Amazing!" said the owner. "You really do possess a great deal of musical talent. I think you could probably do a lot with a mandolin.

"How much is something like this one?" the boy asked.

"The price is right on the tag that's hanging from the tuning key."

The Tramp Prince looked at the price tag and sighed in dismay:

"That's *far* more than I have," he told the store owner.

The store owner then walked over to a table, where many stringed instruments were in the process of being repaired and refinished. He picked up a flat mandolin, still fully strung.

"I want to make it possible for you to expand your musical talent, so here's one you can have very cheap." The store owner advised him, "Its badly scratched up and nicked here and there, but it still plays, okay."

"Hmm," said the Tramp Prince, "How much?"

The music store owner held up two fingers on his right hand, so that the other customers didn't hear the answer.

"Wow! exclaimed the Tramp Prince. "I'll take it," and he carefully counted out the correct amount from the coins in his pocket.

"Here," the music store owner offered, "I'll give you a bunch of used strings for extras — they're mostly still good. And here's a little pitch pipe in the key of G. You tune the mandolin: GDAE. Just remember 'Good dogs always eat.' Then you can't get the tuning wrong. I'll diagram a few chords for you. That ought to be enough to get you started."

The store owner then opened a chord book and copied out a page of simple mandolin chord positions.

"The pick is under the strings," he told the Tramp Prince. "You move your right hand fast back and forth across each string to give it that full tremolo. Then the man demonstrated the process.

"Think you have it?" he asked.

"Well, the idea, anyway," replied the Tramp Prince.

"Come back and play it for me someday!" the owner said half in seriousness.

The Tramp Prince thanked the man and went out of the door, very happy with his new purchase.

"Why did you buy *that*?" Road Toad telephathed. "It took nearly all the money you got today. It's true, that amount of money would not have bought a train ticket all the way home, but we could have gotten a part of the way. Besides, you don't even know how to play that thing!"

"I know, but I can learn. And this way, I can sing and accompany myself. You remember, the time we made the most money was when I sang to the hurdy-gurdy's tunes."

"Yes, and he had that cute little monkey running around in a costume — and carrying a tin cup, too!"

"Alright, so we'll get a little green jacket for you and have you dance an Irish jig holding my cap. How's that?"

"What!... me dance an Irish jig? Why, what a completely stupid piece of unmitigated *nonsense*!" Road Toad fumed in a fit of genuine anger.

"Oh, I'm not really serious," said the Tramp Prince, "but you must admit, you'd look cute in a little green jacket."

Road Toad restrained himself from making any further comment.

After the Tramp Prince had stowed the mandolin safely inside the blanket roll, and walked back to the station, he went to the entrance gate which he had been told led to the north-bound trains. Without even knowing which would be the proper train to take, the boy seized upon an opportunity to board a standing row of passenger cars which had no porters or a conductor in sight. He entered the first car behind the engine's tender, figuring that it would be the least likely to have anyone find him hiding in the 'blinds'.

In another half hour, the passengers began to board the train and a few minutes later, it started pulling slowly out of the station with the Tramp Prince still unnoticed. At the first station, about fifty miles north, the conductor opened the door of the first car's front end and immediately spotted the Tramp Prince.

"Alright, boy, you gotta get off! No one's gonna ride the blinds on this train. Sorry — that's the way it is!"

The Tramp Prince sadly made his way back through the car and exited the train, walking along the track away from the station. He had tramped several miles along the track, when he came upon a farmer leveling a freshly plowed and disked field. Two little girls were filling their toy wagons with rather large field stones. The farmer stopped his tractor when the Tramp Prince approached.

"Hey — do your girls need some help picking up those rocks? I'll do it for a meal."

"Sure," said the farmer, "go up to the house and get a wheelbarrow. Them kids a mine ain't much good anyway. They try awful hard, but they're just too little yet."

All the rest of the afternoon, the Tramp Prince picked up field stones for the farmer. After he had joined the family for dinner, he again began walking the tracks north.

Chapter 35: The Ex-con

Soon, he found himself rapidly walking behind an older man with a bindle. The man was mumbling to himself and continued even when he saw the Tramp Prince beside him. He nodded to the boy, continuing his mumbling. There seemed to be little continuity to the man's rambling verbalizing, the Tramp Prince thought as he walked alongside the man, listening.

"Sometimes... The train will jus' stop. It seems like for no reason. But there's *always* a reason. We jus' never find out what it is. Huh! An' life itself kin be that way. Yuh do somethin'... maybe it's a crime. Yuh do it without thinkin'. Say yer faced with a threat; at least it *seems* like a treat at the time. Pow! Yuh hit the guy. He goes down. When he falls, he cracks his head on a rock. He dies. Yuh didn't try t' kill 'im. They put yuh in prison fer twenty years. When yuh get out yer half crazy. Maybe yuh were already half crazy when yuh went in. Anyhow... Hey kid, I'm Rocko. They usta call me the 'Hard-rock kid--like bustin' big ones inta little ones... know what I mean? But somehow... it got shortened t' jus' 'Rocko'. They call me a thug too. Maybe I am."

When they stopped in the early evening shadows, the Tramp Prince stood in front of Rocko. They extended hands, shook momentarily. Then the two began walking toward what looked to be a jungle from a quarter mile away. The firelight at that distance, flickered in and out from behind the dense brush near the track. The jungle fire was still some distance from a small town's switch yard.

Although there was sporadic conversation between the two vagabonds, Rocko did most of the talking.

"Its horrible in one a them damn places... prisons, I mean. Warehouses fer the insane — an' the vicious. See, most of us in there is a bit crazy; if not before we gets there, at least after we been there a while. You gotta be a little crazy t' commit some a' these violent crimes. Anyhow, prison dehumanizes yuh; the way they run 'em, it don't take long. They say that's how it has t' be. It turns yuh into a wild animal. Yuh can't think no more. All yuh kin do is t' try t' fight back an wait fer yer chance t' try t' escape. But it usually don't ever happen. Yuh jus' stay there 'n' get a little crazier each day."

They walked on toward the hobo jungle, shoes crunching the cinders. When the two reached the blazing fire, they stood close to it, attempting to warm themselves. One of several 'boes also warming themselves by the flames, nudged the Tramp Prince and motioned for the boy to follow him. When they were a distance from the campfire, the hobo spoke:

"Listen, kid, you know that guy you were with is Rocko — he's an ex-con. Best t' stay away from him. Know what I mean?"

"Well — see, he already told me that. So... I don't think there's a problem."

"But kid... ex-cons, they ain't no good. I mean... they're trouble. I mean... I'm jus' tellin' yuh fer yer own good."

"I understand. Thanks. But they do sometimes have an important story to tell. Anyhow, I think I know what I'm doing."

"Ok, kid. Don't say I didn't warn yuh."

As the two walked back to the campfire the older man laid his hand on the Tramp Prince's shoulder and gave him a meaningful look directly in his eyes.

Later that evening, Rocko sat alone with the Tramp Prince by the built-up flaming logs that had been piled onto the glowing coals earlier. Two logs remained next to the fire-pit and Rocko and the Tramp Prince each sat on one. Most of the other 'boes had prepared their meals and either found a spot to sleep or had already moved on. Rocko spoke softly:

"Everyone thinks ex-cons is no good, kid. No one's willin' t' give yuh a second chance. Huh... way I was brought up — terrible poverty — fer me... I never really had a *first* chance! Now, I'm jus' a pariah. See, if they find out yer record... They don't even want yuh aroun'."

Rocko's voice was caustic with bitterness as he gazed dejectedly into the flames.

"Yeah, I killed a guy. I wuz mad. I wuz a stupid young kid. But it don't matter what yuh get in fer. Murder — manslaughter —

armed robbery. Even embezzelin' money. Yer still an' ex-con. An' if yuh get out, yer a pariah. I'm jus' tellin' yuh like it is, kid. Nobody wants t' hire yuh — nobody wants t' be aroun' yuh. Soon as they know about yer record... it's like yuh got sprayed by a skunk. Listen... yuh ever get caught in the system, don't tell *no* one — 'cause everyone's scared of ex-cons."

The Tramp Prince sat in rapt attention listening to Rocko:

"It doesn't seem fair... the boy mused. Why doesn't anyone want to give you a chance?"

"Cause they're scared of bein' robbed or assaulted... or... See, prisons jus' make the prisoners worse than they were 'fore they went in there. It's not jus' the belittlin' by the guards; it's the whole dehumanizin' system. When we do get out, we can't get work... so we have t' steal t' exist. Then we get thrown right back in, again. It's a vicious circle. But I won't be goin' back. I wuz a dumb kid t' get there. But I ain't as dumb no more. Twenty years — it's a lot of time t' smartin up. Even if I'm starvin', I won't steal. Better t' starve *out*, than t' *not* starve in.

"See, kid I wuz born into poverty — an nobody cares about yuh when yer poor. Yuh don't have the skills t' lift yerself outta yer poverty. An' poverty jus' breeds more of itself. Prisons don't help yer head none either. Know what I mean?"

"Yes... I've seen a lot of poverty — and stupidity... and ignorance. But what does society have to gain by not rehabilitating criminals?"

"I dunno, kid. You tell *me*! I ain't got none a' the answers. Yuh start out dumb — yuh usually *stay* dumb — 'less someone comes along 'n' helps yuh. But that don't often happen..."

With a grimace, the Tramp Prince shivered visably:

"I'm getting cold just thinking about this. It's a chill that no fire can warm away."

"Yeah... yeah, I'm with yuh kid. Trouble is, it's been this way fer centuries... an' there ain't no one out there tryin t' change nothin'; 'least not that I know of."

"Maybe," mused the Tramp Prince, "When I finish looking for a new home for my family, I should devote my life to trying to change the penal system."

"Listen, kid, it ain't jus' the penal system — it's the whole society — the culture behind it. *That's* what needs changin'."

The Tramp Prince just sat there. He shook his head negatively: "Where do you begin?"

"I can't tell yuh, kid, I ain't that smart. But I've asked myself the same question a hundred times. The only thing I can think t' do is t' start with myself. See, I don't have t' be part of it. It might not help much, but it's a start. Probably the only start I *can* make."

The Tramp Prince thought for a while: "I guess it takes being a politician or a lawyer to make any real difference. Maybe changing the laws. But even that doesn't change the minds or the hearts of the society at large."

"Yeah... an' yuh know too, kid, when a guy gets elected t' office as a politician — he might have good ideas — might *be* a reformer, but after he's there for a while, he either gets corrupted or he has t' compromise his good ideas n' goals jus' t' stay in office long enough t' try t' do what he wants, 'cause it takes so long t' get legislation passed!"

"Sounds hopeless."

"Yeah — 'less yer some kinda miracle worker. Which you probably ain't."

"And which I probably never will be. So what do we do?"

"Slide by the best we can. That's all I know, kid."

"Just one more thing, Rocko... What do you think's important — what matters in life?"

"Well, that's a helluva question t' ask — we jus' been talkin' about it. But... yuh know... there ain't nuthin' important in life."

"Why not?"

"'Cause it all ends in the graveyard, anyhow. Yeah... that's why."

By now, the landscape was flooded in a cold, bright moonlight that reflected an eerie cast to even the most mundane objects seen in the light of day. The Tramp Prince brushed away a few loose rocks next to the jungle fire and laid out his blanket roll. He slipped into it and was soon asleep. Even before the boy awakened in the morning, Rocko had disappeared.

By the time the Tramp Prince began to rouse himself, several of the 'boes had already begun to restart the fire.

"Watch out there, kid," one of the men called to him, "these here sparks could fly out an' set yer blankets on fire."

In less than a minute the boy was up and had put everything back in his bindle sack. He took out his map again and tried to locate the area where he thought he was. One of the older men came over to him:

"Where is it yer trying t' go, bud?"

The Tramp Prince pointed out the town.

"Phew!" Whistled the hobo, "that's sure a long way. Hey, any a'you guys headed up northeast?"

Two of the men came over and the Tramp Prince explained his destination.

"This track'll never get you there. You gotta take a different route a little later on. Me n' Chewy here — were goin' that way. You stick with us. Chewy spat a slug of tobacco juice close to the Tramp Prince's feet. Jus' don't get too close t' ol Chewy — er you'll get splattered with that brown slime." Both' boes laughed.

The three hoboes later walked the mile into the small town where they managed to solicit meals and soon were in a boxcar heading north. All day long they rode, but toward evening, they got off and again were able to hop another freight taking a slightly different direction. As night fell, the three 'boes attempted to sleep on the floor of the boxcar.

Chapter 36: The Dream

The pitching and rolling of the train slowly lulled the Tramp Prince into a profoundly deep sleep. Suddenly, a voice awakened him.

"You're here! See... I *knew* you'd make it!

"Huh? Wha... where is this? Hey, I know you... the Girl With Long, Curly, Brown Hair!"

"Yeah — I've been waiting for you, sweetheart. Come on, I'll show you around."

The train seemed to be stopped at a very small depot station. Delicate spindles and scroll-sawed fretwork adorned the depot's exterior roof supports and even the backs of the passenger benches.

Ornate gas street lamps scintillated, throwing a pale, warm, yellowish glow over everything the light touched.

"We'll go see the illuminated fountains — they're *so* beautiful at night. Would you like to see them?"

"Sure — sure, whatever you want to show me!"

The Girl With Long, Curly, Brown Hair grabbed the Tramp Prince's hand and pulled him along at an accelerated pace, passing down a street of Victorian and Gothic style mansions. Lights shone through a myriad of large stained-glass windows in many of the homes and the sparkling colors nearly leapt out into the night like a silent carnival along the avenue.

"What do you think of *that*!" the Girl With Long, Curly, Brown Hair asked as she pointed out the dancing lights. "Pfantassiland's pretty neat, huh?"

"Yes — yes it is."

"Well, you'll be able to see even more of it in the daylight — know what I mean?"

"Oh... yes, of course."

The Tramp Prince had still not been able to completely shake himself awake as he moved along in the tow of the Girl With Long, Curly, Brown Hair.

"Say — say... how did I get here? I mean... to Pfantassiland. I don't remember what happened. I was on that train and then you were suddenly shaking me and talking to me."

"You just transported yourself. I told you that you could do it. Remember?"

"Boy — so much has happened to me since the last time I saw you."

"Like?"

"Oh, it'd take hours to explain it all."

"I'll listen. I have hours."

When they reached the fountains and sat along the edge on the flat stones forming the perimeter, the Tramp Prince began describing his adventures since the last time he had seen the Girl With Long, Curly, Brown Hair.

"I've only begun to tell you everything," the Tramp Prince said to his lovely companion as she snuggled against him. "Let's go over to that bench near the walk where we can be more comfortable; it's *such* a long story. And we can still watch the fountain's lights."

After they had moved onto the bench, the Girl With Long, Curly, Brown Hair stretched out on it and pillowed her head on the Tramp Prince's thigh.

"Go on with the story; I won't fall asleep. Oh, by the way — where's your little friend, Road Toad?"

"He's still in my pocket — sound asleep. I'm trying not to wake him."

"So, you were telling me about this hermit guy?"

"Yes, and during our conversation he told me about a woodsman who..."

On and on, the Tramp Prince went describing his adventures until daylight began to show above the horizon line. At one point the Girl With Long, Curly, Brown Hair reached up and pulled the Tramp Prince's head down, placing a light kiss on his lips.

"Now you're made me lose my train of thought," he responded.

The Girl With Long, Curly, Brown Hair merely giggled.

When it became fully daylight again, they began walking hand in hand along the street, the girl pointing out the architectural artistry and all of the paving mosaics. Then the Tramp Prince queried his companion:

"I could never understand what happened to you that night in the old barn. You just... disappeared. There was no trace of you in the morning. Where did you go? I looked everywhere for you."

"Oh that!... Well... you see, I just unintentionally slipped back to Pfantassiland somehow. I really didn't mean to upset you. If I did, I'm sorry — it was like I teleported in a dream. You know what I mean?"

"Well... not really."

"Haven't you ever teleported yourself?"

"No..."

"Silly — that's how you got here now!"

The Tramp Prince stood there with a befuddled look about him that made his face even more appealing to the girl. She reached up and again gave him a light kiss.

"When you finish telling me your adventures, I'll take you to meet a few of my friends here. Some of them are really interesting characters." And she giggled again.

It took another hour for the Tramp Prince to finish telling about his travels.

"Oh, you've *really* been around, haven't you? So how long do you plan to stay *here*?" The Girl With Long, Curly, Brown Hair smiled sweetly and squeezed the boy's hand.

"I don't know how long I can stay — gee, I loved that fountain... the way the water shot up and the colored lights came on and changed and then dropped off as the water lowered. We don't have anything like that anywhere near where I live."

"Lots of things are better here; more beautiful — more interesting... here in Pfantassiland."

"I know... I know. I really wish I could stay — and be with *you*. But it's my family... I simply *must* get back to..."

"Oh, no — you shouldn't have said that! Now you'll..."

At that, the Tramp Prince bumped his elbow on the wall of the boxcar. Chewy bent down and whispered harshly into the boy's ear:

"Hey kid, wake up! There's a bull comin' down along the other siding over there. Come on! Get with us close t' the edge o' the door, an' he might not see us!"

All three of the railroad bums quickly flattened themselves against the wall of the boxcar near the open door. When the railroad bull shone a rather dim flashlight into the boxcar's interior, he saw only an empty blackness. After his footsteps could no longer be heard, everyone relaxed.

"Kid," said the other 'bo, "how could you have slept so sound like that with all the bangin' an' bumpin' over that rough track on the way here?"

"I don't know... I guess it was like I just wasn't here. I mean... I don't know how else to explain it. I was in... Pfantassiland. You don't believe me?" The Tramp Prince looked at the man with obvious facial anxiety.

"Kid... are you feelin' okay?" The man squinted knowingly at his friend. "Y' know, it sounds t' me like yer gettin a little sick."

"No, no! Really, I'm okay! I'm alright. I just had some kind of weird dream, I guess."

"Huh! I'll say!" commented the 'bo.

All three then decided to exit the railroad and make their way into town.

Chapter 37: The Banker

"I guess we'll do better trying to get something to eat if we separate," the Tramp Prince told his companions.

"Yeah," agreed Chewy as he spat a mouthful of nasty-looking tobacco juice at the ground.

"Maybe we'll catch up with yuh later somewhere," said the other 'bo. "Take care a' yerself, kid!"

Later, as the Tramp Prince walked on into the small industrial city after having parted company with the other two 'boes, he soon came to a large, impressive-looking bank building. It's white stone facade had two huge, fluted marble columns on each side of the entrance door. Hanging from a hook at the edge of one wall, was a small sign which read: 'realtor on premises — mortgage loans available'.

"Road Toad! Hey, Road Toad. Wake up! Are you getting my thought?"

"Hmm..." grumbled Road Toad in his half-somnolent telepathic response. "I guess I'm awake. What is it?"

Look at this bank's sign offering real estate and mortgage loans. Should I bother to go in? What do you think?"

"Well... a location around here wouldn't be terribly far from home. But as to a loan — I don't think they'd have any reason to give you one... on the other hand, I suppose it wouldn't hurt to ask."

So, in went the Tramp Prince, and he inquired around the lobby as to who would be the realtor. Having been directed to the desk of a well-dressed middle-aged gentleman, the boy introduced himself and explained his family's needs.

"Oh yes," the real estate agent replied in an almost jocularly flippant manner after looking at the boy's clothes, "I have quite a number of farm listings here in my book. But I doubt that your family would be able to afford most of them." The man began flipping through a ledger-sized loose-leaf binder with typed and hand written pages, some with photographs of the buildings.

"Now, here's one of the smaller farms with a house and out buildings. But as you can see from the pictures, the condition of the buildings leaves much to be desired."

"How many acres, and what's the price?" asked the Tramp Prince with a cool directness.

"Thirty acres and they're asking five hundred for the property."

"Five hundred!" exclaimed the Tramp Prince. "Why that would take *years* for my family to pay off — and leave nothing for repairs to the buildings or for our own needs!"

"Well," replied the real estate agent, "the owner might be willing to negotiate the price somewhat."

"Even so," thought the Tramp Prince, "they can't negotiate the price much because this agent wants his cut in commission out of the price."

"Show me some other farms in your book," suggested the boy.

The real estate agent then went through all of his listings, and almost all the rest were either larger, or at least in much better condition; and all were more expensive.

"Now that I know what you have available," the boy told the agent, "before I even bother to look at any of these places, could I please talk to someone about what it would take to obtain a loan on the less expensive properties?"

"Yes, of course," said the agent with a slight snicker. "Just follow me."

The Tramp Prince followed the agent to another desk with a small sign 'mortgage loans' and a man's name.

"I'm sorry," said the real estate agent, but he appears to be away from his desk for a short break. If you wouldn't mind waiting, though I'm sure it will be only a few minutes before he returns."

After the agent had left, the Tramp Prince sat down in a chair near the desk and began looking around at the elaborately decorated interior of the bank. Its neo-classic style included many incursions into the popular Victorian decorative motifs in the detailing of various arches and capitals. The boy was so engrossed in studying the interior architecture, that he did not see the large, carefully dressed man observing him from the doorway to a room marked: 'Bank President' and the name: 'P. Sterling Geltmizer'.

The bank president had become curious as to why a young man dressed obviously as a tramp, would be seeking a mortgage loan. He walked over to where the Tramp Prince was sitting.

"Hello," he stated, "I'm P. Sterling Geltmizer; I'm the bank president. What may I do for you?"

"Well, sir," the boy responded, "I've just spoken to your real estate agent about the possibility of my family trying to buy a farm. Before looking at any of the listings, I thought it would be wise for me to investigate just a bit of how mortgage loans are negotiated — and how they're, paid off. You see, we have no savings and an extremely limited income."

"Ah, young man, from what little you've already told me, it quite frankly, doesn't sound too hopeful for you. But I do appreciate your honesty. Come into my office and we'll talk about it."

The bank president stepped back into his office, followed by the Tramp Prince. The opulently-dressed gentleman sat down behind his massive, heavily carved oak desk, looking to the boy like some medieval monarch on his throne. The man's handlebar moustache twitched as he started to talk.

"Sit down in one of those chairs, my boy," he began, "and pull it over close to the desk. Now, you see, we do not normally make mortgage loans unless the party taking out the loan has a source of income which will allow him to make the monthly payments. No bank wants to have to foreclose on a property where the borrower cannot make the payments."

"I understand," said the Tramp Prince, "I realize that you're not in the business of having to resell properties a second time. That's why my family was trying to find someplace *very* inexpensive."

"Yes... yes, I see. But you know that you must understand, that if you have no independent source for income — a job, an inheritance — something like that, those small, run-down farms are not capable of generating enough income to make the payments on them — not without some outside money being invested first.

"I know..." said the Tramp Prince dejectedly, "I could see that dilemma at once."

"You know that additionally, you have to be able to come up with the money to pay the property tax each year. If you can't, the government will evict you!"

"Yes, isn't that the craziest thing? What we actually buy, is not the real estate itself, but the right to *rent* it from the government. Of course, that 'rent' does exclude everyone else from use of the property." Geltmizer's facial expression lit up:

"Now there *is* the possibility," the banker suggested, "that if your family has the skills to handle a larger, producing cattle or dairy farm, we might be able to provide a loan for something like that. I know that we have some larger farms, still in production, where the owners have become too elderly to continue and wish to retire, and have no children to take over."

The Tramp Prince closed his eyes and shook his head.

"No sir, none of us has experience with operating regular farm machinery; actually there is only myself, my mother and father to do the heavy work. And as to using animals — well... we just don't believe that its very efficient or humane — to say nothing of the terrible effects on our health. And using dairy products is only a little less inefficient — and is still involved in animal slavery. We see that the world will someday face major economic and climatic crises if this trend continues — and if the human population continues to explode in the way it is now doing."

"What on *earth* are you talking about, young man? What you're saying goes against *all* conventional thinking — at least that *I've* ever heard. Please explain yourself!"

"Sir, please understand that it's not that I don't *want* to tell you, but I simply don't think we have the time to sit here and let me go through the entire lengthy explanation — which is what I would have to do."

P. Sterling Geltmizer pulled out his large, gold pocket watch and popped open the case.

"By jove, son, you're right. I have only ten more minutes before I will have to leave for a meeting of the board of trustees. And you did want me to explain how we write mortgage loans and figure the rates. Alright! On a farm that sells for only three hundred, we would have to charge eight and one half percent interest per year — on say, a twenty year loan. Now, eight and a half present interest, not compounded, on three hundred would be..."

And Geltmizer pulled out a pad and pencil.

"It's twenty four fifty," said the Tramp Prince.

Geltmizer scribbled some figures. Yes, by jove, you're right! How did you manage to figure that so quickly in your head?"

"I don't know, sir... I just... I just... I don't know. It just kind of 'popped' into my head. I can't explain it."

"Well," said Geltmizer, "Try another one. Let's see if you can do it again. A loan, let's say, of two hundred fifty dollars at seven and a quarter percent simple interest on a twenty year loan.

The banker began writing more figures on his pad, but before he could obtain a result, the Tramp Prince chimed in:

"It's about eighteen dollars and twelve cents."

"Amazing! That's *astounding*! How on earth do you do it?"

"Well, I really don't know," the boy laughed. "Maybe I'm just some kind of 'idiot genius'."

"Idiot — certainly not! But... genius...?"

The banker shook his head in astonished bewilderment.

"Son... how would you like to work here for me figuring mortgages and doing other mathematical calculations? I'll pay well. I could probably fire two of my current employees, because *you'd* be able to do more than both of them together! What do you say to that?"

The Tramp Prince sat there — flabbergasted by both the banker's offer and his own unrealized ability.

"Gosh... I... I... don't know what to say. I need a few minutes to think about it... and to do some figuring. How much would I get?"

"Why, I pay each of those other employees twenty-five dollars a week. I'll give you the same and get rid of them!"

"But sir... couldn't you just *transfer* them into other jobs? That wouldn't be kind to just fire them for no reason other than for efficiency."

"Huh! So what's wrong with *that* kind of reason?"

"Why, it's an ethical — a moral situation. Ethically and morally, it's not right!"

"What! Why that's *ridiculous*! There are no ethics or morals at play in the workings of the business world, at least not around here. Don't you already know that?"

"Ah yes," lamented the Tramp Prince, "I'm afraid I do. And what a sad day it is to be reminded of it. Well, good day, sir."

Then the boy walked out of the door, leaving the banker with an open-mouthed expression of disbelief.

Chapter 38: The Return Home

It took several more days of hopping freight trains, hitching rides in delivery trucks and even a thirty mile stint on the running board of a touring car packed with a family after their weekend outing, to bring the Tramp Prince back to within walking distance of his home village.

Walking again most of the day, he finally found himself trudging up the path to his family's garden home.

The first to spot the Tramp Prince was his little sister. The Princess Of The Garden ran down the path to greet him with open arms. Limpy dog followed close behind. The Tramp Prince embraced them both, tears welling up in the eyes of brother and sister.

The boy then went up to the cultivated plot where the King Of The Garden and the Queen Of The Garden were planting seeds in the by now, warm spring soil.

"Ah," said the King Of The Garden, "now the snow has *truly* gone away! Look, Mother, spring has, indeed, finally arrived!"

All the rest of the day, the family planted seeds and talked and planted seeds... and talked. The King Of The Garden explained that even when they had to leave their home, someone else, at least would be able to benefit from the plants.

That night around the dinner table, everyone listened intently as the Tramp Prince continued relating his many stories about his adventures.

The peregrinating son had been back only a couple of days, when up the path to the garden came the Plump Little Man With The Bald Spot. Everyone in the family rushed up to see him with great trepidation in their hearts.

"Hmm," the Plump Little Man With The Bald Spot observed, "I thought you would have vacated this place by now."

"Our son just returned two days ago after spending almost six months searching for another abandoned garden where we could live," said The Queen Of The Garden. "He has made many notes of the other possibilities, but we have not yet had the time to evaluate all of those notes."

"Well, madam," said the Plump Little Man With The Bald Spot, "I have given this a great deal of thought, and I have come to a conclusion, different from that which I had previously decided."

Everyone waited with strict attention to hear the next words of the Plump Little Man With The Bald Spot.

"You see," he began, "I calculated what it would cost me to grade and gravel the long lane up here from the county road so that my motor car could traverse it. Then I added in the cost of building a garage for the car. Also I added to that the cost of constructing living quarters for my chauffeur. In addition, I had to add the cost of bringing in an electric line or buying a large power generator. I also had to figure in the cost of wiring the house as well as putting in plumbing and a water system. Then there is the fact that no telephone service is available out here, plus the great distance I would have to travel each day to commute to my business office in the city. It was soon obvious to me that all of these costs would be prohibitively expensive.

"This is indeed a most beautiful place. But what I have decided is that it is simply *far* beyond the realm of practicality for me to live here. If you people could continue to maintain this beautiful garden so that I could come out here and enjoy it a few times each year — and enjoy a drink of that delicious apple cider — why... there is no reason, as I see it, for you not to remain here."

The King Of The Garden and the Queen Of The Garden as well as the Prince and Princess all threw their arms into the air and shouted with joy. The little Princess took the front paws of old Limpy dog and hoisted him onto his back legs, trying to dance a jig with the old fellow... who looked around with an expression as if to say, "what have I done wrong?"

Then the whole family began to sing: 'For he's a jolly good fellow', and the Queen Of The Garden invited the Plump Little Man With The Bald Spot and his chauffeur to stay for a sumptuous dinner.

The next day, the Tramp Prince called his family together to explain to them his new plans.

"My dear family," began the boy, "I know you would love to have me stay here after my having been gone so long. And I too would love to be able to spend some time with all of you again. But I cannot stay indefinitely. You see, I now have what I consider to be the responsibility of an extended family — my road brothers and sisters... and they sometimes may have a far greater need for my help than you have. I've told you some of their stories — but one never knows where or when their great need may arise. I'll stay a week or two, but then...

"And also, I have a new quest now. I'm looking for a place that I visited only once and that I may never find again. It's called 'Pfantassiland.' I met a wonderful, beautiful girl who lives there and has returned to her home... but I'll search to find her again if it takes the rest of my life." "On top of this, and no less important, as I've already explained to you, it seems imperative that I search for a new home for us in a warmer, subtropical climate. Then we could raise our own tropical fruit and do away forever with heavy winter clothes and spending so much time and energy heating this house."

A couple of weeks later, as he had told them, the Tramp Prince prepared to leave again. The Queen Of The Garden held onto her son's hand, not wanting to let it go for fear that he might never return.

"Every mother has the same fear about letting her son go away – – out into the world," she told the Tramp Prince. "It's the same fear that every mother has had just as long as there have been sons with mothers, I guess... and it will continue, I suppose, as long as there will be human life."

"I know..." said the Tramp Prince patting his mother's hand and looking deeply into her eyes.

"I realize that it's almost useless to say this," his mother continued, "but my love will go with you whenever you travel. I can't wrap my heart up in a package and put it in your pocket... but it will go with you just the same."

His little sister ran up to him: "I guess I'm still too little to go, huh?"

"Oh..." the Tramp Prince smiled at her, "mmm... you're getting a bit more mature — and wiser. But someday..."

"Right now, I feel like a bird in a cage," the child replied.

"You're more like a little bird in its *nest*. But someday, when your wings are strong enough, you too will be able to fly away if you wish. Until then, you need to learn to be patient. The time will arrive more quickly than you realize."

The King Of The Garden grasped his son's hand and smiled. He said nothing. All of his words were funneled into that last handshake..and the Tramp Prince understood the message.

"My heart will always be with the three of you," he told his father, mother and sister, "but I must return to my tramp brothers and sisters; they also need my help and love. I'll still look for a new home for us where we can grow our own mango trees and not have to wear heavy winter clothes or heat our home — somewhere in the warmer places in the world. So, until I see you again... whenever that is…" and he blew them a kiss and turned to walk down the path.

He hesitated before walking past the stone gate post.

"Now, then... Road Toad!" he called out telepathically.

His little friend came hopping up in a few seconds.

"I must leave again to begin another new search. You know that you can stay here if you wish... or, you're welcome to go with me again."

"Hmm... well there *are* a lot of nice juicy bugs around here. But... I think I might go. So where do you suppose you'll be headed

After a reflective silence, the Tramp Prince looked off into the distance as if captivated by a random thought.

"You know... I'm not really sure. I don't think it matters much."

He stooped down to speak directly to the amphibian. Instantly Road Toad made a felicitous leap, landing in the boys jacket pocket. "Alright!" laughed the Tramp Prince, then he became somewhat serious, "See, there's only one place I'm *really* intent on going... but I may never find out how to get there again."

"I know," replied Road Toad with his usual directness, "It's Pfantassiland!"

"Yes," the Tramp Prince admitted, great sadness hovering in his voice.

"Well," observed Road Toad cheerily, "if you ever figure out how to get there again, please, just be sure of one thing..."

"Hmm, what's that?"

"That I'm still in your jacket pocket." chuckled Road Toad, *"and... that I'm awake!"*

The End

Other Books by the Author

(Available in Print and eBook Versions as they are being produced in 2015. Please check HoboJack.com for release dates.)

"Get A Horse"
*Early Automotive, Magazine Cartoons.
Collected, Compiled and Edited by Jack.*

"Time In A Box"
Jack's first Fantasy Satire.

"More Amazing Adventures Of The Tramp Prince"
A continuation of the character and his journeys.

"Obscure Ponderings"
Prose, Poetry and Essays.

"Obscure Wanderings"
Stories and Character Studies in Prose and Poetry.

About The Author

I met Jack 25 years ago. He had lived through more than a couple of lifestyles by then. Born before World War II, his experience and perspective is significantly different from post-war "Baby Boomers." He has seen very little television, so his opinions about politics, music, art and society are rooted in the old movies and radio broadcasts of his youth. After college and years as an itinerant, a welder and junkman, he emigrated to a reclusive and elusive life in the woods with his wife and daughter. In recent years, there was a total reversal of solitude (but not fortune) when his 20 acre junkyard and persona were discovered by national media. Today, millions of people can identify him as that singing antique picker, Hobo Jack.

In a Chaplinesque way, there's an irony to much of Jack's writings. Fans of his affable character, Hobo Jack might be surprised at the depth of his anti-government and sarcastic world view. So, readers be warned, his current works of satire consistently slice and dice the state of human existence. These picaresque satires are not at all for children and should be viewed as social criticism and philosophy disguised as fantasy.

Complex? Several large examples of his work, "Obscure Ponderings" and Obscure Wanderings" are about to be published. These earlier works reflect a romantic, idealized view of the world in prose and traditional poetry. His first publication, "Get A Horse" proved that he has a great, retrospective sense of humor despite a cynical view of history and society overall. These works will astonish anyone who pictures this shabby individual as simply a rural eccentric. Learn more at: HoboJack.com

Bob Whiteside   ArchivalProductions.com

Made in the USA
Middletown, DE
05 July 2015